Michael Jecks gave up a career in the computer industry to concentrate on writing and the study of medieval history, especially that of Devon and Cornwall. He is a regular speaker at library and literary events and has been the Chairman of the Crime Writers' Association. Michael lives with his wife, children and dogs in northern Dartmoor.

Acclaim for Michael Jecks's mysteries:

'Michael Jecks has a way of dipping into the past and giving it the immediacy of a present-day newspaper article . . . He writes . . . with such convincing charm that you expect to walk round a corner in Tavistock and meet some of the characters' *Oxford Times*

'Captivating . . . If you care for a well-researched visit to medieval England, don't pass this series' *Historical Novels Review*

'A tortuous and exciting plot . . . The construction of the story and the sense of period are excellent' *Shots*

'Stirring intrigue and a compelling cast of characters will continue to draw accolades' *Publishers Weekly*

'This fascinating portrayal of medieval life and the corruption of the Church will not disappoint. With convincing characters whose treacherous acts perfectly combine with a devilishly masterful plot, Jecks transports readers back to this wicked world with ease' *Good Book Guide*

'Jecks' knowledge of medieval history is impressive and is used here to great effect' *Crime Time*

By Michael Jecks and available from Headline

The Last Templar
The Merchant's Partner
A Moorland Hanging
The Crediton Killings
The Abbot's Gibbet
The Leper's Return
Squire Throwleigh's Heir
Belladonna at Belstone
The Traitor of St Giles
The Boy-Bishop's Glovemaker
The Tournament of Blood
The Sticklepath Strangler
The Devil's Acolyte
The Mad Monk of Gidleigh
The Templar's Penance
The Outlaws of Ennor
The Tolls of Death
The Chapel of Bones
The Butcher of St Peter's
A Friar's Bloodfeud
The Death Ship of Dartmouth
The Malice of Unnatural Death
Dispensation of Death
The Templar, the Queen and Her Lover
The Prophecy of Death
The King of Thieves

MICHAEL JECKS

THE KING OF THIEVES

headline

First published in 2008
by HEADLINE PUBLISHING GROUP

First published in paperback in 2009
by HEADLINE PUBLISHING GROUP

2

Cataloguing in Publication Data is available from the British Library

ISBN 978 0 7553 4975 3 (B Format)
ISBN 978 0 7553 4417 8 (A Format)

Typeset in Times by Avon DataSet Ltd,
Bidford-on-Avon, Warwickshire

Printed and bound in Great Britain by
Clays Ltd, St Ives plc

HEADLINE PUBLISHING GROUP
An Hachette UK Company
338 Euston Road
London NW1 3BH

www.headline.co.uk
www.hachette.co.uk

This book is for two friends whom I respected hugely.
Both were great countrymen.
Both adored nature in all its forms.
Both had the same respect for the world about them.
Both could see humour in everything they (or others) did.
And I, like many others, suffered from their practical jokes.

Both died too soon.

Martin Coombs
Brian Radford

You're both sorely missed.

Glossary

Crophead   slang term for a priest or other tonsured man.

Harvester   slang for a cutpurse, someone who would slice through the thongs holding a man's money to his belt.

Picker   a thief who would take everything from his victim.

Planter   one who would provide fake jewels.

Cast of Characters

Sir Baldwin de Furnshill once a Knight Templar, Baldwin is now known to be an astute investigator of crimes.

Jeanne Baldwin's wife.

Simon Puttock a close friend of Baldwin's for almost ten years, Simon has worked with Baldwin in many investigations.

Margaret Simon's wife, Margaret is particularly concerned that their house could be under threat.

King Edward II a frivolous, untrustworthy and ruthless King, Edward was loathed by his barons, thought feckless and vain by the clergy, and detested by the French King because of his treatment of his French wife, Queen Isabella.

Sir Hugh le Despenser King Edward's closest companion, adviser, friend and – in the opinion of many historians – his lover, Sir Hugh was probably the most avaricious, dishonest and manipulative adviser that England has ever known.

King Charles IV of France brother of Queen Isabella, King Charles was the last of his line on the French throne.

Cardinal Thomas Thomas d'Angou was an adviser to

King Charles IV of France, as well as
informant to the Pope.

Sieur Hugues de
Toulouse
once an obscure knight, Sieur
Hugues has risen to the post of
castellan of the Louvre.

Sir Richard de Welles
a cheery knight from Devon, Sir
Richard is a King's Coroner, in which
capacity he has worked with Simon
and Baldwin in the past.

The King of Thieves
known as such because of his unique
position in Paris, the 'King' controls
much of the crime that is perpetrated.

Jacquot
Once a contented farmer, now
Jacquot is an embittered criminal
eking out a living in Paris.

Amélie
a prostitute, Amélie is the latest in a
series of companions for the 'King of
Thieves'.

Jean de Poissy
the city prosecutor, or Procureur,
Jean de Poissy is an indefatigable
investigator.

Pons and Vital
two officers of Paris responsible for
inquiring into murders.

Stephen
Jean's servant of many years'
standing.

Hélias
a brothel-keeper and whore, Hélias
has been a friend of Jean de Poissy's
for a long time.

Jehanin
one of many kitchen knaves in the
Louvre.

Raoulet
a messenger in the Louvre.

Arnaud
the main porter, or gatekeeper, to the
Louvre.

Queen Isabella
wife to King Edward of England,
Isabella is deeply unhappy at being

ignored by her husband in favour of Despenser, whom she hates. The Queen has been sent to France on a diplomatic mission to prevent an escalation in hostilities over English possessions in France.

Lord John Cromwell the head of the English delegation, Lord John has already grown to be an ally of the Queen's.

William de Bouden Comptroller to the Queen during her stay in France.

Alice de Toeni a lady-in-waiting, put in place by Despenser to keep a watchful eye on the Queen and all her dealings.

Joan of Bar the divorced wife of Earl John de Warenne, Joan was also put in place by Despenser, but has grown to pity and sympathise with the Queen.

Edward, Earl of Chester son of the King and Queen Isabella, Earl Edward, later created Duke of Aquitaine, is to travel to France to pay homage for the English territories.

Bishop Walter II the Bishop of Exeter, Walter Stapledon is an old friend of Simon and Baldwin, but has also held a number of key positions in English politics. He was the guardian to Earl Edward during the ill-fated journey to France in 1325.

Sir Henry de Beaumont a loyal servant to the King, he has been placed with the Bishop to guard Earl Edward during his journey to France.

Author's Note

There can be few such events in history quite so incompetently handled as the diplomatic mission in 1325 to France of the Earl of Chester.

Never actually created a Prince, the Earl was nonetheless in receipt of every gift a grateful father could bestow. He became an Earl only a few days after his birth, whereas his father, King Edward II, and grandfather were both in their mid-teens. Edward, so it would appear, doted on his little son. However, all that was to change. As King Edward grew in authority after the dreadful Battle of Boroughbridge – following which he systematically hunted down and executed most of the 'rebels' – so he also grew to rely ever more on the judgement of Sir Hugh le Despenser – a judgement which was invariably skewed to the advantage of Despenser himself.

It would be tedious to recite all the crimes of Despenser here. Suffice it to say that the man was entirely ruthless, particularly violent, and peculiarly avaricious in an age when violence was normal and greed not viewed as an especially vile sin. Despenser was notable for his extremes. His behaviour does appear to be deplorable, seen from the safe perspective of seven hundred years.

But after the short war of Saint-Sardos in 1324, all the English territories were at threat. The French had overrun them, with little defence put up by the English – partly because they were starved of funds and men by Despenser.

The result was a protracted negotiation intended to save English suzerainty. But the French King was not hoping for that – he wanted the English off his territories entirely. So it suited his purposes to raise the stakes. He demanded that the English King should travel to Paris to pay homage, as any vassal should to his liege-lord. However, because Edward dared not leave England, he hurriedly created his son Duke of Aquitaine, and sent him instead, under the watchful eye of Bishop Walter II of Exeter.

And thus begins our tale.

The Hundred Years War began only a few years after the events depicted here. Most readers will have heard of the great battles of Agincourt, Crécy and Poitiers, and may find it hard to understand why the English should have been so nervous about losing Aquitaine. There are a number of reasons.

First, was the very real damage that would have been done to the economy. Medieval kings may not have been especially fiscally aware, but they employed a great many men who were – Bishop Walter was one such.

Even in medieval times, accounting was considered a serious business. It is fortunate for us that this is so, because it is often the old rolls of accounts which give us an accurate feel for the period. Be that as it may, the simple fact is that the Duchy of Aquitaine, the rich lands of Gascony, provided more money to the English Crown than the whole of the British Isles. And with a small, loyal population, the Gascons were less troublesome to rule!

The second point, though, is much more important. The English were a small nation, viewed as incredibly truculent, and the King had a hard time trying to keep his subjects under control. If he wanted to send a force to Guyenne, for example, he would need the support of the barons in Parliament.

Without their approval, he could not raise the necessary funds. This kind of dependence other rulers in Europe looked at with incomprehension.

For an English King to propose war against the French, he would have to have a number of exceedingly good arguments and a strong plan of campaign. Not only because of the funding, but also because of the extreme disparity in forces.

At no time in English medieval history did the English King have more than about two and a half thousand knights. There was simply not the population for more. Men-at-arms and warriors on foot would add some thousands, but not many more. Compare that with the French hosts, and the sad disparity becomes obvious. Some ten thousand knights, with tens of thousands of footsoldiers, hired mercenaries from Genoa and Venice, freebooters from German states, all provided the French with the greatest forces in the whole of Christendom.

And they had morale, too. The whole world knew that the French had the best warriors, the largest number of fighters, the most effective armour . . . it was all in their favour. If an English King wanted to fight, he could count on facing forces of five, six or more times his own. It was inconceivable that an English King could equip, transport, feed and field enough men to contest any lands the French sought to take. The only defence was legal. And the English did not have much faith in a legal system which was entirely populated by French lawyers.

There has been a great deal of help in writing this book. I cannot help but mention the excellent books by Ian Mortimer, *The Greatest Traitor* and *The Perfect King* (Jonathan Cape); also *King Edward II* by Roy Martin Haines (McGill-Queen's University Press); *Politics, Finance and the Church in the*

Reign of King Edward II by Mark Buck (Cambridge University Press) among others. Many books have been consulted, and any errors are sadly entirely my own.

One error which I should mention to those who have followed the sequence of the books with enthusiasm, relates to the marriage of King Charles of France to his third wife.

In some cases of history, there are problems. I once spent a month trying to validate a story which I intended to base around an ancient fair, only to discover after four entire weeks of research, that the fair did not exist. It was a Victorian creation.

However, one can usually check on some aspects of life with ease. One such, so I would have believed, would be the wedding day of a King. 'Aha!' I hear you cry. 'Any fool could confirm that . . .'

Well, not this fool. My last two books were leading up to the glorious day of the wedding of King Charles to his wife Jeanne. I had anticipated that wedding occurring in this book. In fact, the wedding scene was to be a significant section of the story – and so it had been planned for over a year when I first embarked on this section of my series.

Alas. 'The best laid schemes gang aft a-gley,' as Rabbie Burns put it so well.

I grew a little perturbed to find that, when I looked through my research material, only one book mentioned the wedding in 1325, and I could not for the life of me find any decent confirmed date. Now, I am a fiction writer, but it is deeply ingrained in me never to put into a book a fact which is historically untrue; I had to check it. Knowing (as I felt sure I did) the year of the marriage, I was confident that the day and date would not be impossible to find. So I searched. I looked at websites. I even looked at Wikipedia (usually a proof of utter despair on my part) and I checked with a number of French sites, working on the basis that they should have the most accurate records of their own Kings' wedding dates.

Not so! I have erased my memory of the total number of alternatives which were given to me. I don't know if someone at some stage has grabbed a handful of dates, thrown them into the air and seen which landed uppermost, or whether it's just Murphy's Law at work ('If it can go wrong, it will'; often corrected by Paddy's Corollary: 'Murphy was an optimist'), but I spent what felt like an age staring at alternatives. So in the end, I went to the Oracle. I spoke to Ian Mortimer.

Those of you who have periodically glanced at my *Notes* will know that Ian is a particular hero of mine. Still, I have to confess that I had not anticipated such glorious and inspiring assistance. After my two weeks of fiddling, Ian was able to bring me an answer in less than one day.

I was out by two years: it was July 1324 (probably).

So if you, gentle reader, feel hard done by in that you have missed the glories of the wedding day of Charles, all I can say is, I did my best!

For those who wish to learn more about this, please refer to Joan A. Holladay's *The Education of Jeanne d'Évreux: Role Models and Behavioural Prescriptions in Her Book of Hours at the Cloisters* (shortly to be printed).

Michael Jecks
North Dartmoor
April 2008

Paris, 1325

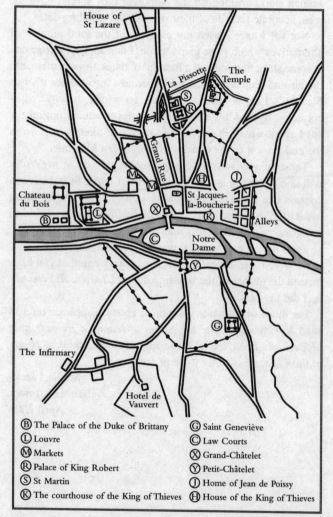

(B) The Palace of the Duke of Brittany
(L) Louvre
(M) Markets
(R) Palace of King Robert
(S) St Martin
(K) The courthouse of the King of Thieves

(G) Saint Geneviève
(C) Law Courts
(X) Grand-Châtelet
(Y) Petit-Châtelet
(J) Home of Jean de Poissy
(H) House of the King of Thieves

House of
St Lazare

La Pissotte

The Temple

Grand Rue

Chateau
du Bois

St Jacques-
la-Boucherie

Alleys

Notre
Dame

The Infirmary

Hotel de
Vauvert

Prologue

Path outside Anagni, south-east of Rome

God's blood, but he hated them. All of them. The religious ones; the *pious* ones. And today he would win some sort of satisfaction for the way they'd treated him.

It was a hot day, and Guillaume de Nogaret wiped his brow with his sleeve as he sat on the horse, waiting for the signal from the man at the top of the rise. September in this benighted land here, only a few leagues from Rome, was always hot. He was used to heat, but not to this overwhelming dryness. He was baking inside the heavy tunic he had bought in Paris.

Some two-and-thirty or so years old, Guillaume had been born in the lovely countryside near St Félix-en-Caraman, but it was not long before he had been captured – when he was orphaned.

The men who had taken him were all the same. Men of the Church who prostrated themselves before the Cross and begged forgiveness for their sins. Well they might! Their hypocrisy and venality were unequalled. Thieves and gluttons, lustful, degenerate, *evil*. They would declare their love for boys like the little Guillaume, asking him to participate in their

---

[1] Saturday, 7 September 1303

unnatural practices, and then beat him with rods when he refused them.

Beatings, whippings . . . all was punishment in their world: children like little Guillaume were there to be educated and shown the right path to take, they said. That was why they must thrash him regularly, they said. There were times he had returned to his cot with his back and buttocks so raw, so severely lacerated, that he could not lie on his back for days. Sleep in those times came hard. He would weep, silently, for making noise in the dorter would lead to another thrashing, crying red-hot tears of misery at the loss of his darling parents. God should not have taken them from him. But God didn't. Men did.

His parents had been good, kind, hard-working folk. Their name came from the small property his father had inherited, a peasant's home at Nogaret, but his father had been better off than that. He had lived in Toulouse; made a fair living, too. Young Guillaume could remember both parents. In the long, lonely hours of the night, he was sure he could sometimes smell faint traces of lavender, the scent he associated with his mother. And sometimes, when he was about to doze off, he could feel the touch of her lips upon his forehead. Those were happy moments. She had doted upon him. He knew that. And he missed her so.

Theirs was a close family. All his father had wanted was for his 'Petit Guillaume' to take over his work and make a good life for himself. Simple desires, the desires of a peasant – but good, sensible ones, the kind that would wash through the veins of any man who had the earth baked into his soul from the first moment of birth. And Guillaume was one such man.

Yes, the boy hated the so-called men of God, who sought to conceal their true natures beneath calm smiles and soft manners. Yet he knew them. They had raised him; they had shown him their weaknesses. And he would exploit them, all of them.

At last! The signal.

Sieur Guillaume de Nogaret nodded to his servant, then spurred his mount. Behind him, the standard-bearer's flag flapped and crackled as the wind whipped around in little gusts. Perhaps that was why he was feeling reflective, Guillaume told himself. This area was like the hills about Carcassone and up to Montaillou. It reminded him of his old home.

But home was miles away, just as his arse was telling him now. Since the great meeting at the Louvre six months ago, Guillaume felt as though he had been travelling constantly, riding hurriedly to do the King's will. Paying out money without worry, hiring men as he may, and recruiting those who had as much hatred as he.

As his horse clattered up the stony path, he had to concentrate on keeping his seat, so when he reached the summit of the little rise, and could gaze about him, the scene was a fresh one.

A thousand – no, fifteen hundred – warriors were waiting in a small valley. They had ridden hard, too, all the way from Florence, where he had paid for them, and they were resting their horses and seeing to their equipment.

'My friend. I hope I find you well?'

Their leader was a tall, elegant, grizzled man of about the same age. He looked over Guillaume's clothing with a quizzical eye.

'I am well, Giacomo,' Guillaume said softly. Giacomo Colonna was the fiercest general in that warlike family. The Colonnas were the second great clan of Rome, and detested their enemies with a passion that was equalled only by Guillaume's. Any opportunity would be seized by them to hit back at the Gaetani family – especially the head.

There was nothing more to say. Giacomo, known as 'Sciarra', the Quarreller, because of his bellicose habits, was a man who believed more in actions than polite conversation, and particularly at a time like this, when he could almost smell the defeat and despair of his enemy. There was a gleeful spring to his step as he rallied his force and pushed and kicked recalcitrant men back on to their horses. In only a short while they were all remounted and then, with a raised arm, Sciarra Colonna set off, with the King of France's man at his side.

Within the hour, they had captured the man they both despised: Benedetto Gaetani, the leader of the great Roman clan, and now known as Pope Boniface VIII, who had over-turned the Colonna and driven them from their great homes and palaces. He had all but ruined them. And not content with that, now he had excommunicated the French King, and was threatening to put the whole of France under anathema. There would be no churches opening for any man. No burial services, no church weddings, no baptisms – nothing. That would be intolerable. The French could not allow it.

It was hard to command obedience from a Pope, but King Philip IV would not tolerate any more truculence. That was why his most trusted lawyer and adviser was here.

To kidnap the Pope.

Anagni

Toscanello di Accompagnato looked about him with astonishment as they entered the palace, struggling, and failing, to keep his mouth closed as he took in the rich paintings, the carvings and statuary. He had never seen such proof of wealth, not even in Florence. The Pope was truly a man to be honoured if he could possess such treasures. God must have showered these gifts upon him for a reason.

Yes, he told himself, the Pope was chosen by God. So he must go and confess this crime as soon as he could.

And it *was* a crime – there was little doubt about that. All over the place, there were men being held, while a few figures lay in the dirt, their blood leaching into the soil about them.

There had been little resistance. The men here had known that they couldn't win, and even the demands of loyalty to their master were insufficient to make a man fight when it was clear that the battle was already lost. So Guillaume's and Sciarra's troops had found their way eased considerably. They entered the papal palace and the great building swallowed them all. Somewhere inside, Toscanello knew, the Pope was being questioned by Guillaume. And soon he would appear, ready to be carried off to France.

Others were looting the place, but Toscanello could only stand and carry on gawping.

He was nineteen this year. Finding a living was hard in his little town, and he had decided to travel to Florence to try his fortune – but with little success. He was still forced to live on the streets, and there were times when he had been compelled to steal in order to eat. So far, he had not been caught, but he knew it was only a matter of time. Then he would have to flee, and eke out some sort of living in the outskirts – or stoop to joining one of the bandit gangs which plagued the lands all about.

But then there had come this proposal. He had been loitering outside a wine shop when he had seen a man whom he knew to be a servant of Sciarra Colonna; the man, noticing him, asked him whether he could ride and wield a sword. 'If you can, and you serve my lord,' he told Toscanello, 'you will be paid in gold.'

That had been a week ago. Now, here he was, in a foreign

land south of Rome, with over a thousand others, robbing the Pope himself.

Some of the men had declared themselves unwilling to attack when they learned who the target would be, but it only took one man being beaten to the ground by Sciarra Colonna for the rest to realise that they were happy to rob even Pope Boniface VIII.

In truth, most were anyway. They were all aware of the corruption of the Pope's rule. He had succeeded to the Papal throne because his predecessor, poor Celestine V, had been so wildly unsuitable. Everyone knew the story. When Pope Nicholas IV had died, no one could agree who should replace him. As usual, the Cardinals had been locked in their room to make the choice, with God guiding their way for them, but with clans like the Colonna and Orsini unwilling to give way and lose influence by choosing someone not of their blood, the process dragged on for eighteen months.

It was Pietro of Morrone who broke the deadlock. The old hermit, highly respected by all because he lived a life so austere it was a miracle he lived at all, wrote to the Cardinals threatening them with God's severe vengeance, should they not hurry and make a decision. To Pietro's horror, they did. They picked *him*.

There was a need for intense persuasion and diplomacy. Pietro was happier in his cave with his whips, so he might flagellate himself without interruption. He needed little food, and existed in a quiet manner, rarely speaking except to praise God and pray. Yet even he could not argue with the will of God, so he agreed, and two years after the death of Nicholas, at last there was a new Pope: Celestine V. He lasted four months.

A simple man, he wanted nothing for himself. His first command, on entering the new Papal palace at Naples, was that a wooden cell be built, in which he could sleep. He was entirely unprepared for the magnificence of his new position – nor for the deviousness and acquisitiveness of his Cardinals.

Unused to the grandeur of his new life, he was entirely overwhelmed. He wanted to be efficient, and signed all the papers thrust before him. Unknowingly, he approved benefices and appointments to the greedy. Some even had him sign blank sheets which they could later sell on for huge profits. The corruption of the Church rose to unthought-of levels. And Celestine grew sickened as he realised how ineffectual he really was.

The fiasco lasted four months. At the end of that time, the poor old man had had enough. He knew that he was no Pope. All he wanted was to leave the debauchery and avarice behind, to go back to his little cave and the simplicity of his past life. He told his Cardinals that he must abdicate. And that was when Benedetto Gaetani became Boniface VIII.

But people muttered that no man could merely resign from a position which God had granted. God's vicar on earth was installed by God, and no human, not even the Pope himself, could resist His will. So they looked on Boniface as being a usurper. The real Pope was still Celestine.

It was worrying enough to make Boniface send to have Celestine arrested, and although it took five months to track him down, at last Celestine was discovered at the coast, desperately seeking a ship to take him over the Adriatic. Brought back to Rome and thrown into the Papal prison, Fumone, there he languished until Boniface ordered his death. The old man could hardly have put up much of a struggle as a pillow was placed over his face and he was gradually suffocated.

So, now people looked upon Boniface as both an imposter *and* a murderer. He had stolen all the wealth he could from the

Papacy, and even made the astonishing claim that, as God's vicar, he held authority over all – even secular Lords and Kings. All must accept his lordship as a condition of their soul's salvation.

Not all agreed. Kings were given their crowns and thrones in the same manner as the Pope: they were given them by God. The King of France in particular was unimpressed. Confrontation was inevitable. And when Philip the Fair decided to take action, his enemies would do well to fly.

It was because of him that they were all here today, Toscanello knew. It was the French King's money which had paid for them all, and it was his servant, Sieur Guillaume de Nogaret, who was directing them. All in order to capture the Pope and bring him back to France.

Toscanello didn't care, though. All he knew was that he'd been given food and wine, and his purse stood to be heavier when they returned. For the moment his belly wasn't complaining, and life was good.

There was a shout from one little shed, and Toscanello saw a figure dart from it and bolt across the court. He looked around, but no one else appeared to have seen the fellow, so he gripped his sword in his hand and pelted along in pursuit.

The other man must have been the winner of the clerk's hundred-yard dash, from the speed he went at. In fact, for all his clerical garb, Toscanello reckoned he must be a lay brother in the Pope's service, for he had never seen a clerk run so fast before – up one narrow alley, then vaulting a low wall which Toscanello himself found challenging, before springing over a series of barrels behind the brewery, and hurling himself bodily at a door nearby. It slammed open, showering dust like a small explosion of gunpowder, and crashed shut again as Toscanello reached it. Unheeding of any possible danger, he kicked at it without slowing, and the door was flung wide.

Under this second assault, a timber cracked, and the whole frame sagged, hitting the ground and remaining still as Toscanello ran on inside.

It was a large storage vault, he saw. There were barrels lined up, some massive ones for fermenting wines, while further away he saw bales of goods imported from all over Christendom. And beyond them, a shadow, and the patter of sandalled feet.

Toscanello grunted to himself, and then set off again, his boots slapping on the paved floor. It was a huge room, this, larger than any he'd seen before. Probably used to store all that was necessary to feed the army of hangers-on which the Pope took with him everywhere. Not that many of them had stayed behind with their master; they had all melted away in the hour or so before the arrival of Guillaume and Sciarra's army. Only the Pope and a few loyal attendants remained, and this one fellow, too.

His behaviour was odd. Most of the clerks here had submitted immediately, hoping that by surrendering, they might save themselves further pain. Not so this one. He was running as though he thought he might be able to save himself somehow.

Toscanello shrugged. There was a door at the far side. He saw it close, and ran towards it, reaching it in time to hear the bolt sliding over.

'Shit!' He experimentally slammed the pommel of his sword into the old wood, and saw it dent and shiver. It was enough. He pounded on the door with all his might, until at last a plank burst apart, and he could reach in. Groping wildly, he found the bolt and opened it, shoving the door wide.

And found himself at the rear of the Pope's palace. A door was slammed a short way away, and he saw that it was the entrance to an undercroft.

'We'll dig him out,' a voice rasped, and Toscanello looked up to see Paolo striding towards him. Toscanello had never liked Paolo, and the feeling was mutual. Paolo had been a paid man-at-arms to a Roman family, and looked down upon all those who were born outside of Rome itself. Still worse, all those who weren't actually warriors. But he had three men with him, who may not have been Romans, but all had the same aristocratic contempt for peasants. Toscanello sheathed his sword and nodded, then turned and walked back the way he had come. It was plain enough that Paolo reckoned there could be a rich reward in following the man.

They were all there for profit, after all. There were men even now, arguing and fighting upstairs over some of the Pontiff's richer clothing; Toscanello could hear them. In the court he could see five or six men bickering over a huge tapestry, pulling in all directions, until another, a red-faced Piedmontese with a jug in one fist and his sword in the other, swathed in bright silks stolen from some secret store, set his sword's edge on the cloth and it ripped, the coloured threads parting all through, and the men falling.

The Piedmontese laughed uproariously, but then stopped as a dagger sliced across his throat, and the fool toppled back, thrashing about as he died. The others laughed then.

All about Toscanello, the place was degenerating. Someone had found the undercroft where the wine was stored, and there were men drinking and brawling in the dirt. From the shouts and screams inside the palace itself, others were rampaging through it, looting as they went. All that splendour, all the majesty of the Pope, was being systematically destroyed. It made Toscanello unutterably sad ... There was a sudden shout from Paolo, and Toscanello turned just in time to see his quarry spring from the door behind which he had hidden, and set off across the court towards Toscanello. But he had only taken seven or eight steps when Toscanello saw Paolo lift his arm. There was a glint of steel as he brought his arm back – and then he let fly.

The dagger he threw was little more than a flat, sharpened steel splinter ten inches long. There was no defined cross, only a rough leather grip. Now the highly polished steel flashed in the sun as it sped on towards the running man, and suddenly the man's steps faltered. He looked as though he would fall, but managed to pick up his rhythm again, running harder. Toscanello willed him to succeed, to reach some place of safety where he might be able to escape, but even as the thought ran through his mind, he saw the man's legs wobble, like a puppet whose strings were loosened. His eyes widened, and he slowed. Blood trickled from his lips, and he staggered, and then was suddenly still. He gazed at Toscanello with what looked like rage mingled with incomprehension, and then toppled to his knees, falling to rest on all fours before very gently sagging down to lie with his face in the dirt.

Paolo walked to him with a beaming smile. 'Said I could hit him, Hugues,' he called over his shoulder to one of his men. 'That's a gold piece you and Thomas owe me!' He pulled the dagger free, then stabbed twice, quickly into the man's back – one to the kidneys, one to the heart – before wiping the blade clean on the dead man's robes. He cast a contemptuous glance in Toscanello's direction, and swaggered away.

He was plainly dead before Toscanello reached him. Rolling the body over, he found himself staring down at a young man of his own age. The eyes were brown, but already fogged with death, and the splash of blood about his face made him look repugnant, but Toscanello forced himself to peer down at him for a few moments, reflecting that this had been a man. That it could easily have been him who died here.

Just a man. A young man with a tonsure. Toscanello shook

his head. The fellow had a crucifix about his neck, and a rosary at his belt. And then he peered. There was a key, too. A large steel key, as though to a door or a large chest.

That was how Toscanello became richer than any man he had ever met.

And why he was slain.

Monday after Nativitas, Blessed Virgin Mary, eighteenth year of the reign of King Philip IV of France[1]

Anagni

Guillaume de Nogaret marched over to the figure lying dead on the ground. He looked at the Sergent. 'Well?'

'They killed him, took the money and bolted. They're not the only ones though – you know that. All the men are sitting here hung-over and riotous.'

'Which ones were they?'

'Paolo's men – Hugues and Thomas – but he's dead too. So only those two. You want me to send after them?'

The King of France's most trusted adviser looked down at the broken figure of Toscanello. 'He was only Italian,' he said. 'Let them go. We don't have the men to catch them.'

[1] Monday, 9 September 1303

Chapter One

Morrow of Deusdedit,
Third year of the reign of King Charles IV of France,
nineteenth year of the reign of King Edward II of
England[1]

Louvre, Paris

At last the woman was gone. He would not meet her here in the Louvre on his way to the chapel, nor in the King's chamber. He was rid of her.

Cardinal Thomas d'Anjou could not help but feel the spring in his step at the thought. Her presence here in Paris had been an embarrassment for too long. The idea that a woman like her should come here and flagrantly ignore the rightful demands of her husband . . . well, it was not to be borne.

King Charles IV had demonstrated enormous sympathy for her. Of course, he always considered any situation from the perspective of chivalry, and what was honourable, so when his sister arrived here in France, King Charles had made her welcome. The fact that she was a negotiator from that despicable tyrant, King Edward II of England, did not detract from the King's evident joy at seeing his sister again.

Perhaps his pleasure was enhanced by the fact that he was himself married again at last. The poor man had suffered so much from the adultery of his first wife. The whole royal family had. She and her sisters-in-law had been found to have committed the foul sin with two knights. Immediately the women were imprisoned, while the men suffered the most humiliating, painful and public deaths ever meted out by a King to a traitor.

King Charles's woman was mentioned only in lowered tones since then. But at long last the Pope had permitted the annulment of the marriage when she had fallen pregnant to her gaoler at the Château Gaillard. The clear, incontrovertible proof of her faithlessness at that point had been enough, and the Pope at last gave his agreement. Now the faithless one was safely installed in a convent far away, and the King had remarried a second time. Sadly, his second wife had died in childbirth. The baby himself had only lasted a short while before also succumbing, and now the King was married to his third wife, the delightful young Jeanne d'Évreux. Hopefully, with her he would prove more fortunate and provide an heir for the kingdom.

There had been so much trouble in the last few years, Cardinal Thomas thought. Ever since the end of the Templars, the Parisians had experienced increasing hardship. Kings came and went, but they were astonishingly short-lived, and none seemed able to father a son. This latest King could be the saving of the line – it was an end to be desired, after all. God alone knew who else might take over the realm.

But his sister's arrival, and her refusal to obey her own husband, must be a shameful reminder to King Charles of his own suffering. Even the joy of his latest marriage must be soured by the presence of his sister, Queen Isabella of England. After all, she it was who had told their father about the women's adultery in the first place.

A messenger came, knocking gently on the door.

'Yes?'

'Cardinal, there is a man to see you. He says he has information for the King.'

The Cardinal made a dismissive gesture. 'You want me to come and see someone *now*? Are you a complete fool?'

'He said it was about a treasure, Cardinal. Something stolen from the King. I thought someone should know, but the steward, the marshals – *everyone* – is preparing for the departure of the English Queen.'

Cardinal Thomas frowned, looking at his reflection in the mirror. There was a little mark on his cheek, and he licked a finger, removing it. 'Very well. I shall come to find him,' he said eventually, and rose. 'There is still some little while before the King and his lady arrive. I shall go to see this man, and then you can take him back to the gates again – yes?'

He waved the servant onwards, and the man led the way along the high corridor, and into a tower. They descended by spiral stairs to the ground floor and turned left, past the kitchens and storehouses, where the din of clattering pans and dishes mingled with shouted commands to the kitchen staff and one hoarse bellowing voice demanding to know where on God's earth his kitchen knave had gone. The Cardinal also saw the black-haired whore who was Hugues's latest favourite, sitting and combing her hair with slow, wanton deliberation near the horse troughs. No doubt she'd been washing away her sins, the Cardinal thought sardonically.

At a door near the great gate, the servant stopped, waiting for a sign. The Cardinal nodded, his eyes closed. 'Be quick!'

The servant opened the door for the Cardinal, and stood back.

Cardinal Thomas entered. 'What on . . . Man, there's been a murder! Call the guard at once!'

'Sir? I—'

'*GO!*'

As the servant hurried away, his feet silent on the sanded ground, the Cardinal crouched by the side of the man on the ground. The fellow was only twenty or so. Not much more, certainly. He had a strong face, but resentment showed in the narrow set of the eyes. There was much you could tell from a man's face, the Cardinal thought; this one had lived with bitterness. 'Where you are going, all bitterness will be gone,' he muttered gently, and pressed his fingers to the man's throat, feeling for a pulse. There was nothing. Just the coolness that was unnatural in a living man.

Sighing, Cardinal Thomas knelt and began to recite the *Pater Noster*, then the *Viaticum*, as he glanced about him at the room where the fellow lay.

'What a place to die, eh? What a place.'

Château du Bois, Paris

Queen Isabella of England stood with her back to the window as she held her arms out for her ladies to clothe her. All must be perfect, after all. She was a Queen.

Yet even a Queen had concerns. For Queen Isabella it was hard to know what to do for the best. If she were weaker in spirit, she would have given up her embassy and returned to her husband. There was so very little money remaining now. That was a permanent worry, because her grasping, miserly spouse had not entrusted her with sufficient funds when he sent her here to Paris to negotiate with her brother. No, instead he had taken away all her revenues, as though she herself might become a traitor. All because she was French.

Perhaps there was no actual malice in it. Edward was not generally malicious. Or hadn't been before his mind had been poisoned by that murderous devil, Sir Hugh le Despenser.

When they had first been married, he had treated her with

scant respect, but she had been so young compared with him. He was four- or five-and-twenty, while she was just twelve. It was not surprising that he preferred the company of others, of older men. And women, of course. She was wise enough to know that. It was four years before she would be able to give birth to their son, Edward. Adam had been the King's first-born son, although poor Adam had died in Scotland on one of the King's adventures to pacify that cold and wet province.

Still, he had appreciated her when his great companion, Piers Gaveston, had died, murdered by his most powerful barons. They had *dared* set themselves against their lawful King! That was something a French baron would never have thought to attempt, but the English were ever truculent and rebellious. Even the people of London would revolt at the slightest opportunity and rush through the streets causing mayhem and murder as they went. It was a land that demanded a mailed fist to control it.

At that time she had done all in her power to aid and support him, as any wife would. The birth of their boy had helped, naturally. King Edward II was besotted with the lad. As soon as little Edward was born, the King seemed to change. He lavished presents upon the man who brought news of the birth, he made grand gestures to his boy, endowing him with lands and ennobling him when he was only a few days old.

But the depredations of Despenser were bound to cause problems, and soon the depth of the Despenser's greed became apparent.

In the beginning he was more circumspect, but as he grew less worried about his position, depending upon the King for support, the people in the land grew to hate him more and more. Eventually his thefts, his murders, his kidnaps and tortures proved too much and the Lords Marcher in Wales could take no more. They overran his territories and brought their armies to London. For a while they held the King to account and forced Despenser's exile. But then, when he returned, he was stronger, more deeply in the King's affection, and all the more powerful.

The Lords Marcher were crushed at the Battle of Boroughbridge, and afterwards began the slaughter. Men-at-arms, squires, even knights and lords, were rounded up and executed as an example to others. The first to die was the King's own cousin, Earl Thomas of Lancaster. It was as though all the King's rage at the way his 'dear brother' Piers had been slain was guiding his mind now. All those who now stood against his new favourite were his enemies, and he would destroy them all. The bodies of his enemies decorated the gates of every town and city in the realm.

It was a hideous shock. Isabella could see the change in every aspect of her own life.

All was the fault of that snake, Despenser, and the foul Bishop of Exeter, the untruthful, greedy thief who set such stock on probity in public, and who enriched himself at the expense of all while he was Lord High Treasurer to the King. It was those two together who caused her such terrible trouble.

Despenser hated her. There was no hiding his feelings. They both knew and understood each other. There might be occasional flashes of mutual respect, but little more than that. Despenser had lured her husband from her, and she would never forgive him. Her ease of spirit was all gone, stolen away by this . . . this *pharisee*. Any joy she had once experienced in her marriage was now nothing but a fading memory.

The Bishop was equally evil, in her mind. It was he who had spoken to the King after the War of Saint-Sardos last year, he who had murmured soft words of deceit. He said that it was unsafe for the French to have an ally in the easily invaded lands of Devon and Cornwall. Perhaps it would be best if they were taken out of the control of the Lady who was sister to the French King, and who was yet the Queen of England. Not because she was *herself* disloyal, of course . . . but she had a huge *familia* to support her. And almost all were French themselves.

Her household was broken up shortly afterwards. All her properties were taken into the King's hands, all her income confiscated, her servants, guards and even ladies-in-waiting dismissed, all bar a tiny number. Even her children were taken from her. No doubt, in order that she might not pollute their minds against the lawful commands of their father. That was how effective the Bishop's sly mutters had been. She had not even the solace of her daughters. And then she was herself given a new household of ladies; now nothing could be written or sent in private apart from some few, carefully concealed notes which the Queen managed to secrete about herself. There were still one or two men upon whom she could rely. Even the woman responsible for her household was installed at the insistence of Despenser. Isabella's most senior lady-in-waiting was his wife, Eleanor. And Eleanor held that most potent proof of Isabella's independence: her personal seal. There was nothing remaining of Isabella's regal position, in truth. It was utterly humiliating.

With the pittance her husband had allowed for this journey, there was little for any form of extravagance. That was why she was forced to leave Paris and find cheaper accommodation elsewhere. Soon, perhaps, she would be forced into returning to her husband. There was no alternative, when all was said and done. At least for now she was only to move a little outside the city, to the Château du Bois.

Meanwhile, there were compensations. Life here in France was far less austere than her existence had been in recent months. Although she could not afford distractions of her own, there were many invitations from others, to parties, hunts, diversions of all kinds.

All she hoped was that the truce should hold a little longer, and that the negotiations should continue. Here she felt free once more.

She would not return to England to be insulted and slighted, to be gaoled in a gilded cage.

Chapter Two

Louvre, Paris

Arnaud, the porter at the south gate to the castle, heard the cries before the messenger appeared, panting and anxious.

'What is it, man?' he demanded. He was seated on a bench behind his makeshift desk, booted feet up on it, his back resting against the wall behind him. Without a candle, the servant could only see a low blur in the gloomy room after the bright sunshine outside.

'A man came to speak with the Cardinal d'Anjou, and he's been murdered.'

Arnaud closed his eyes and shook his head, then said, 'Go and find the guard, tell him to see to the body, and then fetch the city's prosecutor. The Procureur should be present as the matter is investigated. He will take charge. *Go!*'

But when the boy had fled from him, Arnaud suddenly gaped with a distracted air. 'Which man has been murdered?' Then, with a stern expression on his face, he slapped the pommel of his sword in a gesture of decision, called to one of his officers and left the gate in his hands while he himself strode off towards the hall to visit the castellan, Sieur Hugues de Toulouse.

The Louvre had a magnificent hall, as befitted the King of France, and the castellan's little room was attached to the eastern end. It was a small square chamber, with a large table and a stool, and a bed area behind. A fireplace and chimney had been added, and a cheery fire hissed and spluttered, making the porter jealous when he thought of his own chilly and comfortless little room.

Today, though, when he entered, the castellan was busy. A slim, dark-haired beauty was sitting astride him as he lay on the bed behind the desk, and she turned and met Arnaud's appraising gaze with a tilt of her head. He smiled at her. He'd seen her earlier when she had entered the castle. You didn't forget a face and body like hers.

'You want something? Eh? Hurry up!'

'Sieur Hugues, I . . .'

'You waiting for a formal introduction? This is Amélie. Amélie, this is Arnaud, the porter. Arnaud is the man who should be guarding our gate, but instead he's here in my chamber staring at your bubbies.'

The castellan's words and tone proved that he had no desire to discuss matters at the moment, and Arnaud quietly stepped from the room and closed the door.

He would have to come and see him later, when the castellan was less 'busy'.

Procureur Jean de Poissy eyed the messenger without comment for a moment, chewing a hunk of bread with some hard cheese. A tall man, with a long face surprisingly unmarked by scars for a knight who had spent so much of his life fighting in his King's causes, he was elegant and urbane. Unlike many warriors, he was also intelligent.

'Who is the dead man?' he asked.

'I don't know. He didn't give his name.'

'Who killed him?'

'I don't know!'

'Why was he killed?'

'I . . .'

'. . . don't know. No, nor do I, but these are the questions we must ask, heh? So, take me to the unfortunate fellow, and we shall see what may be discerned.'

Château du Bois

The Queen waved her ladies away when Lord John Cromwell was announced. Only little Alicia was permitted to remain when Lord John and William de Bouden entered. There was no need of a chaperone with these men.

William gave her a curious look, and she felt a cold hand clutch at her heart, suddenly fearing that somehow her husband had changed his mind and ordered her immediate return to London. But then she saw that there was an odd stillness about him, as though he was listening to Lord John with his entire soul.

'Your Royal Highness,' Cromwell began, 'I have received some news from England. It is not all good, I fear.'

'Continue.'

'The King has discussed the position here with his council, and they have concluded that the best means of resolving all the issues, is for him to come here himself.'

'The King? My husband will come here?' Queen Isabella gasped. 'But how will he do so? Will he leave the realm under the control of our son?'

'My Lady, I do not know more than this,' Lord Cromwell said. He was quiet a moment, and then looked down at the ground, frowning. 'But . . .'

The Queen maintained her silence, but motioned to Alicia to fetch the jug of wine from the sideboard. Alicia floated over the floor, a graceful figure in all she did, and soon both men were sipping from large goblets.

Lord Cromwell pursed his lips, and then looked up with some sort of resolve in his eyes. 'My Lady, I think you will be ordered to return to England upon his arrival.'

Aha! she thought. 'I fear you are right. And I shall be forced to return to my prison, guarded by those set to watch over me.'

'I think that would be a great shame, my Lady. Further . . .' His eyes slid towards William, and the Lord appeared to take some courage from the impassive man at his side. 'Further, I think it would be a mistake. You are crucial to our negotiations with your brother.'

That was why she was here. To ensure a continued peace with her brother, King Charles IV. After the little war last year, King Charles had confiscated all the English territories in France. It was Isabella's job to try to win them all back. And she had all but succeeded. All that was needed now was for the King to pay homage to the French King for those lands which were held under feudal tenure. The rest didn't matter. And until the King came to pay homage, the Agenais would remain under the control of the French King for now, while the courts decided what should happen to it.

The French had set the date of the *assumptio* of the Blessed Virgin Mary[1] – one month exactly from today. That was the date when he was supposed to be here in France, to perform the formal homage at Beauvais.

But she was sure that he would not come. He was sly, as she knew all too well; cunning enough to escape this. To perform full homage to another King would imply that he was little more than a vassal to the French. A man who might be called 'King', but who in reality held his crown not because it had been bestowed by God, but because he was permitted to do so by his superior. King Edward would never tolerate such a climb-down.

'I shall be delighted to see my husband again, of course,'

---

[1] Thursday, 15 August 1325

she said carefully. Lord John was still the man set to guard her during her journey here, not selected by her, but by Despenser and her husband.

'We have heard that he is to delay his journey. The date for him to meet with your brother is now to be two weeks later, on the Feast Day of St John the Baptist[1].'

The hand was at her heart again. Did he mean that she was to return at once, then? But no! That would be too cruel. She would not go yet. To voluntarily return to a prison would be . . .

'My Lady, I do not think you should return. You should remain here. There is much still to do, and it would be wrong for you to hurry precipitately from Paris. Better that you should wait for your husband here.'

She nodded, not allowing a smile, but as the two men backed their way from her room, she was convinced that the air in her chamber had grown musty and unwholesome. She was suddenly hot, dizzy, and she gasped, swaying, before rushing to the window, throwing the shutter wide and gulping at the air.

'My Lady? My Lady, drink this!' Alicia said urgently, passing her a goblet.

'Wine, Alicia? Wine? I don't need wine now!' Isabella said breathlessly. 'Do you understand? Did you see what my Lord Cromwell was saying? He has moved to our camp, Alicia. Even the head of the King's embassy here in France has moved to support me!'

Louvre, Paris

His mood, always fragile, shattered when the next knock came. Sieur Hugues lifted Amélie bodily from him, stood up

---

[1] Thursday, 29 August 1325

and hoiked his hosen up as he walked across the room to open it.

Amélie couldn't help but laugh as she watched him. The sight of his skinny little legs, the heavy scarlet robe, and his scowling features was enough to make her dissolve. Even when he threw a furious look in her direction, it only served to make the scene still more amusing.

'What do you want?' he bellowed at the poor boy outside.

'Sir, there's b-been a murder!' the boy stammered, appalled at the glower on his face and petrified that he might be beaten for interrupting.

Sir Hugues was still for a heartbeat, and then he glanced over his shoulder at Amélie, his face a picture of horror.

She met his gaze with a blink of surprise. She had no idea why he should look so anxious. He had been here all the time.

Furnshill, Devon

'Wat! Stop that unholy racket!'

If it were not for young Wat whistling in that tuneless, foolish manner, Baldwin de Furnshill would have been perfectly content as he sat at his table. There was much to be done here, plus he had duties as Keeper of the King's Peace, which kept him busy. It was just good to be here, at home, with his wife. For too much of the last year he had been forced to stay away from his family, even undertaking a journey to France to protect the Queen on her way to see her brother, but now he could sit and enjoy the simpler delights of his family. Or could, if it weren't for Wat . . .

Baldwin was tempted to tell him to leave the hall – but that would not do. Wat had every right to sit at table, just as all his servants did. They were there by feudal obligation: theirs was to serve and support him, while his was to feed, house and clothe them. The responsibility of feudal law meant more, so

Baldwin sometimes felt, to the lord of the manor than it did to the servants themselves.

But it was a responsibility which he felt keenly. Any man who had given him his word and hand was fully deserving of Sir Baldwin's reciprocation. Just as Baldwin's own lords were deserving of his unswerving loyalty, so he was deserving of their support and protection. That was the whole basis of English law.

So, Sir Baldwin must give all aid to the Lord of the Shire, Sir Hugh de Courtenay; through him, Baldwin must support the King himself. As must Sir Hugh. And yet Baldwin was becoming concerned that the balance of rights and responsibilities was shifting. There was a growing burden on the part of the King's subjects – all because of Despenser. The rapacity of the man was unwholesome and no one in the country could stomach it any more – except, apparently, the King.

Outside, once he had finished his meal, the air was still cool, and as he waited for his horse to be brought to him he stood in front of the house gazing down southwards, a tall man of some two-and-fifty years with the powerful shoulders of a trained warrior, the thick neck of a knight used to the weight of a heavy helm, and the slightly bandy legs of a man who had spent much of his time in the saddle. His dog walked to him, sitting against his leg and leaning, looking up into his eyes.

Wolf was a handsome animal. He was heavy-boned, and black all over, apart from delightful tan colouring at his eyebrows, cheeks and ankles, with a white muzzle, paws and tip to the tail. And a large white cross on his breast. He panted all the while, as though it was ridiculously hot in the sun. Still a little anxious, he preferred to be with Baldwin at every moment. It was irritating to Jeanne on occasion, but Baldwin had always been a lover of hounds and large dogs of all types.

He had acquired Wolf only a few weeks ago, from the Bishop of Orange, and felt honoured that the brute was so affectionate to him in such a short while.

As he thought this, his eyes rose to the distant view again.

'Husband, you are too pensive.'

He smiled and nodded as Jeanne, his wife, joined him. From here there was a patch of grass that led to the Tiverton Road. It was a small pasture for feeding goats and occasional travellers' horses, but Baldwin always enjoyed standing just here, in front of his door, because there was a fair view over the road. It was easier to see people approaching.

'Are you worried about something?' she said gently.

'Your soft words show better than anything how well you understand me,' he said with a dry grin, his fingers playing at the hair on Wolf's head.

It was easy to be happy in her company, he reflected. Jeanne was a tall, slim woman with red-gold hair, and a face that had none of the merits of classical beauty. Her nose was tip-tilted, her mouth over-wide, with a large upper lip. And yet it was the total of the imperfections that he thought made her unimaginably lovely. Added to her looks, she had a brain which was sharp and astute.

'Is it the King?'

He sighed. There was no concealing his fears with his wife, no matter how dangerous it might be to allow his concerns to become more widely known. 'Yes. I do not know what I should do.'

'What is the need to worry about it at this time?'

'In case I have a man demand that I support him now. This has been brewing for many years. Our Lord, Hugh de Courtenay, has been a keen supporter of the King most of the time – but when Piers Gaveston was being hunted down in the land, it was Sir Hugh who went to try to capture him. When there have been troubles, and the Good Lord knows how often there have been in this unhappy reign, the baron has been at the forefront of the forces trying to hold the King to account.'

'You are worried that he may not support the King?' Jeanne said quietly.

'It would not surprise me. And would that mean that he would demand my loyalty to him personally?'

'What would you do if he did?'

'I could do little. I have made my oath to Sir Hugh and his family. But I do have a higher debt of honour to the King, surely?'

'I am sure you will find a balance, my husband.'

'I wish I were so sure as you,' Baldwin smiled. Then, at the sound of a short scream from inside the house, he spun round and winced. 'I think your son wants you again!'

'He can wait,' Jeanne said with uncharacteristic sharpness. 'What of Despenser?'

'He has no oath from me,' Baldwin said shortly. 'The man is vile. If his mother were to swallow a gold coin, he would dismember her to seek it.'

'Baldwin! That's a terrible thing to say!' Jeanne laughed.

He did not join her. He had not been joking. 'I seek only to avoid any confrontation with him.'

'I think that is sensible.'

'Yes,' Baldwin said, and his eyes rose to the view again. There was no one on the road, he saw.

That was good. Because there was one man he did not wish to be called to see: the Bishop of Exeter, Walter Stapledon.

Chapter Three

Westminster, Thorney Island

Sir Hugh le Despenser was in his small chamber when his clerk found the single sheet of parchment in among the pile of correspondence.

'My Lord?'

'What is it?'

'You have apparently acquired a property in Devon, but I cannot see exactly what this . . .'

Despenser frowned and strode to the unfortunate man, snatching it from him.

'It's from Wattere,' the clerk said helpfully.

His master turned a look upon him that was so sour, the clerk reckoned it could have curdled milk.

The Lord Despenser was not, in truth, looking well. His face had grown pinched and sallow in the last few weeks.

Seeing Despenser glance at him again, the clerk turned back to his work. It was never pleasant to have the Lord's eye upon a man. There was a wealth of suspicion in that eye, and it was dangerous to be thought of as someone who was showing too much interest in him or his affairs. There were enough men and women in the country who were now his enemies.

But the plain fact was, Sir Hugh was a worried man. This in response to news coming in of armies being gathered over the sea, of more and more malcontents who were so disenchanted

with the rule of Sir Hugh and the King that they had fled the
land and were now gathering in ever larger, bolder groups in
France and in other places where the King's enemies
congregated. The trouble was, almost all the world was the
King's enemy. Everyone knew that.

There were reports almost weekly now of ships being
readied for an invasion; and each time Sir Hugh would spring
into frenetic action, distributing messages to the Admirals, to
the Sheriffs of the coastal counties, to knights and others upon
whom he felt he could count, demanding added vigilance,
ordering them to send ships to sea to seek out the forces which
threatened the realm, and generally over-reacting. It was a
proof of his own sense of vulnerability.

That was not all. The kingdom was unsettled. Certainly Sir
Hugh had not helped matters with his single-minded pursuit of
his advancement at the cost of all others. There were many
who had cause to regret hearing his name. Some were
impoverished, their lands and treasure forfeit to the King and
now held by Despenser as reward for his loyalty. His enrich-
ment had come at the expense of so many of the families who
had chosen to set their faces against their King. Others had
been broken physically, their limbs shattered until they agreed
to sign away their fortunes to him, while some few were no
more, their bodies concealed in shallow graves.

But the instability which he had assisted was now growing
alarming. Only this month, Robert Sapy's deputy in Wales had
been attacked in Gloucestershire. His eyes had been torn out,
his legs and arms smashed, and his accounts stolen. There had
been a time only a very short while ago when no man would
have dared to treat such an important man in so dreadful a
manner, but that time was past. Now no one was safe.

And just as he grew alarmed to hear such stories, there was
the threat of the King actually leaving the country to go to

France to pay homage to King Charles IV. Sweet Christ in chains, was the man a *cretin*? If the King were to leave England, Despenser could not go with him. He had been promised death if he ever set foot in France. But as soon as the King left the realm, Despenser's life wouldn't be worth a wooden farthing.

He barked suddenly: 'You! Peter!'

The clerk jumped, startled from his reverie. 'Yes, my Lord?'

'Take a message for Wattere. It is this: "Let him know".'

'Just that?'

'Yes. He will know what to do,' Despenser said. He clasped his hands behind his back.

Peter the clerk watched him surreptitiously. The stance in many would look like that of a decisive man who was considering a new task, but Peter knew him better than most.

He thought Despenser was trying to stop his hands from twitching with nervousness.

Old Palace Yard, Westminster Palace

Edward, the Earl of Chester, strode from the court where he had been practising sword-play with a master of defence, and wiped his forehead with a cloth.

He was already showing signs of the kind of man he would become. Only twelve years old, he was powerfully built, with a long, handsome face framed by thick golden hair. His eyes showed his intelligence: quick, shrewd and observant; he was already a good judge of character. He had been made Earl only a few days after his birth, although his father had been sixteen before he was given an earldom. And it made a difference, he knew. He had inherited responsibilities and duties which most others wouldn't have to think about until they were men.

His other gift was that of diplomacy. Early on, he had

discovered that he must develop these skills to help bridge the gap between his parents, as his father withdrew more and more, growing convinced by stages that his wife was a traitor and considering deserting him.

'My Lord, your father has asked that you join him,' a servant said, panting slightly as he trotted beside the Earl.

'I will go straightway to him, then,' Earl Edward said. He took the next corridor, and in a few minutes was walking into the King's own chamber.

It was a magnificent room. The ceiling was white, with corbels inset, but the walls were painted with scenes from the Old Testament. Carpets lay on the floor, softening the sound of tread, while at the far end was the King's bed. Servants stood silently. When the King lifted a hand, miraculously a goblet appeared in it, the man who had placed it there swiftly but silently returning to stand at the cupboard.

'My Lord King?' Earl Edward said.

'There is no need for too much formality today,' the King said as his son bowed low. 'Today is a day for discussion of the problems I face.'

'My King, you are universally respected . . .'

'I am hated by many.'

'Yet still *respected*,' the Earl said with barely a pause.

'You know the situation with France,' the King said, ignoring his words. 'I am caught in a cleft stick. If I do this, I lose the Agenais. If I do *this*, I lose all our French territories. It is intolerable! Am I not a King in my own right?'

'Not in France, my Lord,' Edward said simply.

'Then I must go and abase myself before my brother-in-law. It will demean the Crown to do so before a foreign power. Can I do it and keep my royal dignity?'

'I am not sure that there is a choice, my father.'

The King did not notice the alteration in tone. A slight

steeliness had crept into the Earl's voice. This discussion was not an abstract matter to him. It affected the realm which he would one day inherit.

'There is an alternative.' The King had stepped to a window near the large fireplace, and now he stood by it reflectively, staring out over the Thames. *'You.'*

'I don't understand.' Earl Edward remained where he was for the moment, gazing at his father with some perplexity.

'Your mother has proposed another idea. It wasn't her own, of course. Her brother, that *shite* Charles, thought this up a few months ago. No doubt he managed to persuade her to his will. You will see that, Edward. Women are invariably weak and suggestible. It is always easier to deal with men, I assure you.'

'What is this, Father?'

'The proposal is, that I invest you with all my territories in France. Make you a Duke of Guyenne. Then you can yourself go to France, meet with your mother, and pay homage.'

'Can you do that?'

'I am King, boy!'

Earl Edward bit back a hasty reply. This was a time to think. *Think!* 'You do not wish to go because it would be demeaning?' he confirmed.

'Yes. But if you go in my place, it will serve to protect dear Hugh.'

'How so?'

'Do you go about with your ears covered?' his father snapped. 'There are many who resent any friend of mine, and I must protect Sir Hugh. He would come with me to France, but I cannot acquire a safe passage for him. The French have an unreasoning hatred for him.'

The Earl forbore to mention the period when Despenser had been exiled and, rather than seek a safe home, had set about raiding shipping from his own great vessel. In one encounter, he stole a wealthy French ship and her cargo. Since then, he had been threatened with torture and death, as befitted a pirate, should he ever set foot on French soil.

'So I cannot go with him. Yet, if I leave him alone here, defenceless and unprotected, he may be captured and destroyed like poor Piers.'

'Poor Piers' Gaveston had been the King's previous adviser, before Despenser. While away from the King and without protection, he had been grabbed and executed after a brief trial organised by some of his many enemies. King Edward would not leave Sir Hugh le Despenser to suffer the same fate.

'So you will remain here, then?' Earl Edward said.

'If I elevate you to a Dukedom, you will have the authority to pay homage on behalf of the whole of Guyenne. That will satisfy the King of France, and it will satisfy me.'

'So you are decided?'

'I think so,' the King said, but then he tilted his head in that curiously undecided way he had. 'I do not see any other path. I *cannot* risk losing Sir Hugh, and your mother and your uncle have both urged that I settle Guyenne on you and that you go and pay homage. I trust neither, so will not!'

'I do not understand . . .'

'Do you think I am a fool? If I sent you to them, your mother would have you under her control. I cannot do that. So I will comply with their wishes. I will go myself. But while I am there in France, I shall leave Sir Hugh as your responsibility. He will advise you in my place, and you will obey all his commands, and see that he is protected.'

He had been talking musingly, as though to himself, but now he appeared to remember his son was present, and span round on his heel. 'You will look after him, yes?'

Earl Edward nodded, but internally he was sickened. Not by

the vacillation of his father, but by his weakness. By the tone of pleading.

Wednesday before the Feast of Mary Magdalen[1]

Chapelle de Saint Pierre, near the Louvre, Paris

Jean de Poissy stood at the back of the chamber as the priest intoned the prayers, trying to ignore the thick fumes from the censer as they wafted past him. The odour was thick and cloying, and caught in his throat like a pungent woodsmoke.

There was little enough for him to see here, but he felt as though he owed it to the dead man to come and witness his funeral. There were all too few others who would come for an unknown man.

He waited as the body was taken out, watching the priest and the peasants who carried it, his mind on the identity of the poor soul. He was keen to find the man's murderer, and yet there was nothing to show who the man was, nor why he would have come to the castle. No one had admitted to knowing him.

All Jean knew was that the fellow had come there to see the Cardinal. That was something to mull over, certainly.

The body was gone, and at last the little chapel was quiet again. Jean leaned back against the wall, staring down the empty space to the altar. This close to the royal castle of the Louvre, it benefited from the wealthy men who came to pray. Gilt shone on the woodwork, the floor was neatly paved and tiled, and the altar itself held enough decorative and valuable metalwork to tempt a saint to theft.

It was the delight of Paris, he thought. And Paris was surely the world's most magnificent city, resting here in the world's

---

[1] Wednesday, 17 July 1325

greatest nation. Paris, the jewel of Christianity. All the world's people envied Paris. They sought her learning in the university, they sought her culture, her beauty. They came from all over the world to enrich themselves, to find a better life. Hardly surprising they came only to Paris, in Jean's view, bearing in mind how intellectually impoverished so much of the nation remained. The people of the soggy lands north were a bickering, unruly mob; those in the east were merely unmanageable, while those to the south, in the too-dry lands – their people were noted for their feuding. Only here in Paris was there order and calm, the centre of the French nation created by Charles Martel.

'Mon Sieur Procureur?' It was a flustered-looking youth clad in a threadbare tunic and bare feet. He had a tousled mop of pale brown hair, and grey eyes with a slight squint, so Jean was unsure whether he was looking at him or not. 'I have been sent to ask whether you have learned any more about the dead man?'

'How did you know I would be here?' Jean asked softly. He stood studying the church without turning to the boy.

'I think . . . I was told you would be here.'

'Ah . . . I see. By whom?'

'The bottler to Cardinal Thomas. He told me to find you to learn whether you have any news of this man's death?'

'You see, this is most interesting. I have this body, the body of a young fellow who wished to see the Cardinal, and yet the Cardinal says he knew nothing of him. And meanwhile, of course, nobody else appears to have any knowledge of him whatever. It is peculiar, do you not think?'

'Me?'

The church was certainly not as richly decorated as the cathedral of Notre-Dame, but for a smaller place, which existed mainly to serve the souls of a community of merchants, it had done very well. It was more modest, but still beautiful. A wide, clean space with all the decoration that man's skill and money could achieve.

There was a thought there, he knew. The thought that the Cardinal was only a more lowly version of the Pope, perhaps. He was as beautifully clothed and bejewelled, just on a smaller scale.

But why had the dead man come to meet the Cardinal?

'Take me to him.'

Chapter Four

Furnshill, Devon

It was early afternoon when Baldwin heard the clattering and squeaking of a large number of men on horseback. His attention snapped to the road, and Wolf followed his gaze, a low rumble in his throat.

There were few noises which Baldwin found so irritating as these. His little estate was a source of calmness and peace for him. Sir Baldwin had been born here, in this little manor, but when the call to arms came from the Kingdom of Jerusalem, demanding aid from Christians the world over, he had gladly taken up a sword. There wasn't much for him in England, after all. His older brother would inherit their father's lands, and for Baldwin there was the possibility of a post in the Church if he wanted, but his martial spirit quailed at the thought of spending the whole of the rest of his life in a convent.

Thus it was that in the Year of Our Lord 1291, Baldwin de Furnshill arrived in Acre, the last city to be encircled by the Saracens. He endured the horror of that siege with fortitude for much of the time, only beginning to sink into despair at the very end. Then, when the heathens exploited a breach, Baldwin and Edgar, the man who was to become Baldwin's comrade and companion, were rescued by a ship owned by the Knights Templar. The warrior-monks saved their lives and gave them peace to rest themselves in a preceptory until they were whole and hale again, and when they were, Baldwin and

Edgar together joined the Order to repay the debt.

For more than a decade they served their Order, until the day when an avaricious French King and detestable Pope conspired to destroy the Order whose only guilt was to have served their God with honour and distinction. Baldwin and Edgar returned to England finally, seeking the sort of peace that could be found only in a quiet rural community.

This noise was a reminder to Baldwin of war and death. It was the sound of armour rattling and chinking, the rumble and thud of a cart passing over rutted roads, the laughter and coarse joking of men-at-arms all together.

'What is it?' Jeanne asked, walking to his side as Baldwin stood in the doorway, watching.

'Quiet, Wolf! I am not sure. I cannot see their flags from here. I would guess that they are men called to fight.'

'For whom, though?'

Baldwin shook his head. The cavalcade continued on its way, heading southwards and west, towards Crediton, or maybe Exeter. They could have been from Tiverton, from Lord Hugh de Courtenay's castle, or perhaps they were from some further manor. All told there were seven-and-twenty, by his count. A fair-sized entourage for a minor lord.

It left him feeling unsettled.

'They're gone, Baldwin,' Jeanne said soothingly. She could see that he was distracted by the sight.

'It worries me, Jeanne. There are so many men riding about the land now, and many have no care for the law.'

'We are safe enough here,' she countered.

'Are we? If Despenser took it into his head to crush us, he could do so in a moment. There are many thousands at his command.'

'You fear for us, I know, husband, but there is no need to. Remain here with us, and all will be well.'

Baldwin nodded, but his eyes remained fixed on the small cloud of dust that enclosed the men-at-arms until they were out of sight between the trees. There was a clutching fear in his belly.

Louvre, Paris

Jean de Poissy was allowed in before the Cardinal had arrived, and he stood in the great room studying his surroundings.

It was the room of a man of power and authority, that was clear. There was the large desk, with books and parchments scattered all about it. A pair of spectacles lay folded on top of one large book, which Jean assumed was a Bible. The fireplace was made ready, although there were no flames. Today was so warm, it was good to enter a room like this and feel the soothing coolness. A large sideboard stood at one wall, and upon it were many silver plates and some goblets which adequately demonstrated the wealth of the man. Large tapestries covered the bare walls on two sides, while on a third there were many paintings of scenes from the Gospels. All designed, so Jean felt, to demonstrate the man's position in the world, like the large goblet with gilding all about it. Interested, Jean walked over and picked it up.

'You wish for wine?'

The door had been thrust wide, and the Cardinal marched in like a General. He was pulling off gloves as he strode past Jean, throwing them on the table and calling loudly for his steward. Soon the servant appeared with a large pewter jug, from which he swiftly dispensed wine and brought it to the two men, Jean's in a smaller, pewter cup rather than the fine goblet he had admired. That was given to the Cardinal. Equally swiftly, the servant walked backwards to the wall, where he stood, jug still in his hands, head bowed.

'This is a fine goblet, is it not? One of a group I once found.

I gave the rest to the Pope himself, Pope Clement of blessed memory.'

'The gift was appreciated?'

'It brought me the position I hold today,' the Cardinal said without boastfulness. 'It often helps to achieve things when you have the ability to smooth the way with money, don't you find?'

'Not in my world,' Jean said.

'No. I suppose not.'

'You wished to see me?' Jean said.

'Yes. I wanted to know whether you had managed to proceed with the investigation?'

Jean studied him. The Cardinal was clad in a Cardinal's clothes, but they had been cut from fine velvets and silks, their colours somehow brighter and more expensive-looking than Jean was used to seeing. The Cardinal was a tall man, with a face that had a certain severity about it. He had the deep brown hair of a man from the far south, and the olive complexion to go with it. He peered at Jean now from narrowed eyes.

'Yes, my Lord Cardinal,' Jean responded coolly.

'And?'

'I am attempting all I may.'

'Also, this theft – I trust you have heard of it?'

'My apologies, what theft?'

The Cardinal made a dismissive gesture. 'There has been a purse stolen from one of my clerks. Any place this size must have its share of thieves, I suppose, but to think that a man would dare take a purse within the walls of the Louvre . . . you must admit, that is alarming.'

'I fear I have not been made aware of this crime, Cardinal. If you are concerned about it, you should report it to the castellan, not me. Now, I know you told me all you could about the man whom you discovered dead, but I hoped that you might have a little more information for me.'

'Such as?'

'Perhaps you can remember something about this man. Were you expecting to hear from somebody about treasure?'

'Did I mention treasure?'

'No, but the servant who came to seek you and brought you to the dead man, told me that the fellow had asked to see you on a matter of extreme urgency – about some treasure. Perhaps you had forgotten this?'

'I do not recall it. Perhaps he did say something, but the sight of the dead man drove all other thoughts from my mind.'

'I see.'

'You seem to believe I know something about this man,' the Cardinal said with a trace of testiness.

'I would expect you to, yes. The man came here from some distance away. He was not from the local garrison, nor, so far as we can discover, was he from any of the households nearby. A foreigner, and yet he could ask for you by name. He plainly knew *of* you, if nothing more.'

'Mon Sieur, many, many people know me. They know me by sight, they know of me by name. I am a man of God, and high in the Church's establishment. All know me, and yet you surely do not think I know them in return?'

'You are of course quite right. Now, this treasure. What could he refer to?'

'I have no idea. As I said, I do not know the man, I do not know where he came from, nor why he asked to see me. Plainly, I also do not know what he spoke about.'

'Naturally. So you cannot help me in any way about this fellow.' Jean nodded to himself. 'Tell me, do you often have men come here to speak with you like this?'

'No.'

'Very strange that he should have come, then,' Jean noted. He glanced about him at the tapestries. 'Very pleasant chamber you have, Cardinal.'

'Thank you. I find it pleasant.'

'Fortunate the man didn't come straight here, isn't it? If he'd been killed here, there'd be blood all over the place.'

'Yes? Well, perhaps it is a good thing, as you say. There was much blood?'

Jean nodded. 'Enough.'

'Oh. I truly did not notice.'

Outside, Jean stopped and looked up at the walls behind him. On the second storey, where he had just been talking to the Cardinal, he was sure that there was a shadow in the window, a shadow that swiftly moved out of sight.

The servant who had escorted him here from the chapel was lounging at a wall, and Jean beckoned him.

'Boy? You look like the sort of fellow who'd be happy to earn a few sous.'

'Perhaps.'

'It involves nothing too strenuous. What is your name?'

'Philippe.'

'Very well, Philippe. I require your help. You will be aiding me in learning all we may about this dead man.'

'No one knows anything about him, though.'

'No. So anything we learn will be an improvement, will it not?'

'But I have my duties!'

'And so do I. Mine have just been altered, as have yours. In God's name, boy, I am seeking a murderer. And now, so are *you*.'

'They won't like it in the kitchen. They're short-staffed as it is.'

'Less sulking, boy. The staffing levels in the Louvre are not our concern. The fact that a man has been killed in the King's castle is more important to us. Especially since we have no idea who he was. That is the first question: who may know him?'

Furnshill, Devon

There were more men passing that day, but nothing on the same scale as the men-at-arms, and Baldwin breathed a sigh of relief as he walked out later in the afternoon and lifted his tunic to relieve himself into the small barrel that sat over to the western wall of the house, near his row of storerooms. The urine would be used later, fermented, to clean clothes, and any excess would be thrown on to the compost heaps. There was nothing allowed to go to waste on his estate.

As he hitched up his hosen once more, letting loose his tunic to cover himself more decently, he heard another horse.

Peering up the road, he saw a mount riding at a steady pace, a young man with fair hair wild in the wind on its back. The man appeared to take stock of the area, staring at Baldwin's house, and then aimed for it, over Baldwin's small field.

Baldwin felt the lack of his sword at that moment, but he was close to his door, and the risk was limited at this time of day. Besides, he had fought and trained for more years than he cared to remember, and he felt sure that he could beat a young fellow such as this one.

'The road to Bickleigh goes up there,' he said as the horse drew up some few yards away. No one would ride right up to a man unless he wished to alarm them. This fellow was polite enough. Perhaps one-and-twenty, he looked as though he had ridden several miles already.

'Sir Baldwin de Furnshill? I have come from my Lord Walter, Bishop of Exeter.'

Thursday before the Feast of Mary Magdalen[1]

Furnshill, Devon

'I am glad indeed that you were able to give me a bed for the night,' the Bishop said.

'My Lord Bishop, it is always a delight to have you visit us,' Baldwin's wife said. She bent to refill his jug, and Baldwin saw how the sun, streaming in from the large, unglazed window, lighted her hair with red sparks.

Bishop Stapledon had arrived as darkness fell. He had, he explained, been travelling from a small vill in the diocese, but they had been delayed in leaving, and it was clear that they could not reach Exeter that night. It was easy to accommodate the Bishop. He took a bed in Baldwin's solar, in the second bedchamber, while his servants slept in the hall with Baldwin's own. Baldwin's men had to be persuaded to share their benches, and some men were forced to huddle on the floor near the fire, but with blankets and cloaks spread liberally, most were comfortable enough. It was as good as the cots in the Bishop's palace, Baldwin considered. He had tried them before, and knew how uncomfortable they could be.

'When you have broken your fast, you will be setting off for Exeter?' Jeanne asked.

'I suppose so,' the Bishop said. His voice was heavy, and now that Baldwin studied him, he was struck by how the last weeks had affected the man. It was only a short while since Baldwin had last seen him, but those weeks had been very unkind to him. Bishop Walter's face was pale, as though he had been sleeping badly for an extended period, and his blue eyes were peering with an effort that was not merely his dreadful eyesight, but was also a proof of tiredness. He looked

---

[1] Thursday, 18 July 1325

down to see Wolf resting his head on the Bishop's lap.

Jeanne saw too, and made a move to remove the hound, but the Bishop shook his head. He appeared to take comfort from Wolf's weight on his thigh. He stroked the huge skull.

'Bishop, I hope you will forgive my observing that you appear quite worn,' Baldwin said.

'My dear friend, you do not need perfect eyesight to tell that. And after all, I am sixty-four this year. It is not surprising that with all the responsibilities I have held, that I should be a little weary.'

He sipped wine, while Baldwin watched him closely. 'Is this because of your responsibilities to the Treasury?'

'Aha! No, that is at least one responsibility of which I have divested myself. There is no more I can do with that, in God's name!'

The Bishop's eyes gleamed with an uncharacteristic anger as he spoke, and Baldwin was surprised. 'You are no longer the King's Treasurer?'

'He decided that he no longer required my assistance. Again!'

Baldwin could not conceal the small smile. Only a few years before, the King had removed the Bishop from his role as Lord High Treasurer, but within a short space, he found he had to reinstate him. Bishop Walter's skill at administration and record-keeping was beyond comparison. 'Why so?'

'The King trusts no one. He is parsimonious, it is true, but his niggardly penny-pinching will lead us into trouble before long. Last year he split the realm into two, for administrative purposes, north and south. But then, although he has created much more work, more administration, more effort, he refuses to allow the hire of more men to do it! Ach! I will have nothing more to do with the Exchequer. And then, he also wants to take more money from the Church, too. All ecclesiastical debts are to be called in. It was too much. So two weeks ago yesterday, I ceased to be Lord High Treasurer.'

'It must have been a most trying period for you,' Baldwin said.

'Not so trying as continuing with a task I could not possibly achieve,' the Bishop said sharply. 'But that isn't why I am as you see me. Have you heard of the violence growing in our land?'

'We have heard some rumours,' Baldwin said, glancing at his wife as he did so. He could see that she was unsettled by the conversation. She stood quietly, but her eyes told of her anxiety.

'I heard last afternoon that another King's official has been attacked. The keeper of rebel castles in the Welsh March has been most brutally beaten and blinded. And he is not the only one. There are attacks in Yorkshire, in the south near London, down towards the coast – there is nowhere safe where the law resides.'

'Surely the land is not so unsettled that you need fear such things?' Jeanne asked quietly.

'My dear, I fear it is worse than you could appreciate,' the Bishop said with absent-minded condescension.

Jeanne could see that he had not intended to patronise her, but his words rankled nonetheless.

'How could it be worse? Are there many similar cases?' Baldwin frowned. 'I have heard nothing of any such attacks here in Devon.'

'Let me put it like this: the King is now moving his prisoners from one castle to another.' Bishop Walter had fixed Baldwin with a steely, unwavering stare as he spoke.

'What does that mean?' Jeanne asked.

Baldwin knew precisely what he meant. 'If the King was confident that the castle garrisons could hold the prisoners securely, he would leave them in one place. If he's moving them about the country, it means he is worried that large forces could be brought to lay siege to any one of the castles, if people grow certain of who is being held there. If he's moving them around, it means he is trying to confuse any potential rebels, not giving them the certainty of which prisoner will be in which castle at any time.'

'It makes excellent sense, Lady Jeanne. However, it is also a proof of his weakness in the face of the men ranged against him.'

'But he is the King,' Jeanne objected. 'Surely few would dare to set their faces against him – especially since he destroyed the Lords Marcher and their forces.'

Baldwin nodded, his eyes fixed upon the Bishop. The King had not enjoyed a successful career as a warrior. The Scots had beaten him severely, not once, but many times. During the last war the Scottish had almost captured the Queen. It was only a miracle that saw her escape – and then it was so close that two of her ladies-in-waiting had died. Only once had he displayed a martial skill suitable for the son of Edward I: at Boroughbridge. There he had defeated the combined strength of the Lords Marcher.

'He succeeded there, yes,' Baldwin admitted. 'But he sowed the problem that is beginning to fruit even now. Isn't that so, Bishop?'

'The King captured many, Lady Jeanne,' Bishop Walter said, and nodded. 'But the simple truth is, his actions afterwards left all those who received his blast of anger with a simmering rage. He took many knights, lords and even the Earl of Lancaster, his own cousin, and executed them. Others he impoverished by taking their castles, their lands, their treasure. I tried at the time to propose that he should show some compassion, especially for the poor women who suffered so much. The widows of his enemies were treated with appalling cruelty. He took all their property, even the dowers which they themselves brought to their marriages. All was removed and used to bolster the King's coffers. Is it any surprise that many resent his behaviour, when he could be so harsh to them? And these same men, whom he deprived of livelihood and wealth, are wanderers now. They have no homes, no fixed dwellings. So if they decide to turn wolfshead and become outlaw, no one knows where they live. The whole nation is beginning to tear itself apart. When a land loses the benefit of the rule of the law, it grows ungovernable.'

'You surely don't truly believe that!' Jeanne said quietly.

'What will you do?' Baldwin asked as the Bishop frowned at the mazer of wine in his hand.

'I will do all I can to ensure that the realm is well governed, to protect the King, and to serve my diocese,' Bishop Walter said.

'When will the Queen return?' Baldwin asked. He had been sent with his friend, Simon Puttock, to France to guard the Queen on her journey to see the French King.

'She should be returning any time soon, I imagine,' the Bishop said. 'If not now, then when the King travels to Paris; he will no doubt bring her back. It is plain enough that she can achieve little there on her own. She has done her best, I suppose.'

'The King will travel there?' Jeanne asked.

'He must go and perform his homage to his liege lord, the same as any other man,' the Bishop said with a faint hint of acid in his tone. 'Some men think that they need not comply with the wishes of their masters, but it is better that they realise sooner rather than later what their duties require. And the King holds his territories in Guyenne and the Agenais from the French King. If he wishes to retain his lands over there, he must pay homage. It is clear.'

'Because the French King has the larger host,' Baldwin said.

'Yes. He has more knights and men-at-arms,' the Bishop agreed, but without an answering smile.

'Will you go with him?' Jeanne asked.

'Me? My dear Lady, I am too old to wander about the land of France. It is enough for me to make a lengthy journey across my diocese – and more than enough to have to attend the King's councils. I seek no more long journeys, by land or by sea!'

Chapter Five

Louvre, Paris

The Procureur stood in the chamber again where the man had been killed.

'What was he doing in here? Why was he not taken to the Cardinal's chamber?'

The servant shrugged. 'If the man was unknown to the Cardinal, why should our master wish to see him?'

'Philippe, you have a point. But why bring him up *here*?' the Procureur repeated. There was no reason for it. This room was not even on the same floor as the Cardinal's chamber.

'What is this room usually used for?' he asked suddenly.

'It was used by a clerk, but he died last year, and it has remained empty ever since, I think. Why?'

'It intrigues me.'

Jean cast an eye all over the place from his vantage point near the door, and then he moved inside, inspecting the plain walls, the simple roof. There was nothing out of the ordinary or hidden here, he quickly decided.

Perhaps there was something about the *location* of the chamber, then, that was significant. Jean went outside again and looked up and down the quiet corridor.

'Philippe – how well do you know this area?'

'I have hardly ever come up here. It's not a part of the castle I have been asked to go to.'

'I see,' Jean said, and swore to himself. It was a problem,

clearly, that this part of the castle was so quiet. It had made it harder to find a witness to the arrival of the man. It would also serve to make it difficult to . . .

'I am the king of fools!' he said suddenly.

Saturday before the Feast of Mary Magdalen[1]

Lydford, Devon

In his own property, Simon Puttock, lately Bailiff to the Stannaries of Dartmoor, and more recently the representative of the Keeper of the Port of Dartmouth, until the Keeper's death, breathed in deeply as he drained his first quart of ale that morning, sitting on his chair in front of the fire, feeling the warmth seeping into his body.

The previous evening had been unseasonally cool, and he was happy to be here – all the more so because when he went out for an early morning ride, a brief shower of rain had left him sodden and uncomfortable. He was painfully aware that he smelled like a drowned ewe, and was keen to have his clothes dried. Worse, earlier in the year a bully called William atte Wattere, working for Sir Hugh le Despenser, had assaulted him, cutting him about the left shoulder and hand. Both wounds still stung, although they seemed to be mending. However, as he looked about him in his hall, he had to reflect that he had known worse mornings.

His wife squatted near him, adding wood to the faggots on the fire. Her rounded figure was straining against the material of her simple tunic, her fair hair already straying from her wimple.

'You know, Meg, life is good,' he said with satisfaction. 'All I need now is a good woman to sit on my lap, and . . .'

---

[1] Saturday, 20 July 1325

He lunged, but Margaret had already squeaked and darted out of arm's reach. 'You have work to get on with,' she objected.

'No. I am without work.'

'Until you know who has won at the Abbey, you have little to do for the monks, you mean. There is plenty to be getting on with here, and as soon as they make up their minds . . .'

'They already have,' Simon growled. 'That is the trouble. Robert Busse has decided that he has won the abbacy, and John de Courtenay has too. It makes it all a little difficult to see who will actually take the throne. Meanwhile, the abbey's funds are all taken by the King while they battle it out. The pair of them must be mad.'

'That's not fair. You know full well that the one who is causing the trouble is John de Courtenay. Robert Busse won the abbacy in a fair election. It's just that John de Courtenay won't accept that he lost.'

'Perhaps, but neither is doing the abbey any good. And meanwhile, here I am, wasting away as the time passes,' he said mournfully. 'So come and squirm on my lap, woman!'

'No!'

He had just attempted an experimental swoop when they were both stilled by the sound of hoofbeats. 'Oh, Christ's cods,' Simon muttered. 'Does this mean there's been a decision about the abbacy?'

'It doesn't look like an abbey's messenger,' Meg said, patting her straying fair hair back under her wimple.

Getting up and walking over to her, Simon admired his woman again. She was five years younger than him, and apart from the natural ravages of time at her face, it was hard to see that she was already some four and thirty years old. Even the three birthings, and the miscarriages between, had not dulled her spirit, nor the shine of her hair, and for the rest he found her body more comfortable now than he did before. He slipped his arms about her waist and rested his chin on her shoulder as he peered through the slats of the unglazed window. 'The fellow is looking about like a lost man,' he commented.

'No, now he has seen us here.'

It was true enough. The man had asked a passerby for directions and now he had kicked his scraggy old mare into an amble and was riding towards them.

From the look of him, he was a lowly lawyer's clerk. Simon had seen enough of that sort when he was a Bailiff, listening to cases in the gaol at Lydford. All kinds of pleaders would turn up there, trying to make a living from the miserable felons who mouldered in the dank prison underground. This shabby-looking man reminded Simon of those who would loiter down in the cells, hoping to find someone who would accept them. Few prisoners, however, were that desperate.

'You lost, friend?' Simon called as he went out from his door.

'I was hoping to find a man called Puttock – Simon the Bailiff.'

'You've found him.'

'I have a message from Master William atte Wattere,' the man said, holding up a small parchment, sealed with red wax.

Simon clenched his teeth and would have left the man sitting on his horse there, but Margaret was at his side, and he could tell by the way her grip stiffened on his arm that she was terrified. He had to show he was not alarmed, and he stepped forward to take the proffered message.

'You want to reply?' the messenger asked.

'No,' Simon said. He did not open the message, but stood silently, waiting. The man shrugged and pulled his horse's head round, departing at a gentle trot.

'Simon!' Margaret hissed. 'What does that man want with us now?'

He bent and kissed her, but there was no passion now; this was a means of steeling himself, he reflected, as he drew Margaret back into their hall.

'Well?' she demanded as he peered at the tiny characters. Simon had been taught to read by the canons at Crediton when he was a lad, but this script was very hard to decipher. It was not the simple Latin of the Church, nor the flowing French of the courts, but a mingling of the two. Knowing Wattere, Simon suspected he had tried to make his note sound more legalistic by the use of florid expressions. It didn't work – but the basic message was clear enough.

'Meg, it's not good news,' he said slowly, as his world fell about his ears.

Wednesday following the Feast of Mary Magdalen[1]

Furnshill, Devon

Baldwin had been relieved to be able to wave the Bishop away. The latter's manner, his paleness and anxiety, had all been so entirely unlike him that Baldwin was worried that the nation was truly beginning to suffer from the collapse of the King's Peace, as he had feared.

When he saw his old friend Simon riding up the grass track to his house, he was relieved to see a friendly face, but his joy was to be short-lived.

'What is it, old friend? Your wife? Margaret is well? And . . .'

'I think, Baldwin, you may find that you have me living near you again,' Simon said with a taut smile, reaching into his

---

[1] Wednesday, 24 July 1325

breast and pulling out a sweat-dampened letter. 'Read it for yourself.'

Baldwin led the way into the hall, reading as he went, and once there, he bawled for Wat to serve them with wine, before dropping into his chair with a grunt. 'And is this correct?'

'I have been to Exeter to find out. I was there all day yesterday, but yes, it seems so. I had bought my house on a lease, and it is renewable every seven years. I had no idea I had missed the last payment. It was due while we were in France, and I forgot about it. If you remember, it was only a short while after we moved to Lydford that our son died, and there were many things that slipped my mind . . .'

'This says that Despenser has bought the house. How did he do so?'

'It was owned by old Harold Uppacott. He died a few months ago, and his son was offered a better sum for it than he would have expected. I don't blame him. But Christ's ballocks, I do blame Despenser. It's just the same as before.'

'I am astonished that Wattere dares to do this, though,' Baldwin grated. His anger was increasing, the more he thought about it.

It was only two or three months ago that Wattere had become known to them. Early in May, when Simon and Baldwin returned to their homes after guarding the Queen during her journey to Paris, Simon had learned that William Wattere, a servant to Sir Hugh le Despenser, had threatened to steal his house from him. It was no empty threat from a brigand, either. Despenser had become accustomed to taking what he wished, and with his position as the King's favourite, there was no means of controlling his intolerable greed. Simon had almost given up his home, but he and Baldwin had managed to have Wattere arrested. Afterwards, they had come to an accommodation with Despenser – or so they had thought.

'What does Despenser wish to do?' Simon said.

Baldwin waved the letter thoughtfully. 'He does not say that you are to be evicted, Simon. Rather, it merely tells you that the house has been sold beneath you. Of course, now you could be thrown out whenever he desired to do so.'

'And you can imagine how that makes Meg feel,' Simon said.

Baldwin nodded. 'What do you want to do about it?'

It was the question Simon had been asking himself all the way here from Exeter. Now he looked away from his old friend and stared out through the great unglazed but barred window. 'I can only think I should remain there for now, and wait and see what happens. There is no point in the disruption of clearing out.'

'You can always return to your farm near Sandford,' Baldwin said.

'Aye,' Simon agreed. 'And if Despenser decides he wants that too, he'll not even go to the bother of buying it. He'll just kill me and throw Meg and Peter out.'

Chapter Six

Gatehouse to Louvre, Paris

Arnaud, the porter to the Louvre, was jealous as he watched her crossing the courtyard. It wasn't enough that Sieur Hugues had money, power, and all the trappings of a lord, he had the best-looking courtesan in the castle too.

She was a leggy, black-haired woman, with the interesting looks of a woman of nearer five-and-twenty than a mere girl. Her expression was bold and appraising, challenging to a man like Arnaud. He adored the sight of her, but Christ in a bucket, she was daunting. Such confidence, such poise.

'You wish for a little wine?' he called shyly as she approached the gate.

To his surprise, she gave him a slow, considering stare, eyeing his boots, his tunic, even his scarred face, and then a smile gradually dawned. 'Why not?' she said.

Westminster, Thorney Island

Sir Hugh le Despenser felt good as he marched to the King's Painted Chamber. The confirmation from William Wattere was welcome news. It gave Sir Hugh some leverage over the Bailiff. If Simon Puttock dared became a thorn in his side

---

[1] Saturday, 3 August 1325

again, the cretin would soon find himself out on the moors, without a roof over his head. And this time, Despenser would be acting within the law. It was a novel experience.

The King was waiting for him, sitting on a comfortable chair amidst a large group of men. His expression, when he saw Despenser enter, was that of a man who saw his only ally among uncounted enemies.

'And what do we have here?' Despenser murmured as he entered. He pulled off his gloves and dropped them, then allowed his cloak to fall to the floor behind him. As he walked forward, servants rushed to take them up. 'A glorious collection of bishops, to be sure. What should this be called, I wonder? A "mass" of bishops? A "celebration"? Or perhaps a "noise"?'

'Your sense of humour has not left you, then,' Bishop Hethe said. Hethe was always very favourably disposed towards the King, and that made Despenser mistrust him. Either the man was dishonest, or, worse, he was in earnest. If the latter was the case, there was always the possibility that he would do all in his power to harm Despenser so that he might serve the King more honourably.

But today he was no threat. Others who were more antagonistic to Despenser were present in that gathering.

Archbishop Reynolds was there, and the Bishops of London, Chichester, Carlisle, Ely and Exeter among others. All chattering and waving their hands like so many monkeys. On the far side of the room, Despenser saw the Earl of Chester, standing listening intently to his tutor, the deplorable Richard of Bury. The fat fool!

He was supposed to be a clever, intellectual fellow, but Despenser thought he was a fraud. He had a great collection of books, certainly, but Despenser reckoned there were too many for one man to read in a lifetime. He'd even said so to the King before now, but Edward was deaf to any comments against the bastard. As it was, Despenser watched him carefully. He didn't trust anyone else to get too close to the King or his son.

'So, what is the discussion concerning?' he drawled as he walked to the King's side and made an elaborate bow.

Bishop Stapledon said tightly, 'The King has reconsidered, and now he feels that it would be best if he were not to leave the country. Instead, another must go.'

That, Despenser thought, must have hurt like a kick in the ballocks. Stapledon certainly looked as though he had been attacked most viciously. His face was as pale as a man who saw his house being burned before him. With his family still inside.

'I am sure that the King knows the most sensible course,' he said smoothly.

'I dare say you are,' Hethe replied.

'I do not think I understand you, my Lord Bishop.' Despenser's eyes were glittering like ice.

Hethe was not one of those who would respond with fear. The pious prickle believed in his divine protection or something. 'I suggest that you are most assured that the King's actions are correct when they suit *your aims*, Sir Hugh. And I believe that you have argued most persuasively against his journeying to Paris.'

'You think that the King doesn't know his own mind? I am surprised at you, my Lord.'

'Do not presume to insult my intelligence, Sir Hugh,' Hethe said with chilly resentment. 'The King must go, whether you wish it or no.'

'It is not *my* decision,' Despenser shrugged, 'and I think you should be cautious of suggesting otherwise—'

'Enough!' The King stood up from his seat and glared about him.

He was still a magnificent-looking man. His eyes showed the nervousness that lay at the centre of his soul, and his face was drawn, but he still towered over the others in the room with him, and he inspired awe, no matter what the gathering. 'I have decided! That should be enough for all of you. Now, on to other matters. What did you wish to say, Archbishop?'

The room was quiet a moment as all those present mentally considered whether it was safe to argue further, but after a certain amount of glancing about at each other, the Archbishop broke the uncomfortable silence.

'Kent is in a turmoil, my Lord. There are wandering bands of discontents and felons who slay with impunity. What may a man do? I have set about building a larger wall to encircle my own manor, but if these desperate men should attack, it would be useless.'

'You want me to provide you with guards? Can you not afford your own? I do not presume to have a monopoly on defence,' the King said sarcastically.

'It is not only Kent, your Royal Highness. It's the whole realm,' another Bishop declared. 'The country is falling into despair, and if there is no peace for your subjects, they may . . .'

'Look to yourselves for your protection, as the King said,' Despenser snapped. 'You are all grown men, in Christ's name! Not maids and churls. You have your own guards. Set them to their duties!'

'If there is no peace in your realm, the land may erupt. Your people will not respect a King who cannot give them peace.'

It was Walter Stapledon, Bishop of Exeter, who spoke, and Despenser gave him a long, threatening stare. 'You and I have always been agreed on most matters, my Lord Bishop,' he said. 'I am surprised to hear you gainsaying me. Think carefully before you continue.'

Stapledon was an old man, certainly, and the last couple of months, especially since he'd lost his job, had made him look his age. But there was still a power in his eyes as he leaned towards Despenser, his head jutting. 'You think to tell me, a man of God, where my duties lie, Sir Hugh? For shame! Keep your mouth closed if you can speak nothing but ill of others. My Lord King, you have decided not to go to France. If that is the case, and you remain here in England, you will lose Guyenne, the Agenais, and more than half your annual income.'

'Parliament will have to increase the money sent to me in taxes.'

'Parliament will not. It cannot. Once you have fleeced your sheep, my Lord, if you continue cutting, all you achieve is butchery. If you try to extort more money from your people than they can afford, you will find that they will rise up. I do not speak sedition, only the truth. You need the French territories.'

'I cannot go. I have decided.'

'Then you must consider another alternative,' Stapledon said, and turned to look at the Earl of Chester, who stood listening intently.

'I will not have him go! I wish my son to remain here,' the King declared.

'Either you go or he does. If not, you lose all, your Highness. This is the single most important decision of your reign, my Lord.'

'And he *has* decided,' Despenser said quickly, but he felt the cold sweat breaking out on his back as the King wavered. Sweet Mother of God, yes, he was reconsidering. After all that effort, Stapledon had hit on the one ruse that could work: mention money to the King, and he'd listen all right. He would ignore comments about other men's welfare, about the King's

Peace being broken with impunity on all sides, about the suffering of the masses . . . but suggest that he might lose a single farthing, and you would have his complete attention in an instant.

'Hold!' the King said. 'I will not have matters bandied about like this. I have no doubt that you all seek to assist me, but what am I to do? I cannot remain here and also be in France. If I leave here, there would be consequences. I am needed in my realm to protect my people, but you say I should also be in Paris to pay homage to the French King. What should I do?'

The Earl of Chester strode forward. 'It's clear enough, Father – your Royal Highness – you will *have* to go to France. The date is set. It would be wrong for you not to honour your own word given to the French King. You must go.'

King Edward stared at his son. He was about to respond with vigour, when his answer was pre-empted.

'The young Earl does speak a deal of sense, with a maturity beyond his years,' said Despenser. 'But there are some aspects of the situation of which he may be unaware. Your Royal Highness, perhaps we could discuss this with him later?'

'Sir Hugh, I fear it is a little late already to be discussing this,' Stapledon stated. He stepped forward. 'You may believe that the Earl is of tender years, but I feel he has demonstrated a most sensitive and sensible attitude. For the Crown to retain the French territories, it is clear that homage will have to be paid to the French King, as he is the liege-lord for those lands. And it would be unthinkable for the English Crown to knowingly or willingly give up the estates won so hard over so many years. The Earl of Chester is quite right.'

The King shook his head violently. 'I am the King, and I have spoken.'

'Your Royal Highness, with respect,' Hethe said, 'we are

your council. It would be wrong for us to allow you to act without our declaring our disagreement, if we felt this decision would adversely affect you. Your Majesty, please hear our views. You know I love you more than my own life. I have served you faithfully and loyally all these years, will you not listen to my own plea?'

Gatehouse, Louvre, Paris

Arnaud watched her walking away on those long legs of hers with a feeling of real misery. She'd been so bright and enthusiastic in his room, it was as though a ray of the sun had dropped in to speak with him, and illuminated his entire existence for those moments.

The only thing that had dimmed her smile had been the mention of the dead man.

'I knew someone like him,' she said. 'I met him in a tavern not far from here in the days before he was killed.'

'You know who he was? You must tell someone,' Arnaud protested.

The smile was there still, but now there was a brittle quality to it, and she looked at him very directly. 'You think so? I met him and his woman. They said that they were here to take money from the Cardinal. You hear that? The Cardinal himself. He stole money many years before, they claimed, and they wanted to blackmail him. Get some of it for themselves. I don't know about you, but I'd be wary of mentioning that to anyone. Cardinal Thomas would make a bad enemy, so I've heard. He could resort to a knife.'

'But if you know the man's name . . .' Arnaud began but quickly stilled his mouth.

'I do not. Why should I? He was only some fellow I got chatting to in a tavern, nothing more. I think he said his name was Guillaume, but I can't be sure. All I do know is, he wasn't

Parisian.' She shook her head. 'Terrible, to think that a man could come all the way here, and be struck down almost at once. So sad.'

Westminster

It was a full hour of the day later that Despenser stepped through the doors and out into the passage to the Great Hall.

'Proud of yourself?' he spat.

Walter Stapledon looked at him with an eye that glinted with anger. 'You dare ask me that!'

'You will see the King leave here and go to France?'

'I would see the King behave as a King, just this once. Edward must go there. If not, his son must. One or other. It matters not a whit.'

'You think that I shall be killed if he goes, don't you?'

'Sir Hugh, whatever happens to you is supremely irrelevant to me. This is a matter of feudal honour and the Crown.'

Despenser glanced about them, and then suddenly gripped the Bishop's robes with both fists. He shoved Stapledon back against one of the massive pillars in the hall, his face so close the older man could feel the breath that rasped in his throat.

'You think you'll be safe when I'm dead? I swear to you, *Bishop*, I shall live longer than you, and you will die in the gutter, missed by no one, mourned by no one. You'll regret this decision for the rest of your days, if you don't get him to think again!'

Stapledon was unimpressed. 'You have threatened and blustered so often in my presence, Sir Hugh, that your words no longer make me tremble,' he said coldly. 'In future, try to persuade yourself to emulate me and see to the benefit of the realm and others before you look to your own advantage.'

'I swear I'll—'

Stapledon raised his eyebrows, and then he spoke with a

calm, quiet certainty. 'I know that excommunication holds no terrors for you, Sir Hugh, but *I* swear on the Gospels, that if you continue to attempt to block the only sensible course for our poor King, I will definitely seek your excommunication, and then I shall also lay a curse upon you of such virulence and authority that all the saints will be unable to raise it from your putrid, stinking soul. You will leave me alone, Sir Hugh, or I shall destroy you utterly.'

'Go, then!' Despenser said, turning and releasing him, raising his hands from the Bishop's robes as he did so, as though fearing that they might have been contaminated. 'You go, old man, and we shall see who wins this battle. It will be a struggle, though, I warn you. I do not intend to see myself captured by my enemies and destroyed just because you seek to promote your own silly little cause.'

'You call honour and the Crown silly? You dare to speak of them with such contempt? Truly, Sir Hugh, you will live to regret such disdain.'

'You think so? Old fool, *you* will regret your presumption in trying to threaten me!'

Chapter Seven

Louvre, Paris

The Procureur was a clearly recognisable figure as he scurried from the front gate of the Louvre and out into the lane that led from the King's greatest château to the city's gates.

It was an inviolable rule that a bastion of defence like the Louvre should always be secure from the city which it was set to defend. In any city there were occasional uprisings, and the castle must stand impregnable.

These were the last thoughts on the man's mind, though, as he followed after the Procureur.

The follower, Jacquot, was a slender man, his frame permanently weakened after the famine ten years before. He had not been able to rebuild his health after that. In fact, sweet Jesus, it was a miracle he was alive at all. All the others were dead, may their souls rest easy. Poor darling Maria, and Louisa, Jacques and little Frou-Frou, all had died. Only he remained out of his entire family.

It was only a matter of luck that he had survived. Jacquot had been on the road from Albi, trudging miserably northwards in the rain, when he had come across a pair of bodies. At that time, there were bodies all over the place. Men and women simply sank to their knees and died, no matter where they were. They'd topple over in the road, and people would barely give them a glance. No one had the energy to help them, and no one cared for them. What was one more man or woman's pain and misery to someone who'd already lost everything? So bodies were left where they lay, unless they were fortunate enough to die in a city which still had a little respect for itself and hoped that the famine would end.

Jacquot had at least seen to the burial of his own. They had all been installed in consecrated ground, his wife being interred under the supervision of the priest. Sadly, by the time Louisa died, the priest himself had expired, and from that moment, Jacquot himself dug the graves and set his children inside, one after the other, all at the feet of his wife's body. After burying Jacques, there was no point in remaining. He had taken his staff and left the cottage, not even closing the door. There was nothing to be stolen. He had nothing.

But on that road he had seen the two bodies, and found himself studying them as though seeing corpses for the first time. It made some sort of connection with his soul. His own children and wife were dead, and now these two sorry souls lay before him. Suddenly, without knowing why, he began to sob. Great gouts of misery burst from his breast like vomit. The convulsions would not leave him. He was reduced to standing, leaning on the staff and bawling like a babe.

And then, when it was done, he found he could not move on. It was hard enough to walk on the level, and impossible to think of lifting a foot so high that he might step over them. At the same time his starved brain could not conceive of passing around them. Instead he stood, transfixed. And gradually a degree of determination returned.

If the King could not provide food, it was up to him to find food for himself. If God would not provide food, it was up to him to seek it. He had been a decent, fair man in his life. When he had money, he had been generous. All those whom he loved had felt the advantage of his largesse. But now he was brought to his knees. There was nothing for him to do but die, unless he took life in both hands and wrung a living from it. There was no point meandering onwards, hoping to find some food. Even the monasteries had little enough to share amongst the thousands who clamoured at their gates.

This conclusion had just reached him when he saw a small building not more than a few hundred yards away. Without quite knowing why, he made for it. Beyond, he saw a wall, and in the wall was a broad gate. He found it was unlocked. Inside was a small farm, with a woman toiling in the fields. The rain was falling in a perpetual stream, and her ankles and calves and thighs were beslobbered with mud as she strained with a harrow, pulling it in place of her beasts. The rain washed over her body, flattening her linen tunic over her breasts, and he stood a while and stared.

Speaking had seemed pointless. The hunger that drove all made throats sore and voices rasp, so he stood silently as she heaved on the rope. And then he walked past her to the door of her cottage and sought food. There was nothing. When she entered, later, he said nothing, and she appeared heedless. For her supper, she had a little pottage made thin, with grasses and some seeds boiled until they almost had some taste. There were no cabbages, no onions or peas to provide ballast to an empty stomach, and bread was a long-dreamed of impossibility. Still, they foraged in among the hedges and fields for what they might find, and somehow both lived for a while.

Then, one morning, he woke to find her cold beside him in the bed. Her eyes were still open, staring at the ceiling sightlessly. He fancied that there was a smile playing about her mouth.

He had left the area and made his way north again. And a few miles later he found himself at a convent. But here the local population had decided to take what they could. He approached to the smell of burning, the sounds of rioting, the crash and thud of buildings being broken systematically.

Two men tried to prevent him from joining in, for he was a stranger here, but either he was slightly better fed, or his desperation was the more potent, for one he knocked down and the other he would have slain, had he had a knife to hand. Instead, though, he took part in the sack of the convent, and within a short space he had joined the people.

It was enough to allow him to survive those two dreadful first years, but he was still scarred by those experiences. And the aftermath, when he had taken to capturing women on the road, waylaying any who appeared to have money about them. Several he simply throttled, stealing their clothing and money; others he took to cities to sell, until by degrees, he made his way here to Paris.

In the past he had been working on his own, but now he had the companionship of a whole class of similar men. These were the dregs of Parisian society, but they gave him their friendship and to a degree he reciprocated it. He began to have a life again.

It was a skewed life. Jacquot embarked on it with two men he met in a tavern. All three drank heavily, and when a whore offered herself, they went with her to an alley, and there, after they had all used her, he himself cut her throat and stripped her naked. The body they threw into a midden, while her few and paltry belongings they took to another innkeeper's wife, a woman they all knew, who washed the clothing and sold it to their profit. It was the beginning of his criminal life in Paris.

Now he was with a brotherhood. The three had become many, all working for the man they called 'The King'. It was said that no matter what the business, if you wanted an act committed within the boundaries of Paris, The King could provide the service, so long as it was paid for.

Jacquot knew perfectly well what the service was this time. There were many amongst his friends who were reluctant to cut a throat, but not he. No, he was happy to release a soul from this pit of misery that was life. And this time there was a good target for his blade.

Jean de Poissy, the Procureur, walked on along the darkening streets. He came and went by the same route each morning and evening when he had to visit the castle of the Louvre, for he was secure, he knew. The Procureur was a powerful man in the city of Paris. He was the leading investigator of crimes, the chief prosecutor of those who were engaged in murder, pick-pocketing, breaking and entering, and any other offence. None would dare to harm him. He might not be invincible, but with the authority of the King and the city behind him, he came as close to being invincible as a man could become.

There was a strong odour of faeces from the slaughter houses as he continued east. The smell hung about here at all hours of the day, but it was just one of the normal, everyday manifestations of life in a city.

He continued past the rising mass of the buildings on the Île de la Cité, and on along the river until he came close to the eastern wall, where he began to head north. Three lanes up here, he took a turn to the east again, and fumbled with the latch to his door. It was dim in the lane here, and he had to concentrate hard to find it and open it wide. A man passed by, but the Procureur ignored him, even when he stopped and turned back.

Jean de Poissy merely assumed it was a beggar, and swore at the man briefly. He had enough on his mind already without worrying about lowlifes.

*

Jacquot smiled as the Procureur pulled the door wide. So this was where de Poissy lived. A pleasant house, he had here. Unlike other lawyers, in their expensive chambers, this Procureur lived cheek-by-jowl with tradesmen and artisans. Strange, but no matter.

Jacquot's knife was ready in his hand, and as he shifted his weight, ready to lunge, the Procureur himself took a sudden sidestep. Jacquot felt alarm thrilling through his body at the idea that his quarry had realised his intention. His first thought was to stab the man and make a bolt for it, and then he realised that it was only the Procureur's servant, come to the door to let his master in.

Sighing with relief, Jacquot made a mental note of the address and slouched off back the way he had come.

The Procureur could be killed whenever he wished.

Tuesday before the Assumption of the Blessed Virgin Mary[1]

Furnshill, Devon

'Dear Christ in chains!' Baldwin burst out as he read the letter.

'Husband!' Jeanne expostulated.

'Don't think to remonstrate, Jeanne,' Baldwin said. 'I'm to go to France again, in God's name!'

Paris

Jacquot entered the little brothel and strolled over to the barrel in the corner of the room.

It was a foul chamber. Straw lay on the floor, but it was ancient, and reeked of piss and stale wine. He poured a good measure of wine from the barrel into a cup and drained it. As

---

[1] Tuesday, 13 August 1325

he did so a wench came running into the room, her skirts up about her hips, her chemise gone, and her breasts bouncing merrily. Behind her was a skinny young man with a mop of sandy hair. He had lost his left ear: the proof that he had had a short interview with the law. Seeing Jacquot, he grinned, then hared off after his prey once more.

If the room was foul, the next few were worse. Each was smaller than the previous one, and held little in the way of furniture, but for a medley of palliasses and blankets piled higgledy-piggledy on the floor. There had never been an attempt to clean the place. The sort of men and women who lived here had little need of hygiene.

In the last room, Jacquot entered more cautiously. This was the room where the King rested. It was dim and airless. Candles illuminated the men standing about: some six or seven, two with the split lips that spoke of an executioner's punishment. These were the guards, the men who would fight anyone to protect their leader, who now reclined on a thick bed of cushions on the floor at the point farthest from the entrance. When he spoke, all was silent in the room.

The King of Thieves was a quiet, sullen man, with the dark hair of a Breton. He had thin features and close-set eyes, which fixed upon one with a strange intensity. No one who had felt those black eyes upon him would forget the sensation. It was like being watched by a snake.

He wore a plain linen shirt and hosen made of good quality wool. His belt had an enamelled buckle, and there were gold rings on each finger of his left hand. At his side was a girl, clearly a new one, recently brought here to the brothel. Jacquot didn't know where she came from. She was only very young, from the look of her, and while the King mused and spoke, his hand played over her breast and stomach, then lower, while she stared fixedly away from him, watching

Jacquot or the wall; anything other than the man who fiddled with her body as another might play with a quill or a knife. She would not complain. Not if she knew the kind of man he was.

'You didn't kill him when you were asked,' the King said.

'I couldn't. There were too many others about.'

'What do they matter? We've been paid.'

Jacquot was not about to contest the money, although he had seen nothing of it as yet. There was a firm belief in the company that all money was to be shared sensibly. For an important commission like this assassination, the money was paid to the King, and when the job was done, Jacquot would receive his share. Not the full amount, for the larger part would remain with the King, but he would take some livres, and with them he could enjoy himself for a while, gambling, drinking and whoring.

'I will kill him within the week,' he stated softly.

'Good. I look on you as my barber. You shave the unnecessary from Paris, as a barber shaves my chin. He removes my hair, you remove the people who aren't needed. I don't want another failure.'

Jacquot nodded. He looked at the girl. The King had set his hand on her groin, and Jacquot saw a little shudder of revulsion run through her frame, as though she had felt a man walking over her grave. Perhaps fourteen summers old, she already had tracks of pain and hardship etched into her soft cheeks and brow.

Fourteen summers. That was the age of his little girl, when he buried her nine years ago.

Suddenly disgusted by his life, he turned and stumbled out. It took three large mazers of wine to help him recover his equanimity.

*

Furnshill, Devon

The letter was almost apologetic in its tone, but there was neither comfort nor sympathy in the brief text.

It was an order which had come to him from the Sheriff's offices at Rougemont Castle in Exeter. There were many words on the paper, declaring the King's position, his authority over the British, his overlordship of Guyenne and all the other territories, but these were irrelevant to Baldwin just now. All he saw was the simple command at the bottom: *The King would have you travel with him to Paris as a member of his guard of household knights. Meet him at Langdon, near Dover.*

Jeanne saw the scrawl at the bottom and blanched. 'I can't come with you, Baldwin. I'd like to, but not with young Baldwin and Richalda. They wouldn't be able to cope with such a long journey, not at their ages. Not at the speed the King will wish to travel. It's just not possible.'

'My love,' Baldwin said, scrunching up the parchment and pulling her towards him. 'I don't want to go, but I cannot refuse the King without good reason.'

'I understand that, husband, but I cannot come too. What else does it say?'

'Only that he wants me to bring Simon too.' Baldwin sighed. 'This is too cruel! Simon will not want to leave while this new matter of Despenser's ownership of his home is troubling him and Margaret.'

'Leave that for him and his wife to sort out, Baldwin. You need to arrange matters for yourself. You cannot worry about everyone else, my love.'

'Very well. But I have to send a messenger to Simon to warn him.'

'Yes.' Jeanne's eyes took on a faraway look. 'Perhaps there is one thing which you might do to protect him, then.'

Morrow of the Feast of St Augustine of Hippo[1]

Langdon, Kent

Neither of the two men were happy as they rode into the yard of the great Premonstratensian house, Wolf trotting happily behind them.

Simon was grim of visage in the face of this latest enforced departure. He had sworn so often, to Baldwin's knowledge, that he would never again leave England's shores on a ship, and yet here he was, set to travel again to France, and at a time when his wife was being cruelly threatened by Despenser. The last time Simon had been away from home, he had installed a lodger who was more than capable of protecting himself – another Bailiff from the moors who had a need of a home. Margaret, meanwhile, had gone to visit Jeanne and taken their son with her.

This time, Jeanne had suggested he should put the local priest in as their lodger. The man would be very glad of a home so near to the church, and Margaret could once more travel to stay at Baldwin's house.

This arrangement did not, however, leave Simon with any sense of comfort. He was here, many miles away from his home, and his wife and family were undefended.

'Despenser promised us that he'd leave me alone,' he said again.

'Simon, I think this only proves that it is not possible to trust anything that he says,' Baldwin replied. 'He is not an honourable man, but a felon who dresses well. He just has so much power that he thinks he can behave with complete impunity. And with the King's support and tolerance, he is quite right.'

---

[1] Thursday, 29 August 1325

THE KING OF THIEVES 83

'Damn him. Damn his soul to hell,' Simon muttered. He had never felt such an overwhelming detestation of any man before in his life. All those whom he had hunted down for murder, for treachery, for crimes of all sorts, had not inspired this sense of utter loathing. To think that the man could have done such a thing to him, for no genuine reason. Simon had done nothing to harm Despenser intentionally. Oh, possibly he and Baldwin had together ruined some of his plans, but that was not their fault directly. They were both officers of the law, and when they discovered acts that were illegal, they were bound to apply the law.

'You must try to forget his actions against you while we are here, Simon,' Baldwin advised, glancing about him. The abbey was filled to bursting with the King's men and they mingled with those who wore the Despenser insignia. 'Do not lose your temper, old friend.'

'I will try not to, Baldwin, but if that self-satisfied cretin shows up and insults me, I will find it difficult not to push my fist through his face.'

'Simon!' Baldwin said urgently. 'Bear this in mind, old friend – Despenser is inviolate. He is the King's closest friend. Any man who makes Despenser an enemy is also an enemy of your King. You want to be an outcast in your own land? Then keep hold of your tongue. Despenser is foul and his acts repugnant, but that is no reason for you to die. Remember that! You do not wish to leave Meg and little Peter destitute, do you?'

'I am sure I recall saying almost the same thing to you, the last time we were leaving the King's presence,' Simon said with a dry grin.

'And you were right then, just as I am now. You reminded me of my duty to my family – now I do the same for you. Do not forget them, old friend.'

'I will try not to,' Simon promised. But there was little conviction in his tone.

Chapter Eight

Saturday after the Feast of St Augustine of Hippo[1]

Langdon, Kent

The years after the invasion of the Normans had seen a flourishing development of religious houses in the country. First were the Benedictines, then Cistercians too, but as time passed on, the Premonstratensians became more and more popular with those who could afford the best protection for their souls. Investing a little money in a house for these white-clad monks was a good long-term prospect.

It was Matilda, the daughter of that great monastic builder, Ranulf de Glanville, who paid for the colony here at Langdon. Simon had heard that they were never overly expensive, which must have been an attraction to some of those who decided to support them. Perhaps they were cheap to feed, since all were vegetarian. And they never required much in the way of laundry, apparently. Their robes were noted for being rather 'lively'. It was a reputation which he preferred not to put to the test, certainly. He would be using his own bedroll, he decided, while they were staying here.

In the event, he and Baldwin took space in the small inn nearby. This entailed sharing a small chamber with five other men, but at least all were from the King's household,

[1] Saturday, 31 August 1325

and should therefore have better hygiene than the monks.

It was a pleasant little place, and their first night had been comfortable enough, with little in the way of irritating habits from the others in the room. Being only a small inn, there was no great bed for travellers, but space for each to spread a palliasse and a rug over the top. It was not the best bed Simon had ever used, but nor was it the worst.

However, even on that first night, worn out from a long, rapid ride to comply with the King's wishes, he found sleep evaded him. How could he rest content, when he had left his wife behind alone?

She had been brave, of course. Meg always was. Her bright blue eyes never looked so clear and shining as when he left her. Her body was slim and taut against him, and her mouth soft and yielding when they kissed. She held him for a moment or two afterwards, looking deep into his eyes, and he knew that she understood he had no choice. He must go – unless he wished to incur the King's displeasure.

Meg had always been sensible. Even in those desperate times when they had been parted, she had not been a nag. She understood the imperatives of a man's life and his duties. In those days, when he had been given the new, awful position of the Keeper's representative at Dartmouth, she had never made him feel guilty about his decision to accept the post. She was sad that he had to leave her and the children, but she appreciated that it was not his fault.

But this time, this parting was harder for both of them. He had already been away for so long, and the country was undeniably more turbulent than before. To be absent from home just now, when Despenser was growing ever more bold in his actions against them both, was enough to drive him frantic. It was not knowing what was happening that made him chew at his lips. For all he knew, his wife and son could have been attacked, along with Jeanne and Baldwin's children.

Then he chided himself. That was stupid. There was no likelihood of that. No. Jeanne had Edgar, Baldwin's Sergeant from his days in the Knights Templar, to guard her and mobilise their peasants against any assault. Meg had Hugh, Simon's long-standing servant – and the bane of his life. Edgar and Hugh together would be plenty adequate, even without Baldwin and Simon.

It did not make his day any the more comfortable, though, to have lain tossing and turning on a flattened palliasse while all about him, men gently snored.

They were unlikely to hear much about their duties that day, they both knew, but the lack of direction was enough to make Simon peevish. The food was no good, the ale worse, and the people here should be making more effort to assist the King's own guards, he thought grumpily.

'Simon, we shall be here for some little while, I expect. Try to ration your ill-temper, rather than venting it all today, eh?' Baldwin said at one point with a half-smile.

'If I could keep it in, I'd be a deal happier,' Simon said.

They were able to find a clerk late in the morning, just before noon, who was apparently aware of the King's movements.

'To France? No, I'm afraid he's not going,' the man said.

'Sweet Jesus!' Simon burst out. 'Who can tell us what is happening? We've come here at no notice to accompany him to France, and now we're here, you say it'll not be for days?'

'No, I didn't say he wouldn't be going for *days*,' the clerk said. He was a pedantic old soul with a thin fuzz of hair encircling his bald pate. Now he frowned at Simon with a meditative expression. 'When I said he wouldn't be going, I meant it. He's unwell.'

'How unwell?' Baldwin snapped.

'Unwell enough to send two ambassadors to explain how bad he is, and to swear to it on their oaths.'

'Two, eh?' Baldwin said without conviction.

'So we'll not be going, then?' Simon said hopefully.

'I don't know. You need to ask the King, don't you?'

'Very well. So where is he?' Simon asked.

'He is with the Abbot in the Abbot's chambers, I expect. But you aren't allowed in there. It's private.'

'So who *can* we ask?' Simon enquired with poisonous charm.

And so it was that by the time they were needing their lunch, they found themselves sitting with Bishop Walter Stapledon of Exeter.

Louvre, Paris

The Procureur left his house and made his way gradually along the lane, heading towards the little shop where he customarily stopped to break his fast.

Today he was late. He'd woken with a headache, the natural result of an evening out with his old companion Raoulet the Grey. They had known each other for many years, but those years had not taught them to be cautious of too much cheap wine. Therefore, this morning, his head was atrocious, but his bowels were even worse.

As he walked gingerly along, one thought continued to whirl about in his mind. The man killed in the Louvre was almost certainly lured to that particular room in order to be slain. That little chamber was so quiet, so remote from the main thoroughfares, that it was ideal for an assassination. But *why* had he been killed? And whose idea was it that he should be taken to that room? Was it the messenger, or had someone else decided to bring him to that chamber? If the messenger, did it mean that the messenger himself had killed the man?

It was making his headache worse.

This lane was broad at first, and then it narrowed. Overhead, all light was excluded by the buildings which leaned towards each other like toppling cliff-faces. Jean often wondered why it was that they didn't collapse more often. They must be almost half-eaten away by beetles where they weren't rotted by the damp. Yet the ancient timbers seemed to survive, and the instance of fatal cave-ins was minimal. Only a few people died each year, so far as he could tell, and not many of them actually died *in* the building. All too often it was the fools who heard the rumble and creak of a house about to submit to the inevitable, and who rushed to watch it fall. It was easy to stare at the wrong house, expecting it to teeter, while the one behind them collapsed, with fatal consequences.

Eventually, as he walked along this lane, the Procureur knew he would see a spark of white up ahead, which would gradually reveal itself as the massive block of the Louvre. A fortress fit for an emperor, it was enough to make any man gaze with pride and admiration.

Admiration today, however, was overwhelmed by the sense of turbulence in his belly. As he glanced upwards, he was struck only with the immensity of timber, plaster, lathes, wattles and planks that loomed menacingly over him. The distant sight of blue sky was no help; it made him feel dizzy and sickly at the same time.

No, best to keep his eyes on the ground.

Men shouted, women bawled their wares, selling from baskets bound about their necks, and urchins pelted along the cobbles amid the filth in their bare feet. There was one little room up here, Jean knew, which had fallen in on itself one evening. There was no one else about, and no witnesses. In the evening there had been a hovel there; next morning there was a mess of wood. Took them three days to find the last of the bodies. It was the mother and the baby of the family, and when they got to them, they found that the mother had been killed in the first moments, a balk of timber crushing her skull. The baby, though, some said, had lived for a while. They found its head at the mother's breast, as though still seeking milk from the corpse.

It was a proof to Jean de Poissy that no matter how cultured and civilised the city, there was always an edge of cruelty about the place. He loved and despised it in equal measure most days, for while there was much to stimulate the mind and inspire a man to greatness, there was also much to cause revulsion. A city in which a babe could die in such miserable loneliness was not one in which to bring up children.

But since he had no wife and no children, it was not a concern for him at the moment. He would marry sometime. Not this year, though. He enjoyed his life too much to be tied by a woman. Better to be free.

Just then, he spotted a group of men huddled in a corner, and he automatically became wary. They appeared well-off, from the look of their clothes, but that was no sign of honour. It was all too easy to disguise an evil soul in silks like those of a gentleman.

They were paying him no mind, however. Their attention was fixed on another man. Thinking briefly that they might be felons looking to waylay another wanderer down this lane, Jean glanced around at the man they watched.

To his surprise, he saw that the latter was staring at *him* – and only then did he recognise the man who had been loitering outside his home the other day. In that same second, he saw the glint at the man's side, and put his hand to his own sword, half-drawing it. It was enough to set the fellow to flight. One of the richly-dressed young men attempted to catch him, setting a foot to trip him, but the stranger was up and away before any more could be done.

Langdon, Kent

Taking up a crust of bread and dipping it into his mess, Simon winced as a stab of pain lanced through his shoulder. The wound would take a long time to heal completely. Despenser's man had cut him well.[1]

'Simon? Are you all right?' the Bishop asked.

'It's that scratch I got from the bastard Wattere,' he said. 'Despenser's man.'

'I am sorry,' the Bishop said, a little shamefaced. He had held William atte Wattere for a while, and then released him, even though he could have kept him a little longer.

'You know that Despenser has bought Simon's house?' Baldwin asked pointedly.

'He is a very greedy man,' Bishop Walter said. 'But surely that means he will not harm the house now, Simon?'

'I think it means he will evict us at the first opportunity,' Simon grunted.

Baldwin added, 'It is why Simon did not wish to come with us. He feels sure that his wife is not safe.'

'Could I help? I could have a man check on her for you.'

'I would be glad of it,' Simon said shortly. 'So, tell us what has happened.'

'It takes little enough time,' the Bishop said. 'The King had decided to make his way to Paris, and there to pay his homage to the French King, as is his duty. But there were some of us who were nervous that to do so would endanger his life. There are stories that if the King sets foot on French soil, he will be

---

[1] See *Prophecy of Death* by Michael Jecks

attacked. Some fear that he will be captured and treated as a prisoner of war, ransomed like a knight taken on the battlefield. It would be an appalling situation.'

'So a group of advisers told him he should be anxious? And he immediately gave up his honourable commitment to go to King Charles?' Baldwin said.

'It would be better to keep your voice low if you are to make such comments, Sir Baldwin,' the Bishop said harshly. 'Those of us who argued in all good faith to protect the King may not meet with your approval, but do me the honour of believing I argued from conviction, not evil intention.'

'He sent to apologise to the French?' Baldwin said after a moment or two.

'Yes. Two men have gone – Bishop Stratford and John de Bruton, one of the canons from Exeter. I think you may know him?'

Baldwin recalled a thin, pale man with a sallow complexion who looked as though he might benefit from a visit to a warmer city than Exeter. 'What now, then?' he asked. 'Why are we here?'

'That's what I want to know, too. Surely this wasn't so sudden that we couldn't have been told before we left our wives and our lands?' Simon blurted out.

'If you were not to go, you would have been warned. However, you will still be needed.'

'We were sent for to guard the King on his way to Paris,' Simon pointed out. 'If he's not going, there's not much for us to do.'

'The King is not going, but *someone* must go to pay homage. And the King's representative has asked for you to be his guards – as have I.'

Baldwin frowned. 'You mean the Earl?'

'Yes. The Earl of Chester must go, if the King won't. And

after this latest prevarication, the King would certainly be in danger. In fact, his ambassadors should already be with the French King now, and with any good fortune they will have made their offer.'

Chapter Nine

Monday before the Feast of the Nativity of the Blessed Virgin Mary[1]

Louvre

Jean had not enjoyed a restful weekend. His sleep had been shaken by the memory of the flash of steel, and now, although he had been to church and prayed all the previous morning, he still felt sore-eyed and rough.

The attack had shocked him. It was not the first time he had been attacked in the streets, nor would it be the last, of that he had no doubt, but the suddenness of it had made him fear for his life, and like some slow-moving dream, he could still see the huddled figure with its hidden weapon . . . then the man bounding away, like some strange apparition. It was enough to set his teeth chattering when he woke for the third time in the watches of the night. It was times like these, he thought, when the presence of a woman in his bed would have been a comfort.

Today, he would take his servant with him. Stephen had the appearance of a bullock, but the mind of a tax-collector.

'You're coming with me today,' Jean told him.

'Very well, Sieur. Who will prepare your food while I am with you?'

---

[1] Monday, 2 September 1325

'You will. Your duty is to follow me to work and see that I am safe, and then to return for me when I walk home again.'

'And the rest of the day you will be unprotected?'

'There is no need for sarcasm, Stephen. You will be content to know that I shall have the whole of the King's household within shouting distance. But they are not on hand when I walk to and from the castle. You understand?'

'Of course, Sieur. That makes perfect sense.'

The Procureur looked at him suspiciously. 'Good. Prepare yourself, then.'

There were many times like that, when he was not sure whether his servant was mocking him or not. Usually it was safer to assume that he was, but make no comment. Today, Jean did not feel up to arguing logic with the fellow.

But what he did want was to think through this notion that the murdered man had been lured to a quiet chamber where the foul deed would be easy to accomplish.

Who had taken him there?

After a morning's assiduous questioning, the Procureur learned from Philippe that a stranger had been seen in the main hall on the day of the murder.

'Master Castellan?' he called quietly.

The castellan, a tall, aristocratic man with the dark face and beard of a Breton, crossed the floor to join him. 'M'Sieur le Procureur – how may I help you?'

It was hard when speaking to someone like this to remember that he was just a man like any other. Jean was intimidated by rank. He was too aware of his own lowly background. Even when a clerk in his cups had told him that the easiest way to remember a man's true position in the world was to imagine what he looked like sat on a privy, his robes hitched up about his waist, he still found himself feeling awed by men like this castellan.

'My . . . my Lord, I would like to ask you about a man who was found dead while waiting to meet the Cardinal d'Anjou. I have heard he may have been seen here in the hall with you.'

'With me? I don't remember him.'

'Are you sure? A couple of servants and a cook's apprentice all agreed that they saw him talking to you that morning.'

'Ah . . . you are correct. There was a stranger in here. He asked the way to the Cardinal's rooms, and I sent him to the gate to ask for a servant who could direct him. But I didn't know him. He was nothing to do with me.'

'Did he make an impression upon you?'

'Only that he was quite well-informed. He seemed educated. Not a felon and bully, but a man of letters and some intellect.'

'I see. Well, I thank you,' Jean said with a little bow. He could not bow lower, because he saw no reason to honour a man who had lied to him. The servants and the apprentice had all been firm on the fact that the castellan had taken the man by the hand and led him away.

'So, Mon Sieur, why would you lie to me about that?' he wondered aloud, then turned back to look at the castellan. It was interesting for him to see that the castellan had chosen that same moment to turn and gaze back at him.

Louvre, Paris

The King, Charles IV of France, stood tall. Even without his boots, he was almost five feet eleven inches, so he towered over most of his knights, let alone the general populace.

His eyes passed over the men who instantly dropped to their knees. The clique of cardinals and clerics all bowed their heads, but true to form wouldn't bend their knees, and he stared at them stonily for a moment or two. They were unrepentant, he was sure, but that was a fact of life. He must try to accommodate them in public, while twisting their arms in private.

His father had been more successful than he. At times he had fallen out with the Pope and the whole malign, meddling coterie of priests. The Church wanted to dominate every aspect of life. That was its primary aim. After Pope Boniface VIII had announced his Bull, *Unam Sanctam*, there was little else the King could do other than defy him. The meaning of the Bull was, that all men and women on the planet owed their loyalty and fealty to the Pope before any other. Even Princes, Kings and Emperors must bow to the Pope, because he was the primary representative of God on earth. All who wished for their soul's salvation must submit to the will of the Pontiff.

No other Pope had dared go so far. And few Kings worried themselves about it. After all, they had been anointed by God. All were chosen by God. The Pope did not intervene, and thus he had accepted tacitly that they were entitled to their positions, whether he now argued against them or not. So the secular Princes and Kings sat back and watched with interest.

Not so Philippe IV, Charles's father. The French would never submit to a Pope whose position he owed, in some measure, to French diplomacy. The King ordered his leading lawyer, Guillaume de Nogaret, to make a case against the Pope, and he found it embarrassingly easy. The Pope, Boniface, had taken the position when the previous Pope was still alive. Celestine, the holy, the ever-pious, had fled the Papacy because he feared the corruption. Boniface had captured him and taken the Papacy as his own, and then had his predecessor murdered.

Thus he was guilty of two hideous crimes. While Celestine had been formally wedded to the Church, Boniface had adulterously taken the Church from him; and second, Boniface had been responsible for the slaying of his predecessor.

Infuriated, Boniface threatened dire consequences on the whole of France, but de Nogaret moved against him quickly, and neutralised the Pope.

King Charles beckoned the Cardinal, and Thomas d'Anjou crossed the beautifully tiled floor to join him.

'Your Royal Highness?'

'I understand that there are two men here from England to see me. I would be grateful for your company while speaking with them.'

'I would be delighted to aid you.'

'I am sure you would, Cardinal. However, if you do not feel able to demonstrate the correct degree of respect to me and to the Throne, it may be difficult.'

The Cardinal bowed low. 'Your Highness, I apologise if my demeanour appeared to show too little respect. I honour you deeply, both as a man and as a King.'

'I am glad to hear it. Where are these two?'

The men were soon brought in, and the King stood eyeing them with a chilly expression for some while without speaking. Then, when he did open his mouth, it was to say in a mildly annoyed tone: 'I was expecting my brother, the King of England, and yet I find I have a Bishop and a cleric. What, has King Edward suddenly died? Has he fallen from his horse and broken his pate? Or is he, perchance, sitting with a terrible attack of the gout?'

'Your Royal Highness, my King sends his humble apologies, and declares that he has been overwhelmed by a terrible affliction in his belly and lungs. The physicians are with him night and day, your Highness. Otherwise he would certainly have come here to attend to you.'

'In truth? How the poor man must be suffering, then, to

miss out on the opportunity of meeting me. I had thought he was simply avoiding the homage which was due to me so many months ago. But no matter. Perhaps it is better this way. I shall simply confiscate all the territories which were to have been returned after his homage.'

It was then that the envoys begged to explain that there was a new proposal. 'If our King creates the Earl of Chester as the Duke of Aquitaine, and settles all his lands and titles on the Earl, the Earl himself can come and pay homage to you as his liege lord. Surely, that would settle the matter?'

The King stared down at the man. 'This was my proposal many months ago. At the time, your King was reluctant to agree. What has made him compliant now?'

'His desire not to prolong the difficult negotiations, nor to upset your Royal Highness.'

'And the hope that I will marry my son to his daughter, I have no doubt.'

There was no answer to that. King Charles knew that King Edward wished to forge a stronger bond between their thrones by marrying his daughter Joan of the Tower to Charles's son. Bishop Stratford had been bribing men in the court to support the proposal, but his success would be limited. Charles was too well aware of all to whom money had been paid.

It was some little while later when the audience had finished that the King turned to his most trusted adviser. 'Well, Cardinal? And what do you think of this?'

'It is remarkable that they have sent these men to make the proposal. I would think that by the time a response is sent, the boy will have his Ducal coronet. It makes the matter more interesting for you, of course.'

'In what way?'

Cardinal Thomas gave him a look. If he could, he would have been ironic in response, but instead, he chose to set out the facts clearly. 'If the boy comes here, you will have him, and his mother. The English can struggle and argue all they want, but the Queen of England, your sister, detests her husband's friends and advisers. With the King's heir under her control, you will have a stage ready for any number of stratagems.'

'My thoughts precisely. I shall send to England to agree to the settlement of the English territories on the son, and then I shall welcome my nephew with open arms as soon as he arrives. However, you do miss one important aspect of all this, old friend.'

'Such as?'

'Once the boy is here, I also have a duty of care to him. I cannot allow any man to harm or threaten him. His person will be as inviolable as my own. For were anything to happen to him, the blame would immediately be put to my shoulders. And I do not wish for that, Cardinal. So there must be formal warnings to all, that I will not tolerate even any rudeness to my nephew.'

The Cardinal nodded, blank surprise on his face. 'But why should you seek to have him harmed? Who could think such a thing?'

'There are many, Cardinal. It is a pity, however. It would have been so pleasant to have King Edward here, and to make him squirm as he paid me homage. And especially if he had brought that arch-schemer and thief, Despenser with him. Or, better, the foul Bishop of Exeter. He is a man I would like to see punished for his treatment of my sister.'

'He has mistreated her?'

'It is Walter of Exeter, who sought to deprive my sister of her lands, her money, and even the comfort of her household. Stapledon persuaded the King to remove her children so that the evil French mother couldn't teach the Princes and

Princesses treason against their father. Can you conceive of such a mind? That he could think such treachery would be possible from her?'

'Shocking,' Cardinal Thomas agreed. He found such allegations easy to believe.

The King clapped his hands. 'Very good. And now, I would like to hear from the Procureur what he has learned about the dead man in my castle. I am not so rich in my population that I can afford to lose the occasional visitor. Where is the man?'

Langdon, Kent

'I hope I find you well, Sir Baldwin?'

It was good to note the quick shock on his face, Despenser thought. Always he tried to instil respect for his position and authority, but to see a man like this knight, a renegade who had once been a Knight Templar, cringe even slightly was satisfying indeed.

The other, the little Bailiff, looked as though he'd bitten into a sloe, his mouth was so puckered. It made him look like an old man with an arse for a mouth. Fool! He had plainly heard about Despenser's purchase of the lease on his house. 'Bailiff. How is your lovely wife?'

'She is well, we thank you,' Baldwin said quickly, stepping between them. 'Sir Hugh, I hope the King is recovered?'

'He is greatly improved, I think. He is in with the Abbot just now.'

'That will give him much comfort, I am sure.'

'And you, Sir Baldwin. What are you doing here?'

'We were summoned. Originally we were to guard the King on his way to Paris – but now I understand that he has decided not to go.'

'Quite so. And yet there is a fresh embassy to go in his place.'

'Yes,' Baldwin said, but did not elaborate. He wished to see whether the Despenser had any other snippets which could be useful.

'So you will return home soon, then, I imagine?' Despenser said.

Simon caught his glance, and looked away, jaw clenched.

'I will have to come to Devon to see the lands which I own, I suppose,' Sir Hugh went on languidly. 'I may ask you to put me up in my new house, Bailiff. You will not mind leaving it for a week or more, will you? And now I must be off. *I* have much work to do in the King's service.'

He marched off, gathering up two henchmen as he went. One was chewing at a straw. He had thin, sandy hair over a circular, freckled face, and he stared impassively at Simon from pale blue eyes. As Despenser passed him, he smiled and nodded, as though content that his original opinion had been confirmed. Then he slowly turned and followed the man.

'I will have his head one day, if he so much as looks at my wife,' Simon hissed through gritted teeth.

'Enough, Simon. Think of better thoughts. Such as, returning home to see your wife yourself.'

Louvre, Paris

Procureur Jean stared at the ground before him as he approached the King. The tiles were beautiful, he thought. And as many before him had done, he wondered next how many had found these lovely tiles to be the last sight they enjoyed. For the King was known to be ruthless.

Still, he was meant to be fair as well. He wasn't as cruel as his father had been. In God's name, Philippe IV had been very harsh!

'My Lord King?'

'You have been investigating the death of the man, have you not?'

'Yes, my Lord. I am trying to learn what I may, but it is not easy. No one admits to knowing him,' de Poissy said. Over behind the King to the right, he saw the castellan, and locked eyes with him for a moment or two. 'It would be a great deal more easy if I could learn who was his friend and who was his enemy. Motives tend to flow from such understandings.'

'I see. Could you please try to hurry yourself? I have a Prince coming to visit me before long. It would be pleasing to me to know that there was no murderer wandering my palaces with an insatiable urge to kill.'

There were some sycophantic chuckles at that, and Jean felt himself bridle. It was normal, of course, for the Lords about the King to enjoy the discomfiture of any other man, but he did not see why he should be held responsible personally.

'But of course, my Liege,' he said.

Fairness, justice and equity had nothing to do with the King's court, of course. This was a warlord's hall. The King was the supreme baron in the land. And here he held supreme power. None could gainsay him; none could talk back. In Christ's name, a man couldn't even meet the King's eye unless he wished to have his head taken off. And right now, although Jean was a knight in his own right, he did not wish to call too much additional attention to himself.

'There is another thing, Procureur. There have been some thefts from guests of mine here within the Louvre,' the King continued, and now his eyes were moving over the assembled audience. 'I would like them stopped. I believe the good Cardinal here told you?'

'Yes, my Liege.'

'Then try to learn who is responsible. There is a space on

my gallows for this man. I will not have a thief in my house at the time of my sister's visit with her son.'

'I shall do all I can, your Royal Highness.'

So saying, Jean bowed his way from the presence, while the Dukes and Counts and others simpered and smiled, and when he reached the door and had backed out through it, and the door had closed before him, he knew only pleasure that he had endured another audience.

He took his sword back from the door-keeper, and thrust it into his sheath – for no one might approach the King with a sword without his express permission – and left the great hall.

Outside, he breathed in the rich air, filled with the odours of woodsmoke, charcoal, horse dung, blood and human excrement. This was a great castle, the Louvre. The work went on, through every day. The braziers were lighted for the smiths, and even now grooms and scavengers were collecting the piles of horse droppings in their hands and transporting it to barrows ready to be wheeled out to the dung heaps. The garderobes were being cleaned, too. As they did every day, serfs were gathering up shovel-loads of human waste from beneath the chutes, and dumping it into buckets to be carried to the middens. Little was left to waste even in the King's household.

The Procureur had been about to return to his office, but standing here now, he watched as servants, visitors of different degrees, and traders entered by the main gateway.

It was interesting, he noted. Some would pass in front of him here, others head over to the right of the gate, while the senior people, those who had important business for the King or his representatives, would be taken by a servant up to the main entrance of the castle itself.

He was still smarting from the embarrassment of the attack on him in the street. It was so careless of him, not to have realised earlier that he was being followed. Had it not been for his interest in the fellows on the street, he would very likely now be dead. And that was something which Jean took very seriously.

Jean had been born to lowly stock. He was the son of a serf, but he had managed to educate himself, thanks to the help of an accommodating priest. And seeing his potential, the priest had himself recommended that Jean should be permitted to have an education. Not only had that fired his imagination and enthusiasm for learning, to his astonishment, he found that he was good at it, too. He had rapidly risen and been sent to the university here in Paris, where he soon realised that he was better at the reasoning than at the simple arts of debate. He enjoyed applying logic to complex conundra, and gained a reputation for aiding others with strange little perplexities. After some while he had come to the notice of the City's mayor, and then his career had begun.

It annoyed him that, having been a resident of Paris, knowing the dangers of the little streets and by-ways, he should have become so entirely smug about his safety, when he knew how many people every day were robbed and beaten up.

There was a call, and he glanced around. Another merchant had reached the main gates, and now a young kitchen knave was scurrying to him, listening while the richly dressed man spoke to him.

Jean studied the merchant with a measuring gaze. He was clearly a wealthy man. Probably high in one of the guilds, if he had to guess. His cloak was trimmed with fur, his shoes beautiful, with long toes. His hosen were parti-coloured, green and red, while his cotte was a glorious scarlet with silver threads that caught the light with flashes of fire as he moved. He had that innate arrogance that men born to wealth always possess, and as Jean watched, the fellow jerked his head at the knave, and the lad scampered away to do his bidding. Noticing Jean, the man eyed him lazily with a raised eyebrow, but seeing he was not worth cultivating as an associate, soon turned away, losing interest.

Jean nodded to himself. Yes. The man was clearly one of those who held his own position in such high regard that there was no need for anyone else to give him respect.

Still, when the knave returned, he observed the youngster leading the merchant off in front of him, and over to the great hall.

Not the kitchens, he noted. The knave must have been used merely as a handy messenger by the man. Which was interesting in its own right . . . possibly something to be considered.

He would have done so there and then, but as he was knitting his brows over the niggling thought that sprang into his mind, he was aware of a man bellowing at him. Glancing up at the gate, he saw old Godeaul, the Sergent from the area near the Grand Châtelet.

'What is it?' he demanded as Godeaul ran to him.

'A woman, Sieur. Murdered down near the bridge.'

Chapter Ten

Langdon, Kent

'Ah, I am glad to see you both,' the boy said condescendingly, and Simon had to shoot a look at Baldwin to stop himself from sniggering. Not only would it have been rude, it would also have been very foolish. A man would not willingly insult the next King of England.

The Earl of Chester was almost thirteen years old, but his manner held all the haughtiness of his father. He was taller than Simon remembered, although it was only some two months since he had last seen the Earl, but as Simon knew perfectly well, a lad could very quickly shoot upwards at this period of his life.

He was good-looking. The fair hair of his father, the regular, slightly long features, and the steadiness of his gaze all added to the lad's allure. Simon could easily imagine that in a short while, he would be tempting the serving girls from any nearby establishment. But his looks and manner were of little concern to the Bailiff just now. What he wanted was to hear that his own presence was unnecessary.

'You will ride with me when I leave this country to go to France to meet my uncle,' Prince Edward stated. 'I will need to have protection, I am told.'

'His Royal Highness is fully aware of the risks of the road,' Richard of Bury put in.

Simon did not like Bury. The man was a large, florid-faced

cleric, who appeared to hold his piety and love of learning as others might grip a shield. He was watching Simon now, his small, brown eyes shrewd and knowing.

'How many of us will there be?' Baldwin asked.

'We haven't decided,' Bury said.

'My Lord?' Baldwin pressed, ignoring him.

'I have a need for a fair entourage. I am to be travelling as a Duke, after all,' the Earl said. 'I think I shall need four knights as a minimum, and then the servants . . .'

The list was a long one, but Baldwin was not interested in the finer details. 'Which other knights will travel with us?' he enquired.

'I had thought to bring Sir Henry de Beaumont. And of course the Bishop of Exeter will join us.'

'They are good men,' Baldwin agreed.

'Oh, and I would like to have Sir Richard de Welles, also.' The Earl was looking up and over Simon's head as he spoke, as though mulling over this additional choice.

Simon looked up, forgetting to show due respect. 'Him? Why?'

'I beg your pardon, Bailiff?'

Simon realised his error. 'I am very sorry, your Royal Highness, but I am just surprised at your choice there. Sir Richard is a man of . . . of great courage and—'

'Precisely, Bailiff. He is a man of courage and fighting ability. He would be an ideal companion on a journey such as this, I would think. You have a comment to make about him? If you know of some fault in his character, or a dangerous secret, you should share it with us now.'

Simon swallowed and shook his head. He could hardly declare that he had a great respect for the knight's drinking abilities, for his capacity for strong ale, burned wine, and breakfasts of immense proportions the morning after, when all decent folks were still nursing bellies that complained at the patter of a flea's feet. And heads that threatened to explode at the rumbustious clatter of a sparrow's feet landing on a branch. 'I have enormous regard for Sir Richard,' he managed with a slight croak in his voice.

'I am glad. And now, gentlemen, I would be grateful if you could prepare yourselves to leave England in the next week. My father will soon give me the two counties of Ponthieu and Montreuil, and after that we shall be leaving for Paris.'

Simon knew it then. This was a boy, little more than a child. And he was about to leave his country to go to a strange land, where he would be carrying out an important duty for his country and his father. It was a stern, responsible task – but for a boy of twelve years, it was more than that: it was *exciting*. Especially since he would hopefully guarantee his own inheritance.

He mentioned this later that afternoon as he and Baldwin stood at the bar in the buttery, Baldwin sipping at a leather cup of strong, red wine, Simon gulping from a quart jug of the King's best ale.

Baldwin looked at him a little strangely. 'You believe he's thinking of the realm and his Crown? I tell you this: I think he has more important considerations in his heart.'

'Such as? What would be more important to a fellow like him than his realm?' Simon scoffed.

'The thought that he will be able to see, kiss, and converse with his mother for the first time in many months – that will weigh more heavily with the Earl.'

'And we'll be there . . .'

'To look after us,' said Richard of Bury.

The chubby cleric eyed them both short-sightedly, and Simon glowered in return. 'You were eavesdropping on us. Don't you trust us?'

'Bailiff, I have been seeking you out. Don't you think that we are to be allies on this journey? My only interest is the safety of the Earl of Chester, and yours is the same, surely?'

Baldwin gave a smile and apologised. 'We are sorry if we gave you offence, Richard. The simple truth is, we are both out of sorts. We would infinitely prefer to be ensconced in our homes with our wives and children about us. This trip – it is just one more lengthy journey which we would fain have left to others.'

'But the Earl himself asked for you both. He felt happier with your company.'

'He barely knows us,' Simon said with a bad grace and turned his back to lean on the bar.

'True. But he knows his mother's opinion of you both, which is very high. And he knows something of your characters because I have been teaching him how to understand men. What's more, he is well aware that you are no favourites of the Despenser.'

'Sir Hugh le Despenser is a close friend of his father's, though,' Baldwin said lightly.

'Let us not mince words, Sir Knight,' Richard said, his voice dropping. 'Despenser is an evil cancer in the heart of the realm. You two are known to be hated by him. Yes, even here people can receive messages of such a sort. And yes, the Earl is happy to have men with him who will be less devoted to Despenser.'

'What do you want from us?' Baldwin asked.

'Just this: that you keep an eye on the Bishop. He is dedicated to the destruction of the Earl's mother, and Earl Edward will not allow that. It is your task to . . .'

Simon turned back, eyes narrowed. 'Are you suggesting that we should spy upon him? Bishop Walter has been a friend to me for longer than I can remember.'

'I am glad for you. To others, the good Bishop may not appear so kindly. One such person will become your King. Remember that, Master Bailiff!'

'Richard, we are grateful to you,' Baldwin said sharply. 'We will do all in our power to protect your student.'

He watched as the clerk nodded and walked away. 'I think, Simon,' he sighed, turning to his old friend, 'this could become a strangely dangerous mission.'

'May he swyve a goat!'

Gate of the Grand Châtelet

The body lay at the rear of a small, dark alleyway.

Jean stood with the Sergent while a physician studied her, concluding his examination with a grimace and a muttered, 'Whoever did this was in real earnest.'

Jean could see what he meant. Despite the lack of light, he could see that the girl had been stabbed many times. Her torso was punctured with lots of little wounds, each about an inch in length, one even penetrating a nipple.

For that was the other thing: this young girl, and she could scarcely have been fifteen, was entirely naked. It was a sight that made old Godeaul's breath rasp in his throat. As Jean knew, the Sergent had three daughters of his own. The man was gripping his staff with whitened knuckles.

'Who did this, Godeaul?'

'If I knew that, Procureur, his body would already be in the river!' The old fellow said hoarsely. 'I would not allow a man who could do this to a young girl to live.'

Jean nodded and peered closer, crouching down at her side. The bones of her right hand were crushed; blood was clotted all over her, and smeared across her belly in two lengthy sweeps. That was, he thought, where her murderer had wiped his blade clean after thrusting it into her. And it had been a frenzied attack – he could count twenty stab wounds quite easily, but there would be more, all over her upper body: her breasts, belly, shoulders, throat and head. One had ripped through her right cheek and laid the teeth open to view.

He felt ashamed of himself for subjecting her poor naked body to this close study, but he knew that he must make sense of her position, her wounds, even the choice of this alley for her resting place, if he was to find her killer.

And find her killer he must. As Sergent Godeaul had said, the man who was capable of this sort of attack should be found and slain like a rabid dog before he could kill again.

Langdon, Kent

They had left the bar, and were making their way back to their beds when Simon heard a quiet call. Wolf turned and growled, a low, deep rumble.

'*Baldwin!*' Simon hissed, his hand going to his sword.

'There is no need for that, Bailiff,' said the Bishop as he approached.

'Bishop Walter, I am sorry,' Simon said.

'Walk with me, both of you. I have need of a little contemplation, and your heads will aid me.'

They followed him as he paced along the grassed lawns, his head bent.

'Bishop, is there something you wish to ask of us?' Baldwin said after some minutes.

The Bishop sighed. 'Yes, there is. It grieves me to say it, but we have too many men on this journey. I am content with Sir Richard de Welles. He is a stout-hearted man, and has experience of reading how other men will react, from his position as Coroner. And I believe he will stick true to his oath.'

'Of course.'

'You will, too, I know. There is nothing you would do to harm me,' the Bishop continued, as though he had not heard Baldwin. 'It is the others. You know, I am wary even of Sir Henry de Beaumont.'

'Why? Sir Henry is a man of good reputation.'

'Yes, he is. But a good reputation is only as good as the last man who reported it.'

'What do you fear, Bishop?' Simon asked bluntly.

'It is not my fear,' Bishop Walter said quietly, 'but I am anxious, that if I die, then the Earl's life could be in danger, and the realm with him.'

Chapter Eleven

Wednesday before the Feast of the Nativity of the Blessed Virgin Mary[1]

Paris

The Procureur had three mysteries to consider now, where one alone had taxed him before. There were the two corpses, and the matter of the thefts, as the King called it. The only positive aspect was that at least the second death had nothing to do with the King. The first, the death of the young lad, must take precedence, because it was an embarrassment to the Crown. Jean had spent all the previous day trying to find out more. But without success.

On the day that the man had arrived, he had been taken to the chamber where he was presumably murdered by a servant. This same servant was no longer at the Louvre, Jean had discovered. He had been despatched to the King's special hunting ground at Vincennes, one of the servants sent ahead to prepare the little palace for the vast numbers of guests shortly due to arrive. Meanwhile, three others stated that they had seen the man in conversation with the castellan, Hugues – but he had denied all but a fleeting contact with him.

This morning he had made a decision, and sent a messenger to Philippe at the Louvre. The boy was rebelling against these

---

[1] Wednesday, 4 September 1325

constant investigations, but Jean had demanded, and received, the support of the head cook, and now Philippe was seconded to his service. Jean had ordered the lad to watch the castellan and report any visitors to him. It was likely that the castellan was merely involved in some form of corruption and trying to conceal that, rather than being a murderer – but at this stage of the investigation, anything was possible. And yet the witnesses were all convinced that Hugues and the stranger had greeted each other like old companions.

Anyway, to Jean the dead woman was a worry of a more immediate sort. He was not at all happy to have a madman walking the streets of Paris who could slash and stab a defenceless young girl so viciously. Once she had been cleaned up, he had counted sixty-three wounds on her. An appalling number. Her hand was crushed, too. But not by a single massive injury; there had been several different blows: one to each knuckle, one to each finger, one to the bones of the hand, and so on. The blows had been rained down on her to inflict maximum damage or pain.

He was walking from the Grand Châtelet's chapel, in which he had viewed the corpse again where it lay before the altar, and now, recalling that poor little body, he stopped and wiped a hand over his eyes. She was so pretty, so young and innocent looking. He could feel hot tears rising at the memory of how she had been forced to suffer.

But tears wouldn't bring her back, nor erase the memory of her suffering.

If only there was something, *anything*, which could give a hint as to who she was, and who her killer might be.

There was a natural assumption that an unknown girl like her, found dead in an alleyway, was more than likely a prostitute. Women like that were five to a *sou* in Paris. They came in from miles around to the city here: girls who had argued with their parents and fled the home; girls who were threatened with rape by local men of influence, and needed to escape; girls who met persuasive young men who told them of the life they could enjoy together in the city, and who then sold the girls . . . So many young women, so many victims. There were few indeed who would survive here to make a life for themselves.

But there *was* one woman who might be able to help him find out who she was. Hélias was one of those who knew everything that went on. She could always aid a man – in so many ways . . .

He mustn't think of her, though. There was too much to be done.

And then he stopped. He was in the middle of the main street which ran west from the Grand Châtelet. Shops and stalls lined the sides, and people wandered and mingled all about. Women in gaudy colours strolled among the stalls where merchants and haberdashers plied their trades. The dressmakers called to them, the cloth-sellers held up bolts of material, the wine sellers extolled their wares, as did the girls with baskets of small, sweet pastries, and the boys trying to sell honeyed thrushes and ortolans – and over them all was a haze of dust rising all the while. The sun was warm on his face as Jean looked up at the sky. Here the road was wide to allow the passage of wagons, and he could actually see the sun up in the sky. Its brightness made him wince.

He was Procureur. There was a responsibility on him to investigate any murder when the King demanded it, but there was also a need to protect the public of this city. He had two bodies. So far, he had got nowhere with either of them. He did not even know who the dead man was, nor why he was in the castle. Meanwhile, here was a young girl. It was possible that he might be able to find out who she was, why she had died there in the demeaning little passageway. And if he could, to hell with everything else.

Tomorrow he would see *her*. Hélias. The whore who knew all.

Louvre, Paris

Cardinal Thomas rose from his praying and crossed himself reverently before leaving the little church.

The Procureur was asking all sorts of questions, which was good. Soon he would discover the identity of the dead man. It was fortunate that Thomas had been able to prime three servants to let de Poissy know that the castellan had seen the dead man that morning. After all, Sieur Hugues had told him that he'd seen the fellow. Hugues knew him, all right, and had made sure that he'd been taken to the chamber in which he'd been invited to wait for the Cardinal's arrival. Of course, when Cardinal Thomas did arrive – the poor fellow was dead as a nail.

The Procureur would soon make the connection. Cardinal Thomas for one would be glad to see the castellan taken away in chains. It would serve the man aright for his attempt at blackmail.

It was only a shame that Cardinal Thomas could not himself give the castellan, Sieur Hugues, to the Procureur as a gift. But to do that would inevitably leave him open to danger, and the possible extortion of even *more* money. So it was best to leave matters as they stood, and hope for the best.

*

Thursday before the Feast of the Nativity of the Blessed Virgin Mary[1]

Paris

Hélias lived in a small building on the other side of the city wall, a little north of the Château du Bois, in a filthy area that was close to collapsing into a bog. The soil here was always damp, as though the Seine had inundated it. But no, it was just some freak of the area. No one knew why it was.

There were many who lived down there among the grim little hovels. They were the people who had not been born inside the city walls; those who had, had an immediate advantage in life. They were the ones who would form the aristocracy of the city when they grew up. The merchants, the members of the guilds and fraternities, they all rose to their elevated positions as a result of the location of their birth, not merely by dint of effort. If hard work entitled a man to wealth, position, power, Paris would be ruled by the poorest, Jean thought.

Perhaps this would happen in the future. For the present, the city was ruled by those who already had money. And those lesser beings whom they needed – to clean the streets, to sweat and toil and die while others took advantage of their efforts – existed here in these dank streets.

Hélias was sitting on a stool in front of her little house when Jean de Poissy arrived. He could see her there as he strolled up the reeking street, avoiding the puddles of rainwater, of urine and of worse. The city employed men who would scrape up every piece of dogs' faeces to be sold to the tanners of leather, but here outside the city the men weren't paid to come, so the place was about as wholesome as a . . . as a tanner's yard, he supposed.

---

[1] Thursday, 5 September 1325

She was a large woman now. Still handsome in many ways, although at nearly forty years she was long past her best. Yet, for a woman to have survived so long in her chosen trade, that was a marvel. And for her to have saved enough from lying on her back to buy this little place and fill it with other young hopefuls, was nothing short of miraculous. For her to have remained unbowed and proud was still better.

The figure which had tempted so many men when she plied her trade in the streets was sadly worn. Her large breasts sagged, and her belly was swollen like a mother ready to be confined, while her face, which had once been so soft and full of promise to the young men who came to be entertained by her, was bloated with wine and the inevitable effects of too many hours lived at night rather than day.

And yet yes, she *was* still handsome. Her eyes had the gleam which could make a man stop and look again. There was a liveliness in the set of her head, an overt manner of licking her lips as she considered a man, a brazen manner of staring at his cods when she should have been meeting his eye, which still set a man's blood boiling.

'I don't often see you up here, Procureur,' she said. 'You wanting wine? Or something else?'

'What else could a man seek at your door, Hélias?'

'Ah, you smile now, naughty man. There was a time when we were both in our twenties when you wouldn't have waited and smiled, though, wasn't there? Then you just took me by the hand and led me to the nearest bed. It's true!' she added more loudly, in case her neighbours hadn't heard.

'Hélias, I don't deny it.'

'No. But you'd still prefer one of the younger fillies now, rather than this old jade, wouldn't you?'

'I would prefer the practised to the student, every time. And

I doubt me not that you have the most practised rump of all the wenches in Paris, Hélias!'

'I don't deny that. If you have a skill, I always say, you should use it. Some can sew, some can knit. Me, I was built for other purposes!'

'True enough.'

'Not that I need to do any of that now. Hey, come and sit with me, Procureur. It's too hot to be standing and talking. Sit and have some wine.' She bellowed in through the open door behind her. 'I'll have a girl bring you something. Not the usual piss I feed the gulls, either. Real stuff.'

Her house was adequately equipped as a tavern, for a madam needed the drink to aid the clients to fetch off swiftly enough so her girls could charm another. 'There is no point having stock waiting on a shelf,' she was fond of saying.

'So, then, naughty man. What do you want? A blonde, a red-head? I have a fresh girl from the south, if you like. Black hair like a . . .'

'You know which girls turn up in the city, Hélias. I have one. Killed.'

Her eyes dimmed a little, but then they hardened. She took a long pull at her cup of wine. 'How old?'

'Entirely fresh, I would say. Perhaps fifteen?'

'Hair? Eyes?'

Jean gave her a full description, and as he spoke, she frowned in concentration.

'There are many of that age. They appear at all times of the year, although more so in the summer and autumn. I think they are less keen to test themselves against the snows if they can avoid it. No clothes, you say? Then it's possible she was new here, and didn't realise a whore could die for stripping in the wrong alley. There are all too many men who seek to protect their territory and their investments by killing any little draggle-tail who seeks to make use of their bit of land. Money paid to a new wench is money taken from their own, they reason. But this sounds less like a cock-bawd protecting his money. He'd just cut her throat – get the job done. The idea that he should stab so often . . . that sounds more like a madman.'

'That's what I thought, Hélias. If he isn't found, he may do this again. That is what worries me.'

'I'll let the girls know. All of them. Meanwhile, where is this chit? I'll go and see her.'

'Why?'

'To see if I know her, of course. And to pay for a Mass too. No one should die without a decent send-off. Don't care if she's one of mine or someone else's, she ought to have a service.'

'Good, Hélias. You do that. And I should be off.'

She looked up at him, and there was that deliberate set to her head again, an evaluation in her eyes. 'Do you *need* to go?'

'What are you offering me? A second-rate trainee, or the real thing?'

'You wouldn't be satisfied with a student, would you?'

'And you'd see to me for free?' he asked, wide-eyed.

She gave a throaty laugh. 'Get away, you villein! The day I offer my arse for free is the day you leave the city to live in the countryside.'

Lydford, Devon

Margaret, Simon's wife, was out with the milkmaid when the sound of hoofbeats reached her ears. She set the maid to work with the butter churning, and then hurried out to where Hugh, Simon's servant, stood with a staff close to hand, scowling at a pair of riders. The priest had not yet arrived to take over, and she had not packed or prepared for the move to Furnshill. She had wanted to finish all the main tasks about the house and farm first, like seeing to the harvest of the fruit and nuts, the slaughter of the pigs and the careful threshing of grain and its storage. All was nearly complete now, but there were still many jobs to be finished, and her back was breaking under the effort.

She recognised one of the men at once. It was tempting to run back into the house and gather up her son to protect him. Instead she stood her ground, her face set.

'Wattere,' she said steadily. 'What do you want?'

William atte Wattere grinned without humour. 'I have a message for you from my Lord Despenser. He wishes that this house be emptied.'

'I cannot do that. My husband is not here.'

'Yes. We know that.'

Margaret swallowed back her fear. 'You threaten a woman when she is all alone? What *courage*!'

Wattere smiled. His left forearm was still wrapped in a linen cloth from where Simon had slashed at him earlier in the year, and the pain had not left him. It was little satisfaction to know that Simon's hand and shoulder were both injured from Wattere's sword.

'Lady, I don't threaten. I'm making a promise. You go, or your house will be taken from you by force. And I will take whatever payment I want,' he added, eyeing her body lasciviously.

She felt her skin crawl at the thought of his hands on her.

*

Vigil of the Feast of the Nativity of the Blessed Virgin Mary[1]

Dover

Baldwin and Simon had not slept well after the Bishop's comments about the Earl's life and the realm being in danger if he himself, were killed. Neither wanted to talk about it the next day until, much later, Baldwin gave Simon a look and the two left their stools and went outside.

'If you want to talk about Walter's words yesterday,' Simon began, '*don't*! I have no desire to contemplate someone killing him.'

'And yet it is a natural fear on his part,' Baldwin said. 'The Bishop is no friend to the French, and the King of France knows that. More, he is still less a friend to the Queen. It has been largely by his efforts that she has been deprived of lands and wealth. The French King would be entirely within his rights to deprecate the treatment meted out to his sister on the advice of the Bishop.'

'Perhaps so, but I don't want to think about such matters. They're not for me,' Simon said. 'Our job is to guard the Earl, and that is all.'

'Simon, I do not disagree. However, how would it look to the King if we permitted someone to kill his most respected churchman? We shall need to take care.'

'I find it hard to imagine that anyone could try to kill Bishop Walter, in any case,' Simon grunted.

'And I too,' Baldwin said, crouching to rub the ears of his dog. Wolf sat and stared up at him, panting slightly. 'But we should be wary nonetheless.'

'I am likely to be wary the whole time I am away,' Simon said glumly.

---

[1] Saturday, 7 September 1325

Louvre, Paris

It was nearly dark when Jean had finally finished his work. The light was dim in his chamber with only three cheap candles, and he was relieved to be able to snuff them and rise, rubbing at his eyes. The scrolls he could leave there. No one was likely to try to break into his room to steal them, in his opinion. No, better to leave now and make his way homewards.

Since the second attempt on his life, he tended to avoid the smaller alleys, sticking to the larger thoroughfares where there were more people. Yet he was aware still of a certain anxiety. There was something about knowing that a man had set his heart upon your death that took the lustre away from even the best and brightest day.

Today he and his man walked quickly from the castle gates and into the city. And it was as he passed the great city gate that he saw a small shape dart under a guard's polearm, and rush towards him.

For an instant he was tempted to reach for his sword and sweep it out, until he realised with a closer look that this was a young girl, and if she was armed, her weapons were very well concealed, since she only wore a thin linen shift, with no sleeves, belted about her waist with a cord.

'Sieur Procureur?'

'I am,' he answered, lifting a hand to tell the guard to hold back.

'I come from Hélias. She asked me to tell you this: the girl was not a whore. She was a recent visitor to the city with her husband. They were called de Nogaret, I think.'

'Sweet Jesus!' Jean blurted.

So that was it! The two corpses were those of de Nogaret and his wife.

*

Furnshill, Devon

Madame Jeanne de Furnshill was entirely engaged in the careful selection of the apples and pears that were to be stored, seeing to their careful wiping so that any dirty ones wouldn't pollute the others, and taking out all those which were bruised or damaged in any way. They would be eaten now, or used to make cider for the farmers on the demesne. She had just set the last from the present basket in the rack in the roof, when she heard the clopping hooves and rattle and squeak of harness and chains. Frowning slightly, she put the damaged apples into the basket, and carried it down the old ladder with some caution. A new ladder would be needed for next year, for this one was rotted with worm holes.

Outside, she was still wiping her hands on her apron when Margaret Puttock appeared around the corner. 'Margaret! You are sooner than I expected – were you not going to come in another couple of weeks?' Jeanne was surprised. Then, remembering her manners, she said hastily, 'You are most welcome! Come here, come here!'

She could see the weariness on Margaret's face as she hurried to the horse to greet her. The miserable old devil of hers, Hugh, was grumbling at the cart behind, with her son Peterkin at his side, but all were clearly glad to be here in Furnshill. Jeanne sensed Baldwin's servant Edgar behind her, but before she could ask, he had taken Margaret's horse's bridle, and was holding the beast steady for her.

'Jeanne, I am so happy to be here. I feel safe at last,' Margaret managed, before bursting into tears.

Chapter Twelve

Jean le Procureur's house

Later, as he sat in his chamber, rubbing at his eyes to clear them, he could recall the story of the late Guillaume de Nogaret. Born of a family which had been denounced as heretics, the young Guillaume was removed from them and placed in the care of the Church. Naturally, both parents were executed.

A clever boy, he rose quickly through the Church, and was educated to a high standard. As a result, he entered a career in the law, and after some years came to the attention of the royal court. Soon he was the King's most trusted adviser. When there was a hard task, de Nogaret would be called upon to assist. It was he who drew up the spurious accusations against the Jews and had them thrown from the country, their debts all cancelled, the money diverted to the Crown. And then there was the matter of the Templars. It was Guillaume who had drafted the accusations against them. By all accounts, his enthusiasm for persecution of those in the Church knew few bounds. And then he had been sent to Italy, too, to capture the Pope.

Jean picked up his pen again. This was very important, he knew. The full matter of de Nogaret's son must be recorded, since his father had been responsible for a major incident in the autumn of 1303 – the seizing and punishment of the Pope. It was a shocking affair, of course, but it had shaped the world today.

The old Pope, Celestine V, had been a hermit, and was more or less forced to accept the post by the cardinals about him. A mere matter of months later, he had been persuaded to relinquish the job, and his successor, Boniface VIII, had taken his place. However, many believed that a Pope was chosen by God, so it was not possible to abdicate. They considered the new Pope to be a cuckoo in the nest, and sought to find and reinstate the old one. Celestine had gone into hiding, but he was found and taken back to Rome, where he died shortly afterwards. All thought he had been murdered on the orders of Boniface VIII.

This successor was an acquisitive man utterly ruthless in his search for wealth. For him, the turn of the century was a fabulous bonanza, in which he sold privileges and made vast sums. But he was as determined to bring secular rulers to book as he was to fleece Christians generally. He issued a ruling that proposed the Pope to be superior to all earthly rulers. And in so doing, signed his own death warrant.

His behaviour had been causing concern for years when he issued this latest provocation, and the French King was willing to take up the challenge. De Nogaret was given his instructions, and a short while later he was at Anagni, where the Pope was finalising his plans to bring Kings to book. Boniface's palace was attacked and ransacked, his wealth taken, and he was himself captured. He died a matter of days later, some said because of a blow from de Nogaret or his allies. Others said he was driven so mad by the loss of his vast fortunes that he killed himself, driving his brains out by slamming his head against a wall.

Jean finished his notes. 'De Nogaret was at Anagni,' he murmured, 'but de Nogaret has died. Possibly the dead man was Guillaume de Nogaret's son. But what was he doing, here in Paris? Why did he seek to meet the Cardinal – and why did the castellan deny knowing him?'

Jean set his reed aside and rubbed at his temples, studying what he had committed to the scroll.

It made little sense. No, he must search deeper, and answer those questions. He sighed, exhausted, and rolled up the scroll, storing it away safely in his chest before yawning, finishing his wine, and preparing himself for his bed.

Furnshill, Devon

'So your house is gone?'

Margaret nodded unhappily. Peterkin was asleep in the solar already, and the two women were sitting on a bench before the fire, drinking some of the end of last year's cider. 'Wattere came and threatened me with my life – and with rape. I had to leave before anybody was hurt by him.'

Jeanne felt her heart go out to her friend. To lose everything now, just when the work of harvest was complete, was a dreadful blow. It was one thing to lose a house, and another entirely to lose the crops which had been husbanded so carefully in the last months. 'Was anything saved?'

'What could we rescue? I had to pack all our belongings and get out as quickly as possible. There was nothing I could bring. Not with only one cart.'

'Well, when the Bishop is back with Baldwin and Simon, they will see to your house and ensure that all is returned.'

'That is good, Jeanne, but what can they do against Despenser? He has ruined us, and there is nothing we can do to defend ourselves. We have lost *everything*!'

*

Monday following the Feast of the Nativity of the Blessed Virgin Mary[1]

Paris

Jacquot sipped at a mazer of wine as he entered the chamber, affecting an ease he didn't feel.

The King did not look in his direction. He was studying the breast of the girl who lay at his side, exploring it with the frowning innocence of a young boy. But he knew when Jacquot entered.

'You failed!' he snapped. 'You swore he would be dead within the week. But that was – what? Three weeks – four weeks ago?'

'I will kill him.'

'When, do you think?'

'As soon as he walks abroad alone. As soon as he's unprotected. What, do you want *me* to be killed?'

The King was driven to smile. 'That,' he explained, tracing the line of the girl's nipple with a forefinger, 'is your concern, not mine. All I know is, I took money for this service, and you haven't done what you were supposed to, have you? Perhaps you're too old now, Jacquy? *Are* you too old? Does the thought of death at the hands of the Procureur fill you with dread? Or is it just that you don't want to be a part of my little force here? Do you think you could take over from me, perhaps? Have control of my men?'

All was spoken in that quiet, sing-song voice that showed his real anger. There was one thing that maintained the King's authority in Paris, and that was his power to promise results. If a man paid for the destruction of an enemy, the King would guarantee it. And that promise, that certainty, kept the money coming in.

[1] Monday, 9 September 1325

'If it was a crophead, you'd have done it in a moment. But I suppose a priest is easier, eh? They don't have such . . .' his finger had dropped to the girl's navel, and now she bit at her lip as he moved lower . . . 'such ability at defending themselves, eh? No, a Procureur is more hazardous. Perhaps you are scared?'

'I fear nothing, King. Not even death,' Jacquot said. And it was true.

Ever since he saw his last child into the grave, he had held no illusions. A God who could permit the deaths of his little ones and force him to suffer so much, was no God for him. What use was a God, in any case? God had seen to the deaths of so many, and always the innocent died first. There were some who said that God was testing men, but to them Jacquot would ask: *why*? If He wanted to test a man's soul, He should pick a man who had been alive long enough to have some sins, not a beardless child.

Jacquot could survive now, mainly by his wits, but also by the exercise of his skills. There was no assassin on the streets of Paris who could compare with him. In his profession he was pre-eminent, and he knew it.

'You have failed, though – whether you are fearful or not. So, I have to wonder what I should do for the best. You see, there are others who want to serve me. The Stammerer over there – he would like to serve me. He is keen to test his knife in another man's blood.'

Jacquot did not even bother to glance at the fresh-faced, smiling boy in the background. He knew Nicholas the Stammerer perfectly well. Nicholas was the kind of man who would pull out a man's nails – not from any need to extract information, but purely from interest – to see how much pain his victim could endure. He was only sixteen years old, so Jacquot had heard. 'You want to entrust the Procureur's death to *him*?'

'I begin to wonder whether he would not be a better agent for us. He has some dedication – but I have begun to doubt your strengths, you see. He is a young lion. You . . . you are more of a boar, I think. Wily, powerful, but brutish and slow.'

Jacquot smiled. 'And you think Nicholas is faster? Then try him, King. Try him. And when he fails and dies, ask me again. But next time I will need more money, I fear. Much more.'

Louvre, Paris

The castellan was a short, heavy man called Hugues de Toulouse, who was the proud owner of a goodly paunch. All men aspired to such a belly: it proved that the owner was a rich man, that his family was well-provided for. Jean le Procureur eyed it with a degree of jealousy.

'Mon Sieur,' the castellan said as he marched into his little chamber and found Jean waiting. 'You have something you need?'

'For my investigations, you mean? No, not really. There were just a few questions I had about the man who died. Did you know who he was? I have learned that his name was Guillaume de Nogaret.'

'Shit! In truth? But he was young!'

'He was not the old man who served our King's father, but perhaps that Guillaume's son?'

The castellan puffed out his lips, shaking his head, and then made his way to the shelf behind his table, where a jug of beer stood. He filled a horn and drank it off, before refilling it, his back to the Procureur.

This was a huge embarrassment, were it to come out. The castellan knew that the son of the old King's chief lawyer might not be considered important himself, but the mere fact that he was related to a servant of the old King's would make his death more suspicious, were anyone to learn about it.

'I knew his father,' he said at length. 'He was an arrogant bastard at the best of times – like all those who get too much education and get pushed up the ladder when they've not the sense to make good use of it all. Bloody fools. Got to give him that: Guillaume was a bright lad. He picked things up. And when he went after the Jews, or the Templars or the Pope at Anagni, he made sure of his position first, and then he was as sodding relentless as a mastiff. If he got his teeth in, there was nothing would shake him loose. Complete bastard for that, he was.'

'You liked him?'

The castellan eyed him sourly. 'You mad? You trust anyone in the King's closest circle? Of course I didn't trust him or like him. No, he'd have shoved a knife in my back as soon as he heard I had something he fancied.'

'Did you know him here at the court?'

'After Anagni, yes. I wasn't here before that.'

'You were there, then?'

'Why do you say that?' the castellan asked suspiciously.

Jean smiled. It was natural for any man to grow alarmed when he was asked about dead men whom they had known. 'You mentioned Anagni, and it was as though that was an event in your life, not merely something that happened to de Nogaret. You were there, I infer?'

'Yes. I was one of the King's men. There were many of us there. And there was so much booty, all of us became richer for our efforts.'

'Booty from the campaign?'

'From the Pope's palace. He was a thieving old scrote, Pope Boniface. Had the best collection of cash, gold, plates, goblets – you name it – of any Lord I've ever seen. Didn't save him, though, murdering old bastard. We found him and raped the place! Happy times, they were.'

'Did you know de Nogaret had a son?'

The castellan shrugged. 'Should I? I last saw de Nogaret some while after the arrest of the Templars, a long time after Anagni, but by then I was already fairly wealthy myself. Didn't have to ingratiate myself with him.'

'His son was already a boy by then,' Jean said pensively.

'What of it?' the castellan demanded. 'You suggesting I had something to do with the lad's death? Because I was here, and there are witnesses to it. The morning he was killed, I was here in the hall with the King.'

'Sieur Hugues, please, do not upset yourself,' Jean said soothingly. 'I was thinking aloud, that is all. Is there anything else you can tell me about the boy or his father?'

'Nothing. I hardly knew them.'

'Very good. And now I must leave you. You will have much to do, I have no doubt.'

'Why are you asking me all this about de Nogaret? Has someone said I was there?'

'No, I merely wanted to learn all I could about the man, so I could try to understand what he was doing here.'

'Hah! Trying to get money, I expect. What else? That's all petitioners ever do, isn't it? He was probably coming here to ask to see the King to explain how, sadly, his father had fallen into poverty, and ask could he have a hand-out.'

'Perhaps. But why would he then go to the Cardinal?'

'Thomas knew his father too, just as I did.'

'He did?'

'Before he was a Cardinal, Thomas was a priest, and knew the court as well as any other chaplain about here.'

'Interesting!'

Back outside, Jean stood in contemplation. There was much

to consider, not least the fact that the castellan appeared anxious about something to do with the matter.

As he thought about all he had heard, he saw a dark-haired beauty enter the passage and walk down towards him. She was not well-dressed, but the graceful measured pacing of her feet made her look more elegant than many a lady of the castle. She looked at him without recognition or interest as she passed, and then made her way into the castellan's room. It made Jean's brows lift to see her confidence – and the fact that she was not evicted from Castellan Hugues's chamber made them rise even higher.

If he had to guess, he would have said that she was a prostitute, from a certain hardness about her, and the swagger of her hips, and he found it a little disconcerting, not to say shocking, that the castellan should entertain such a woman in the King's castle.

Tuesday following the Feast of the Nativity of the Blessed Virgin Mary[1]

Dover

Baldwin stood and watched, chewing slowly at a long strand of hair from his moustache as the King rose and held up his hand. In his clear voice he made his declaration, sounding firm and resolute. He was in every way the symbol of perfection. The ideal King.

'Made a miraculous recovery, eh, Sir Baldwin?'

'I think we should listen to his words, Sir Richard,' Baldwin answered. He was thinking that never had a tyrant looked so kindly.

'Maybe so. But he don't look like a man who had to miss

---

[1] Tuesday, 10 September 1325

an important meeting with the French King, eh?' grinned Sir Richard de Welles.

De Welles was a tall man, some six feet one inch in height. He stood with his legs set a shoulder's width apart, as stolidly planted there as any tree. He had an almost entirely round face, with a thick bush of beard that overhung his chest like a gorget. His eyes were dark brown, amiable yet shrewd, beneath a broad and tall brow. His face was criss-crossed with wrinkles, making him appear older than he really was, for Baldwin knew he was actually younger than his own age of two-and-fifty. Sir Richard's flesh had the toughened look of well-cured leather that only a man who has spent much of his life in the open air would acquire.

He also had the endearing conviction that his booming voice was inaudible to the rest of the men standing about.

'The Bailiff didn't look too well, did he?'

Baldwin allowed a faint smile to pass over his lips. 'I rather think that was your fault again, Sir Richard.'

'Me? What did *I* do?'

'He is not quite so well accustomed to strong wines as you, perhaps?' suggested Baldwin, happy in the knowledge that his own moderation the previous night had prevented any liverishness on his part.

'Not so well accustomed? Sweet Jesus's ballocks, Sir Baldwin, we hardly had enough last night to persuade a nun to run to the privy. Hardly any at all.'

There was a hiss from the man at Sir Richard's right. 'Can you keep quiet? We're trying to hear what the King's saying.'

Sir Richard's expression did not alter. His beaming countenance turned to his neighbour, a fellow in his early twenties, and Sir Richard looked him up and down for a moment in silence. 'Did you speak to me, my young friend?' he asked at length.

'Sir, I would be grateful if you could be silent until the King has finished,' the man growled.

Sir Richard's smile widened. 'And so you should, my young friend. You look damn familiar, though. Let me see, have we met?'

'No.'

'But we must have . . . no, don't say a word . . . have you ever been to Exeter? I am Coroner there, you know.'

'No.'

'Aha! Then it must have been while I was in court, then. Were you ever in Axminster? Chard? Honiton?'

'No,' the man said, and his teeth looked to be set like a man with lockjaw, Baldwin thought.

'Then at the King's courts? Did I meet you at his hall at Westminster or York?'

'No, I haven't—'

'I know. It was in a battle. Were you at Boroughbridge?'

'*No!* Now will you—'

'You weren't at Boroughbridge? Were you at Bannockburn, then?'

'Sweet Jesus! No!'

'In that case, lad, I wonder where I, a warrior, a man high in the esteem of the King, a man who has been to battle on the King's behalf, and who has served him these last thirty years past, I wonder where I could have earned your contempt?'

'I . . .'

'Should keep your bread-hole shut when your betters and elders are talking, boy. So, Sir Baldwin, Simon is not feeling himself?'

'I fear he regrets entering the third and fourth alehouses with you last night,' Baldwin admitted.

'He looked more like a corpse than the last two-month-dead body I studied before coming here,' Sir Richard said musingly. Then he brightened. 'Still, I always say that the best cure for a sore liver is a little more of the same. It never fails to cure me when I feel a little out of sorts.'

Baldwin smiled. To imagine the Coroner 'a little out of sorts' was like imagining a raging bear at the baiting rolling over and cradling its head. It was inconceivable. He turned his attention back to the scene before them.

The Earl of Chester had just stood, and now held his hand high while those nearer him cheered and the noise rippled round the rest of the men standing there.

'There we are, then,' Sir Richard declared, clapping his own hands loudly. 'Hooray! Hooray!'

'Yes,' Baldwin said. 'He's no longer a mere Earl – now he is a full Duke.'

It was a week and a day since the Earl had been given the two counties, but with this ceremony, the King had settled upon him all the rest of his extensive territories in France. Now, with the whole of the British Crown's possessions in his hands, the Earl, a Duke of France in his own right, could meet with King Charles and pay homage for all his English possessions. He would be the first English Prince to own such a fabulous demesne.

'Makes him an attractive target, don't it?' Sir Richard said as the crowds separated.

'I do not think he need fear dangers here,' Baldwin said, looking about them with a small smile.

'I was thinking of France, as well you know. I may live in Devon, but I know dangers when I see 'em. And just now, with the French snapping at the borders of all the King's lands, this little lad would be a tempting morsel for them to pluck up, eh?'

Baldwin shrugged. 'Sir Richard, all we can do, you and I, is guard his body as well as we may. I personally think that the French King would do all in his power to protect the boy and save any embarrassment. It would be a blow to his reputation, were he to treat his own nephew dishonourably.'

'Aye. True enough. But his men could do it for him, couldn't they? Especially all the renegades and traitors. Even that blasted Mortimer is over in Paris, so they say. Despenser keeps having fits of terror that the man will return. He pretends he's not afeared, but you bring up mention of the Mortimer and watch Despenser's face. Enough to sour a vat of ale! Not that I blame him, mind. The idea that the King's best and most effective general might land in England and be on your trail would be enough to make most fellows quail.'

'Not you, though, Sir Richard.'

'Who? Eh? Me? No. I hope not, anyway. I ain't a threat to any, because I am content. I don't need to have anything more than a comfortable berth for me backside of an evening, a jug or two of good wine, and perhaps a small brunette to warm me when the evenings get chilly. Not too much to ask, is it?'

Chapter Thirteen

Thursday following the Feast of the Nativity of the Blessed Virgin Mary[1]

Dover

They were fortunate. All managed to clamber aboard the ships without injury, and Simon and Baldwin were there as the King bade farewell to his son. It took some little while, with exhortations that the young Duke wouldn't enter into any marriage contracts, nor accept a guardian without writing to confirm his father's approval. Not that it would be forthcoming – he made that clear enough. There was also a small ceremony, at which the priest from the port came to bless them all and their passage, but Simon paid little attention to that. His mind was fixed on the sea already, and all the speeches and chatter as letters were given to Bishop Stapledon and Henry de Beaumont for the Queen, washed over him like a great tidal wave. Just like the ones he could see from here, he thought with a shudder.

The small fleet was soon at sea. All too soon, in Simon's opinion. With luck they would cross the Channel in no time, and be back on land again.

That was at least Simon's most fervent wish. He could not remain below, and in preference, he made his way, green-

---

[1] Thursday, 12 September 1325

faced and horrible, in time to spew over the side before they had picked up full speed.

It was a consolation that some others were also here. He was by no means alone, even though the sea looked a beautiful blue and had only a very few white wave-crests. The sailors running about the decks on bare feet, and rushing up the stays to the sails, laughed at the sight of so many land-based men vomiting, but Simon was so far gone, he did not care.

'Hah! Bailiff. Feelin' a little better? I've a joke or two to tell you to pass the time, if you wish . . .'

Simon glanced over at the Coroner. He had a hunk of bread in one hand, with a thick slice of bloody beef wrapped about it, while in the other he gripped a jug full of wine.

Simon only wished, as he heaved again, that when he died – and please God, may it be soon – he might be able to haunt Sir Richard *de Damned* Welles and visit upon him the full wrath and hatred which he felt boiling in his blood at this moment.

Paris

He had done nothing, intentionally, since hearing from Hélias. Procureur Jean knew when he was treading on dangerous ground, and this was as dangerous as any in his experience.

The name of de Nogaret was well known in France. The devoted servant of King Philippe the Fair, he had been a lawyer of such skill and understanding, that few if any cases were lost once he had taken them on. The King so admired him that he had him knighted and installed as his own trusted adviser.

It was shocking, therefore, to learn that both the boy and girl from this favoured family had now died, such a short time after arriving in Paris. What were they doing here, de Poissy asked himself, and why were they killed?

Those were the tasks he set Hélias to discover, and he had faith enough in her abilities to leave her to it. If she did not learn anything about the two, no one else would. She knew all those who might be able to answer his questions.

It was very late in the afternoon when he finally received a message to go and visit Hélias again. Pulling a woollen cap over his head, he took up a staff, shrugged a cloak over his shoulders, and set off to the gates.

At the road outside, he saw the burly shape of a man lurking in a doorway towards the city's gates, and immediately turned left, up to the north, away from the fellow. But he was sure that he was followed.

At home he had an old, broken mirror, and he had tried bringing a shard of it with him in the mornings for a couple of days, but it was so small that he could discern nothing in it when he held it up and glanced behind him. But when he tried a larger piece the next day, he found people staring at him in the street, and began to fear that he might at any moment be grabbed by a sergent and questioned. They probably thought him mad.

So instead he had hit upon this. Yet it was not foolproof. He just prayed that the man was actually behind him, had truly seen him.

Hélias's road branched off this one at a crossroads, where today there was a pair of carters brawling in the street. One had broken a wheel, and the load from his wagon had fallen all over the roadway, a mixture of hens in cages, eggs broken and crushed, and a mess of butter trampled into the mire. Like many others, Jean paused to watch, cheering on the larger man, who seemed to need little by way of encouragement. He had already managed to turn the other's mouth and face into a bloody mess, and now he had grabbed the smaller man by his shirt, and was pounding him in the belly, while two Sergents watched indulgently.

The crowd was as happy with the entertainment as any at a baiting. And it gave the Procureur time to shoot a look behind him, and – yes, there he was! The man was leaning against a building, lolling like a drunkard, arms crossed over his breast, with the weary, semi-vacant look of a man who had enjoyed too much of his master's wine.

It was enough to make a man weep. Jean the Procureur sighed, passed around the two men as the smaller collapsed onto all fours, vomiting, and the other carter drew his boot back for the final blow. The Procureur hurried now. Here the lane was partially cobbled, and he had to watch his footing where the fist-sized stones had worked loose. At one particularly bad spot, he had to spring over a large puddle. It was a little consolation that a short while afterwards, he heard his pursuer make a similar leap, but heard the man's boots fall into the water, followed by a short curse.

'You took your time,' Hélias said as he reached her door.

The Procureur nodded, trying to look relaxed as he glanced back along the road. There was one man, and then the fellow he'd expected to see, a bit further back. Good! 'May I enter, Hélias? I'd prefer not to discuss this business here in the street.'

'Get inside, then,' she said. There was little humour in her tone. 'This is not the sort of affair I like to involve myself with, you understand?' She led the way in through the door. Once they were safely secluded in a tiny little chamber at the back of the house, she passed him a cup of wine and sipped at her own. 'You know what this makes me think of? Those bad days when Philippe the Fair lost it.'

Jean nearly choked on his wine. 'What?'

'Oh, come on! Philippe lost it completely. He reckoned he could take whatever he wanted. Well, he was the King, wasn't he? First it was the Jews, and no one complained. Then it was the Templars, and some folks got uppity about that. But not too many. No, a lot of us were pissed off with the Templars already. All they did was wander round the place showing off with all their money, didn't they? I wasn't going to lose any sleep over them. But I think he went too far when he took all the Templars' money. That got the Pope's back up, and then made everyone start to think, Well, if the Templars are up to no good, what's to say the other monks aren't – and the nuns – and the priests – and if *they're* gone to the bad, what of the Pope? Some folks even wondered about the King. After all, if he was accusing everyone else, perhaps there was only one man to blame. And the Templars were monks. Most people trusted them.'

'Hélias, they were found guilty of worshipping idols. They were *guilty*. Don't you remember the ones they burned?'

'And the King himself died a little later, didn't he?'

'That was different. That was a broken heart, I think.'

'Yes. He learned much. Like his sons' wives were all more keen on waggling their arses than a Toulousain tackle.'

'Toulousain tackle?'

She looked at him. 'You know what I mean. A tart from Toulouse. Anyway, his grandchildren were assumed illegitimate and disinherited, his daughters-in-law were divorced . . . he saw the end of his line. Must have broken his heart. Would any man's.'

He was frowning already. 'But what's all this got to do with my men?'

'You know that they were both called de Nogaret? Husband and wife. He was named for his father: Guillaume. She was a pretty little thing in life called Anne-Marie. They arrived here in the town shortly after the visitation of the Blessed Virgin[1]. I saw them about the place occasionally. They were living out near the Sainte-Opportune. A grotty little inn, not to my standard, but clean enough, I suppose. Not that his wife would have enjoyed residing here, eh?' She cackled suddenly. 'I think we could have helped them with the finances, though. She had the sort of backside that would have tempted the Bishop of Sens.' She nodded to herself, and then a look of mild reproof crossed her face. 'Not that he would be necessarily hard to tease, from what I've heard.'

With difficulty, Jean pulled his attention back to the matter in hand. 'The couple – de Nogaret and his wife. What happened to them?'

'I came to hear of them when they had not been here long. They let on to others that they wanted to seek an audience with the King. They had some news for him, so they said. They seemed very keen.'

'What was this news?'

Hélias shrugged with a wry grin. 'You think they were stupid enough to tell anyone? They were stupid enough, it is true, to let on that it involved the King, and that it involved money – a lot of money – but nothing more.'

'Perhaps they wished to bring money to the King, and someone heard and executed them so he could take it all to himself?'

'Perhaps. And then again, perhaps they sought to *take* money from the King or someone else. Plainly, somebody thought that there was a good enough reason to kill them both.'

'You think they were murdered by the same person?' Jean enquired.

---

[1] Visitation – 2 July

'I would say that as a Procureur, I would make a good investigator. And as a whore, you would be useless. But I can whore as well, which means I am without a doubt the better of us two. Do you really mean to say you do not think that these two died for the same reason?'

'I had not connected the two. One died in the castle, the other in an alley. I assumed she had been killed by a jealous lover, or perhaps a madman bent on enjoying her youth. While the man was simply slain for . . .'

'For what?'

'Money, greed. Perhaps for some political motive, since he was the son of de Nogaret.'

'May the devil piss on him and stop him burning too quickly,' Hélias spat.

'You had reason to hate him?'

She crossed herself, but her feelings were made clear by her expression. 'He was the cause of much pain and suffering. Never trust a lawyer, is my motto.'

'You think he was worse than others who had similar jobs?'

Hélias looked at him. 'There are many who will kill for money or power – not so many will do it for simple pleasure.'

Jean left the little house with much to consider. There was a lot of sense in Hélias's words. He now believed that the deaths of husband and wife were too coincidental to be separate, random events. It was plain that they must be connected, and that connection meant that there was someone who was keen to make use of some information which they had.

The crucial problem, of course, was that he had no idea what the information could be, nor how to glean it. Unless he could find someone who knew the killer of the de Nogarets, and persuade him to talk.

There were many judicial methods for opening a man's

mouth. Foolishly, many thought they could withstand the terror of the wheel, or the agony of flames. No man could. The only effective means of preventing massive anguish or death, was to get over the shameful confession early in the process. Far better to do that, than be left to suffer unnecessarily. The outcome would probably be the same, for most criminals, but the sensible man would hasten the end and welcome death sooner rather than later.

Yes. He was content that there were plenty of ways of acquiring the knowledge he needed, provided that he could first capture the right person.

Deep in thought, the Procureur walked with his head down, aware only of the conundrum of the deaths, and a hollow sensation in his throat. It was deeply unpleasant to be strolling along here, convinced that he was being followed by a murderer, but there was little else he might do. When a man sought an assassin, he was best served to leave himself open to attack, but with enough protection that, were an attacker to try to kill him, the fellow would soon learn the error of his ways.

He could hear them now. The steady pattering of feet growing nearer, the firm plodding of another – unhurried, resolute and calm.

Christ in a box, the man was going to be late! Jean thought, and turned, his hand going to his sword.

There was a lad. Almost on him, teeth bared in a grimace of desperation and determination, a small figure, with thin, pinched features and gleaming brown eyes in a foul, smeared face. It was not his face that Jean saw, though, but the sharp knife in his hand. It was held up in his fist, and suddenly the Procureur felt powerless. The point began to fall towards his chest, and he felt like a mouse catching sight of the owl swooping down. He could not even groan, so great was his

THE KING OF THIEVES

terror. The knife was all. He could see its edge catching the light and glinting, as it plunged down towards him. All was slow, all was hideously clear. The knife held his destruction. He would die now, and all because his servant—

There was a clanging tone, and he saw a metal-studded pole appear. It stopped the blade a foot from Jean's face, and he felt as though he must faint at any moment.

The staff rose, and Jean watched his impassive guard heft it up and away, before slamming a fist the size of a ham into the side of the attacker's head. Jean saw the lad's head jerk, then swing back, into the fist once more. His eyes rolled up into his head as his mouth fell wide, and suddenly his entire body wavered like a ripple on water. It lurched to one side, then the other, and then gracefully collapsed.

'Where in God's name were you?' Jean demanded, and then felt the bile hot and acid in his throat as he thought of the knife thrusting into his body.

Turning, he vomited on to the roadside.

Chapter Fourteen

Second Tuesday following the Feast of the Nativity of the Blessed Virgin Mary[1]

Bois de Vincennes, near Paris

Simon was almost prepared to believe in the superiority of the French race as he approached the great manor of Vincennes.

It wasn't the size and the wealth that struck him here. Rather it was the extreme elegance of all he saw. Ever since they had landed at the coast, the people all over the country had turned out in their hundreds to see the young Duke who would become King of England. There was an immense proprietorial pride in him, as though he was actually a Prince of France, not of England. All knew that his mother had been a Princess of France, after all, before she became Queen of England. Perhaps it made sense.

The country was rich. There were little vills spread all over, and he knew that the churches were filled with precious plates, jewels and cloths. No matter that the peasants looked more cowed than those whom he knew in England, their religious houses waxed rich.

It was noticeable, though. In England, the peasants were shifty, untrustworthy churls for the large part. He would never

---

[1] Tuesday, 17 September 1325

have wandered alone in darkness in England, and even in daylight there were many places which a man would be sensible to avoid. Here in France he had a different impression. It seemed safer, somehow. Perhaps it was just the tension he felt because of the threat to his home and his wife, but there was definitely something about this land which made him feel comfortable.

And the people were so welcoming. Women came and gazed at Duke Edward, some spreading flowers beneath the hooves of the knights as they passed by, others calling and waving as though they fully expected him to become their own King before long. It was very peculiar.

Perhaps it was partly the presence of Queen Isabella. She was a pretty little thing, sitting on her horse in such a gracious manner.

She had looked a little surprised when she saw all the men with her son on the ships. Simon was not the most observant man in the world, as he would happily admit, but even he saw how her smile became glassy and brittle when she saw Bishop Walter Stapledon stand at the gangplank. She had been waiting there patiently, Simon could easily imagine, without any outward display of fretting, all the long wait until the ships came into view. And then, when she saw them she must have been overwhelmed with excitement, but all would have been concealed behind that firm, reserved exterior. Until her son was in her arms, naturally. And then the others appeared and strode up to greet her. All welcomed with a polite nod of the head, all bar Stapledon.

The Queen detested Stapledon. Simon had been aware of it before, but never before had he realised just how deep that hatred ran. And it was a shock to him to see that her feelings were reciprocated. It was all Stapledon could do to nod to her, and even then he didn't so much as smile. Nor did he bow in

the manner that was customary when a subject met his Queen.
Simon noticed that, and more. But he wasn't alone.

'Did you see that?' Baldwin whispered.

'He should be careful!' Sir Richard said. 'A Bishop is still
a man, and a man who insults his Queen is insulting his King
as well.'

Baldwin gave Simon a brief but significant look. They were
both of the same mind: a man might insult *this* Queen with
relative impunity. The King had no love for her any more.

But if there was safety from the King, Simon soon realised
that others were less inclined to tolerance. The English men-
at-arms were unbothered, watching as the stevedores began
offloading horses, boxes and trunks, together with bales of
cloth and gifts, but the French warriors felt that their King's
sister had been snubbed, and there were mutterings among
them, and many dark scowls passed over towards the Bishop.

Their journey to the south and east from Boulogne had been
slow, but only because there was no need to hurry. All was
planned meticulously. In fact, as soon as the ship was docked
and all were on land again, Simon and Baldwin were asked to
attend the Queen in a conference to discuss just that.

Sir Henry de Beaumont and the Bishop were already there,
as was Sir Richard de Welles, who grinned broadly at the pair
of them, while a little distance behind the Queen, Richard de
Bury, the Duke's tutor, stood warily, his eyes shifting from one
man to another as people spoke. He looked nervous to be in
such company.

'Sir Baldwin, Bailiff,' the Queen said. She was sitting on a
small chair with delightful carved arms, a comfortable little
seat for travelling, that would fold up in half for packing. She
sipped from a silver tankard of wine. 'I am glad to see you
again.'

At her side stood her son. He had a stiffness about him, and

Simon regretted that the boy who had been so keen and eager on the ship, was now restrained, like a hound freshly muzzled.

On board ship, he had been filled with excitement at the great craft. The rolling and plunging that made Simon's belly roil, seemed to thrill the boy. He walked from the castles fore and aft to the ratlines and stood with his arm through the ropes, laughing at the spray that dashed in his eyes. He appeared to come alive still more when the wind blew a little harder, and although the Bishop and his own tutor begged him to go with them at least so far as the decking, and ideally to the cabin aft, he refused point blank. There was no need, he declared. If it were dangerous, then their whole journey was also insanely dangerous, and he would prefer to be up here on deck to see the looming rocks than below, where the ship could be crushed for a man's lack of attentiveness.

Now, though, his eyes were dulled as he stood and listened. It might have been a different fellow entirely. Not surprising, though, Simon reckoned. The lad had come here keen to see his mother – and now he had, he must realise that there was no chance of her returning to England with him to try to force a reconciliation with the King. His hopes of peace in his family had been dashed.

'I am glad indeed to see you both again,' the Queen said. 'I was unsure who might be sent to guard my child.'

'He has been the soul of good manners and behaviour,' Baldwin said.

'That would be a change for him. It was ever the case that my son would play in the trees and at any sport that was most dangerous,' Queen Isabella said lightly.

'Madam, your son is educated now to appreciate mature behaviour,' Stapledon said. He did not look in her direction as he spoke, but eyed Simon and Baldwin.

'I am glad to hear it,' the Queen said shortly. She too would not look at the Bishop, but instead moved on immediately to discuss the route they must take, the deployment of the men, the stores which would be needed. Once she was content, she dismissed the men, somewhat haughtily, Simon felt, but that was no surprise. After all, she probably wanted some private time with her son. And he with her, too, from the look of him. He kept giving her little sidelong looks, at her hair, at her profile, at her hands on the arms of the chair. All as though he didn't believe she was really here with him. As though he had thought she was dead.

However, this was not the end of the discussion for the Bishop. 'There is one last matter, your Royal Highness,' he said, and produced a small roll sealed with the King's mark.

'What is that?'

'The King has written to you, I think. This is a safe conduct for you to return home.'

The Queen stood, her face suddenly pale. 'You think to send me away just as my son arrives in this land? You think you can order me to leave just as my son needs my help?'

'With the greatest respect, your Highness, the Earl of Chester needs the help of professional diplomats, such as myself and Sir Henry.'

'With respect? Well, *Bishop*!' It sounded as though she spat the word. 'I say to you, *without* respect, that I have been born as a diplomat, that I have been raised as a diplomat, and that I have been raised in the Royal Families of England and France. There is nobody I do not know, and there are many from whom I can demand – not ask, but *demand* – help. You, on the other hand, are not a popular man in this country. You will not presume to command me to do anything.'

'No, my Queen. But this letter . . .'

'You may keep it. I will not look at it now. *Mon Dieu!* Do

you realise that this is the first time I have had an opportunity to speak with my son in months? And you would have me leave the country as soon as he arrives.'

'The King was expecting you to return to your home, my Queen,' Stapledon tried one last time.

'The King should have been a little more considerate. I shall return shortly, no doubt. But in my own good time. Now, you may leave us.'

And that had been that at the time. The men had all walked away to leave the Queen with her son and his tutor, while her eyes, red-rimmed and gleaming with anger, remained fixed upon the back of the Bishop.

However, Simon was sure that the affair was almost over. The Queen would have to take the note from her husband soon. No wife could think to ignore her man's legitimate commands, not for long. Soon she must submit and go home. And then the serious negotiations could begin.

Furnshill, Devon

Margaret heard the hooves clattering up the path to the house from the hall, where she sat trying to concentrate on mending an old blouse, and for a moment she felt a curious mingling of trepidation and excitement, torn between the hope that it could be her husband and Baldwin, and terror that it was another man sent by Despenser, this time to ruin Baldwin.

'Margaret? Here is the man who was to live at your house,' Jeanne said, entering.

'Sir,' she said, falteringly.

The man before her was a heavy-set priest. He wore only a rough tunic, but he was clearly a monk, and looked at her with that slight dispassion that was the normal manner of a senior churchman who never usually encountered women. After the introductions were over, he shook his head with some confusion and asked why she was there at Furnshill. 'Were you not going to wait for me at your house?'

'I am very sorry, but the house was taken from me,' Margaret said, and the words made the tears flow again. She had to bend and wipe at her eyes, her apron bunched in her fists, while Jeanne explained what had happened. As she spoke, the man's face hardened.

'This is true?' he asked.

Margaret nodded, still not trusting her voice.

He waved imperiously at Edgar, who stood in the doorway. 'Wine!' He had a curious accent, a Roman-sounding tone from all the Latin he had spoken over the years. 'Very well. Then I shall have to evict this man, whoever he may be.'

Margaret was tempted to laugh. 'You don't realise, sir. This man is very dangerous. He attacked my husband with a sword, and would have slain him.'

The man stood up. 'Really? He had best not try such a thing with me, or he will find himself in great danger.'

'I think that this man doesn't worry about danger.'

'Then he will learn quickly! I am Raymond, Cardinal de Fargis, in the service of God and the Pope. If he tries to threaten me, he will find himself in gaol faster than a whore in a cathedral.'

Temple, Paris

The cell was a large one, sixteen-feet long and as many wide, set into the north-west corner of the great keep.

Just the atmosphere made Jean feel chilled as he entered the place. There were marks scrawled into the walls here, the despairing words of prisoners who knew that their time was almost over; men who had entered this place as rich as any knights, who had loyally served their master, only to see him turn against them for a simple financial reward.

The Templars had been held in this room, and in others, their hands in manacles, chains at their ankles, and they were forced to stand by and watch as, one by one, their comrades were dragged forward to be tested by the inquisition. Jean had seen the records of some of the trial, and he knew the details that would not have been noted down: the way that a man's scream could rise sharply to the ceiling when his flesh was being scorched; how a man would whimper and weep, even the strongest, when he was slowly beaten, his bones broken one by one; the little 'click' of a tooth breaking its link with the jawbone as it was drawn out; the soft squelch of blood and gristle as a nail was pulled from a finger. The sizzle of cooking meat as a foot or hand was thrust over a brazier, after a pat of butter had been smeared over a slash in the flesh to make it fry more efficiently. Oh, the monks wouldn't be involved in the brutality, of course. That was a matter for the secular arm of the law. No, the monks would merely ask the questions, ever so softly and gently, and watch and listen and smell as the prisoners were slowly broiled, burned, broken before them.

And now he was instigating his own little process of torture. All in the name of the King.

The prisoner had been hanging there from the butcher's hook for over a day now. His arms must have been in agony, especially since they were so tightly bound. His ankles had swollen to an alarming extent, and Jean seriously wondered whether they would ever reduce to an ordinary size.

'You will have to talk sooner or later, Nicholas,' he said.

They had learned his name with embarrassing ease on the first day. That was the day on which they merely beat him with fists and ropes. Fists were good at first, but when the two men with him wanted to kick the man as well, Jean had shaken his head. He wanted information from this man, not for him just to become a third corpse. The questioning had begun. 'Who are you? Why did you want to kill me? What do you know of the man in the Louvre? What was his name? What of the woman who died?' On and on, he asked the same questions, and for the first day he had a policy of not believing a word he was told.

On the second day, he believed the man when he gave his name. '*Nicholas*. They call me the Stammerer.'

He had looked at Jean with his face screwed up against the light of the candles. Jean thought – a strange idea, this – that the boy was actually speaking like someone talking to an ally or confederate. There was no complicity in this room, though, except for that which lay between torturer and questioner. The men who wielded the metal and stretched this poor scrawny body, breaking pieces of it, little by little, and him, Jean, the Procureur.

'Why did you want to kill me? Who was the man in the Louvre? What was his name?'

It was the same questions, repeated. Each time a response was given, he made a note of it. And then, when the answers seemed to be falling into a pattern, he would change the order of the questions, trying to catch Nicholas out, snapping them out and waiting to see how long it took for the reply, listening for that pause that said Nicholas was having to think, to remember something he had invented, or whether the fellow was responding honestly.

'He was de Nogaret. That is all I know.'

'And the woman?'

'His wife. We were paid to kill her . . .'

This was the first time that it wasn't 'I'. It was interesting. More interesting, if he was honest, than much of the slobbering, self-justifying ox-shit he had been forced to listen to. Jean stood, his legs and arse aching from spending too much time on a stool. Crossing the floor, he leaned down, hands on thighs, and peered up at the dangling head.

Blood trickled from a wound over his temple. Both eyes were puffed and blued from the regular beatings, and there was a reddened welt on his shoulder where a heated rod had been lain. The rest of his back was thankfully in darkness, and Jean needn't look at that, nor at the man's grotesquely swollen genitals.

'Why?' he asked quietly. 'What would it serve you to kill me?'

'The King was paid. Just like he was paid to kill de Nogaret.'

'Who paid him?'

'Someone from the castle. Don't know who. Servant came to pay.'

Jean nodded. 'Who is the "King" you talk of?'

'I can't say.'

'You can. You will.'

'I can't say.'

Jean rose and shook his head. Looking over the boy's head, he saw the two torturers. Neither was an expert at this art. Both were trained in the fields of Montfaucon among the great poles that stood there. The old wooden uprights were gone, replaced with stone in the last year. Now there were sixteen uprights, the King could have a full complement of sixty-four corpses swinging in the wind when he so desired. And all were on view from the north of the city. When space was needed, the bodies could be cut loose, and then the rotting flesh was cast into the city's midden that lay close by. On a hot summer's day, when the wind came from the north, Jean would cover his face with a cloth against the noxious fumes.

These two had learned their arts there, stringing up the boys and men who were guilty of foul, degenerate crimes like stealing a loaf. Better that a man should starve than rob his fellow. Jean had lived through the famine. He knew what it was like to see people starve to death. If a man had managed to keep a small store of foodstuffs, and another sought to rob him of it, that man deserved his fate at Montfaucon, so far as Jean was concerned.

'Leave him until morning,' he said now, considering the broken and ravaged figure before him. 'But show him the brazier and all the implements. I want answers by the end of tomorrow. Show him and let him dream of them tonight. And cut him free. He can't run anywhere tonight, and the freedom will hurt more than leaving him hanging.'

He left the chamber and the stench of sweat, piss and faeces, with relief. With every step he took away from that revolting room, he felt a little of the foulness falling away from him, until he found himself up in the open, and took in deep lungfuls of the fresh air. He was no torturer. The whole process made him feel sick. But the job worked – that was the trouble. It achieved results.

Louvre, Paris

The castellan strode into his room to find her there, waiting as usual. 'What are you doing here?'

Amélie stood and walked towards him languidly. 'Don't you want me any more?'

It was tempting. Galician born, she had the body of a heathen harlot, but the face of an angel. Black hair that gleamed, an oval face with lips as red as a rose, she was utterly beautiful. Christ knew, it was tempting . . . but he didn't have time. 'You have to go to your master. To the "King",' he said harshly. 'Tell him that one of his men has been taken, yes? He's being held in the Temple, where they're torturing him.'

'What of it? Nicholas will break and die,' she said, reaching up to his neck and placing her cool, cool hand behind his head. Her black eyes stared into his.

'Get off me, wench! Sweet Jesus! You think this is the time for that? If this man is taken, we're all in the midden, you understand?'

'The "King" is no fool, Sieur Hugues. He has already sent a man to deal with Nicholas. The boy will stammer no more!' She drew away from him as she spoke, and walking to the shelf on which lay his jug and cups, she poured two, and brought them to him. 'Come, drink, relax, and then do what you want with me. I have all the time we need.'

'What do you want with me?' he demanded, but with less anger, as she took his hand and led him to the back of his room where he had a palliasse rolled at the wall.

She said nothing, but unrolled the bedding and knelt on it. As he watched, she crossed her arms and lifted her linen tunic over her head. Beneath it she was naked.

Temple, Paris

The figure at the doorway tapped quietly. 'I have a livre for you if I can see the man they're torturing.'

'What do you want with him?' the porter demanded, taking the little leather purse and reaching inside. He took up a coin and stared at it hard, before experimentally biting into it. Seeing the result, a grin of delight spread over his face.

With directions, it was easy to find him. Through one open door, down some steep stairs, into a great vaulted room that might as well have been a hall, he thought. Inside, two men were using bellows to warm a charcoal brazier, while the Stammerer stared in horrified fascination from his ravaged face.

Sighing, Jacquot strolled inside. 'Gentlemen, this fellow was a friend of mine. Can I let him have some money for food and drink while he remains here at your service?'

'Who are you?' The nearer of the two men clearly had the sharper brain. Now he blocked Jacquot's path, a length of chain swinging from his fist.

Jacquot said nothing, but showed his second purse, a bloated little pouch. The man took it, then turned to his companion and showed him the contents. 'This for us?' he asked Jacquot.

'If you give me a few minutes with him, yes.'

'A few minutes, then. But we'll be listening, mind.'

The two walked out from the room, leaving Jacquot with Nicholas the Stammerer. They had not yet released him from his hook, and he swung gently, his head loose, a ball of exquisite agony.

Seeing he did not have the lad's undivided attention, Jacquot took a large ladle of water from the barrel near the door, and dashed it into Nicholas's face.

In the past such an insult would have merited an enraged response, but now Nicholas had sunk so far into despair that he could only mumble and avert his head.

'So, Nicholas the Stammerer. How are you today?' Jacquot said with mild enquiry. He looked at the wreckage of the man and shook his head. 'You should not have tried to take my prize, little man. It was not a sensible course. I do not like to destroy, but when there is money at stake, and *such* money . . . well.'

He already had his long, thin knife in his hand, and he weighed it in his palm for a moment. 'You are dead, Nicholas, already. There is nothing anyone can do for you. But the King and I do not want our names mentioned. So I will stop your mouth.'

'No!'

The knife slipped down from above his shoulder, gently sliding in between the collarbone and the shoulder blade.

Nicholas lurched to draw away, but that put strain on his hands. He screamed wildly, and thrust his body upwards. His mouth opened, madly, his neck muscles thickened and strained, his veins stood out like ropes, and his head swung from side to side in maddened denial, as his heart thudded with thunderous irregularity, working against all reason, as though his soul could contain the damage done by the skewer-like blade that had sheared through muscle and lungs to puncture it.

Chapter Fifteen

Second Wednesday following the Feast of the Nativity of the Blessed Virgin Mary[1]

Louvre

Hugues was tempted to go and see the 'King' and throttle the bastard. It was all very well, him being so cocksure about the danger posed by Nicholas the Stammerer, as Amélie had intimated, but that didn't make the castellan any calmer. He had too much to lose, damn the man's soul!

Although he had not been so lucky as some. Hugues thought back to the sack of Anagni, the capture of Pope Boniface VIII. When the others had found the man Toscanello, and taken the key from him, there had been no one about at Anagni. No one at all, and although Toscanello had denied finding anything, the shifty little shite had been unable to stop himself sweating. Anyway, Paolo had always hated him. That was why he'd wanted to search for himself. And found the chest.

Most money chests were made of steel with more steel bands to enclose and protect them, and a great locking mechanism that was designed to keep all safe inside. Not this. It was a simple wooden box, not much larger than the chest a man might keep in his bedchamber. Perhaps two feet tall, two

---

[1] Wednesday, 18 September 1325

more deep, and a yard and a half wide. No decoration, just the enormous hole for the key.

'See? It's just an old chest,' Toscanello had said, and had made as though to leave the room. But he was shaking.

Paolo had stopped and stared though, less sure. Just because this was lying in an undercroft didn't mean it was empty. He was keen to open it up. So he did. The great key fitted the lock, and they could all hear the mechanism moving four enormous lugs out of their slots. And then he lifted the lid.

Hugues had never seen so much money. It actually hurt. There was a desire like a knife in his groin. He'd never known avarice like this, not since he'd craved another's wife, and then he'd had to kill her man and rape her before killing her too. But this, this was different. It was so pure, this gold coinage, so shiny and bright, he could hardly bear the thought of touching it.

In the chest itself there was the coin, but then as they searched further in the storage room, they came across other chests, other boxes. One contained a set of plates, all gilded and valuable as diamonds. Another contained goblets, another held jewels. All the wealth of a Pope was in here. All the money Boniface VIII had accrued from selling indulgences and promotions at the turn of the century, taking advantage of the centennial fever that struck Christendom, it was all here.

And in the chamber, there were only the four of them: Paolo the leader, Hugues, Thomas and Toscanello. That much money was enormous, even split four ways.

But all knew the risks. And any who was unaware would have realised the danger as soon as the detestable de Nogaret began demanding to know where all the booty was. He wasn't here just for the better glory of the King of France; he was here at Anagni to make himself fabulously rich. And he would have the head and heart of any man who tried to prevent him.

It was some while before they had reached Paris afterwards. De Nogaret was disappointed with his rewards, still fuming over his inability to find much of the Pope's fabled wealth. He couldn't. Hugues and Thomas had concealed it well. He soon learned to seek other means of gaining the money he craved. Hugues and Thomas later returned to the place where the money was hidden, and rescued their shares – which they were able to put to good use.

It was twenty-two years since that fateful meeting at Anagni, and Hugues was damned if he would see all he had built up destroyed by a drunken sot who fancied himself 'King of Thieves' and dropped others in the shit from incompetence.

Temple, Paris

Jean stood in the room and gaped. 'Who let the assassin into the chamber?'

The executioner shook his head. 'There are always people who try to get inside. Some are legitimate – they want to go and provide some food for the prisoners. You know how it is.'

'Yes, but no one should have been allowed in there. Not *there*, where the King's prisoner was being questioned. You know that, in Christ's name! So how did this happen?'

'As I told you, we found the prisoner dead in there this morning. Someone had stabbed his heart with a long, thin blade. It was only a matter of a spot of blood at his shoulder. I would have missed it myself, but one of the guards saw it there. There was nothing we could do.'

Jean dismissed him angrily. All too often prisoners could suddenly die, he knew. Sometimes it was an angry guard who went over the mark when a man was complaining. Guards were not hired for their sense or kindness. If a weeping man carried on for too long, he could be given something to weep about. Occasionally prisoners could die for no other reason than disease. Or malnutrition, or the cold or wetness. All were natural enough in a dungeon. These deaths weren't the result of particularly bad treatment.

But this man's death left Jean with more work.

First he must find out more about the Stammerer, and then see if he could do the same about this man called the 'King'.

But first, perhaps, he should see if he could learn a little more about de Nogaret and his wife.

Tuesday before the Feast of the Archangel Michael[1]

Bois de Vincennes

Baldwin took his place at the edge of the dais with an eye on the crowds all about. They were all in the courtyard of the great hunting lodge, and the arms of the French manor house reached out on either side, the fourth side being blocked by a large wall. Flags drooped in the still air; it was unseasonally warm for late September, and Baldwin could feel a trickle of sweat running down his back.

There were so many people here. Wolf was behind him, and Baldwin kept turning periodically to make sure that he did not spring into the middle and cause a mêlée. He had no desire to see a fight break out because of his beast. Not on an occasion of such importance.

Opposite him were a large contingent of French nobility, all watching the English visitors with suspicion. Baldwin was glad that he was wearing a new red tunic. His old one would have made him feel too much like a country churl in the midst of all this splendour. Armour gleamed with a blue light, the French nobles' clothing was clearly the best available, and even in his new tunic, he felt slightly shabby.

---

[1] Tuesday, 24 September 1325

In the event it was all over quite quickly. Simon Puttock and Sir Richard de Welles, the Coroner, turned up just as Duke Edward, Earl of Chester, arrived and strode to the throne where the King of France waited, Edward's mother at his side. Before all the men present, the King held out his hands. The Duke knelt before him, and raised his own hands in that universal symbol of fealty, his palms pressed together as if in prayer. The King placed his own hands on either side of the Duke's and looked about him at the audience of witnesses as the Duke spoke in his high, unbroken voice. And it was done. Immediately the King announced that his warriors would be withdrawn from all the lands held by his nephew, and control would revert to the Duke.

Baldwin glanced at Sir Richard. He had conspired to bring a small haunch of ham with him, and was surreptitiously chewing at it as he listened.

'Well, Sir Richard, was the ceremony to your taste?'

'To me taste? Not so fine as a good jug of English ale, eh?'

Simon squared his shoulders and stretched. 'Maybe now we can soon return home, Baldwin. Surely the Queen's business here is done and we can serve her on her way home.'

'That is to be fervently desired,' Baldwin agreed, but even as he spoke there was a sudden noise.

It was the Bishop of Exeter. Walter Stapledon strode forward and bowed to the King. 'Your Royal Highness. I have here a letter from King Edward, which demands that the Lady Isabella, his Queen, should return at once to England.' Stapledon waved the note high, and then held it out to the Queen. 'Your Royal Highness, the King says that he will tolerate no delay. I have money to pay your outstanding expenses, but I have been commanded only to pay if you will come straight back to England with me to return to your

husband, as you are obliged to do. I am afraid the King does
not offer you an option, your Royal Highness. He *demands*
your obedience.'

There was a complete silence for a moment. It was as
though all the world was waiting to see how the Queen would
react to this rudeness.

She responded coolly, staring at the note in his hand with
some contempt. And then she looked at the Bishop with eyes
that seemed to dart fire.

Sir Richard gave a low whistle. 'If he was hoping for a
quick service of his own, I'll wager he'll need a new filly.'

His crudeness about the Queen was shocking to Baldwin,
who was about to remonstrate, when the Queen spoke. Her
voice shook with rage, beginning so quietly that all must strain
their ears to hear her words. And then her voice grew,
swelling, until all could hear, and her disdain and anger were
clear to all present. It lay there in her perfect enunciation
and slow, deliberate speech.

'I feel that marriage is a joining together of man and
woman, maintaining the undivided habit of life, and that
someone has come between my husband and myself, trying to
break this bond. I *protest* that I will not return until this
intruder is removed, but discarding my marriage garment,
shall assume the robes of widowhood and mourning until I am
avenged of this . . . this *Pharisee*!'

Stapledon held the little roll high overhead, then turned to
the King for support. 'My Royal Lord, you know that a man's
first duty is to his wife. Surely no wife can look for support
when her husband has determined that she must go to him?'

The King of France looked to Baldwin as though he might
explode with fury himself.

'D'ye think the Bishop knows of the King's past?' Sir
Richard said to Baldwin. 'Poor devil – his first wife was found

playing the dog with two tails with a knight, after all. Won't like to be reminded, I reckon.'

'I don't think he could be unaware,' Baldwin retorted. 'Why he has chosen such a high-handed manner is beyond me.'

Simon was more sanguine. 'Because he's never had a wife, Baldwin. If he had, he would understand the folly of such language and such a conspicuous venue for his demand.'

The King looked at the letter, and then at Stapledon. His voice was cool, but calm. 'The Queen has come to my court of her own free will. I will not send her away if she chooses to remain. She is a Princess of France and my sister. I will not exile her.'

Baldwin winced. 'That is your answer, Simon.'

'Christ's ballocks. We're stuck here, aren't we?'

Furnshill

Margaret was surprised to be told that there was a man in the hall to see her. Jeanne had sent a maid to fetch her, and Margaret strode indoors with a frown of concern on her face. It was unlikely to be a messenger from her husband, so she had a feeling that the fellow would be from her home.

'You are Madame Puttock?' the fellow asked, eyeing her haughtily.

He was a youngster, this cleric, but one of those who thought he knew the importance of his own position in the world.

'Yes.'

'My Cardinal, Raymond, sends his deepest regards and wishes me to tell you that your house is entirely to his satisfaction. He will be most happy to remain there for some weeks until accommodation can be provided at Tavistock Abbey.'

'Oh!' Margaret said. She was dumbfounded. 'But what of the men who had taken it over?'

'They learned to regret their impetuosity.'

'I don't understand.'

He sighed, but as Jeanne appeared with a great jug of ale, he brightened appreciably. 'The Cardinal is here to adjudicate between two candidates at Tavistock Abbey. The last abbot, may he rest in peace . . .'

'I know. He was a kind, good man,' Margaret said. She had always liked Abbot Robert Champeaux, and she and Simon had been sad to learn of his death.

'There are two men who claim the abbacy. Robert Busse won the election, but John de Courtenay chooses to contest it. The Cardinal is here to listen to the evidence and decide who deserves the post. He answers only to the Pope. He fears no man.'

'Nor does Wattere.' Margaret remembered with a shudder the man leering at her.

'Wattere was the man who took your house? He has learned to respect the Cardinal. He is in the gaol at Tavistock Abbey now.'

'What happened?'

'The man chose to try to draw a sword. My master called on the stannary bailiffs of the local court and reminded them that the Abbey of Tavistock owns the stannaries. They were happy to arrest Wattere and his men for the Cardinal, and then transported them to Tavistock for him.'

Margaret could only gape.

Paris

The King of Thieves ran his hand along the thigh of the whore at his side. She was a new one, this Amélie. The last had given up, exhausted by the hours he kept, but the King didn't care. It was better for his natural urges that he spend them with new women at every opportunity.

This latest was a Galician. Strong, fiery, not at all compliant, she would take a little breaking in, he thought. She'd been the go-between for the castle and him for some weeks now, but perhaps he should keep her here with him a while. She had the temper to match her body.

'So you succeeded, Jacquot. I congratulate you.'

Jacquot walked along the room until he stood before the King. 'You should trust me more. He was a pathetic copy of me. He would never have made the mark.'

'Perhaps so,' the King said. He put his head to one side, staring at the woman's black hair. It gleamed as though oiled, and he set his hand into it. 'It's good that you've removed the little stammerer. Yet you have still not managed the first commission. The Procureur is still alive.'

Jacquot smiled without humour. 'It will be done.'

'Good. Go to it, then.' The King motioned idly with his hand and the man turned and left him.

He was the only one who dared do that. The others all gave him some sign of respect, limited in a few cases, it was true, but they still gave him some proof that they accepted him as their natural leader. Not Jacquot, though. He was always the loner, the one who was watching, never involved.

Soon a couple of watchmen were due to come and see him. There was always business. Never a moment for rest. The King let his hand sweep down the flank of the Galician girl, then smoothed his palm over her upper thigh to the soft, inner flesh. He always loved this part of a woman. So free of blemishes, so lovely and sleek. He had a few minutes, surely. His hand rose to her, and her head turned to him, lips slightly open, eyes dull and staring into the distance.

Oh, the bitch had ruined the moment. He drew his hand

away and clouted her hard on the rump, making her squeal. Women were so stupid. They didn't understand what a man wanted. Not a real man like him. His anger flared, and he punched her in the mouth, jerking her head away from him.

And then he saw her turn back to him. There was a trickle of blood at her mouth, and she wiped it, then smiled and licked it away. And in her eyes there was a pleasure he had never expected to see reflected. It was like looking into his own eyes. She pinched him, and he felt his heart begin to pound.

Yes, he'd keep this one at his side.

Bois de Vincennes

The King of France stormed from his hall, pulling off his gloves as he went and hurling them at an unfortunate servant. 'Well? What do you have to say?' he snarled at Cardinal Thomas d'Anjou. The latter had that look on his face, the self-righteous one that was so infuriating, and the King enjoyed a brief vision of the Cardinal bending over the figure of some wench, that same bloody expression on his face, as though he wasn't a man like all others.

'It was a most unfortunate display – and yet may well play to your advantage.'

'Oh, *yes*! Much to *my* advantage, this. My sister, Queen to Edward of England, refusing to obey his order for her to return. It is bad enough that she is here, consorting with any men who are disinclined to accept their own King, her husband, as though set on reminding me that I used to wear the cuckold's horns. Now she wants it to escalate into a full-scale political dispute or war!'

'It would be a war you would win, my Liege.'

'But it would be hellishly expensive, and I have other affairs that demand my energy. She has antagonised that fool the Bishop.'

The Cardinal smiled. 'Did you see his face? Like a man who's bitten into a juicy pear to discover it tasted of wormwood! Hah! That was worth the seeing.'

'Yes. It's true, that was worth a chest of treasure, just to see the bile in his face! Stapledon is one of those who has caused shame beyond measure to me and my sister. The man thinks he can insult me with impunity and then come here on a diplomatic mission! Well, he is safe from me, but if he *was* threatened here, I don't think that the Queen's supporters would lift a finger to aid him. Except for Sir Baldwin, perhaps.'

He knew that Sir Baldwin and Stapledon were friendly. It was one of the Cardinal's own spies who had brought that information to him.

The Cardinal smiled and nodded.

He was a strangely self-possessed man, the King thought. Charles had known him for many years, both as a diplomatic and a legal adviser, and had only rarely found him to fail. His spies were everywhere – they were probably only marginally less effective than the King's own, although nothing like so speedy and accurate in their information as those of, say, the Bardi family. But then bankers always had the best of everything. They could afford it.

No man in the world was indispensable – but the Cardinal came very close to being so. For the King he was the most competent adviser on every aspect of Church politics, he was shrewd when planning about England, astute on Scottish affairs, and utterly objective and ruthless in the pursuit of French interests.

'What would you do now that the fool of a Bishop has forced Isabella's hand?' King Charles asked after a moment's consideration.

'My Liege, it is very hard to know what to recommend.

Naturally the King of England is entirely within his rights to demand that his wife returns – but he is not in a position to ask that you force her to comply. She is still a free woman, and a Princess of France. However, it would be of no service for others to believe that you assist a woman against her husband. And were you thought to be plotting to remove a neighbouring monarch, that would *not* enhance your reputation.'

The King nodded. He beckoned a servant, took the goblet of wine and drank. 'So?'

Cardinal Thomas watched as the servant walked away before answering. It was a measure of his caution that he would not even speak in front of the King's servants. Foolish, in the King's view, since a servant would know that he would have his tongue cut out, and his nails removed before having his limbs broken on the wheel if he opened his mouth at the wrong moment and caused any embarrassment to the King. They were more careful than the King himself about not divulging anything.

'My Liege, you do not want any hint of complicity in planning the downfall of your brother-in-law, so I advise you to make it clear to your sister that her presence is an embarrassment to you. She will understand.'

'So I should exile my sister from her own country,' King Charles said. This was dispassionate advice at its best. The Cardinal had a heart as cold as a toad's.

'Not exile, no. But remove her from your immediate orbit. Otherwise the King of England might end up with a case that justified his own actions. Your sister wouldn't wish for that.'

'What do you mean by "his own actions"?'

'Her lands, her treasure, her income,' Cardinal Thomas shrugged. 'All have been sequestrated by the King. If she were to plot here, the King of England's spies will soon hear of it. And then he could declare all her possessions forfeit. If she were to wander away, to a place such as Hainault, where the English King is less likely to have spies in place, she may be safer. And so may her son.'

'Yes. That is fair,' the King said. He motioned to the Cardinal to leave him, and stood a while in splendid isolation in the middle of the great room.

His sister must go, that much was certain. Apart from anything else, her behaviour was growing tedious. The repetitive complaints about her husband, the whining, the sidelong mentions of her lack of funds – it was all getting on his nerves. And then there was the matter of Sir Roger Mortimer, and his sister's relationship with the man. Mortimer had been arrested, left to moulder in the Tower of London, and then engineered an escape a matter of days before he was to be executed. But this man had been the King of England's best warrior! He was the King's own General in Ireland, the man who had managed single-handedly to halt the warfare out there, and therefore the one man whom the King of England most feared. As for the Despenser – he and Mortimer had a feud that went back to the time of their grandsires, since Mortimer's grandfather had slain Despenser's on the field of war.

But it was one thing to have a sworn and bitter enemy of the English here in France to twist the tail of the English King, quite another to have a man who appeared to be inveigling his way into the Queen of England's affections, if not yet her bed.

The Bardi spies were usually the best, but those which the King had set to watching Mortimer were the finest, the most skilful at their craft. And having once been forced to wear the cuckold's horns, King Charles was sensitive to any suggestion that his sister might be doing the same to her husband while here at the French court.

It was not to be borne.

Chapter Sixteen

Wednesday before the Feast of the Archangel Michael[1]

Bois de Vincennes

Stapledon walked up and down the chamber, while his clerks watched anxiously. There were three of them, all sitting at the large table, waiting for instructions, but for now there was nothing. The Bishop didn't trust his voice still. The embarrassment of the previous day sat like bile on his soul. So now he paced, his hands clasped before him as though in prayer, but the language which rolled about in his mind was not that which he would usually use in the presence of God.

It was not his fault. The King had decided to send him here to see to the diplomatic problems involving the Queen, and ask that she return home. He even had access to the King's bankers so that he could raise money to cover her present expenses and those of her journey. But she was a dangerous, difficult woman – sly, cunning and hard to deal with. The *vixen*!

'Ha! Me lord Bishop, I think she has you there!' Sir Richard declared as he entered. He crossed the floor to the sideboard, where he inspected the dishes in the hope of finding something sustaining.

'Sir Richard, I do not need your advice on the matter,'

---

[1] Wednesday, 25 September 1325

Bishop Walter said coldly. 'Where are Sir Baldwin and the Bailiff?'

'With the Earl, and keeping an eye on the others with the King, I dare say. The Queen's a pretty little thing, but I wouldn't want *my* son left with her and her brother as my boy's guardians, so I suggested that the two of them stayed with Earl Edward. I believe they were going to go falconing.'

'And you didn't want to join them?'

'Me? Chase after a bird? No, although give me some good greyhounds and a fleet destrier, and I'll chase deer all over the place. I've been asking, and there are quite a good number here. Perhaps I'll have a chance of setting the hounds on 'em, eh? That would be a glorious ride. In the meantime, I'll have to just occupy meself as best I can around here,' he added mournfully.

The Bishop nodded curtly and strode to the large table. On it were the letters which he had been asked to bring. A clerk looked up hopefully, and received a baleful glare in return, as the Bishop picked up the sealed parchment for the bankers.

Leaving the chamber, with Sir Richard wandering behind him like some enquiring mastiff, the Bishop swept through the corridors until he came to the Queen's chambers. He knocked, and the little blonde woman, Alicia, the lady-in-waiting who was so often at the Queen's side, opened it.

'Tell your mistress that I would speak with her,' he said abruptly.

'I think she may be a little indisposed, my Lord Bishop,' Alicia said.

'I have funds for her if she makes herself available.'

As he had expected, the letter in his hand was the key to opening her chamber, and in a short while he and Sir Richard were in the Queen's gracious apartment. She stood, dressed as a widow, all in black, as the two entered. Behind her were

Alicia, Lady Alice de Toeni and Joan of Bar, King Edward's niece. And all stared at him without expression.

Dear God, he thought, *the bitch has poisoned all of them against me!*

It had been almost a year ago now that he had argued with the King that her household should be broken up, and new maids brought in to serve her. As Stapledon had said, the woman might be Queen of England, but she was still French by nature. Her heart was French. All those who were French should be removed from her household, and replaced with loyal English servants. That was why he'd been forced to demand a full safe-conduct from Queen Isabella when the King first suggested that he come here to treat with her. Until then there had been threats that he would be captured and tortured if he ever set foot in France, for his offences to the Queen.

'I hope I see you well, my Queen.'

'I am well. Alicia said you have money for me? That is good. I need funds to maintain myself in the manner to which a Queen should be accustomed.'

'Yes, my Lady. I am to help you here as I may, so that you can return home to your husband all the more speedily.'

'I shall consider the matter as soon as I have my debts paid,' she said firmly.

'My Lady, your husband, the King, has asked that you return home forthwith. Here is his letter.'

'I do not wish to read it, Bishop, but I will have my money, if you please?'

He looked down at her hand and then back up into her eyes. Cold, they were, as ice. 'No.'

'You refuse *me*, your *Queen*?'

'I was told quite definitely to give you money only when you agreed to return to England. I am not at liberty to give you money to support you here while you refuse. Especially after the manner of your refusal yesterday. That was a sad embarrassment to me, to your husband's loyal servant!'

'Then it would appear that there is little more to be discussed.'

'Quite so,' the Bishop said. He was shivering, he was so cross. That this damned *woman* could dare to deny him – and her King – what they reasonably asked, was outrageous. Quite outrageous!

'What are your plans, my Lady, if you will not go back to the bosom of your family and your husband?' he asked with frigid calm.

'I have much still to do, my Lord Bishop. There are matters to negotiate with the King here. Fortunately he is prepared to help support me as a Princess should be. I am safe here in France, you see. Safe from attack – and from the depredations of those who would rob me of all my properties and income.'

Bishop Walter curled his lip at that, but said nothing. He knew that his reasonable and sensible actions in seeing all her lands in Devon and Cornwall sequestrated had rankled, but that was not his concern. 'And how long do you intend to hold this charade?' he said, indicating her widow's clothing.

'Until the King is free of the base traitor Despenser and I can once again take my throne in Westminster Hall.'

'Come home now.'

'You heard me yesterday. I will not.'

'Then all support is cut off. The King will advance you nothing.'

He stared at her hard, and then span on his heel and strode out, Sir Richard, grinning broadly and winking at Alicia, following more slowly.

'Sir Richard?' the Queen said as he reached the door.

'Yes, my Queen?'

'Do be careful around the Bishop. There are many here in France who do not like him.'

'I'm always careful, my Queen,' he said with a smile. He left the room just as Sir Henry de Beaumont appeared in the corridor outside. 'Ha! Sir Henry. You coming to see the Queen too?'

Sir Henry had paled, before smiling in return and nodding effusively. 'Yes. I was here to speak with her and ensure that she was safely guarded. Can't have just anyone breaking in on her.'

'No, there are too many Frenchies here for my liking!' Sir Richard chuckled, and set off in the Bishop's wake.

But Sir Richard, for all his amiability and an exterior composed apparently of elephant hide, was a law officer, and as astute as any. The hesitation of Sir Henry had not been missed.

Paris

He knew what the 'King' was thinking, half the time.

Jacquot stood in the shadow near the gate of the Louvre, watching the crowds passing by, waiting for a sight of the Procureur, musing over the 'King's' behaviour.

He was growing ever more irrational. When Jacquot had first arrived here, the 'King' had been greedy, but wary. No one could survive with immoderate demands at all times. It was necessary for a man to be sensible. The 'King' had known that. He had become the main gang-leader in the area because he had the ballocks and brains for the job. Over the years, two rival gangs had ruled the city. One controlled the northern part of the city, the other the south, the river forming a natural boundary for them. And for many years this was an adequate separation. There were tens of thousands – perhaps hundreds of thousands – living in Paris, and a number were devoted to a life of crime.

All operated under the aegis of one or other criminal 'family'.

Jacquot had arrived just as the situation was changing. It was impossible for him to earn money, except by robbery, and when he fell in with others in a similar position, he took the same attitude to his victims as he had in the past to animals while living on the land. There was a duty to make any necessary killing as swift and painless as possible. That was his creed, and he stuck to it.

However, others were less humane. The 'King' was one such.

Jacquot met him once, swaggering about the lanes with a woman at his arm. He was about seventeen then, and life had been good to him. He had been a cutpurse for a while in the southern family, and progressed to breaking locks. But for him the small beer of the southern half of the city was no good. He wanted more. Always more.

So the 'King' began to make inroads into sections of northern Paris, striking up relationships with the thief-takers and Sergents, making little advances to test them every so often. Once a man had taken a small bribe from him, it was harder for them to return to the northern family and denounce him, and the 'King' was very shrewd. He took care which men he over-used.

His genius lay in his new idea. While all the others were content with their lot, making a few sous a day and wallowing in wine and women at night until all was gone once more, the 'King' saw that a more amenable approach to his income would be to take the royal shilling. So he became a thief-taker himself. Only a lowly one, naturally, but the position and the royal staff that went with it were both enough to guarantee him an easier passage about the city when he wanted. And in that position he could take more stolen goods and trade them on his own behalf.

There had been a bloodbath when the two families realised someone was taking their business. For weeks, corpses were found lying in the streets or thrown into the river, to be discovered further downstream. And then, when the two old families were so weakened by internal wrangling and the loss of so many of their men, the 'King' appeared to take over, with a new group of hard men, men who were keen to impose their own rules on the city. From that moment the north and south were united in the one large band, and where the rivalries had threatened their business, now they controlled all. It was the beginning of the 'King's' reign.

Jacquot had watched all from his own distance. He had no need of the 'King's' aid, nor did he want to become associated with a group of men who could well prove to be entirely untrustworthy. The idea of becoming involved in a group which then sold him to the law, or perhaps thrust a knife into his back when he didn't expect it, had little appeal. It was only when he realised that it would grow ever more dangerous to work on his own, and that unless he had the support of the 'King' he could be turned over to the Sergents, that he chose the easier route of joining the 'King' and becoming a loyal servant.

Not that he was entirely committed, of course. A man should always look to his back when he lived as a felon.

Bois de Vincennes

Baldwin had enjoyed a good morning out in the woods. Although he had no falcons, it was enough to watch others sending their birds high into the air, then observe them plunging down to break the backs of the rabbits set loose for them.

The only hair in his soup was his brute Wolf. As soon as he saw the birds, the beast was determined to be off after them, and when the game was killed, he would try to lunge free.

'You should tie the blasted thing to a tree and leave him until we're done,' Simon said at one point. 'Better still, leave him there permanently.'

Baldwin stroked Wolf's head. 'Do not listen to him, old fellow. The good Bailiff feels grumpy this morning.'

'So should you, hearing that there's little chance of our returning homewards any time soon. Do you think we could speak with the Duke? Perhaps he would release us . . .'

Baldwin glanced at him seriously. 'True. He might. And then, consider: what if he came to some mishap while he was here, and we were safe at home? What would the King say to us then? Would he understand how you and I had left his heir alone with a reduced party to protect him? Or would he hang us from the gates of Exeter City for all the world to laugh and jeer at?'

'Baldwin, my wife is troubled . . .'

'So is Jeanne, Simon. And both are many leagues distant. So the best course we may take is to serve our Duke and pass our time sensibly until we may take ship again – for it will happen. Perhaps we can raise the subject when we speak next with the Queen.'

The two friends spent the rest of the morning with the Duke and the King of France, and later, when the hawks were resting in the Mews, they ate a hearty midday meal with the second service. For while the King and Duke were eating with the Queen, Simon and Baldwin stood behind the Duke on guard. Only when the higher nobles had eaten their fill and left the tables were fresh mess-bowls brought in for the likes of Simon and Baldwin.

It was after they had eaten, and when Simon had suggested

a walk about the old hunting lodge that they came across Sir Richard.

'Ha! You look like a man who's eaten a hog by yourself!' the knight declared, poking Simon's belly with a finger as hard as a staff of oak. 'You're a trencherman after my own heart!'

'I doubt it,' Simon muttered, but the knight was already looking at Baldwin. 'I think there may be a problem here for us, Sir Baldwin. Care to come with me on a walk, both of you?'

Chapter Seventeen

Louvre, Paris

Now, at last, he was beginning to see the story.

Jean the Procureur sat back in his chair and steepled his fingers over his breast. It was an affectation, but the fact of keeping his fingers perfectly still helped him from being distracted.

'The man was de Nogaret's son. His wife was with him. Within a few days of arriving here, he visits the Louvre, and there he is killed. A short while after that, his wife too is slain. Most viciously.'

Hélias, when asked, had cheerfully confessed to knowing seven assassins in the city. They were occasional clients of hers. One apparently preferred men, so he had never visited her establishment, but she wasn't going to try to persuade him otherwise. There were plenty of men with hot blood in the city without seeking new clients.

According to Hélias, the common view was that de Nogaret's wife had simply been unlucky and met a cut-throat on her way along a quiet street. There was no more to it than that. Jean himself, however, had seen plenty of deaths in his time, and to him, this one had all the hallmarks of a crime of passion, not of some random robbery and killing. If the husband had died in a similar manner, with bloody wounds all over his torso, that would be significant, but he hadn't. His death was clearly a great deal more professional. As was the despatch from this earthly realm of Nicholas the Stammerer.

Oddly, Hélias had not been able to help him over *that* death. Sweet Mother of Christ! It had made the Procureur furious to learn that the security up at the Temple was so lax that a man might walk in off the street and commit murder with impunity. The two executioners must have been bribed, but it was not so easy to punish them, as men with their lack of scruples and their minute moral flexibility were hard to find.

Still, the death of Nicholas the Stammerer had been clean and tidy: a simple thrust down with a terrible, thin blade. It would have to be a long blade, too. There were some who said that to break open a man's heart it would take only an inch and a half of metal from the front. More, apparently, from the back – but from above? He wondered how long the blade would have to be: six inches? Ten? But all men carried blades as a matter of course. There was little point attempting to look at the methodology, except to consider the manner of death. The two men killed cleanly with a single blow: the woman slaughtered in a frenzied welter of blows.

'Are you sure you know no more about the married couple?' he had pressed Hélias. He would ignore Nicholas the Stammerer for now.

'What can I tell you? The pair of them seemed pleasant enough, although desperately hard up. They did keep talking about how much easier their lives would be soon, but never told anyone why, nor how much they would be improved.'

'No mention of gaining money directly, then,' Jean mused. 'But who would, in a tavern in a strange city? That would be to invite death.'

'Then perhaps they did confide in someone, eh?' Hélias had said shrewdly.

'Yes,' he said now. 'Someone was told. Someone knew what was going on.'

He frowned up at the ceiling, considering all the different aspects of the matter, and it was only when he thought again about the footsteps of de Nogaret, that the frown deepened.

If he had arrived here in the castle, he would have requested some help to find the chamber where the Cardinal would meet him. And Jean had already decided that the chamber was perhaps selected for de Nogaret by his assassin, because it was far enough away from everything and everybody.

The first person he had considered for the murder was the messenger who brought the Cardinal to the body. First the man took de Nogaret to the chamber, and then he slew him, before going to fetch the Cardinal.

Except there would have been blood. The messenger was seen by many, and all admitted that he was clean. So that was the first mark against him.

'Second,' he murmured, closing his eyes, 'we have the problem of the servant killing him for no reason. Why do that? The man appears to be perfectly normal, so far as I can see.'

If he had wished it, the boy could already have been dangling from the meat hook in the Temple, but there was little to be gained by harming a lad of decent birth. It wasn't the same as torturing a fool and knave like the Stammerer. And at the present, he had no reason to suspect the servant of anything other than working correctly in his post.

'So, servant finds visitor at gate; servant takes visitor to a remote chamber; servant fetches the Cardinal; Cardinal and servant return to the room and find de Nogaret dead. Why? And why in that particular room? And slain by whom?'

It was a foul, confusing mess, and the more he considered it, the less confident he felt about learning the truth.

There was no point in remaining here. The dark was beginning to fall. He must leave the castle and find his way home. Perhaps while he slept, a partial solution might occur to him; some little detail he had missed.

He closed his door behind him, locked it, and crossed the court to the gate – and then, as a man entered, he stood a little aside.

'Friend, do you know where I can find the exchequer of the Duke of Brabant?'

Jean was tempted to snarl, 'Do I look like a servant?' but then he spotted a young knave from the stables. 'I think you will find this boy an excellent guide,' he said, and was about to turn away, when he realised what he had just done. The visitor thanked him and walked away, casting a curious look at him, as though wondering whether he was moon-struck.

It was his own foolishness that made Jean swear quietly and lengthily. He had seen it only a few days ago. When a visitor arrived, if he knew little about the castle and the people in it, he would automatically ask a mere boy to show him the way. A knave from the stables, or one from the kitchens, either would suffice.

Surely that was what de Nogaret had done. A newcomer to Paris, overawed by the city itself, then by the great palace of the Kings of France, he would have gazed about him with fear, anxious that he might make himself appear foolish. And so he would have turned to someone who was lower in the social scale at the castle: a knave.

Jean cast a look about him as the dusk began to settle. He would hurry homewards, and then consider this. Perhaps, he thought, the solution was approaching him after all.

Bois de Vincennes

'Are you sure of this?' Baldwin asked.

Sir Richard set his head to one side and didn't respond.

'I am sorry, Sir Richard. I forget you too are a Justice.'

'I am used to questioning men, and I know when they are lying to me, Sir Baldwin. Trust my judgement here. Sir Henry de Beaumont is no more an independent guard of the Duke than I'm a tailor. The man is up to his eyes in something.'

'Such as?'

'Such as plotting to support the Queen while she's here, I should think, Sir Baldwin. The woman's as cunning as a fox, and will use her wiles to protect herself and her son. Now, this means that it's only you, me, the Bailiff here, and the Bishop who are independent of the Queen. It's not enough to serve the Duke as he should be served. I think we ought to warn him. Maybe leave France.'

'I do not think so. We have no need to fear the King,' Baldwin objected. 'He will not harm his sister or his nephew. No, we are safe.' Then a thought occurred to him: it was one thing for *them* all to be safe, but quite another for the Bishop of Exeter. He was hated throughout France for the stand he took against Isabella. And she would be unlikely to do much to help him.

Simon was nodding to himself, but his expression was glum. 'If we cannot trust to Sir Henry, we have to look to ourselves. But perhaps that is the Queen's ambition, to force each of us to take her part, and then leave no one here independent to protect the Duke. Perhaps keep him here, away from his father.'

'At least the King's traitor, Mortimer, is not here,' Baldwin said. 'But no matter. I suggest we should remain together, all three of us, as much as possible – just to ensure that our own lives are not threatened. And we must tell the Bishop as soon as is possible.'

'Yes. That makes perfect sense,' Sir Richard said. He cast an innocent look upon Simon. 'Perhaps we should visit the castle's bar and take a little wine to settle us after this unpleasant shock, eh, Bailiff ?'

Simon threw a look of mingled horror and disgust at Baldwin. His belly was only recently recovered after his last visit to a tavern with the iron-gutted Sir Richard.

'I think that would be an excellent idea,' Baldwin said, and left the chamber with a fixed grin on his face.

Cardinal Thomas d'Anjou was enjoying his visit to the Bois de Vincennes since his discussion with the King about the Queen of England and Bishop Stapledon. It was not always the case. He had been one of those who struggled to get on with King Charles and his companions. Not surprising, perhaps, bearing in mind the fact that the King's friends were all of exalted rank, and his own family were little better than peasants.

Yet in France there were some who looked beyond the position of a man's parents. In Thomas's life, that guardian angel had been the kindly priest of his tiny parish church. Some priests had so little learning themselves that they were not merely unwilling, they were unable to spot the brighter children, but not Père Hugo. He had noticed the young Thomas's facility with numbers and with a pen, but rather than pick him out and thus ostracise him from his circle of friends, the priest made a point of speaking with *all* the boys, and occasionally holding small parties for them, at which he would let them play with slates and chalk.

But it was Thomas who had the ability. There was no doubt about that. And when he was praised for his efforts, he began to want to continue, to learn more. Reading he found difficult, but writing was a joy. He loved to make curling letters spread over a tablet or sheet of parchment, the patterns a delight to the eye. To elevate his work to a higher level he would add pictures: dragons breathing fire, boars snorting steam in the winter, horses rearing with a knight in the saddle. Later, when his tutor saw these works, he had scowled and beaten Thomas for inventing things which would be unpleasing to God.

'He has made this marvel of a world for us, His people, and you spend your time inventing new worlds? Make yourself more complete, boy, by studying His works, by copying His creatures.'

The beatings were regular, of course. All boys learned how to cope with the pain. But it did not dissuade the young Thomas, and as soon as he could, he had announced to his Vicar that he would like to be educated as a priest himself. And a priest he became after some little while, but he did not remain a priest for very long. Soon he was studying again in the Vatican. And he came to the notice of the Pope.

In those days, the Papacy was a shoddy organisation. Not enough piety, too much avarice. And yet to be there, to be living with the Pope, that was an enormous honour, and one which he was unwilling to give up lightly. He rose through the ranks, crowning his career with this position of Cardinal, here at the court of the French King, as adviser to King Charles, diplomat, and spy on behalf of the Pope.

It had been a good life. And now, with all fortune, perhaps he could see a long-hoped-for peace. The bitter rivalry between the two Crowns of England and France would be set aside at last, and maybe a new Crusade could be launched, against the heretics who'd stolen the Holy Land. That was an aim devoutly to be desired.

The Queen of England's position was difficult, though. Her being here could prove to be an embarrassment before long. There was enmity between herself and her husband, the kind of bitter dispute that could end a marriage. And while her presence in France could be a thorn in the side of the English King, it was infinitely worse for the King of France, for it was a constant reminder of the matter of the silken purses. The last thing which the King wished for was any reminder of that horrible affair . . .

Thursday before the Feast of the Archangel Michael[1]

Paris

It was a cool morning when Jean the Procureur woke, and he clad himself in thick clothing in a hurry, bellowing for his servants to prepare his fire and some hot water with wine as well as food.

He hated the winter. The cold seeped into his bones, and the feeling of darkness all around made him anxious. There were plenty who felt the same, he knew, but that was little consolation to him.

It was the lack of daylight which really oppressed him and brought his spirits low. The fact was, he enjoyed warm sunshine on his face, and the winter meant little if any. So much of the day was spent in darkness: rising in the dark, leaving for work in the dark, returning in the dark, sitting at home with only the firelight and perhaps a candle or two for illumination . . . all was misery and black fear. Ghosts and witches abounded, so they said. It was easier to believe those stories in wintertime.

Stephen, his servant, the burly man who had been following around after him and who assisted in the arrest of Nicholas the Stammerer, was a devoted fellow. He stood about now, helping his master into his jacket, tugging the old cloak over his shoulders, and standing back to consider the effect

---

[1] Thursday, 26 September 1325

before hurrying down the steep staircase to the ground level, where he stirred the thin porridge and warmed some spiced wine.

'At least the sun is abroad,' the Procureur said, once he was sitting before his fire.

It was throwing out a feeble warmth, he thought to himself. The faggots of twigs had burned through already, and it seemed that there was little heat in the remaining embers. He kicked at the coals, then threw a last faggot on top and enjoyed the sudden crackling rush of hot air that left his face feeling scorched and shining.

'Are you going back to the Louvre?' Stephen asked.

'Yes. I have had a new idea about the death of the man de Nogaret,' he said. It was a matter of pride to him that he should have had the thought, and he did not mind demonstrating his cleverness. 'You remember that he arrived, and was murdered before the Cardinal could reach him?'

'I have been considering it with anticipation ever since you divulged your conundrum to me.'

'Don't talk ballocks to me, Stephen,' the Procureur rasped. His servant might have the appearance of a churl from the gutters of Bordeaux, but there were few cleverer men in Paris, he knew. And sadly, Stephen knew this too. 'The lad was killed, I think, because the period between his arrival and the appearance of the Cardinal was greater than people thought beforehand. Consider: if another led the visitor to the room, and then asked a second messenger to go to the Cardinal, that might leave more time. The first messenger could have been the killer, for all I know. He slew de Nogaret, and then hurried off to ask someone to fetch the Cardinal.'

'Possible, certainly,' Stephen considered. 'But who would want to kill de Nogaret?'

'There are many who remember his father, I would

imagine. Was there some ancient debt to be paid? Someone may have been happy to slip a blade into him.'

Stephen nodded, but not with enormous conviction. There were, the Procureur knew, too many possible failings in his logic. Because that was all it was: a string of logic. There was nothing substantial on which to hang an allegation.

Still, it was a starting point, and when he marched to the Louvre, with Stephen in his wake, he paid less attention to the people around him as he considered the day's work ahead. At least the King was still away at his hunting lodge. That was a relief. It meant that Jean would have a little peace before he must present his findings.

The porter at the main gate to the castle was a burly man in his late thirties called Arnaud. He had a thick beard, which he grew partly to conceal a jagged wound he'd won in the battle of the Golden Spurs at Courtrai twenty-odd years before. Where some men prized their scars, Arnaud seemed to find it only a source of shame.

When Jean arrived at the gates, Arnaud was standing with two of his men, waving the morning's rush into the castle grounds.

'Ha! You again, Procureur? Haven't you finished your inquest yet?'

'Perhaps you yourself can assist me with my enquiry? I have to know what would have happened to the visitor when he arrived here at the gate.'

'We'd have sent him on his way, of course!' Arnaud said. He showed his teeth for a moment in a grin. 'You mean something else, of course?'

'Of course.'

Arnaud glanced behind him, then jerked his head, and the two men stepped forward and took his place, herding the people through. 'So?' he asked again, once they were inside his little chamber in the gate's tower. 'What do you want now?'

'The man de Nogaret. When he entered the castle, I assumed that a servant who happened to be here at the gate, would have taken him to a room, and then fetched the Cardinal himself?'

'It is perfectly possible.'

'Do you have any servants waiting here right now, in case a visitor turns up? If a man came here at this very minute, what would you do?'

Arnaud considered him and a slight frown passed over his face. 'What are you suggesting, old friend, eh? That I or one of my men took this fellow to the chamber and killed him?'

'No,' Jean said. He paused. The porter was a useful contact, but not a friend, no matter what he might call Jean. To upset him would make life and entry to the castle more difficult in future, and was best avoided. He needed to placate the man's feelings. 'The thing is, you see, I need your help to understand this. The servant who brought de Nogaret to the room: what was his name?'

'Raoulet, I think. He works under the steward in the hall.'

'That's him. Do you remember him being here when de Nogaret arrived?'

In answer the porter jerked a thumb over his shoulder, towards the queue of people walking into the castle. 'Do I remember Raoulet being here? No. Do I remember de Nogaret? No. Do you expect me to remember all these faces tomorrow? *You* can, if you wish, Procureur, but I doubt I'll remember more than a dozen. There are too many.'

'Very well – do you remember any who might have been on the other side, then? Inside the castle's court? So that a man walking in might see him and ask directions? I saw a fellow doing just that the other day. He asked me where he should go, and I regret to say I was unable to help him.'

'You should ask Raoulet himself. He would know. I see all sorts here. Christ's teeth, I even saw a whore directing a man the other day. People will ask directions of anyone.'

'I will do. Can you fetch Raoulet now?'

'He'll be in the buttery, I expect. Would *you* be waiting outdoors on a cold morning like this?' Arnaud said bitterly. The gatekeeper was obviously proud of his grievances, and any opportunity to air them would never be missed.

Jean smiled. 'I think he has the best idea. That is good, then, master Porter. I will go and ask him. I'm sorry I wasted your time, but I was only seeking to learn what could have happened.'

'That's all right,' the porter said gruffly.

'For your help, I'll have some wine sent to you later. The cold! A man needs wine to keep it out, eh?'

'That is kind. Very kind. You know, there was one . . . I can't be certain it was the same day, you understand, but there was one kitchen knave waiting out there one day. It's such a while ago now, but I did notice the lad out there, loitering.'

'Loitering?'

'He was a young lad. Eight or nine years old, I'd guess. Not that it's easy to tell nowadays. But he reminded me of one of my own boys. Little devil! He was out there kicking stones about like there was nothing better for him to do.'

'And he could have offered to take a man somewhere?'

'He could have – but I didn't see it. And he's only a kitchen knave, you understand.'

'I fully comprehend. And this boy – do you know his name?'

'Aye – the devil himself! He was out there that morning because he was waiting to be thrashed by the cook for leaving the spit to turn on its own instead of being there to keep the meat cooked evenly. He is that sort of boy, little Jehanin. And I heard the cook bellowing for him later.' He frowned quickly. 'Haven't seen him since, though.'

The cook ruled supreme. He stood, a large, rotund man, with a thick towel tied to his waist by a cord of rope that also held a large knife, and a shirt of linen all besmottered with gravies and blood. Sandy-haired, with blue eyes that were so faded they were nearer grey, his flesh was pale and unhealthy, while his lips were the rosy red of a maid's. Still, he had the voice of a herald at war; arms on his hips, roaring and cursing all who came near.

Seeing Jean enter, he glowered truculently. 'What do *you* want?'

'I was hoping to see the chief cook.'

'Congratulations. You've succeeded. Now, piss off! We're busy.'

'So I see.'

It was, in truth, a scene from hell. All about the cook, young boys ran, some carrying joints of meat, some bags of beans, one or two staggering under the weight of yokes which held buckets filled with water on either branch. The fires were roaring, four of them all in a row, and there were massive cauldrons on two, while enormous viands were set to rotate gently about a third. The fourth appeared to have been lighted for no purpose, but the heat from it reminded Jean of a tale he once heard the priest tell of Hades. All was mad bustle, with a sudden gust of feathers which flew into the air from a table at the middle of the room, where three boys were plucking and drawing geese next to four men who were washing, cutting and slicing vegetables. Steel racks were poised like instruments of torture, and among all the

204   *Michael Jecks*

youngsters, older boys and men hurried to carry out the cook's instructions.

'I would like to speak with you.'

'I don't have time.'

'It is about a murder.'

'And this is about breakfast, you fool! Can't you see that? Now clear off out of it, before I call the Sergent!'

'I am the Procureur, and the King has ordered me to investigate this case. If you wish, I can go to him and tell him that you have deliberately obstructed me. After all, it will not harm you – a new cook is hard to find.'

'You pissy little prickle! Do you think you can scare me? Eh?' He turned and caught sight of a man listening with interest. 'Jacques, get back to your work! If you think I'm going yet, you'll have a nasty shock!' Turning back to Jean, he snarled, 'It is easy to find a man who *says* he can do this job, but much harder, to find someone who can actually *do* it!'

'All I want is to speak to the kitchen knave called Jehanin.'

'Do you? Well, so do I, man. When you find the little shit, you can tan his arse for me. That'll warm him up for when I thrash him and take all the flesh from his backside for running away.'

In the porter's room, Arnaud poured himself a large cup of wine and drank it reflectively. And then, while he still had the resolve, he set the cup down, and left the gate. He muttered a few words to the men left to guard it, and then crossed the court to the main castle building.

The great hall had been a source of wonder to him when he first saw it. It towered up, and its white stone gleamed when the sun shone on it. Today, though, he was not thinking about the building. Instead he walked inside and looked about him until he saw the face he was seeking.

'Hey, old friend. A word.'

Hugues looked up with quick interest at the tone of his voice. 'What?'

'I've just been talking with the Procureur. He wanted to know about a kitchen boy. The lad had helped fetch Raoulet on the day that man was killed.'

'What about it?'

'Well, I saw your girl with the kitchen knave.'

'What?'

'That raven-haired beauty. She was with him. And now he's missing.'

'He was a boy. They disappear all the time. You saying she killed the dead man? No? Then don't be so stupid!'

Chapter Eighteen

Friday before the Feast of the Archangel Michael[1]

On the road from Vincennes

It was wet, and miserable, and the Bishop could feel the steady trickle of rainwater running down the back of his neck.

'I am too old for this,' he muttered to himself.

It was nothing more than the simple truth. He was in his sixties, and most men by his age were either dead, stupid, or cosseted at home, enwrapped in blankets, while doting wives and children, not to mention grandchildren, fetched and carried all that was needful.

Not him, though. Early on he had chosen the path of mental and spiritual toil, and forsaking the comforts and ease of the secular life, had embraced the world of an ascetic.

It had been hard. When he was first elected Bishop, he was so hard up for money that he was forced to borrow from the good Bishop Reynolds, who was consecrated on the same day. But he had done his best in the years since. He had endowed schools and a college in Oxford, and he was proud of his reputation of being a hard-working Bishop who knew every parish in his diocese. And the rewards had come. Especially while he was the Lord High Treasurer.

This, though, this was his worst ever experience. He was

---

[1] Friday, 27 September 1325

hated in France, as he knew all too well; the Queen detested him, a sentiment with which he was entirely comfortable, bearing in mind he reciprocated it wholeheartedly. In his opinion, she was a vain, unpleasant example of an untrust-worthy species. Women were, as all knew, a flawed and failed version of the male sex, and the Queen, being half-French, was doubly so.

All the way from the Bois de Vincennes they'd been watching him. Hooded eyes, narrow and suspicious, were on him as he walked around the court, as he mounted his horse, as he trotted from the hunting lodge, and now, on the road, they were on him still. There was none in the French court in whom he could place his trust. This was a mission in which all depended upon him and only a very few men – Sir Henry, Sir Baldwin, Sir Richard . . . and Simon Puttock, of course. The Bailiff had always been very dear to him.

They rode due west, the rain gusting, the pitter-patter of raindrops tapping at his hat making him hunch still lower, while the drips that touched his flesh made him want to recoil, they were so icy. It felt as though it might begin to snow at any moment. His boots were already spattered with mud, his hose sodden and shapeless under his robes, and he felt as miserable as a man could, but at least there was the promise of a fire and spiced wine when they reached their journey's end. And he had the protection of safe-conducts from two Kings and the clothing of a man of God to promise the Pope's own vengeance on any who dared to think of an offence against him. Yet still he felt worried.

There was something going on here that escaped him. The Queen seemed supremely confident – more than was warranted by her situation. It was only to be expected that she would be feeling happier, of course. She was back with her own folk, away from the court of her husband which she did not understand. How could she? A spendthrift and feckless woman could never appreciate the constant battle which her poor husband fought every day with income and tight restrictions on his budget, nor the worries which assailed King Edward every day.

Yet her buoyant mood appeared to be more than simple confidence brought on by her return to this country. Something else must be going on. Her life had been a steady, trotting journey, and suddenly she was bucketing off into the woods at the side, and the Bishop did not understand it. Not at all.

Clearly she could not remain here. Queen Isabella might be a dreadful person, but she was, even Bishop Stapledon had to admit, a devoted mother. She would never agree to leaving her children behind in England. She had one – and that the most expensive bargaining counter of all, naturally, being the King's own heir – but that did not mean she could happily concede the others.

She was still guarded by Lord John Cromwell; her ladies-in-waiting were still the women installed by the King and Despenser to keep a wary eye upon her, and she still must depend upon her husband for her money. Without his good-will, she had nothing. And Stapledon had strict instructions: she must agree to return before a single farthing was advanced to her.

So why did she look so pleased with herself?

Ah! Thank God! Ahead at last, he saw the city in all its glory, the walls, the great towers, the stain on the sky that spoke of a thousand, thousand fires, the noise of men shouting, and of all the other activities of a busy, thronging city. And beyond it all, he could see the bright, white towers of the Louvre.

He had never thought he would be so pleased to see any city in the whole of France, but today, he was so deadly keen to see a fire, he was almost ready to shake hands with the Devil himself.

Louvre, Paris

The weather was miserable, and Arnaud was happy to remain in his little chamber for most of the day, although when the entourage appeared and the King's outriders swept in through the main gates, he had to shift himself to make sure that all his guards were ready on the doors.

There were so many, and all with their finery sodden and dripping. What weather to be travelling! He wouldn't have gone out in this, not for all the King's money from Normandy. It was one of those fine rains that blew straight at a man horizontally and cut through his clothing like a dagger piercing oil.

He saw Jean, and tutted to himself. The Procureur was standing, a small frown on his face, as though he was assessing the incomers, trying to work out whether they were capable of the murder of the man in the chamber at the rear, or whether they were dangerous in some other way.

Jean often had that sort of appearance. He looked like a man who would stare at a problem for hours, in the hope that it would explain itself to him. A dowdy little fellow, Arnaud thought. He should have got married. Let a woman have a go at him. Then he would have looked a little more presentable – although the poor fool probably thought he looked the picture of elegance.

A Bishop rode in, and sat upon his horse shivering, while three clerks busied themselves about him, one fetching a little stool, one a fresh cloak, the last hurrying into the castle itself, probably, so Arnaud thought, to bring out a jug of warmed wine or something similar. The Bishop looked ancient, after all. He was probably near to exhaustion.

Jean was still hanging around, gormlessly staring, and Arnaud grinned to himself when the Bishop took offence.

'Well? What do you see that is so fascinating, man?'

Jean looked startled. 'Pardon?' he asked.

'You are staring at me. I assume you have some reason for doing so?'

'My apologies, my Lord Bishop. My mind was a thousand miles away. I did not observe you.'

'Do not lie to me, man! I saw you staring at me! What was your reason? Eh? Come on out with it, you cretin!'

Jean held out his hands in a pacifying gesture. 'I do not understand your concern, my Lord.'

He glanced about him as though calling upon all those present to witness this curious outburst, but then a younger lad rode up to the side of the Bishop. With a shock Arnaud realised by the coat-of-arms as well as the three men who followed him as a guard, that this was the fellow all had been discussing: the Duke of Aquitaine, the boy who would be the King of England when his father died.

It was the Duke who spoke first. 'Is there a difficulty here, my Lord Bishop?'

'No, no. I am deeply sorry if I led you to be concerned, your Highness.'

The little scene was intriguing. Arnaud stepped outside to listen.

Jean was speaking, 'I do not know how I have offended, my Lords. I am a mere officer standing here watching guests arrive.'

'It is well. I am sorry for any upset the Bishop may have given you. I am sure he would be more than happy to apologise very fully.'

The Duke stared at the Bishop with a steadiness he had learned from his father. The latter had said once, that none of his men should be too comfortable in his presence.

The King had led Edward, while he was a mere Earl, out to the walls of the Tower of London, and they went to a guard standing lonely in the corner of the wall where it met a tower.

'Are you well?' the King asked the guard. He had a strangely gentle voice when he wanted it. At times his harshness and crudeness could appal, but if he wished to please or cajole, his manner was much softer. He used it now.

'Yes, my Liege. I am very well,' the man replied.

'It is a lovely evening,' the King commented.

'Yes.'

'With a full moon.'

'Yes.'

'So you can see for miles as though it was torchlit.'

'Yes.'

'So perhaps you should keep looking out there, *you fool, and stop staring in towards the castle's keep!*' the King bellowed suddenly. 'Because, you cretin, the enemy will attack from out there, not in here, won't they?'

The Prince was tempted at the time to bolt, his father's behaviour seemed so extreme. He wanted to run and hide, but his father had given a twisted grin and a slight wink. 'No, boy, you stay with me,' he said quietly a moment or two later. First, he pointed out along the guard-walks. 'Look! All the men here heard me with that man. Do you see a single man idling? Is one of them peering inside? No. Now, come with me.'

They descended into the court, and from there walked to the tower in which the jewels were stored. Outside were two more guards, both alert, presumably because they had heard the King's roar earlier from the walls. They allowed the King and the Earl inside, and the King led his son along the shelves, opening the chests and displaying the proudest possessions of the Kingdom.

In a chamber inside the treasure house sat a pair of clerks, writing by candlelight at a table.

'I hope I find you well?' the King asked when the two had upset their inks and a candle in their haste to rise in his presence.

'Very, your Royal Highness,' one said nervously.

'And you have all your works finished? The hour is late.'

'No, we are completing our inventory for Sir Hugh le Despenser,' one said.

The King's face registered nothing, but for a heart's beat there was no sound, and Earl Edward shot a look at him. The King had not known that Despenser had set these two here, he realised.

'You are not finished? Then how can you feel so well? You still have work to do,' the King muttered, and left them to their labours.

'I had thought to spring myself upon them and make them jump, but see how they repaid me? They did not even realise they shook me!' he murmured to himself.

'Your Highness?'

'It is nothing.'

The Earl had been surprised to see his father like that. It was an odd occasion. The King at one moment so supremely confident that he had destroyed the comfort of one guard's mind, and then, while trying to repeat the experience, he had himself been embarrassed. And perhaps it was little surprise. Because the man in whom he had placed so much trust was the same one who had ordered the cataloguing of the Crown Jewels. It was a small enough matter, Earl Edward knew that. And yet, he wondered then, as he did again now, whether his father had ever seen that inventory, or whether he waited, hoping against hope that the Despenser had not made use of the inventory to appropriate a few of the choicer jewels for himself.

But the incident on the guard-walk had taught him about the impact of the voice of a man in power, and that lesson Earl Edward had not forgotten. What's more, this was the man who had shamed his mother.

'My Lord Bishop, are you quite well?'

'Yes, my Lord.'

'Your mind is not disordered?'

'No, my Lord.'

'And you have no upset of the humours?'

'No, my Lord.'

'And yet you rail at this poor man as though you consider him a felon. What was his crime?'

'He committed no crime, my Lord,' the Bishop said, and turned bitterly angry eyes upon him.

'You bellow and rant and for no reason, you say? And you also say you are not unwell?'

'No.'

'Then, Bishop, I think you should make a fulsome apology to him.'

'Yes, my Lord.'

'So, Bishop? Have you anything to say?'

Baldwin had watched from behind the Duke, and now he spurred his mount onward. 'I shall take care of my Lord Bishop, your Highness,' he said.

'Good. Please *do* take care of him,' Duke Edward said. 'After all, he has not yet supplied my mother with the money which she requires while she remains here.'

'I may not,' the Bishop said.

'You *may* not? Or *will* not?'

'The King made me swear only to release the funds after your mother the Queen agreed to return home, as I have said.'

'I think you should reconsider your priorities, my Lord Bishop. Some may take unkindly to your attitude,' the Duke said. 'I think you should go indoors and rest and reflect. After all, one day you may find that you depend more upon me and my mother, my Lord Bishop.'

'Thank you, Duke. I shall.'

'And remove all those wet things. We do not want you to have a coldness about your humours, do we? I need you fit.'

The Bishop watched as the Duke and two of his guards trotted away to hand their mounts to the ostlers.

Baldwin slipped from his saddle and bowed to the man who had sparked the little scene. 'Sieur, I am called Sir Baldwin de Furnshill. I apologise if my Lord Bishop upset you. It is only that we are tired and wet after our ride. I beg that you forgive us.'

'There is nothing to forgive. Please do not trouble yourself,' said Jean with a grave, deep bow in return. 'Sieur Jean de Poissy at your service.'

He nodded to the Bishop politely enough, and then strode away.

'Bishop, are you sure you are quite well?' Baldwin asked when Jean was out of earshot. He saw the gate-keeper watching, and when he caught his eye, the fellow shuffled away.

'The man was staring at me as though he . . . no. No, you are right, Sir Baldwin. It is nothing to do with him. It is my concern. The Queen will make my life here as difficult as possible. And yet I must remain, for I have a duty to the King's son.'

Bishop Stapledon clambered tiredly from his horse and began to wander towards the guest rooms, a bent man, suddenly showing his age.

It made Baldwin sad to see him so downcast.

Chapter Nineteen

Vigil of the Feast of the Archangel Michael[1]

Louvre, Paris

All through the night and for much of the morning it had rained solidly, and Baldwin, as he walked from the small chamber in which he and Simon had been installed, felt glad that the weather had warmed a little with the rain. Yesterday, when they had been riding here from Vincennes, it had been cold enough, so Sir Richard said, to freeze the teeth in a man's mouth.

He had appeared to be a little out of sorts recently. Certainly he had been a great deal quieter for the last few days, and if he had been unknown to Baldwin, the latter might have uncharitably assumed that the man was hung-over. The knight was usually such a loud, rumbustious soul, but he had to Baldwin's knowledge told only four jokes during the ride to Paris. It was clearly the effect of the news about Sir Henry de Beaumont. If that knight was now in the Queen's purse, it would make their positions more difficult. All of them were aware that the Queen was gathering about her a group of loyal men, and the little group charged with the defence of the Earl was growing so tiny in comparison with the hosts at the command of the French King and his sister, Queen Isabella,

---

[1] Saturday, 28 September 1325

that at any time an attack against the Bishop must succeed, just as an assault against the Earl of Chester to take him into the protection of the French King, for example, could not fail. Baldwin, Richard and Simon could not on their own protect either of their charges.

There was a fine spitting rain again, and Baldwin began to hurry his steps towards the hall, where he hoped to find Simon and the Bishop. They were to meet there.

On the way, he saw a dapper man of about his own age, standing staring at the gateway with a perplexed frown. It took Baldwin a moment to recognise Jean de Poissy. Jean looked as though he was concentrating so hard, he would not have heard the thunder of a cannon shot.

Baldwin walked past him, debating whether to reintroduce himself, but finally decided against it.

He had been to the French castles many times when he was younger, because as a Templar, and one who was at a moderate level in the hierarchy, he had often travelled to deliver messages or join in diplomatic discussions, but he had still not lost that sense of awe at the great entrance to this castle. He passed under the massive archway, and into the broad open space within.

The castle had, so he recalled, been built as a bastion against the English and Normans under King Richard. Perhaps it was a memory of the perpetual warfare that was conducted in those days which had led the French King to seek to obliterate all the English territories held by him. In future, King Charles IV could hope to reign over a single, united country. Not that it would last for long. The kingdom was so riven by disputes between rival barons, that it must inevitably collapse. The more the French King sought to enforce his will on his powerful magnates, the more likely it was that France would suffer from a similar fate as England, where King

Edward had recently crushed resistance. But to attempt such a bold move here in France carried more risks. In England the rebels knew that internecine warfare was illegal, and all hesitated to raise a banner against the King. In France, Baldwin was less certain that a rebellious mob would be so easily quashed.

For now, though, he could revel in the beauty of this great white giant just outside the greatest French city.

He was making his way to the hall, when he heard a shout go up from a large building in front of him. There was a shriek, then a series of shouts, and a pair of young boys came pelting out, rushing past Baldwin and out through the main gate. He had little time to wonder whether their rapid disappearance was due to an errand, or whether it was a proof of some infraction, but the expression in their eyes had seemed to speak of terror.

A moment or two later, they were back, this time with Jean panting slightly in their wake. The three ran on to the hall, which Baldwin now recalled was the kitchen.

Intrigued, he followed them.

The kitchens gave out a blast of heat like no other. Four enormous fires roared, and it was only the height of the ceiling, and the pointed roof with its own chimney in the centre, which saved all the kitchen staff from suffocation. The hole at the top allowed the worst of the heat to escape.

All the staff were at the back of the room, surrounding the figure of Jean, who was crouching down and peering at something on the floor. Nearer Baldwin, a large, pink man stood wiping his hands on his apron mechanically. He had a long knife in his belt of cord, which led Baldwin to assume he was the master cook, and now he drew it out and began to systematically cut up some fruit, muttering to himself the while.

'It is not my fault. How can I be blamed for something like this? What did I do? All I did was threaten the little brute. Yes, I threatened him – so what? We all have to chivy and chide. It is the way of things.'

'Friend, is there some problem here?' Baldwin asked, as Wolf entered behind him and expressed an enthusiasm to get to know the carcasses of meat rather better. Baldwin prodded him away with a toe.

'Who're you?' the cook demanded, his knife gripped tightly, the point turned slightly in Baldwin's direction.

'Just a man who is worried that you may need some help in here,' Baldwin said, craning his neck to see what was happening behind.

'Why should we need help? I already have the city's Procureur with me!'

Hearing the voices, Jean looked up, frowning, and then recognised Sir Baldwin. 'Ah! The knight from the journey yesterday. I am glad for your offer of help, but this is nothing, merely a kitchen knave who has died.'

The man was firm in his speech, but his eyes told the lie. He was desperately sad at the death of the boy. It was endearing. Baldwin had seen too many dead bodies in his time, and he thought that this Jean looked like a man who felt much the same. Then Jean's eyes moved away from Baldwin and down to the small figure at his feet.

In front of Baldwin the cook's knife had not wavered. Baldwin said, 'I am sorry, my friend. Even knaves can be affectionate and all too greatly missed.'

'You think I miss one of my knaves?' the cook said. He looked up at Baldwin, and Baldwin saw the tears in his reddened eyes.

'When an accident happens and a young friend dies, it is not wrong to mourn.'

'This was no *accident*, knight. You want to see what happened to poor little Jehanin? My little Jo? Come!' He threw his knife down on the board in front of him.

The cook took Baldwin to the space in front of Jean and pointed down. The other kitchen workers were all about there, some few with their aprons held up to their mouths, some openly weeping.

In front of them was a large chest, and inside it lay a young boy. He was dead – Baldwin could see that at a glance. It was the colour, the greenish paleness of the face, the darkened flesh where the blood had sunk, the swollen belly and body where decomposition had set it. All this he took in and noted. Yet it was the sight of the leather thong about the boy's throat that shocked him. And the way that the man had to prise it away, where it had sunk into the flesh of the neck.

'In my land I have been known to seek murderers,' Baldwin said. 'I am what we call a Keeper of the King's Peace. I have the responsibility to hunt down those who threaten the realm and the rule of the law.'

'My name is Jean, as you know, and I am the Procureur here, the prosecutor. I investigate crimes and seek those responsible, and then challenge them in court,' Jean replied. He stood, feeling his old legs protesting. 'This is a terrible thing. Such a shame, to see so young a life snuffed like a candle.'

'But a candle may be relighted,' Baldwin agreed, staring down at the boy. 'He has lain here some while.'

'Yes. You may tell from the degree of swelling of the body. I had to work hard to remove this thong from where the flesh had engulfed it. Also there is the odour. It is sweet, *non*? Like old pork that has not been salted correctly.'

'Yes. What was he doing in the chest?'

'That is something the chef and his boys must tell us,' Jean said with determination. He looked up at Baldwin, and there was a degree of challenge in his eyes now. 'I shall go and enquire of them.'

Baldwin found himself quickly removed from the kitchen, dismissed. It was a novel experience.

Later, walking through the darkened streets, Jean ruminated on all he had seen. There was no one apparently who could tell him when the chest had been last opened. It was used to keep certain expensive spices locked away, but they had not been used in some while. The chest had only been opened today because the King had returned. In the days before his arrival, it had remained locked.

Jehanin had been a conscientious little fellow for the most part. A gullible lad, he was keen enough most of the time, and a danger to all at others, for he would go into a daydream about his old home or his mother at regular intervals, and then he would be perfectly capable of making a gravy with arsenic, or a jelly from red lead, without thinking. There was no malice in him, and whenever the cook had seen others trying to lead him into misbehaviour or fighting, he had robustly refused. If Jean had not known the cook to be a more than usually forthright man with maids in the area – for he had checked on his inclinations after meeting him that first time – he might have believed him capable of pederasty, but there was no evidence to support this.

And so, it would appear that a man had managed to kill the boy, and then threw him into the chest in the kitchen when no one was there. It would be easy enough, the cook had said. Any time of the night up until the later watches when the bread-makers arrived, the kitchen would be empty.

'And the chest? Would it have been locked?'

'Why, yes. But I sleep in the side room there, and someone could have come and removed my keys from beside my bed without waking me.'

'You do realise how this makes you look, Cook?' Jean had said sternly.

'What? Me sleeping there, me having the key to the chest, me being the one who shouted at him most, that sort of thing?'

Jean had grinned slightly at that. 'Well, yes. Why should I not think you guilty of this crime?'

'First, if you can find a single man to say that I beat the boys more than they deserve, the man's a liar; second, do you think I'm stupid enough to kill a boy and then hide him for some days, only bringing him into my own place of work when no one had already found him?'

'You mean he wasn't there for long?'

'I don't know. But he wasn't there when the King was still here. The chest was in use all the time until the King left the castle to go to meet his nephew. Ask any of the kitchen staff, they can all confirm that.'

'I thank you. I shall do so,' Jean had said.

And now he reflected on all he had heard. There was a great deal to absorb, though, and as the rain began to fall again, he started to hurry his steps.

Since the arrest of Nicholas the Stammerer, he had for some days walked cautiously with Stephen behind him, but in the last few days his caution had left him. Stephen was behind him, he knew, and that knowledge in itself was enough to make him confident.

Jacquot saw him approach from six hundred yards away. His hearing was not good, but his eyesight was adequate to recognise a man by his gait and bearing from many yards away, and today he recognised his quarry.

He eased himself out of sight in among some shadows at a doorway. The street was becoming quieter as men hurried home to avoid the curfew, and now he saw the Procureur's servant striding along. A strange man, this, with his vacant expression and loping walk, because Jacquot had heard him talking to his master, and there was clearly a good brain in his head. He probably enjoyed leading others to assume he had little in his skull.

There was no point in killing him. Jacquot's main ambition was to remove him as a threat. He couldn't allow him to prevent his assault on the other man, nor to cry out or alert him.

Jacquot waited silently as Jean walked past, head down, and it was not until Stephen passed by him that he sprang out. In his hand was a small leather sack with a clod of earth inside. Jacquot cast a look about him for anyone watching, and then took three swift steps and swung.

At the last moment, Stephen turned and saw him. He was about to shout – he got so far as to open his mouth – to warn his master, when the clod of earth struck his head. His legs wobbled and he toppled.

Jacquot did not stop. He had removed the guard, now his attack was safe. There was a bend in the lane coming up, and he dropped his chin, hurrying his pace, eyes fixed upon the target. Jean was a dark blur in the distance. A torch was alight at the corner, where a tradesman felt anxious about waylayers in the entrance to an alley, and the Procureur walked around the light, staring into the alleyway, aware of dangers.

There was another torch at the next entry, and Jacquot hurried his steps, bouncing high to reduce the sound of his approach. Jean appeared to pay no attention, but as they came close to the next alley, he walked away from the entrance again, staring in for any danger there.

He would never have seen Jacquot, who slid in between his back and the opposite wall, never have noticed the quick flash of the blade, and possibly, very possibly, he was dead before his brain had realised that the blade had been thrust home so expertly. All he knew was that a hand had grasped his breast for an instant, and then the sliver of steel, darkened over a candle flame, pressed down, and there was a sharp pain in his shoulder, his muscles, and then his heart . . . and Jacquot gripped his body as it collapsed, easing it gently into the shadows. The blade was released, the knife wiped twice, briefly, on Jean's shirt, and Jacquot muttered the *Pater Noster* as he watched the trembling of the corpse, listened to the rattling of the heels and heard the snoring of the last breath.

Then Jacquot rose and walked quickly up the lane to the next street. He was content. The job was done and he was about to become considerably wealthier.

Chapter Twenty

Feast of Archangel Michael[1]

Louvre, Paris

Baldwin and Simon enjoyed a quiet day. They participated in the Mass held in the castle's chapel, although Baldwin was keen to remove himself afterwards. There were many churches in Paris, he told Simon, and all were more elegant than this one in their appearance, more religious in their devotions, and a damned sight warmer to boot.

There was no doubt that the weather had changed now. Even the Duke wore a thicker tunic and a cloak lined with a band of glorious tan fur. It was that time of year when a man stopped thinking about what might be fashionable, and set his heart on more practical wear.

The Queen was ever religious, of course, and Baldwin was sure that she would be spending her day of rest reading some of the Gospels and remaining quiet until the hour of the meals. Meanwhile, he determined that Simon and he would take their ease among the streets of Paris.

'It is a great city, this, Simon. One of the very finest the world can show us. All about you there are magnificent buildings, as befits the city of Philip Augustus and Charles Martel. There are few in the world who could equal the exploits of those two.'

---

[1] Sunday, 29 September 1325

'Who was Charles Martel?' Simon asked.

'Martel was a great warrior. It was he who stopped the Moslem invasions of the Christian lands. If not for him, the Saracens might even now rule France, Simon. And if that, what would have prevented them from overrunning England too? He met them in a battle at Tours, which is where they were stopped, and Martel pushed them back until they were over the other side of the Spanish March. Then he turned his attention to the Germans, and fought them until they were kept away over the Weser, and brought safety and stability to the northern borders too. That was all many hundreds of years ago, but we owe our Christian faith to him, in large part. God chose him to protect His lands.'

Simon was wearing a sceptical expression.

'At all times, the French have been the guardians of our religion,' Baldwin added helpfully. 'Philip Augustus was the first Holy Roman Emperor. He conquered all the heathens and created the Christian lands we know today.'

Simon grunted.

'Come, Simon, at least attempt a display of interest. I have been forced to learn much in order to entertain you today.'

'Oh, this is new to you?'

'Not entirely,' Baldwin grinned.

Simon grimaced. 'I am worried, Baldwin, and walking about here will not help.'

'What troubles you? Is it Meg?'

'Yes. Every moment I spend over here I begrudge. I want to be at home again. I am anxious that she could be in danger, or at the least, fearful of attack from Despenser and his men.'

Baldwin was about to make a comment when there was a loud roar. 'There you are! I was lookin' for you both. You going out for a walk about the city? Excellent. I will be with you in a moment.'

'Sweet Jesus,' Simon groaned.

'Do not be so antisocial, Simon,' Baldwin said. 'The good Sir Richard de Welles is a kindly man, and he is a loyal servant, too.'

'My head has experienced enough misery caused by him already,' Simon muttered.

'And he brings our Duke, too,' Baldwin said.

It was true. As Simon turned to look, he saw the young heir to the throne walking a little in front of Sir Richard. Behind them both was the tutor, Richard of Bury, and a short distance further back, Sir Henry de Beaumont.

'Had to think of a reason to get the Duke out of that place,' Sir Richard confided to Simon later. 'Didn't want him closeted with that snake de Beaumont. No telling what the man might get up to.'

He was worried, but so was Baldwin. There was a real risk that this embassy to France could be fracturing along a number of lines: those loyal to the Queen, those loyal to the King, those loyal to the King's son. And in that environment, he was sure, the only certain loser would be the son.

Sir Henry had fallen back as they walked among the great buildings and crossed the bridge to the Île de la Cité. Here Richard of Bury began to expound on the history of France and of the great cathedral of Notre-Dame. Simon listened with half an ear, Baldwin saw, and gradually he himself fell back until he was next to Sir Henry.

'Sir Henry, what do you think of this?' he asked.

'It is a splendid memorial to that marvellous Lady.'

Baldwin nodded. 'She must be proud to be so praised. Few women can expect such glory.'

'Few indeed.'

Baldwin glanced across at him. The knight was quiet, but every so often he cast a sidelong look at Baldwin as though wishing he could speak his mind without fear.

At last, as the Duke and Sir Richard strode on ahead, Richard of Bury drawing their attention to some new decoration or another aspect of the cathedral, Sir Henry de Beaumont said quickly, 'A word, Sir Baldwin?'

'If you wish.'

'There is much wrong with our kingdom. In past times, barons have risen up against their ruler when that ruler became less than deserving of their total support.'

He paused hopefully, clearly anticipating some comment from Baldwin, but the knight merely nodded agreement without speaking.

'Of course, at the time, many of them were looked upon as disloyal. But there is a higher loyalty, is there not? To the Crown itself, and not to the mere figure of the man who wears it at any particular time. You and I, Sir Baldwin, we have both made our own oaths, have we not? To the Crown and to—'

'The King. And yes, it is a matter of honour that we uphold those oaths,' Baldwin said uncompromisingly.

'Can we? Can *you*? You know what that man Despenser is doing to people all over the kingdom, Sir Baldwin! Men and women, kidnapped, murdered, their estates broken up, their children orphaned, their inheritances stolen – and all while the King looks on without compassion or care. So long as his friend Sir Hugh le Despenser is safe and happy, he is happy too. Is it any way to rule the nation? The people deserve better, Sir Baldwin. They deserve the rule of law!'

'And you would impose this rule of law by breaking the most important rule of loyalty? You would impose it by breaking with your King?' Baldwin said with heat. 'What kind of rule would you put in its place? A tyranny of another sort, no doubt. What credence can I put in the judgement of a man who would contemplate removal of the legitimate King placed there by God Himself?'

'You mean you would prefer to see the Despenser there at the seat of government?'

'Of course not! The man's insanely avaricious.'

'His greed is without limit. He will not be satisfied until he has consumed the whole of the kingdom.'

'Perhaps so, but that is no reason for me to prove disloyal to the King. I will not.'

'Without the aid of men like you, what will happen to the kingdom? What will there be left for the Duke? What will there be left for the people of our island?'

Sir Henry had stopped now. He was speaking with all the passion and persuasion he could muster, and Baldwin could not stare into his eyes without feeling a compulsion to agree.

He stared up at the cathedral. 'Sir Henry, our people have lived through the depredations of the Vikings, through the invasion of the Normans, and will survive any number of trials caused by the King and his friends. If you say, do I think that there is a better way to rule, then I would have to agree. If you suggest that the Despenser is uniquely venal and vile, I would have to agree. But if you say that there is only one manner in which the country can be saved, and that it involves removing our King, I would have to reject that. I will not agree to the proposition that a man has a right to rise against his lawfully anointed King. That way lies insanity.'

'Perhaps. But if it does, it is a more wholesome and rational insanity than the madness which we suffer right now. The rule of law is broken, Sir Baldwin. The men whom Despenser has deprived are wandering, landless, shiftless, and hopeless. They rob and break into homes for food, and the more confident the Despenser grows, the more he steals, and the more wandering men there are with no money, no hope. It is a tragedy for the whole kingdom, Sir Baldwin, and you propose to stand by and watch it unfold, doing nothing to protect those who most need our support?'

'And whom would you put in the King's place?' Baldwin snapped. 'Another knight who desired an earldom? A knight who desired nothing for himself, so he could be all the more malleable to another hand? Or another? Who would you have sit on the throne and accept a sip from this poisoned chalice?'

'There is another already.' Sir Henry's eyes flicked towards the Duke, standing with Sir Richard and his tutor.

'You would have that child put on his throne? And who then would hold the power? Oh, you sound so plausible, Sir Henry, but all you suggest is false! A boy of not yet fourteen on the throne of England? He would need a man with great power and authority behind him to maintain the Crown, and that man would have to fight all those who were against him and wanted a return to the old system. You would have the boy risk his life to protect your hide for a few years?'

Now he had come to his point, Sir Henry spoke swiftly. 'There is a way. If his mother were prepared to protect her son and see that he was given a smooth ride to the throne, then all would be well. I say we should remove the Despenser, and if necessary – only if necessary – remove the King as well, and have the Duke installed under the wise direction of his own mother and a small council. All to govern in the interests of the nation. That would be best.'

'Of course – if you wish civil war to lay waste to the majority of the island. Are you mad? Do you seriously believe that you can persuade enough barons to agree to this lunacy? You would have war in moments of the boy being placed on the throne.'

'Do you think we are so foolish, Sir Baldwin—' Sir Henry

began. The words choked him in his throat, and he paused and looked away. When he met Baldwin's gaze once more, there were tears in his eyes, and he spoke more slowly, more quietly. 'Do you think that you alone have any honour and integrity? Do you think you possess a monopoly of chivalry? I tell you this, Sir Baldwin, if there was any other way I could see to remove the Despenser and have the realm return to peace, I would wholeheartedly pursue it. If I could believe that the King would rid himself of this canker, I would remain content. If there was some evidence that he would once again return to enjoy the affections of his wife, I would be joyful. In Christ's name, do you think that I want to ruin the realm? But look at it, Sir Baldwin! *I urge you: look at it sensibly!* What other action can be taken, than the forcible removal of Sir Hugh le Despenser and, if necessary, the removal of the King himself. The realm is dissolving before our eyes, and you want to quibble about a chivalric ideal!'

'Do not think to lecture me, Sir Henry!' Baldwin spat. 'I was fighting for Christianity against heathens in the Holy Land while you were yet in training with wooden swords! I learned my catechism in the Siege of Acre. I have seen what happens when a kingdom collapses, I have received the buffets of fate already. And you dare to accuse me? I am older than you, and if there is one thing I have learned in my life, it is that it is better to support the ruler, no matter what. As soon as the ruler is toppled, all suffer. And I will not be a part of any alliance which seeks to overthrow the man to whom I have given my oath.'

'Then may God forgive you, Sir Baldwin. Because I do not think that many others will.'

Later, when the Duke and his tutor and Sir Henry had returned to speak with the Queen, and Simon and Sir Richard had rejoined Baldwin, Simon was surprised to see how sombre he was.

'Do you feel all right?'

'I am quite well. But I am fearful.'

'I thought that was my province,' Simon said with dry sarcasm.

'Perhaps today I feel the need of some anxiety of my own.'

'Was it the whippersnapper?' Sir Richard asked. 'I saw him havin' a word all quiet, like, and wondered what that was about.'

'Yes,' Baldwin said quietly. He glanced about him. 'If the King sought to protect himself and his son by having Sir Henry and others here to serve him, I fear that the ploy has failed.'

There was no need to explain. All three understood the dangers. 'What does this mean for us?' Simon asked after a moment.

'That we may well be entering very dangerous territory, Simon. If there is to be some form of assault on the Crown, all those who have proved loyal to it must inevitably be endangered. And that means you, me, and our families.'

Simon closed his eyes for a moment, lost in his own private fear. He saw in his mind's eye his home, emptied and desolate, his wife and son on the road with a handcart holding their few possessions . . . and he saw himself. His head on a spike at London Bridge, along with all those of other men considered traitors. There would be no life of honour for his son. His wife, his lovely Meg, would die in poverty, bemoaning her fate, perhaps blaming her husband for the misery to which she was subjected. There was nothing else for his family, he knew, if he was labelled as a traitor by some new administration.

'Aye?' Sir Richard belched. 'And so what? Eh? Come, Sir Baldwin. You're old enough to have lived through worse times than this, eh? If some lyin' bastards try to steal the kingdom, they may succeed, and they may fail, but they won't bother with the likes of us. They'll be worrying about all the rich fellows first. Don't you worry, Bailiff. You'll be all right too. You're little better than a churl so far as these mighty lordings are concerned. And you know what they do respect? Loyal service, man. Anyone who tries to take the Crown will want all those like you to be on their side in the future. So, me friends, don't worry yourselves, but drink up! And let's have a toast to the stability of government, eh?'

But even as Sir Richard hefted his great quart pot and urged them to do the same, Baldwin saw his true feelings in his eyes. Sir Richard, for all his protestations of ease, was more worried than Simon and Baldwin.

Chapter Twenty-One

Outside north-west Paris

Hélias had a client who had stayed with her all night, one of her long-standing men, as she liked to call him, and she had just bade him farewell at the door when the whisper on the street reached her ears.

'What's all this?' she demanded. Bernadette, one of her girls, a buxom brunette with eyes of startling emerald, stopped talking to her cully and turned, ashen-faced, to Hélias.

'The Procureur, Hélias. He's dead.'

'Don't talk stupid, wench. Who'd kill him?' she scoffed.

'There are a few who'd like to remove a man like him,' the client said. He was a flash fellow, with bright yellow and scarlet clothing, apart from an old cowl of faded green. He had been digging in his purse, and now he lifted a coin with the demeanour of a man who had performed a magnificent conjuring trick. 'Ah! An hour of your time, girl!'

Hélias rudely shoved him from her path. 'Be still! Tell me, who could have done this? Has anyone confessed?' She was torn between scorn and the dawning horror that Jean might actually be dead.

'No, of course not. What, you think someone would kill Poissy and then rush to the officers and roar, "It's me! I did it!"'

'You, Bernadette, get inside and fetch the other girls. She can do you later, man. For now, you want to have her for free?'

The man's eyes were fixed on the girl's bouncing figure as she hurried inside to get the other girls. 'Is this a trick?'

'No. I want to know who killed my friend.' Hélias took a shuddering breath. 'Anyone who can bring me information about him will be rewarded – and you will be first. If you go to all the taverns in the city – start with those nearest to where he died, and then go to the farther ones – you can have her for free, and any of her friends you like. You understand me?'

The man nodded wildly.

'Good, then *go*! Now, Bernadette, where the hell are you?' Hélias bawled.

Louvre

The Bishop had slept well, but upon waking he felt as unrefreshed as ever. He rolled in his bed, grunting and grumbling until he rose from the mattress and made his way over the floor. There was a jug and bowl on the table at the window, and he threw open the shutters, staring out into the castle's courtyard.

For all his life, he had been a servant. At first he was merely a servant of the Church, and as a student, he had proved adequately to himself how important learning was to the youthful mind. Later, when he became a Bishop, he had decided to take more interest in other spheres of public life, and especially the government of the realm.

There were many who decided to go into politics in order to enhance their own position or to enrich themselves. In Christ's name, he had known many of them himself: from the slovenly, dull-witted fools who thought themselves so grand if they could but earn a few pounds without work, to those myriads who were callow, corrupt and venal. It was an astonishment that the realm ever succeeded in anything. And a miracle that its enemies had thus far failed to destroy it.

He knew that he had acquired an unenviable reputation. Many loathed him because they thought he was a thief who had stolen taxes in order to endow himself with wines and fine foods. In London he was especially detested for the Eyre which he had been instructed to hold into all the customs of the city. It had been held at the King's order, but that was no consolation to the folk there. They hated him, and made it clear enough to him that, were he without the King's protection, his life would be worth little.

The irony was, his motives were pure. He had been a loyal servant of the Crown, seeking to increase the efficiency of the system of taxes so that less was wasted, less was stolen, and less was merely misplaced. Instituting a new system of records had made a vast difference to the King's ability to collect his revenues, and thereby had helped to protect the kingdom. The King could now fight wars which required large investment. There was always a need for money, and now the King had it. All that, Bishop Stapledon knew, was because of *his* hard efforts – no one else's.

And he had not used one single penny to feather his own nest. That was an easy allegation to make, he knew. Standing at the basin, he filled it with water, washing his face and armpits, round the back of his neck, and then peered into the water as it smoothed over, the ripples and distortions fading. In the makeshift mirror he saw his face. Older than it should appear, he thought, longer and more haggard. He had none of the colour he used to have; all was washed away with the worry and trials of journeying and negotiating – or trying to.

A drip ran from his chin and splashed in the middle of his reflection, and it was gone. Suddenly he had a premonition that this was how his own life would be. One day he would still be here, hale, hearty – maybe even happy. And the next, he would be gone. Eradicated so effectively that he might never have existed. Who would remember him a month after his death? A year? Nobody after a few tens of years, surely. The Canons of his cathedral would recognise his name, presumably, and perhaps the work he had undertaken at the Exchequer would ensure that he was not instantly forgotten in government, but beyond that, there would be little enough to show that he had ever lived. That he had breathed the air, that he had worked so hard to make other lives better. Nor that he had come on this latest perilous mission, risking his life in service to his King.

Drying his face on the towel by the basin, Walter Stapledon felt an unaccountable sadness washing over him. He was very lonely here in France. Everyone hated him for his support of his King against their Isabella. But what else was a man to do, other than support his King? It was every subject's duty to do as he had. He knew that, and he could not regret it. He *would* not.

Pulling his robe on, and shrugging the heavy material to drape more evenly over his shoulders, he mused a little about the state of his own life.

The matter of the little man the day before rankled. There had been no excuse for his ridiculous display of petty arrogance. He decided he would have to pray for some humility and a little calmness. It was quite wrong, to jump at a man merely because he was watching him.

Yet his mood would not go away. He had been anxious ever since the harridan Isabella had responded to him so rudely in front of the French King's entire court. It had been shocking to find her speaking to him in that manner. Shocking and unreasonable. And disquieting.

He was still aware of that feeling of anxiety as he walked down the stairs and along the passageway to the courtyard at midday with two of his clerics. Morning Mass had taken the edge off his sense of unhappiness, but not the feeling of being a stranger in an enemy's camp. Today it would have been enough for him to see only one friendly face to make him throw off his grim presentiment of evil, but there was nobody he recognised. He searched among the men standing about – and then he saw Sir Henry de Beaumont.

'Come,' he said to his clerks and servants, his *familia*, and crossed the yard to Sir Henry, a smile on his face.

To his surprise there was no reciprocal joy on the face of the knight when he saw the Bishop approach.

'Sir Henry. I hope I see you well?'

'Well enough, Bishop.'

There was a curtness in his manner which was unlike the suave knight whom Stapledon had met in England. Sir Henry was an ally of some months, and had always been polite. Now, he was short to the point of rudeness, and the Bishop could feel his hackles rise. However, before he could make any further comment or enquire as to the reasons for his changed attitude, there was a series of cries from the gateway, and some new visitors arrived.

One was a short, black-haired man with the build of a church's column. His thighs alone were the size of a small tree-trunk, and the width of his shoulders was proof of great strength. He had blue eyes, permanently lazily lidded, that peered about him, and looked as though he had a smile that was always ready to intrude.

The second man was taller, with the long, gangly arms and legs of a youth. His face was darker, but not swarthy, and he had a mild expression, rather like so many young men the Bishop had seen in different villages over the years. He looked like one of those who suffered from less brainpower than he deserved.

A tall fellow went to speak with them, a grizzled old

veteran of many of the French King's wars, from the look of him. He spoke briefly to them, and then cast an eye about the place, beckoning two guards and a messenger.

'What is this?' Baldwin asked, appearing behind the Bishop's shoulder.

'I have no idea,' Bishop Walter said, shooting him a look. Behind him Stapledon saw Simon and Sir Richard de Welles. Simon gave him a grin, which was so comforting, the Bishop felt suddenly almost weak with gratitude after the rudeness displayed by Sir Henry.

The old fellow had been seen by the gatekeeper, who was talking to him and the other two now. All four appeared to be speaking very swiftly, and the gatekeeper held up both hands suddenly, stopping all further discussion, before jerking his chin and then pointing, shouting one word as he did so. '*Là! Là!*'

He was pointing at the Bishop and Baldwin.

There was an inevitability about the progress of such an investigation, as they both knew. Simon was not articulate in colloquial French, although he had not found it difficult to make his desires known, but Baldwin was entirely fluent and comfortable with the language.

The Bishop, as befitted a man who had spent so much time abroad from his earliest years as the chaplain to Pope Clement V, and later on diplomatic service for the King, spoke French like a native, as he was able to demonstrate now with some gusto.

'You suggest *what*! You dare to accuse me, the Bishop of Exeter, of a murder? You say that I would waylay an innocent on some road I have never travelled, and for what? In order to repay some perceived slight? Do you think a man of God has no scruple? Is that how you view your clergymen in France today? When I was last here, man, I was viewed with respect, and now you tell me I am the suspect in a murder inquest?'

'I think, my Lord Bishop . . .' Baldwin began, but the furious Bishop held up a hand peremptorily and he subsided.

'This is not merely a gross insult to me, it is a shameful insult to my liege Lord, the King of England. It is also an insult to Queen Isabella, whose servant and guardian I am while I am here, and to the Holy Mother Church, and a deliberate insult to the Pope himself. I am shocked and appalled that this kind of accusation could be considered, let alone that it could be actually posed to me.'

The two men were standing before him. The shorter was still grinning, and Baldwin kept his gaze fixed upon him, because in his experience, men who wore that kind of look were usually smiling with their mouths only; however, this one appeared to be genuinely enjoying himself. He could, of course, be that rarity among officials, Baldwin thought, a man who could conceal his true motives and aims even from his own eyes. That sort of man was exceedingly rare – and enormously dangerous.

'My Lord Bishop, we have made no accusations. I would obviously not wish to suggest that you could be guilty of anything so foul as this simple waylaying of a pair of men on their way home. And yet, we have already heard from Arnaud and others of your argument with the Procureur – and yesterday he died. What was it that you accused him of?'

'I accused him of nothing. I was tired and irritable after a very long ride, and I was surprised to find myself being observed when I arrived here to the Louvre.'

They were in the great hall now. The only aspect which gave Baldwin some satisfaction was the fact that the King of France and Isabella were not present. However, both must have their own spies here in the chamber. In truth, Baldwin was not sure any longer who was loyal to King Edward, and who was more devoted to Isabella. Those whom the King had selected to travel with the Queen and their son were all, so far as Baldwin could tell, becoming increasingly devoted to the Queen, at the expense of any commitment to the King himself.

The Bishop was almost spitting with rage. 'You dare to accuse me, then? This is what diplomatic protection means, is it? That I can be dragged here against my will and forced to answer these ridiculous questions? I shall not! If you wish to speak to me, you will need the sanction of the Pope himself, and I will write to him myself explaining the ludicrous position into which you have cast me. To think that I, a Bishop, could be accused of such dishonour, is a disgrace!'

There was a quiet soughing at the back of the room, Baldwin noticed. He peered over the heads of the men encircling the Bishop, and saw a group of people passing through the crowds.

'Make way for Queen Isabella!' was suddenly bellowed, and Baldwin saw Lord John Cromwell appear, a staff of office in his hands. Immediately behind him was the Queen, and Cromwell stood aside as the Queen arrived in the open space. Whether by design or fortune, she had appeared at the side of the two officers of the city, staring in a confrontational manner at the Bishop.

'My Lord Bishop, what is this?'

'I am the victim of a dreadful injustice, my Lady. These men have heard of a minor altercation I had with a man the day we came from Vincennes, and now seek to accuse me of that man's murder.'

'Is this true?' she demanded.

'No, my Lady. The Bishop here is upset that we have sought to ask him about the dead man. He was, you see . . .' and here the man hesitated, clearing his throat. Baldwin, studying him closely, was sure that he saw a tear or two in his eye. 'He was a good man, diligent in all he did, and widely respected. And now he is dead – only one day after a small dispute with you, my Lord Bishop. It seems a coincidence, you see?'

Baldwin saw the Bishop's perturbation in the way that he chewed at his lip. It was unlike Walter Stapledon to be at all distraught, and Baldwin began to understand the pressure he felt.

In the last months Baldwin had been let down by the Bishop. The man had proved himself to be unreliable, untrustworthy, and more a vassal to Despenser than friend to Simon and himself. And yet there were strong bonds which united them.

The Bishop looked to Baldwin, and there was a mute appeal in his eyes. Baldwin felt his heart begin to pound rather painfully, but he could not refuse that plea.

'Let the good Bishop leave, friends,' he said, stepping forward. 'I have some experience in seeking murderers. Let me help you.'

Chapter Twenty-Two

Paris

Jacquot walked into the chamber and was surprised to see that the King had the same wench as before draped over his arm. This one must be more durable than most, he thought to himself. As he eyed her, she rolled over slightly, and her dark eyes were on him from beneath a tumbled mess of black hair.

However, at that moment his attention was concentrated more on the mood of the men in the room than on her. The atmosphere was edgy. He could see that one in particular – perhaps a friend of the Stammerer? – was staring at him angrily. The King himself was mild in manner, but there was something in his eye that put Jacquot on his guard. Not that he allowed it to show in his face or his actions.

'You owe me for the two jobs,' Jacquot announced.

'Ah, so the Procureur is dead?'

'You know he is. All Paris is talking of it,' Jacquot said flatly.

'And the second?'

'The Stammerer. The one you sent to do my work.'

He was right. The man at the edge of the room was practically foaming at the mouth. It was quite amusing, really.

'I see. So you want me to pay you for the removal of one of my friends?'

'You commanded his execution. You owe me for it.'

'And what would an executioner demand for the death of

his friend – the same fee as usual? Poor young Nicholas hardly deserved his end, did he?'

'I gave him the fastest ending a man could hope for,' Jacquot said with silky calmness. There was a serenity about him as he settled on his legs, waiting.

'Perhaps you would like the same?' the King sneered.

Jacquot saw it coming. There was a shadow in the corner of his eye, and he ducked to avoid it. It was a mace, only a smallish, tubular one, perhaps an inch in diameter, and six inches long, with nail-like spikes protruding, but set on a shaft of beech two feet long, there was enough momentum in it to crush his head like an apple. It swept over him, one spike catching his shoulder as the man tried to change his point of aim, and the pain burned.

He was up, turning as he rose, his dagger already out and thrusting. It plunged into the man's gut, and he ripped it upwards, his left hand grabbing the man's mace-hand as it crashed into the wall. Then the mace was his, and the attacker was on the ground.

Whirling, he brought the mace around, clenched in his left hand, the dagger slick and slippery in his right, and a man shrieked with pain as the iron spikes tore into his forearm, the massive weight shattering the slender bones, ripping through the flesh and peeling it away, from his elbow to his wrist.

Another was at his side. He could not swing the mace in time. Instead he dropped his stance, his right knee bending, and thrust with all his body's mass behind the dagger's point, straight at the fellow's groin. The blade skidded on the man's thigh-bone, and a gush of blood proved he had hit the artery, before there was a snap like a small cannon-shot hitting a wall, and the man's tendon was gone. He slumped, sobbing, his hands over his wrecked body, and the blood pumped in a steady flow from between his fingers.

Jacquot continued the whirl, and rose slowly from his crouch, the dagger held up at his breast, the mace high, in the overhand guard. Two more men stood at the walls, but they did not challenge him. The King himself was still lying on his cushions, the wench at his side breathing a little faster, her little pink tongue touching her upper lip, her eyes bright with excitement. So that was how she survived, Jacquot thought to himself. He had never liked women with a taste for violence, but it explained the woman's longevity.

'My money,' he said again.

The King glanced at him, and now there was a chilly dispassion in his gaze. 'What do you think, Amélie? Should he have it or not?'

'No,' she said. She rolled a little to study him more closely. He could look along the length of her body, and she saw his gaze, lifting an arm to make her breast tighten, an invitation. She was breathing faster, but it was not fear, he saw. No, rather it was a sexual excitement. She had been thrilled to see the men fighting. Women like that made Jacquot feel sick.

'She says I should keep my money,' the King said.

Jacquot glanced about him, then gripped his knife more tightly, and stepped on the King's foot. 'Then I'll cut off each toe. That will be payment enough for now.'

He set the blade at the first, the little toe of the right foot, and began to press.

'All right, you bastard! Yes, you can have it, but let me go!'

He pointed to the man furthest from the door out. This was not one of his protectors, but one of his counting-men. The King maintained several who were escaped clerics, renegades who sought to avoid a life of boredom by joining his little group. The sad fact was, few if any realised what a life of excitement might entail. This fellow was a youth of only some two-and-twenty summers. He was about the age Jacquot's son would have been, had he lived.

Dropping his foot and walking to the lad, Jacquot held out his hand. It still held the dagger, and he realised it made him look intimidating. He did not care. The mace was a dead weight in his hand, so he tossed that to the wall, and reached out with his left hand for the purse the boy held.

He saw the movement in the boy's eye. It was tiny, just a fleeting glimpse of a reflection, but it was enough to send him diving to his left, and the weapon missed him completely.

At the floor, he rolled swiftly, and just missed the second blow. It was a war-hammer, an evil tool, with a great square lump of steel on one side, a four-inch spike on the reverse, and a sharpened blade protruding from the head for a good six-inches which held a razor-edge. The man wielding it was, short, but heavy, and his eyes were quick and alert. This wasn't one of the King's young drunks, but a wary and competent opponent.

Jacquot sprang to his feet, regretting his confidence in reaching for the money. He should have been more cautious. The blade waved in front of him, the two edges of steel catching the light as it moved. Each had a quarter inch of rebate where the man had whetted it, and it held Jacquot's attention like a snake as it wove from side to side, in and out. And stabbed.

Close, so close. He had only just moved in time. And now he was running out of space to reverse further. The hammer was set on a long shaft, and gave the man an extra three feet of reach. Jacquot needed a weapon with similar length, or some other means of attacking. He was not near the door, and all about him were the bodies of the men he had beaten off. Their groans were dismal in his ears, making him wonder if his own would soon join theirs.

No. He was not ready to die. Not yet. He felt a foot slip, and could smell the odours of death about him. There was the tinny, metallic scent of blood, the foulness of faeces where death had relieved one of the contents of his bowels. Without glancing down, he knew that the floor was dangerous here.

Without considering, he took a couple of quick steps back, and allowed the hammer-man to chase him, and then reversed his dagger quickly, letting it flick up in the air, before catching it by the point. Then he drew his hand back and let it fly straight at the man's groin.

Some would flinch to see a blade whirling towards his face. Many would duck or slip to the side – but there was no man who could prevent himself from trying to avoid a weapon aimed at his manhood. This fellow was no different. His hammer was pointing at Jacquot, but when the dagger was released, the hammer was withdrawn as he tried to knock it away with the shaft nearer his right hand. The hammer was away, and Jacquot did not wait to see where his dagger struck, or even if it did. He sprang at the man, grasping the shaft too. Their feet scrabbled on the bloody floor, and then the fellow was forced back, his legs flew away from him, and he landed badly on his back. His dagger was on the floor, but Jacquot still had his thin blade. Except he couldn't reach it while also holding this shaft. And if he released it, he was sure the man would kill him in an instant. All he could do was fight. He head-butted the man, he kicked, kneed, bit and butted again. The man was not going to relinquish the hammer, but neither would Jacquot. In the dark, lying among the blood and the shit, the two scrambled for the better purchase, both desperate to win control, both knowing that the one to weaken must die.

And then his knee hit something. It was his dagger. With a last convulsion that felt as though it must tear all the muscles of his back and shoulders, Jacquot heaved at the hammer. The shaft moved up just slightly, enough, and Jacquot bent his legs, and then leaped with them as high as he could. He came down with both knees bent, pulling against the hammer's shaft to bring himself as hard as possible into the man's belly.

It worked. There was a foul gasp of agony as his knees hit the man's lower gut and groin, and then he gave a keening shriek while trying to protect himself.

Jacquot didn't care. He snatched up his blade, and now thrust it twice, thrice, four times, into the man's upper chest. There was a long, rattling noise, a harsh hacking that seemed to tear at the man's breast, and then nothing.

'You seem to have destroyed all my guards,' the King said.

Jacquot hefted the hammer in his hands. It would have been easy to kill him, but there was no point. It would prove nothing. It would not even make him any safer. As soon as the King was known to be dead, Jacquot would become one of those who would never be trusted in another gang, a man who was safer if eradicated. The King would not waste good money on killing him. There was no profit in it. But if the King was dead, others would likely decide to dispense with Jacquot as well as his services.

He walked to the cleric who watched him with eyes made luminous with terror. Gently he eased the purse from the boy's fingers, and hefted it. 'I hope it's all there,' he said grimly. He surveyed the floor. 'You really should think about cleaning up this place. It stinks in here.'

'Tell the lad on the door, Peter the peasant, to get in here and clean this lot away,' the King said without interest. He was already fondling his wench, who writhed under his hands with a passion Jacquot had not seen her exhibit before.

Jacquot nodded. And then he kicked the King as hard as he could in the face. He heard the woman gasp, and it was not from horror.

'Never try those tricks on me again, King. And never renege on a business arrangement again. Next time I will give you so much pain, you will wonder that the life has not left your body.'

The King tried to speak, but his mashed lips would not respond. He bent and spat out a shard of tooth. And then, as Jacquot stepped back to leave the room, he saw the wench gentling the King and licking at the blood on his lips with a smile on her face.

Chapter Twenty-Three

Louvre

'Where did he die?' Baldwin asked.

The short man was called Pons, he had learned, and now he and Simon were ensconced on a large bench while Pons and his companion, who turned out to be a quiet, self-effacing man called Vital, sat on stools at the other side of the table at the little tavern near the Louvre's gates. Sir Richard had joined them as soon as he heard of the accusations against the Bishop, while Sir Henry de Beaumont had been asked to stay with the Duke and keep His Highness close to the Queen and her guards. The Bishop himself was remaining in self-imposed solitude in his chamber, away from the gaze of those who accused him with their eyes.

'The Procureur was struck down a few streets north and a little east of here.'

'His purse?'

'Still on his belt.'

'And witnesses?'

'None whatever. At least, none who admit to seeing it.'

'He was alone?'

'No, he had his man with him, but the evil son of a Basque whore managed to have the man knocked on the head before killing poor Jean.'

'His servant is alive?'

'Yes.'

'Good. Perhaps he will remember something?'

'When he can see straight and stop vomiting, perhaps,' Pons said, permitting himself a faint smile.

Baldwin nodded. 'This was no random attack, you think?'

'No. It was premeditated. I am sure of it.'

Now Vital spoke up. He had a soft, singsong quality to his voice. 'Jean was a most effective prosecutor. The city knew him well, and especially all those who live in the twilight. You know? The men who live and work and struggle in the alleys and cellars and rarely come up into the daylight.'

Baldwin looked at him briefly. There was a poetical turn to the man's speech. 'An assassination, then?'

'It is how it looks,' Pons said. He looked at his companion, then at Baldwin with a vague shrug. 'There are few enough who'll help us to seek out the killers.'

'And yet you accuse a good Bishop whose sole offence is that he was in the same city?'

'No. I will seek out and question all those who have ever shown any dislike for Jean. Any man who has had a dispute with him recently, any who has shown him disrespect, and any who has been arrested or found himself on the wrong side of Jean in recent years – all will be questioned.'

'I wish to speak with his servant,' Baldwin said.

'That can be arranged,' Pons said.

Jean le Procureur's house

The rooms to which they brought Simon and Baldwin were set in a rougher part of the city, over towards the eastern gate.

Simon had never been to this part of Paris before. He was made to feel quite at home with the close-built dwellings, their jetties reaching out overhead just as they did in London. However, this was not an area of wealth and easiness. There were on every side the signs of people striving and failing to earn enough to live on. The doors were of timber that was rotting; hinges were rusted or bent; windows had broken shutters; the roadway itself was lacking many cobbles, and the path was puddled and filthy with shit and the stench of urine.

Yet for all that, there was a certain atmosphere among the people who lived there. Women shouted and cackled, young urchins ran barefoot, giggling and shouting, and even the men seemed to be cheerful enough.

'Ha! Not a bad part of the city,' Sir Richard considered. He stood looking about him with a satisfied smile, thumbs in his belt. His eye was drawn like a bee to honey to the small tavern only a few doors away.

'It is not as poor as some districts,' was Pons's comment. 'There are people here with a reasonable income. They may not be so rich as the merchants down nearer the river, but they are better off than many others.'

'This was his?' Simon asked when they stopped outside a house and knocked.

'Yes. This is where the Procureur used to live,' Vital said shortly.

'His servant is here?' Baldwin asked.

It was Pons who responded. 'For now. I don't know where he'll go when he's better.'

A watchman opened the door, a surly, ill-favoured man with a cast in his eye and a developing hunch-back. He took them up to a clean, bright solar where they found the servant. He was clearly not going to be leaving any time soon.

He lay on a good bed, and Baldwin assumed that in the absence of his master, the servant was installed in his master's bed.

This Stephen was a very tall man, and well built. That much was obvious from the way that his feet were close to overhanging the bottom of the bed while his head rested on the wall.

However it was clear that he had not always been known for his honour and integrity. His upper lip was split – a common enough punishment for criminals in Paris, Baldwin knew.

'You were the servant to the Procureur, I hear?' he began his questioning.

'There was no one else would take me, Sieur.'

'You were guilty of some offence here?'

'Yes. I was a successful felon, I fear. However, Master Jean rescued me.'

'How so?' Baldwin said.

'He met me in the street and beat the living daylights out of me. From that moment I thought it was preferable to work for him, than against.'

'It didn't help him two days ago, friend.'

A cloud passed over the servant's face. 'No.'

'What do you remember?'

'Of that evening? We were walking back as usual. My master often had me walk with him, because this is a dangerous city, just as any other.'

'You were at his side? A little behind him? What?'

'I was some thirty paces behind. My master was concerned because some short while ago he was almost killed by a man in the street. He felt sure that his life was at risk. And for that reason he wished me to remain some way behind him, so that if I saw a man try to assail him, I would have the space to attack, but the assailant himself might not realise that I was there.'

'And yet the assassin clearly did know you were there – that was why he knocked you down so swiftly.'

'It may be so.'

Sir Richard fixed the man with a steady gaze. 'Did you see the assailant? Did you recognise him?'

'No. I neither saw nor recognised him. If I did, there is nothing would keep me here in my bed,' Stephen said.

'Then can you tell us who it was your master was afraid of?'

'Sieur Jean was working on a strange affair at the Louvre,' Stephen said, and explained about the body of de Nogaret. 'After that, his wife's body was also found, and my master believed that there was some connection between the two deaths. When we started to investigate, a man began to follow my master – a thin man, wiry. Like one of those who had been forced to starve and never won enough food afterwards – you know?'

Baldwin kept his face carefully empty of all emotion, but he could not help a slight grunt at that name. *Guillaume de Nogaret*. A man so steeped in villainy, even the devil might refuse his companionship.

If the dead man was that same de Nogaret, Baldwin himself would have been happy to slit his throat.

Sir Richard glanced at Baldwin, hearing his intake of breath. 'You all right?'

'I was thinking of the famine,' Baldwin said shortly. 'Too many on our streets look like that – emaciated.'

'Aye.' They all knew of men like that, who had starved and been marked by it during the famine years. 'A sad time.'

'Tell us all you can about what happened,' Baldwin said.

'The fellow tried to attack my master twice, he thought, so after that he had me follow him wherever he went. He hoped to catch the man. As it was, he found another trying to kill him, a fellow known as Nicholas the Stammerer. We caught him and learned all we could, but then he was found dead. Someone had killed him with a thin blade slipped down from here,' he finished, touching his finger just above his collarbone.

'Not a normal place for a killer to strike, eh, Baldwin?' Sir Richard commented.

'Hmm? Not that I have seen, no,' Baldwin said. It amused

him to see how Sir Richard had immersed himself in this affair. Clearly it was possible to take the Coroner out of England, but not the urge to investigate from the Coroner himself. From his point of view, the name of the dead man was more intriguing.

'Interesting,' Sir Richard said. 'So you had this other fellow, and he died, and yet the first one was not caught?'

'No.'

'What did you learn from the one you did catch?'

'He was a felon who worked with a small gang, so he said. There was a man who sought the services of a killer, and he said that another was sent to fulfil the contract, but failed. My master and I believed that this failure was the man we both saw originally. And so later this Nicholas was given the contract instead. He took over when the first failed.'

'And died in his own turn,' the Coroner said. 'You say it was while he was being questioned?'

'Yes. The assassin murdered him while he was hanging in chains in the interrogation chamber.'

Sir Richard gave a low whistle. 'That shows some balls, eh? Wandering into a torture chamber and slaying the felon there.'

'I suppose so.'

'What can you tell us that will help us find the murderer?'

Stephen looked at Sir Richard, then over at Pons and Vital. 'If I knew anything, I would use it to find the man myself. All I know is, the Stammerer told me that the gang had received payment for the murder. So find the Stammerer's men, and you may find the killer. Then, perhaps, you could find the man who killed my master as well as killed the Stammerer himself.'

'I will, friend,' Pons said. 'If he is in Paris, I shall find him and deal with him.'

He nodded to the others and he and Vital left them alone with Stephen.

Baldwin saw a spasm pass over the wounded man's face. 'Would you like some wine?'

'I just want to sleep and to wake to learn this was all a foul dream,' Stephen said bitterly. 'All I ever wanted was to serve my master. Without him, I do not know what I can do.'

'There is one thing you may do,' Baldwin said, leaning against the wall. 'You can tell me all you know of your master's investigation.'

'That is easy. His notes are all there,' Stephen said, pointing to a large chest in the corner of the room.

Baldwin walked to it and lifted the lid. Inside were a number of scrolls, each covered in a neat, delicate script. 'All these?'

'Only the one at the top. My master used to keep notes on all the crimes he investigated.'

Baldwin found one with 'De Nogaret' clearly marked at the top, and removed it. 'I thank you, friend. This will aid us. Is there anything more?'

'No,' Stephen said, sinking back on his pillow, a pasty, green colour returning to his face. 'All you need is in there.'

Tavern near the eastern wall by the River Seine

Jacquot slipped along the alleyway until he reached the little doorway. There was an ancient crone in the corner, and he nodded to her as he passed by, dropping a couple of sous into her bowl as he went.

'Merci, m'Sieur,' she muttered.

Madame Angeline had been here for as long as anyone could remember. In the past, a long time ago, she had been the leading attraction of the brothel which had stood here, but that was before her third babe and the infection in her womb which had all but killed her. It was said that after that baby she had felt so much agony in her belly that she could never service her men again. The brothel had turfed her out, and she had remained there on a little box, begging from all those who had once used her, never threatening to tell wives or lovers, but merely sitting mutely, hoping for money to support herself. Her babes died one by one as the famine struck the city, just as so many other youngsters did, but she seemed ever more determined to remain here where she had known happiness, laughter and fun in her youth. The brothel closed, reopened, closed again, and now was a tavern where some women offered themselves, but only on an unofficial level. They paid a commission to the tavern-keeper.

He had to clamber down a steep staircase to the undercroft where the barrels of wine were racked. The place held that warm fug of sour wine, piss and smoke that was the odour of drinking to any man. He snuffed the burning applewood with appreciation, thinking again of the days of his youth. In those days, with a large orchard nearby, he had often taken old boughs for his own fire, and the scent was like the smell of his childhood.

Here the wine was not the cultured flavour of the more expensive vines in the south and west, but the stronger, peasant wine of the small farms outside Paris. For some, they were too powerful, smelling so strongly that many would turn their noses up at it, but not Jacquot. The weaker wines and more cultivated grapes could be left to the rich, to the knights and merchants who liked to discuss the different tastes they said they could discern. For Jacquot, the purpose of drinking was to recall happier days.

There were rushlights and a few foul-smelling tallow candles which added their own pungency to the reek, and he took a quart of wine to a barrel and leaned on it, while he supped the wine and felt its urgent heat slipping in through his veins. This was the best of times – the moments when blessed oblivion started to rush towards him, when pain and grief would slip away and he could feel the wonder of forgetfulness. Forget his intense loneliness.

The King shouldn't have tried that. It was a shameful act, to try to kill him for merely demanding the full reward for his efforts. Sure, he had been slow to achieve the original aim, but that was because he was a perfectionist. He had to know his target in extreme detail before he could think of launching any form of attack. And usually, of course, he was desperate for the money to allow him to return to a little hovel like this one, in which the bad memories could be erased and good ones revived by the use of suitable quantities of red wine. Now he had his money, he could remain here for a full week, he reckoned, sensing the weight of the purse at his belt.

'Hello, Killer.'

His reactions were a little blunted, but even if he was sober, he wouldn't have immediately drawn a knife – not with a low, sultry voice like that. 'What do you want with me?' he asked.

The King's woman was taller than he'd realised. This was the first time he had seen her either fully clothed or standing. She was a better-looking wench than he had thought before. There was a feline elegance to her, in the way that she walked, in the way she gestured with her hands and arms while talking, and in the measuring gaze of her dark eyes. Her lips were full, soft and red, and he wondered what they would taste of, were he to crush them under his own. As he looked all over her, he saw her little tongue flick out and wet her upper lip in an unmistakeable invitation.

'I want you, Jacquot the Killer. Amélie wants you.'

He gave a dry chuckle. 'So you can take me to the King's men? The King sent you, did he?'

'The King is the old King. There is always a new King waiting in the wings,' she said, leaning forward and running a long forefinger down the side of his face, tracing a line from his temple to his jaw, and then down, under his chin.

'I am no King.'

'But you could be. With my brain, you would make an excellent King. All who opposed you could disappear, while you took over the King's income.'

'And then, when you found another more suited to you, you would leave me for him?'

'I have no interest in others,' she said, and licked her lips again before biting at her bottom lip and smiling.

He drank off his horn of wine and poured himself more. 'I have no need of you or of money or power. All I seek is here,' he said, lifting the horn again.

'Then you are a lucky man. Most men want something,' she said.

'I have already had all, and lost it,' he snapped. 'I know that the pain of loss is stronger than the pleasure of possession. Much stronger.'

'So it's better not to have anything? Just in case you lose all again? That is no recipe for happiness,' she said slyly.

'Go and lie with a goat, you whore. You want me for some sick passion based on blood.'

'Yes – I want blood! You give me blood, and I'll give you my body. But take me and you can have all Paris at your feet. You know it's true. The King is stupid. He thinks he can hold everything together by the exercise of his will. He thinks, the fool, that if he wishes everything to remain the same, it will do so. But it will not! The world changes. The world moves on. Kings live . . . and then die.'

'And you think this King is due for retirement?'

She smiled lazily, and then dipped her finger in his wine, before bringing it to her lips and gently sucking it. 'I think he is soon to lose his throne. Don't you?'

Chapter Twenty-Four

Simon and Baldwin's chamber, the Louvre

'Well?' Simon asked at last.

Baldwin was sitting in a window seat, making the best use of a pair of candles and the very last of the dying sun to read the fine writing, squinting to make sense of the small characters. 'Eh?'

'What does it tell you?'

'That the man de Nogaret was found dead in a chamber where he ought not to have been. The Procureur postulated that the room was deliberately chosen, since it was far from all the daily work at the Louvre, so no one would hear the murder. Second, that Cardinal Thomas d'Anjou was brought there by the same servant who had led de Nogaret there. The Cardinal was in his chamber, but went straightway with the messenger to the room, where they found the body. The messenger was a man called Raoulet, apparently. And the Procureur was aided in his investigations by a kitchen boy called Philippe. Hmm.'

'Not a lot there, then. Is that all?'

'He mentions a woman helping him – someone called Hélias.'

'Interesting, but hardly enough to help us to resolve that crime or to prove the Bishop's innocence in the matter of the Procureur's death.'

'No. Clearly we shall have to search elsewhere for aid,' Baldwin said.

Morrow of the Feast of the Archangel Michael[1]

Louvre, Paris

The Cardinal was standing at his fire when Bishop Walter entered, warily.

'I am most grateful for your time, my Lord Cardinal.'

'Bishop Walter, please, take a seat and let me help you.'

'It is a terrible position I find myself in, my Lord, in truth,' Stapledon said as he sat, glancing about him.

The room would have served for a King's private solar. Decorated beautifully, with paintings on one wall depicting the Blessed Virgin Mary with her little baby, and thick, glorious hangings on the others to keep the cold at bay, it was a room in which a man could sit and relax. The cupboard held a wonderful display of plates, some gold, others no doubt gilt, and jugs with jewels and splendid engravings upon them – the rewards due to a man who had accomplished much.

Stapledon was no failure himself, in worldly terms. His own palace at Exeter was also full of the trinkets and toys of a man who had succeeded in his chosen career. Not that his was a career, of course. It was a vocation. Still, Bishop Walter had risen to be the prominent Church leader of the nation, and it was a role he held proudly.

'You will know that I am experiencing grave problems,' he began. 'I have a crucial duty to the King to guard the young Duke. It was my task to bring him here safely, and then to travel with him home again. And meanwhile, I was given the letters for the Queen which would order her to return home too.'

'It did not work very well, this part of your mission,' the Cardinal observed.

'In truth, it did not. You were there when she berated me?

---

[1] Monday, 30 September 1325

How the woman could be so insulting to a man of God, I do not know. I have never sought to harm her, only support her King and the realm.'

The Cardinal nodded, eyes cast down as he listened. 'You are sure that there is nothing you have done which could have incurred the lady's wrath?' he asked coolly.

'All I have done, I have done to support the King. It is my duty as an English subject.'

'There is a higher duty, of course, to God Himself.'

'And I have ever sought guidance from Christ's vicar on earth,' Stapledon said.

'The Pope has made comment?'

'The Pope has tended to agree with me that there must be some easing of the relations between the French and English Kings. Christianity needs peace between two such powerful nations. How can we ever hope to launch another crusade with France and England at daggers drawn?'

'Yes. But did the Pope suggest that you should remove, for example, all the lady's French servants?'

'That was a sad necessity. Cardinal, you would not expect us to agree to harbour potential spies and assassins in the household of our Queen?'

'And the removal of her children?'

'It was thought necessary, both to save her the embarrassment of having to edit her own thoughts before her children so as not to be seen to be treacherous to either her husband or her brother, and to protect the children from any malign influences.'

The Cardinal looked at him with raised eyebrows. That, he thought, was a likely story. 'For their protection, then. Good. And what of the sequestration of all her belongings? I heard that all her lands have been taken. All her income is removed, and now she travels where her husband permits, pauperised. Is it true that this too was your idea?'

'Not entirely my idea, no. And yet, there is sense in it,' the Bishop replied.

'And yet after all these issues, which I have to admit the Queen *does* lay at your door – if not at that of Sir Hugh le Despenser – you now wish for me to intercede for you with her? Why now?'

'The affair has grown greatly more dangerous. Not only is the matter of the Queen's continued refusal to go home a source of grave concern, now I find,' and here the Cardinal was delighted to see the Bishop hesitate, glance about him rather wildly, and swallow hard before daring to continue, 'now, I say, I find myself accused of the murder of a man whom I did not know, and all because I happened to speak with him briefly on the day before his death.'

'You shouted at him, I heard. Were you not shouting?'

'Yes, yes, yes, I did shout – I confess it. I was anxious after the dreadful scene with the Queen accusing me so ferociously before King Charles. What else would make me snap so? I had suffered a sore interview with the Queen, and then rode here in the rain, and my humours were all unsettled. I think that any man looking into his heart would agree that my slight rudeness was understandable. But to suggest that I could *murder* a man like him is ludicrous! How could anyone suspect me of such a foul crime?'

'With the greatest of ease,' was the response tingling on the tip of his tongue, but the Cardinal merely shook his head sadly. 'I am so sorry for your predicament, my friend. I shall pray for you, and in the meantime I shall try to use my good offices to secure a less precarious situation for you. I think that the best route would be for me to petition the Queen herself and ask her to see to it that your status is respected. The very last reaction we need is to see you arrested.'

This was clearly one aspect of the matter which had not

occurred to the Bishop. He blenched, and the Cardinal had a quick fear that he might vomit all over his floor-coverings, but the concern was short-lived. The Bishop swallowed, brought himself under control, and left a short while later.

Cardinal Thomas stood up respectfully as he walked from the room. It was hard to imagine how a man usually so astute and shrewd in the affairs of state for a not-insignificant country like England, could have so marvellously failed in his latest endeavour.

The Queen, of course, was a vital element of his problem. While she was at loggerheads with him, the Bishop could not hope to find peace. But the Bishop himself was the source of his own downfall. He had harried the poor woman all through her life in England. It was almost certainly true that he had intended to make the realm safer for all – but the Cardinal was no fool, and he knew too that the Bishop was an enormously wealthy man in his own right – although he had not been rich when he was first raised to his Bishopric. All his money had come from the different jobs he had undertaken for the King.

There was the sound of the latch, and he turned and smiled as the door opened. 'You heard all?'

'Your Eminence, I am most grateful,' Queen Isabella said as she entered.

'I am glad to be of service,' the Cardinal said, bowing low.

'I shall be very pleased to compensate you for your trouble when I once again have some funds of my own,' Isabella said. She beckoned her guard, and in a few moments the Cardinal was alone again.

Foolish woman! Wearing widow's weeds as though her husband was truly dead was merely an affectation to gain the hearts of strangers. It was a silly demonstration – and yet it might prove effective. It had most certainly proved successful to the French people. They had all taken her to their hearts, much more so than the Cardinal would normally have expected. The sight of a wonderfully attractive woman in her prime of life was always enough to make a Parisian man kiss his fingers in appreciation, but when she was clad all in black, raising her to that level of near-approachability, near-avail-ability . . . that worked on a man's heart like an aphrodisiac, the Cardinal thought cynically. Christ Himself alone knew what the English would make of it.

He knew what the English King would make of it, of course!

But that was not his concern right now. At this moment he must concentrate on the situation that was developing.

All was in flux. All was danger. War was brewing – but he did not know between which parties.

Sir Baldwin and Simon spent the morning with the Duke of Aquitaine, and it was some relief to them both when they were able to leave the Duke in the care of his mother, and seek a quiet corner.

'Are you all right, Baldwin?' Simon asked.

'Of course. Why shouldn't I be?'

'It's just that since yesterday, when we saw the dead man's servant, you've been more than a bit withdrawn.'

Baldwin eyed him closely. Then he sighed and said. 'The fellow who was found dead here at the castle? It was Guillaume de Nogaret. A man of that name was the one who drew up all the accusations against the Templars. He was the King's lawyer, the architect of the full terrible injustice of those times. Simon, I think he must have been the father of the dead man.'

'Not the man himself?'

'No. Guillaume senior died some years ago.'

'So now the son and his wife have been slaughtered,' Simon mused.

'And it is nothing to do with us,' Baldwin said with brutal certainty.

'Because we are in France?'

'No. Because the man was a liar and a perverter of the truth. I would have nothing to do with him, alive or dead, nor with his son. Why should I aid his descendant, after he caused the destruction of an Order which was so far above his comprehension?'

'Hah! Thought I'd find you two here!' Sir Richard bellowed, in what he optimistically considered to be a quiet tone.

Baldwin felt Simon stiffen at his side. 'Would you care to join us, Sir Richard? We are taking a little wine.'

'No such thing as "a little wine". Wine should be drunk in profuse quantities, Sir Baldwin. Move over, Bailiff. Give a man a little space. Hey, did I tell you the joke about the young squire who was about to inherit? Eh? He was forced to think about marriage, and then met a lovely wench: you know the sort, eh, Bailiff? One with thighs that could crush a destrier between 'em. Bubbies like great soft puddings, and the sort of face that would tempt Saint Gabriel himself to come and—'

'I think we get your drift, Sir Richard,' Baldwin interrupted smoothly.

'Eh? Oh, right. Well, he met this girl with lips that could suck the worms from an oaken beam, you see, and he said to her, he said . . .' Sir Richard began to guffaw at the joke as he approached the end. 'He said: "Maid, I may not look much now, but in a year or so, my father will be dead, and then I'll be as rich as grease, so how about you marry me?" And you see, she was very taken with him, and she asked for his name, and all his details, and then, two weeks later, he learned she was his new stepmother. Eh? Eh?'

Baldwin smiled in appreciation of the pain on Simon's face.

'You seem wonderfully recovered, Sir Richard. You were not content when we saw the chasm open between our Queen and Bishop Stapledon.'

'No, but I reflected hard, Sir Baldwin. You see, there is nothing I can do about that. Ach, I'm no diplomatic man. To be good at that, you must be an expert at dissembling before others. And that's not my way. No, I know what I am good at, though, and that is keeping the King's Rolls on sudden deaths. Yes, I can investigate a murder without trouble. You know that. You and I, we've looked at a few corpses together, haven't we? Well, that's why I'm in better spirits now.'

'Because of the murder?'

'Aye. If there's a dead man about, I can help to find the killer. And if it means I'm helping Bishop Walter at the same time, then I'm happy.'

'Is there more for us to look at?' Simon asked. 'I had thought that the others, Pons and his friend, were set to find the killer of the Procureur.'

'Where there's a corpse too many, there's work for others, is what I say,' Sir Richard said.

Simon looked at him blankly, and then gazed at Baldwin, who shook his head. 'No, Simon, I can freely confess that I have not the faintest idea what he is talking about.'

'Well, there is the Procureur, whose killer we must discover if we may, to help our Bishop, who is suspected of the crime, but since we know so few people about here, it's not easy without any sort of assistance. But we could perhaps help if we could take a view of the body.'

'You've a means of allowing us to see his body?' Simon asked with a marked lack of excitement. In all his years as Bailiff and since, he had never enjoyed the sight of a dead man.

'Aye,' Sir Richard said, but he was looking meaningfully at

Baldwin, not Simon. 'Someone told me once that if you want to find a man's killer, you should always look at the corpse first, because he's the last witness to the murder. And if you can get *him* to talk, you're half the way to finding the assassin.'

Chapter Twenty-Five

Paris

Jacquot walked from the tavern as the sun rose to noon, but today he was sober enough. He had only returned here for a morning's reviver.

She was a trim little tart, that much was true. Amélie'd wagged her tail at him, and made her intentions clear enough. If Jacquot was to kill her man, he could have her for himself. Not the best proof of fidelity a woman had ever given to a man, but for all that there was a harlot's good faith behind it. Which meant the bitch would be happy with him for a while, for exactly as long as he satisfied her cravings and desires. Let him fail in that duty, and she would undoubtedly rush to hold the same conversation with another likely fellow with brawn in his arms and little in his head.

That was going to be a problem – the fact that he, Jacquot, had too much going on in his head; he was no slow-thinking churl like the others. As soon as she sensed that he was capable of thinking for himself, her desire for him would wane. Ach, he had known too many women like her since he'd come here to Paris. They were all out for the same things: money, security, control. And if you gave it to them, they just wanted more. There was no future for a man like him with a woman like her.

Once, he had planned to get back to the little village where he had been so happy with his wife and family, but that was

when he had first set out on his career as a killer. He had
thought then that he would kill a few people, gradually
increasing his fee, until he had earned enough to be able to go
back home, find another wife, start afresh. It was a beguiling
notion.

As were all dreams. No. He had learned while still a young
man that there was nothing that God had given that He
couldn't take away again. So he would remain here. One day,
perhaps, when he had gone on a bender for a week or more,
his heart or his brain would give out, and he would discover
the wonderful solace of death. No heaven for him. He would
be there in purgatory, so he believed, and maybe his soul
would be dragged down to hell. When he was drunk, he didn't
care. He ranted and raved at the skies when he was in his cups,
because he didn't give a sou for a God Who could ruin him in
this way – and for *what*? To see whether he, Jacquot, was good
enough? Sweet Jesus, he *would* have been good enough, if
God hadn't stolen his entire family.

His thoughts returned to the woman, Amélie. She wanted
him to kill the King and allow her to run all the King's
activities.

He would be best served to kill *her* instead, Jacquot considered. Yet to take over the King's demesne was an attractive
notion . . .

The three men were studying the Procureur's body, which had
been washed and lay in his chamber.

Sir Baldwin and the Coroner were intent on their task;
Simon less so. To the Bailiff, the corpse was, and only ever
could be, a man who had died unnecessarily.

True, he, Baldwin and Sir Richard shared a common
purpose. They tried to impose a little order on the world. That
was what a dead man was, after all. He was a disturbance. To

the King's Peace, to the natural order of things. He was a father removed, he was a son taken away from a doting mother. He was an emptiness where there should have been noise, laughter, joy. Even tears on occasion.

Simon had not come to this conception early. It had taken the death of his first-born son to make him realise that there was more to life than merely walking through it easily. Sometimes a man needed hardship, but dear Christ, Simon did not want to have any more. He couldn't bear to lose another child.

The loss of his boy, the original Peterkin, had left him befuddled and sad, and it was only the exercise of his intellect in different investigations, he now realised, which had given him a fresh purpose. He needed the excitement of seeking a killer, a robber, a draw-latch. But most of all, he needed to find the killers.

Sir Richard was formed of similar clay, although he was far less bothered by any personal, emotional motivations. In essence he was a simple soul. He had a firm belief that those who broke the King's Peace should be hunted down. A man who was prepared to break the rules was a man who was a threat to all others, so far as he was concerned, and he would do all he might to challenge and punish them.

Of them all, Simon knew that Baldwin had the strongest urge to find murderers. Having been Knight Templar, Baldwin had an abhorrence of any form of injustice, and that worked as strongly in him for those who were the victims of crime as for those who were innocent, but found themselves convicted of crimes they did not, indeed, often *could* not have committed. Baldwin hated to think that an innocent man could be punished.

'Hah! Damn strange to be starin' at a body like this without a clerk to hold my hand,' Sir Richard commented. 'Most of the time they're less use than a tarse at a convent, but just every so often there's something handy they come up with.'

Baldwin nodded his understanding. 'That is why it is often so useful to study a body with another man. Two pairs of eyes see more than one alone.'

'And I see that this fellow was stabbed bloody efficiently. God's ballocks, will you look at that? A very fine, narrow blade, that was. But long, to reach down to the man's heart, wouldn't ye say?'

Baldwin peered closer. The wound itself lay atop the shoulder, a small, diamond-shaped cut, perhaps a half-inch in length, that had entered the triangular hollow between neck, collarbone and shoulder blade. But the depth would have to be some nine inches, he guessed, to puncture the heart. 'The one blow. It was deep, clearly. You can see the blue beginning of a bruise where the cross struck the man's shoulder. For a man to use such a point for his attack is surprising, though. Most would merely slip the knife up from the front, or under the shoulder blade . . . the risk of missing the heart and having the victim struggle and fight would put most men off delivering the killing blow this way.'

'It was done by a man well-used to such attacks, then.'

'I would think so.'

Baldwin remained staring at that stark body, the wound standing out so clear on the pale flesh. 'It's tempting to find a twig, or a glass rod, if there is such a thing to be had, just to measure the depth of the wound.'

'But the age . . .'

'Yes. It's been such a long while since the man was killed, the clots will be deep in the wound already. It's one thing to test a dagger thrust in a man's belly, but another to look at this kind of stabbing. Still, we're looking at a narrow blade, not much more than a half-inch in breadth, and long enough to puncture a heart from above. It gives us an idea of the type of knife that was used.'

They remained a little longer, making sure there was nothing of importance they had missed, before leaving the little chamber with its grisly inhabitant.

Outside, Wolf lay happily panting, tongue lolling, great forepaws widely spaced. Seeing the three return, he lumbered slowly to his feet, shook himself, and padded softly to Baldwin.

'Look at this fellow. Gentle, mild-mannered, loyal, even though he scarcely knows me . . . and then consider the men who infest our world. Men who will kill for money or lust, for the sake of an argument or a wager. Yet we're told that this poor beast is the failed creature.'

'What do you mean?' Simon asked, pulling the door to behind him.

'Man is made in the image of God, Simon. That is what we are told. And yet think of it. No dog would murder because it coveted another's blanket or bone. It would fight to defend its master without reneging just because some other offered it money. Some dogs will guard their master's body even though he has been dead for an age, and the dogs will die trying to continue to defend it. Such loyalty, such devotion. But the vicars would have you believe that a beast like Wolf here can never pass the gates of heaven because he is only a dog. They would say that he can have no soul. And yet the meanest of men with the lust of a demon, and the greed of Despenser, can get to heaven if he will only ensure that he dies in a state of grace. I tell you, it makes no sense to me. If God is so committed to accepting only humans to His gardens of paradise, and will not let dogs in, I am not sure I want to go there. I would prefer to remain in purgatory with the soul of a brute like Wolf here, and my old Uther, may he rest in peace, and all the other hounds, mastiffs, alaunts and raches which I have known and loved in my life, for all eternity. Better that than risk meeting with some of those I have known who walked on two legs,' he added. The thought of Guillaume de Nogaret had not left him. The idea that de Nogaret might be in heaven was so appalling, it almost made him want to reject his soul's salvation.

'Baldwin,' Simon said, eyeing him with perplexity, 'what has brought all this on?'

Sir Richard was also watching him askance, although in his case, it involved looking at Baldwin from the corner of his eye, tilting his chin upwards, and drawing the corners of his mouth down. Catching sight of him, Baldwin gave a weakly smile.

'It is nothing, only that the poor man inside there is dead, and appears to have been a kindly soul. There was nothing about him to cause offence except to the law-breakers. He was good, by my measure. And yet he is dead now, and if his killer is shrived and dies in a state of grace, the two may well meet in heaven, while this good soul Wolf will not. Well, a pox on that!'

Simon exchanged a look with Sir Richard. He was nonplussed. He had never heard Baldwin swear, to his knowledge. That was his own preserve. And it was most unlike the knight to complain about anything, especially not any religious matters. For Baldwin, although the memory of the Popes was dubious at best, and the behaviour of the French King Philip IV was painful in the extreme, he had never made a negative comment about God, so far as Simon was aware.

It was a hard time, to be sure. Others Simon had known had lost their faith in God, as they buried their children or wives after watching them gradually fade away and die after the atrocious weather a decade ago, that brought crop failure and famine. Towns and cities lost hundreds or thousands of inhabitants. Simon had learned that there was a city in the far north of the French kingdom called Ypres that had lost one tenth of its people to the famine in one month alone. The famine had continued to ravage the lands of all Christians for two years and more. How could men *not* lose faith? Simon's own beliefs had been staggered and bruised when his little boy died, for it was hard to understand how a kindly God could take away a little angel like that.

Sir Richard cleared his throat. 'Did I ever tell you about my wife, my Hannah? No? She was my love from my earliest years. Met her when I was seven, when I was just being shown how to fight with a sword two-handed. She was daughter to a local cowman. I thought then, I would marry her. Eh? And you know what? I did. Happily married we were, for twelve years. Never had children. Just never happened for us. A sadness, but we had enough pleasure.

'Well, one day I was away from my home. Left the demesne in the hands of my wife and my steward – a thieving little scrote by the name of Jack of Lyme. I trusted him, but he repaid me by killing my wife and robbing me of all my treasure. He stabbed her . . .'

The knight looked away from them and swallowed. For the very first time Simon heard the sadness that lay at Sir Richard's core.

'Aye, he robbed me of all I held dear. Still hold dear, in fact. Just one thing, though. I had a monstrous great brute. Mastiff, he was, a tan devil named Bill. Well, Bill must have heard something in there, because he went in, and he saw Jack in the room with my wife. And Bill bowled in to see what was up, found her dead, I think, and went for Jack. Damn near took his arm off. Jack killed him, poor old Bill, but Bill put paid to his escape. We caught him less than ten miles distant, pleading with a peasant for some aid for his chewed arm. I didn't wait for the law that day, I fear.'

He turned slowly back to Baldwin. 'This is not a perfect world, my friend. We both know that. But I tell you now, Sir Baldwin, God would not refuse my Bill in heaven. And if Jack got there, probably by trying to bribe Gabriel at the door, Bill would chase him out in a moment.'

There was a sudden firmness in his voice, and now he spoke in more his usual manner. 'And if Saint Peter himself tried to tell me to cast me old Bill out through the gates, I'd black his eye for him.'

Baldwin smiled. 'Sir Richard, you are a good, kind, and generous soul. My apologies for my black mood. I have not earned the right to be melancholy.'

'Hah! We're all here, ain't we?' Sir Richard said. 'But there's little need for sadness. We're on the brink of war, in the city of our enemies, with the estranged wife of our King, surrounded by men who're apparently deserting the King to lend succour to his wife, and trying to learn why someone has killed a good and decent man whom we never got to meet in a tavern. Plenty there to celebrate, I'd say!'

Chapter Twenty-Six

Paris, near the River Seine

The King wiped at his nose again, still feeling the fury that had swept through him when the mother-swyving son of a whore had left last night. The bleeding wouldn't stop.

Amélie had tried to soothe him, but the bitch was no good with potions and bandages. All she was capable of was pouring a fresh cup of wine, and when his mashed lips had touched the liquor, it stung so much, he threw the cup at her, swearing when he missed. She had walked from the chamber after that, and hadn't returned until now.

It took an age for the bodies to be taken out. Luckily the King had a shed next to the river, so all the men had to do was cart the fellows out at night and drop them into the water. Even that had proved a problem. The river was low, apparently, and one of the bodies fell into the thick mud at the water's edge. Matters weren't improved by the fact that he wasn't entirely dead and began to wail. Probably came to as the cold water hit his face. Old Peter the peasant clambered down a rope and cut his throat for him before he could bring the Watch, and then half-dragged, half-slid the body to the water, where he pushed the fool off. Then Peter himself almost drowned in the mud and had to be rescued. The whole thing was a farce. And it was not made any better by the reflection that bloody damned Jacquot had bested them all.

You had to be impressed. The man was ancient now, and yet

he could fight and win against several men at a time. The King was not keen to see his forces whittled down any farther, but there was a matter of pride at stake here. There were those who would hear of the incident and might form the opinion that the King's crown must be slipping. And a crown, once fallen from a brow, could be picked up by any with the power and strength to carry it. There were many in Paris who felt sure that they had just that authority.

Curse Jacquot. He was the best man the King had ever had. But there was no doubt, he would have to die.

'Where were you?' he growled at Amélie. 'I wanted you last night.'

'You made no sign of it. I thought you wanted me to go, so I went.'

There was an indifferent note in her voice that made him want to hit her again. 'Come here,' he said.

'Why?' she asked as she crossed the room.

He reached out and grabbed her hair, twisting his fingers in it and drawing her nearer. 'Where did you go last night?'

'To a tavern. Why?'

'Looking for a dog to cover you?' he sneered.

'Looking for a man, perhaps.'

'You dare seek to make me wear the cuckold's horns?'

'Did you marry me, then?' she hissed.

'You cow! You strumpet! You craven, shitty little slut! You want some of this?' he snapped, and drew his knife. The point had just touched her chin, when he felt something poke at his belly, and looked down to see her own knife at his groin.

'Kill me, and you'll be paunched, little rabbit,' she said with icy calm.

'I can kill you in an instant.'

'Yes. And I can gut you so you die over days, in agony,' she said.

And she was right. He had seen the exquisite torture that a knife in the guts could bring. There was no cure. Not when a man's bowels had been spilled. It was enough to make him respect her again – if not trust her. He didn't trust any woman.

He shoved her away and rammed the blade back into its sheath before demanding more wine. At least his mouth was healed enough for that now. Meanwhile, she walked away and lay on her flank on the skins that made up his bed in the corner. Christ's arse, but she was beautiful. Wild, dangerous and lethal as a hawk. What she wanted, she would take.

'You are lucky I didn't kill you then,' he said.

'Am I?'

The King usually killed his women because they were too dull. This one would have to die soon because she was too unpredictable. She made him nervous.

Yes, Jacquot first, and then her. But Jacquot's death would take careful planning. Whom could he set upon his assassin?

Paris

Vital eyed the men and shook his head.

'I do not think that they know very much, Pons,' he said.

'I think you may be right, Vital.'

'Will you release us, then?'

The speaker was a short man, with a face that appeared to have been burned by acid when he was a child. One eye was milky-white, although his hair was still unmarked by the frost of age. He was probably only some two-and-twenty years, Pons thought to himself. And already an expert in so many aspects of thieving and murder.

All these men had been swept up by the watchmen of the city in the last day. There were some forty or more in different gaols all about the town. Some were wanted already, and one was destined for Monfaucon, to be broken on the wheel for his offences, but most were like this little man: idiots who had so little ambition and intelligence that their crimes were obvious to all. However, they were useful, since they were likely to know more than most about the men who were capable of killing a Procureur.

'Please? You have nothing against me.'

Pons and Vital exchanged a look. 'No,' Pons said. 'You will remain here until we are satisfied that there was no collusion between you and others to murder the Procureur.'

'But we know nothing! *Nothing!*' The man swore as Pons and Vital nodded to the gaoler, and the heavy door swung shut with a dull thud. The keys rattled, the bolts slid into their niches in the wall, and the gaoler began to lead the way up the damp staircase.

'Wait!'

Pons turned. 'You want something else?'

'You must realise you cannot keep us here for long?'

'My friend, King Charles himself has demanded that we take all measures to ensure that the killer is found. You have no rights in this. You will remain until we remember you and consider letting you go free.'

'But we . . .'

'*Bonjour, mon ami.*' Pons smiled, and set his face to the steps again.

Les Halles, Paris

Jacquot rested, watching a bear baiting, then wandering idly along with the crowds, viewing other entertainments.

The city was such a vast place. Cut in half by the great swirl of grey river, the islands in the middle where the cathedral and King's main courts were based, this was the centre of Christendom now that the Holy Land was lost. Men and women congregated here, for Paris held all hopes, all desires, within its walls. Jacquot had arrived looking upon Paris as the place where he could find a new life, and it had given him that. However, in return it had taken all he had. All his honour and integrity had been eroded until there was now only this: a husk of a man, full of self-loathing, desperate for salvation but not having any idea how to achieve it.

If he had found just a fraction of love, of friendliness, he might have been different.

Walking about this area, he studied others now. They drew his eye as they had not for many years. Men and women, smiling, laughing. Children at their sides, gambolling and capering in the thin sunshine. Men buying flowers and sweetmeats for their wives. One man bellowing with laughter, throwing his son into the air, while the lad screamed with delight.

It reminded him of another time. Another life. When he had his own children, when he had hurled his boy up into the sky. But now, all he could remember was the same boy's face, blue-grey, peering up sightlessly from the winding sheet as Jacquot wept and threw soil into those dead eyes. Up in the air, then into the ground. It made a fist in his breast, a fist that clenched about his heart.

Jacquot was lost. He was in the city's market and he was lost. He recognised nothing. Panic was his sole companion as he span on his heel, desperate to be away, to be anywhere other than this. He wanted to run, to pelt off in the direction of his rooms. Or a tavern. Anything. Anywhere. Panting, he felt like a wolf in a trap, frantic with the urge to flee, but utterly incapable of doing so. His legs would not obey.

And then, the horror of his loneliness in the midst of all this joy left him, and he was calm again. He felt the fist open in his chest, his breathing return to normal, the cool sobriety return. There was nothing here for him to fear. The only danger for him was the King.

Last night Jacquot had felt secure. Now, he knew he was in grave danger. The King would have to eradicate him just to prove that he was still the King. Thus, Jacquot had two choices. He could leave, or he must fight.

He would fight, then. It was not in his heart to leave this whore of a city. He had run all the way here ten years ago. He wouldn't be forced to run away again.

The King was past his time – Amélie was right about that. The King must go, and perhaps Jacquot would take Paris in his place.

Chapter Twenty-Seven

Louvre

Baldwin was still in a pensive frame of mind when he and the others returned to the Louvre. Once inside, he looked down at Wolf and said to the others, 'We should remain here, I think. There is no point in making ourselves unpopular with Vital and Pons when our task is to do all we can to protect the Duke. It is his safety that we are here to ensure.'

'Aye, true enough,' Sir Richard said. 'But if the Bishop is accused of complicity or worse again, it's best that we know the details, so far as we can, of the investigation.'

'I suppose so,' Baldwin said. He looked up at the massive white walls of the castle.

'Something wrong, Baldwin?' Simon asked. He was growing quite anxious for his friend. It was unlike him to be so introspective.

Baldwin turned to him with a lift of his eyebrows. 'Should there be? No, Simon, I was merely reconsidering my priorities. There are times when it is absolutely right for a man to leave his duties to investigate a matter such as this death of the city's prosecutor, but there are other things which demand our attention, as good Sir Richard has reminded me. Our place – *my* place – is here, in this castle, ensuring that the Queen and our friend Bishop Walter do not come to blows, and seeing to the defence of the Duke of Aquitaine. It is not my place – *our* place – to investigate the deaths of men in this castle. Come – let us find the young Duke now.'

The Queen felt utterly contented, in a manner she had not known for months, sitting in her chair, her son at her side in a similar seat, listening to the bickering of her musicians as they debated amongst themselves what they should play next.

'Mother, do they always argue like this?'

'No, I feel that it may be your presence which has caused them this additional pressure,' she returned. As she said this, she bent her head a little in the direction of the gittern player. The musician swallowed, and hurriedly struck up some chords. Around him, the other men gradually followed his lead. While they played, the Queen turned her head towards the little huddle of ladies-in-waiting.

'My Lady?' whispered her maid, Alicia.

The Queen nodded, and Alicia began to usher guests, servants and hangers-on away, to give the Queen more space. Of the two ladies-in-waiting who were moved, Lady Alice de Toeni looked quite shocked; beside her, though, Lady Joan of Bar gave the Queen a slight wink.

'She is happy to tolerate your foibles, I see, Mother,' the Duke said. 'Are you feeling unwell?'

The Queen smiled. He was not yet thirteen, and yet he had the observant eye of a man a great deal older.

'I feel better now that those people have been removed. I thought I was to be crushed when they all came in behind us.'

'But why include the ladies-in-waiting?' he wanted to know.

'I do not trust them all. If you need to converse with me, my darling, you should always try to do so through Alicia. She is my friend and dearest companion. Do *not* speak with Lady Alice de Toeni.'

'She's a creature of my father's?'

'Yes. And not to be trusted,' the Queen said, scarcely moving her lips.

It was true. When King Edward had sent the Queen here as his emissary, so he had fenced her about with his own people. Among her ladies-in-waiting, the only one in whom she could confide when she left England was Alicia, a sweet child who knew, moreover, that her own happiness depended entirely upon the Queen. She adored one of Isabella's guards, Richard Blaket, and that gave the Queen a certain control. Alice de Toeni, by contrast, was utterly devoted to the King, and the Queen suspected that she was a spy.

Lady Joan of Bar was a different proposition. Formerly the wife of the Earl Warenne, some ten years or so ago she had managed to leave her vile brute of a husband.

'If the matter is urgent, you may be able to trust Lady Joan,' the Queen added.

'Her? But wasn't she selected to join you by Sir Hugh le Despenser?'

'Yes. But she suffered so much from her husband, I think she now feels sympathy for me and remorse for accepting the task of coming to spy on me. She will not harm me, I believe.'

'That is good. I will bear these women in mind.'

'What of you, my darling? What news is there?'

'I have heard that the Despenser is in another panic just now. He fears that at any time the Lord Mortimer will arrive on our eastern shores to overrun the country with a ragtag and bobtail host of Hainault mercenaries. He writes to all the Admirals warning them, I hear.'

'He is a frantic fool,' Queen Isabella snorted. 'And the sooner he is removed the better.'

'He is my father's friend, Mother.'

She noticed the sudden use of the personal. 'You are quite

right. And yet he rapes the whole nation. Your father's friend treats it as his own private plaything. How many more loyal servants of your father must be dispossessed and exiled because of Sir Hugh le Despenser?'

'Sir Hugh has the right to protect himself. Mortimer would have seen him hanged.'

'It is a mutual ambition.'

'Perhaps so,' he said. But there was no answering chuckle in his tone. He looked listless and fretful.

'Darling, you are worried?'

'Mother, I have seen the effects of the wars on you and the King, as well as on my friends in the household. Good men are dead because of the squabbling between the Despenser and the Marcher Lords. I would not have any more good men die.'

'What of the realm?'

He glanced at her, and suddenly she saw a man in those shrewd blue eyes. 'I feel I should be asking you that, Mother!'

She smiled, turning back to the musicians. Putting out her hand, she took his, but only for a moment. There was no answering pressure from his fingers. It was not a lack of love for her, but the mere reminder that she was not his only parent, and that he had loyalty to his father too.

'Mother?'

Ah, she thought, here it comes.

'Mother, Bishop Walter has asked me to speak with you, to request that you meet with him. Will you do so?'

'What does he want with me?'

'I think, only to speak. He is deeply worried, too. He wants to see if he can heal the rift between you, he says.'

'Oh, really?' she spat. 'Will he return to me my tin mines? My estates? My children? My money? What of the men of my household, the ones exiled by his advice, the others held in

English gaols? All guilty of the atrocious crime of loving me and wishing to serve.'

'He is a different man from the arrogant Treasurer of a year ago, Mother. Now he sits quietly. I think he realises his treatment of you was not fair. And he is terribly fearful of the matter of the man who was killed.'

'I had heard something of that,' she said. 'But you think that he is malleable now? He will be honourable in his dealings with me?'

'I hope so.'

She smiled. 'Hope is so misjudged a commodity, do you not think?'

'I feel sure that the Bishop is better acquainted than I.'

'So I should speak with him again. That is well. I shall, you may tell him.'

'I will ask Richard of Bury to see him.'

'This Richard . . . you are content to keep him?'

'He is a good tutor, Mother. He is diligent,' the Prince said with a slight droop of his mouth. 'Too diligent on occasion, when the sun is warm and the deer waiting to be hunted. But he teaches well, and forces me to consider the importance of a martial spirit and love of the arts. I have learned all about Alexander, about the Romans, about King Arthur. I sometimes feel I must wade and wallow in their history all my days.'

'So long as he is loyal.'

'I think he is the most loyal of all my servants.'

'Good. We will have need of loyal men before long.'

'What shall I tell the Bishop?'

'That I will be pleased to see him in two days. I will let him know where and when. And now, let us give ourselves up to the music.'

'Very well.' He listened silently for a moment or two. Then:

'Mother? Where on God's clean earth did you find these men?'

Wednesday after the Feast of the Archangel Michael[1]

Paris

Stapledon stood licking his lips in the antechamber to the Queen's rooms, keen to get on with the interview, and yet fearful of it. It would not be a meeting of minds, of that he was sure.

'Bishop? Please follow me in here,' a servant called from a doorway, and Bishop Walter rose from his bench and glided after the man, his heavy robes concealing his feet.

'My Lady, I hope I see you well?'

'Dispense with the pleasantries, my Lord Bishop. You and I know each other well enough to realise they mean nothing. What do you want?'

'My Lady, I fear for your safety,' the Bishop said. 'It is one thing to return to a beloved country, to visit a brother, to see all the places which have appealed so much, but at this time it is dangerous. War is still possible.'

'You have little faith in my diplomacy, then.'

'It is not that, it is the value which you hold. You are too important, my Lady, to be left here in Paris.'

'Oh, that is not a matter of concern, my Lord Bishop. Since you refuse me my own income from my estates in Devon, and since you also now will not extend to me the money which my husband allocated for me, I am forced to live away from Paris for much of the time. The King, my brother, is not so parsimonious as to see me resort to beggary to keep myself fed and clothed.'

---

[1] Wednesday, 2 October 1325

This was a pointed comment, and the Bishop flinched. 'My Lady, all I did, I did for the good of the realm. It was my duty, and I discharged it as I thought best. I am very sorry if any action of mine was enough to disturb you.'

'Not for long, my Lord Bishop. I was a little discommoded to have all my children sequestrated, I confess, but what is that for a woman, compared to your mature judgement.'

'My Lady, let me . . .'

'*No*, my Lord Bishop. Let *me* explain to *you*. I want the money which the King my husband sent with you. I want it in my coffers, because that will allow me to fulfil my duties to him. It will also permit me to ensure the safety of my son. I and he will not be here forever, and we must leave a good impression. That means largesse, feasting, entertaining. Have you ever known an impecunious ambassador? Yet you insist on making me one such. It is not satisfactory.'

'My Lady, I would gladly, but the King was most insistent. He said that you must return.'

'I say I wish to have the money first.'

'Your Royal Highness, sadly—'

'So you will refuse. That is a great shame. You know, of course, that the French court blames you for the death of the Procureur?'

'That was nothing to do with me!'

'Really? All say you were seen quarrelling violently with him. And all Frenchmen know how argumentative the English are. And how prone they are to grabbing weapons and attacking.'

'But on the day he died, I was—'

'I am sure you have a perfect alibi, Bishop. However, it will not suffice. A man with your wealth can easily afford an agent to do your bidding.'

'My Queen, will you not please consider returning home?'

She looked at him, and now allowed a small smile to stretch her mouth. 'Of course I will. As I said in the court, just as soon as that *pharisee* is gone, I will be happy to go home.' She rose. 'I will not return to my husband until Sir Hugh le Despenser and his father are gone from the kingdom forever.'

Temple

Pons returned to the gaol alone when the message reached him. Vital was asleep, and there was little need to wake him, so far as Pons could see. There had been many similar messages in the last day or two, and always it was a whining cur of a peasant demanding to be released.

The streets here were crowded about with tall, timber-framed buildings, but as he approached the river and the Île de la Cité, the streets broadened suddenly, and the walls about him became stone. The gaol where this man was kept was at the northern gate to the Île, the Grand Châtelet. Here, Pons nodded to the guard, and was soon inside.

Walking down the circular staircase was treacherous in the extreme. The water was a constant sound here, with droplets falling from the ceiling, and green slime clinging to the stonework all around. Pons was sure that if he was to be left here for any time, he would be driven mad. The sound of water dripping, the wash of the river, the clanking of chains, the constant smell of faeces from the buckets in the little cells, all would contribute to a feeling of intolerable despair.

'What is it?' he said.

'I want to speak to you, master.'

It was the youngster with the white eye, he saw. The lad had his face to the grating in the wooden door, like a man trying to escape by forcing his way through the ironwork. His lips were outside the cell. Perhaps that was it, he wanted to be free so desperately that merely pushing his lips to the free air outside was enough.

In the glittering torchlight, the man's one good eye rolled with anguish. Of course, Pons thought, the others in the cell would be interested to know what the boy thought he could sell . . . and if he was to betray another, his life would not be worth a brass sou.

In the last few days, many of the prisoners gathered up by the Watch, were already so desperate to escape their cells that they were calling Vital and Pons to relate any snippet. So far, none of it had been of any use whatever. If there had been much chance of a breakthrough, he would have woken Vital, but now, seeing this man's yearning to be free of the cell, he was glad he had not done so. This was another useless dead-end, if he knew anything.

'What's your name?' he asked.

'They call me Le Boeuf.'

'Well, Boeuf, if you get out of that cell because you tell me you know something, and then I learn you don't, you'll be straight back inside – and next time you ask to see me, it'll be a week before I come down here. Got that? I dislike having my time wasted, and looking at you, I have to ask myself: "What can this piece of shit know that can possibly help me?"'

'Please!'

Pons studied him a moment longer, wearing his 'dicing' face. An expressionless face was particularly useful when gambling with some of the sailors at the riverside, but now Pons was using it to intimidate. Making a decision, he span on his heel and was off up the stairs, the guard hurrying behind him, while Le Boeuf screamed after them.

'That man, you know him?' Pons asked the guard as they reached the street level.

'He's just a low-life. I suspect him of cutting a few purses, pocketing a few trinkets, perhaps. But mostly he's just a nuisance because of his attempts at begging. I've seen him before now, with a patch over his good eye, pretending to be blind, grabbing at any matron who passed.'

'So it's hardly likely he has anything of use,' Pons said.

'I doubt it,' the guard agreed. He was a large, broad man with swarthy features and a face that had been scarred badly by a sword or dagger blow many years before. The scar tissue had marred his face, a great horizontal mark that reached from one cheek almost across to the other, breaking his nose on the way. His face was enough to scare Pons, let alone the men downstairs.

'Have you had any deaths in that cell yet?'

'No. But there's a couple who're coughing badly. Could be they're getting the prisoners' disease.'

Pons reflected. 'Ach, we had them all taken so that we could listen to their tales. I may as well learn what I may. Bring him up here to me.'

'*Sieur.*'

The man called Le Boeuf had been punished before, Pons saw. His right ear had been heavily clipped. The entire lobe and much of the rear of the ear was gone. That was good. He knew what he might suffer, then.

Pons said nothing for some moments, considering the man. Le Boeuf had great manacles on his wrists, and the heavy chain dangled almost to his groin. At his ankles were more chains, hobbling him most effectively. The blood was staining his bare feet where the metal bands chafed his flesh.

Apart from that, he had only terror in his eyes. It was there in the way that his eye avoided Pons's own, the way that he kept looking longingly over Pons's shoulder towards the daylight outside, but also in the wideness of his eye and his panting. This was no ordinary terror. Perhaps he suffered from that fear of small, dark spaces which afflicted so many?

'Well?' Pons said sternly. 'You said you had something to tell me.'

'Will you release me from that cell if I tell you all?'

'If you can tell me who killed the Procureur, I will have you freed and see that you are well rewarded too.'

The young man glanced over his shoulder as though stiffening his resolve by reminding himself what the alternative was.

'Then I will tell you. There is a group in Paris which runs all the crimes.'

Pons lifted an eyebrow.

'It is true, Master. The man in charge, he is called the King, and he has many men at his command. Those who cut purses or rob, or the others who break into houses, they all have to pay him. He takes what they steal and sells it for them, and they receive a part for themselves. If they steal money, they must pay him. If they have whores, they must pay one-fifth of their takings to him. All the crimes in Paris are to his profit.'

'You tell me that the thieves of Paris have a King?' Pons said cynically. 'Guard! Put this man back with the others!'

'No! He lives in rooms near to the eastern wall, down by the river. The thieves go to him at night. Those who disappoint him are taken to a warehouse at the river itself, and their bodies thrown in.'

'I suppose he kills them himself?'

'No. He has his own executioner, just like our King Charles. It was that executioner who slew the Procureur.'

Pons felt his breath stilled in his breast. 'This executioner killed the Procureur? How do you know?'

'I saw him. I was in the alley when it happened.'

Chapter Twenty-Eight

Louvre

Baldwin was relieved to be told that Richard of Bury had the Duke fettered that morning. Instead of the usual chase about the King's parks hunting deer, or the apparently endless round of engagements and feasts in his honour, the Duke of Aquitaine was to be left with his tutor to learn more about the position of France in Christendom, and the politics of his new estates.

'It is time he learned what his new responsibilities are,' Bury had said, overruling the arguments of Sir Richard, Sir Henry de Beaumont and the Duke himself. Fixing Duke Edward with a steely eye, he continued, 'Because Princes who do not study their realms with due diligence and care may find that they lose them!'

Baldwin would have smiled, but for the expression on the Duke's face, which consisted of a mix of resentment and shock, from the idea that his hold on Guyenne and the other parts of his territory could be as precarious as his father's had been.

'Come. You had better teach me all you may, then,' Duke Edward said at last. And as he walked from the room in Richard of Bury's wake, Baldwin heard him add, 'And mind you teach well, Master Bury, for if I lose my lands because of a failing on your part, I will have my payment from you directly!'

It made Baldwin grin to hear it. The Duke was far too young for such an awesome responsibility, but he did have the intelligence to keep himself from arrogance, and the humour to win friends.

'What you grinnin' about?' Sir Richard asked.

'Just reflecting on our Duke.'

Simon snorted and gazed quizzically at the door through which the Duke had left. 'Was Bury serious when he said the Duke could lose the lot?'

'His father did,' Sir Richard pointed out.

'But I think the young Duke is stronger in temperament,' Baldwin said. 'I can recall listening to tales of the King with *his* father, Edward the First. The two Edwards were often at loggerheads, I heard. And at one time, the old King grasped his son by the head and tried to pull his hair out, he was so frustrated. King Edward the First was a long-lived King. It must have been a sore trial to his son, our present King, to have waited so long in his father's shadow.

'Ha! So you think he may do the same to his own son in his turn?' Sir Richard enquired.

'No, I don't think so,' Baldwin said thoughtfully. 'I think our King was a more turbulent youth. He was forward and headstrong, while this Duke of ours is much more aware of his responsibilities than his father ever was. The latter sought only the trappings of power so that he might enjoy his leisure in whatever manner he wished. Our Duke seems much more thoughtful, and considerate of other people's feelings and desires.'

Sir Richard grunted, but then his mood lightened. 'Well, now, since we're free for the morning, what do you two say to a walk to the kitchen to see if they've got a honeyed lark or two for us? I could happily eat a snack.'

Simon reflected warily that the way to the kitchen also

took them past two very good wine shops and a tavern, but the idea of a slab of meat and a hunk of bread was most appealing. And a quart of ale to wash it down would be pleasant, too.

Baldwin was behind the other two when they reached the kitchen. He had enjoyed a dream of his wife the night before – just a fleeting gallery of little memories, a snap of her smile, the impression of her body, her hair in a breeze – and it had left him feeling vaguely melancholic and unsettled. Thus it was that when Sir Richard and Simon blundered their way into the kitchen, Baldwin himself waited outside.

There was a curious weeping noise coming from somewhere, he noted, and he wondered where.

Like all kitchens, this was built close to the main hall where any feasts would be held, but was a completely separate building in case of fire. All castles, all halls, had separate kitchens for this reason.

This was a large rectangular block, which was clearly quite old. Built of stone, it had a tiled roof against the risk of sparks erupting from the chimney and setting fire to a thatch. The weeping seemed to be coming from behind it, so Baldwin, frowning slightly, peered around the corner.

And there slumped on his backside, head bowed, was a boy who could not have been more than eight years old. He was dressed in old linen, with a blue stripe of some cheap dyestuff which had already begun to fade.

'Are you well, boy?' Baldwin asked.

With a squeak the lad sprang to his feet and backed away, farther into the gap between the kitchen and the castle wall.

'Don't worry, I am not here to harm you,' Baldwin said soothingly.

'I should bloody hope not!' came a voice from behind him.

It was the cook. The big man stood looking suspiciously at Baldwin, his hand close to his knife.

'Master cook, there is nothing for you to fear,' Baldwin told him. 'I heard this knave weeping, and sought to help him.'

'He's fine.'

'Is he?' In some circumstances, Baldwin might have thought that the cook had been bullying the boy, but now, seeing how the knave ran to the man and hid behind him, gripping his shirt tightly, and how the cook himself ruffled his hair fondly, he grinned. 'That lad looks as though he'll be a sore trial before he's a grown man.'

'He already is,' the cook admitted. He looked down and jerked his head. 'Go on, Raff! Get back inside. I've been hunting for you.' He sighed with exasperation when the lad had disappeared. 'I am sorry, sir, I thought you might be . . .'

'Yes?' Baldwin enquired. And then he flushed a little as he realised. 'You thought I could have been seeking to hurt that boy?'

'Well, we have had a lad from the kitchen taken and murdered,' the cook said bleakly. 'I wish I could learn who did that. Whoever it was has no soul and no humanity. That bastard took a little boy with the sweetest nature in this city, and slaughtered him like a pig.'

Baldwin unbent a little. 'I saw the body. I was here when the Procureur was taking the child from your chest. I had forgotten, may God forgive me. There has been so much happening, with the Procureur being killed as well. So, tell me, the murderer was never found?'

'No. Little Jehanin died without justice. Now he's in his grave, and no one will bother to learn who did that to him. Who cares about a fellow like him when he's not the son of a baron?' His voice thickened, and he looked away.

'Friend cook, I am truly sorry. Perhaps it was merely an accident, as I first said?'

'His throat was stopped by a cord, you remember? How could that be an accident?' the cook sneered.

'I have known such accidents. In my own lands I investigate deaths and try to make sense of them,' Baldwin said. 'Was the cord a type that you use in the kitchen?'

'No. I have several cords which I use to bind carcasses – small for poultry, larger ones for venison and the bigger animals. There are ropes too. But this was none of them.'

'You are sure?'

The cook looked at him. 'The cords in the kitchen are all good quality, fine linens and the like. That which killed the boy was a rough one, made out of hemp or flax, I think. It was unlike anything I have in my kitchen, I can swear. And what sort of accident would lead to a boy being throttled like that?'

'At home, I found a miller's boy who'd been playing with a rope, and it became snagged on the hoist without his realising. When his father used the hoist, it lifted the boy as well, and there was nothing the father could do. A terrible accident. Then I saw a boy who was playing at swinging on a tree's bough with some string. Not high, he had to bend down to the rope, but he slipped, and his neck fell on to the rope, and he swung about, the rope tightening, and as he panicked, the rope choked his life away.'

'Jehanin was not playing on a tree, though. And there is no hoist in my kitchen.'

'I merely demonstrate that accidents can happen. Was he unpopular?'

'No, he was a lovely lad. All liked him.'

'I know you did, for I saw your distress at his death. But could one or two others among the staff have been jealous of your affection?'

'No. He was not a favourite, if that's what you mean. I merely liked him. But I like all my charges. I would be a poor master to them if I hated them all,' the cook said with asperity.

'You speak truly,' Baldwin agreed. Then, 'So could this have been someone who had a reason to detest *you*, and sought an easy means of upsetting you through the boy? I have known weakly men try to do just that.' Into his mind there sprang a picture of Sir Hugh le Despenser. It made Baldwin wonder whether he had taken Simon's house in order to get back at Baldwin.

'I am only a cook! Who would hate *me*? All I do is make people's lives more pleasant by cooking for them. I could not have offended anybody like that.'

'Is it possible that you might have had something valuable in your kitchen? Perhaps someone tried to steal something and was seen by the boy, so he killed the witness?'

'The only items of value in my kitchen are my meat and spices, and I'd swear that nothing's been stolen.'

'And you are convinced that Jean could find no reason for the lad's death? The Procureur was a most competent-looking man.'

'He gave no reason. I think it was that very day that he died, though. Perhaps he would have learned more, had he not been murdered.'

Louvre

Cardinal Thomas d'Anjou left his little chapel and returned to his own room. A clerk followed after him, and, knowing his habits, brought a small tray on which were a bowl and a goblet. D'Anjou washed his hands, dried them on the towel which the thoughtful clerk had provided, and then took the goblet.

It was one of his favourite pieces, this. A delightful cup of pewter on a solid stand, and with gilt to highlight the scene engraved around it. Faultlessly executed, it depicted the story of St Francis, from his early years rejecting his inheritance from his cloth-merchant father, to his preaching to the birds and his taming of the wolf of Gubbio, and the appearance of the stigmata.

Sitting now, he sipped from the goblet and considered that life. That a man could be so devoted to God that he might throw aside all his father's great wealth, was astonishing in such a backward age. It was two hundred years ago that St Francis had been born, while his parents were abroad in France, which was why he was named for the land. And he had heard a voice while he was in a shrine telling him to rebuild a church, so he had gone and sold some of his father's cloth to pay for the rebuilding. And that, naturally enough, led to his father's rage, and soon afterwards the two separated. Francis went so far as to throw off even the clothes which his father's money had bought for him, and he had to rely on the charity of the Bishop just to clothe himself.

He was clearly a deeply religious man. In the Cardinal's view, he was almost certainly insufferable, too. He had met some ascetic, religious types in his time, and often they were the most difficult and truculent of all. There was no negotiating with them. Which was why the Pope generally preferred the slightly more worldly when it came to diplomacy. They were easier to deal with.

The Cardinal sipped again, and was about to settle back to consider some messages recently arrived from the Pope, when there was a respectful knock at his door.

'Yes?'

'Cardinal, the Bishop Walter would like to speak with you.'

Thomas d'Anjou pursed his lips. Then he nodded silently

and finished his wine. There would be time later to read the letters.

'Bishop,' he said as Walter Stapledon arrived.

'Cardinal.'

The Bishop was feeling ever more anxious. The impression that men were looking at him askance was increasing, and had grown now to include almost all those in the English delegation, bar Baldwin, Sir Richard and Simon Puttock.

'Cardinal Thomas, I am very sorry to trouble you again.'

'What is it, Bishop? I am a little busy this evening.'

'I am deeply concerned. The Queen has not responded positively to my discussion with her.'

'Ah. But your difficulty with the accusation of being involved in the murder of that man – the Procureur – that has gone?'

'Yes, I think I am no longer considered guilty of that, I thank God. Yet still, I do have the duty to act as guardian to the Duke while he is here, and then to take the Queen home. Yet she will not allow any discussion of such a—'

'Then you must hold yourself in preparation against the day that she agrees at last.'

'You have seen how she habitually wears a widow's weeds? How easy do you think it would be to persuade her to come back to England when she refuses even to make the effort to show that she is willing to tolerate the Despenser?'

'From all I have heard, your Despenser does not make it easy for her to return. And not he alone,' the Cardinal said pointedly.

'Sir Hugh acts in the best interests of the realm as he sees it.'

The Cardinal eyed him steadily. 'Let us dispense with polite forms, Bishop. The Despenser sees only his own interests and his own benefits. He does nothing for the good of the realm.

That is clear enough even here in France. I would myself not command a dog to return to his power. And you want the Queen Isabella to submit to him? I find your demands upon her astonishing.'

'I only submit the desires of her husband, my King,' Stapledon said tersely.

'Only him? Not the wishes of his *great* friend Despenser? And how convincing do you think that will sound to her?'

'Cardinal, this is a matter of a husband and wife. A man and woman bound by holy—'

'Matrimony, yes. I know. And it is also true, is it not, that your Sir Hugh le Despenser has already attempted to have the Pope annul the marriage? Sir Hugh, not the Queen's husband. Sir Hugh sent his emissary to the Pope, did he not?'

Stapledon gaped in shock. 'But . . . he could not! There could be no justification for such an act.'

'Absolutely right. There is no justification. And yet it happened. Curious, no? So, you see, Bishop, I will not aid you to have the Queen sent back to the land where her position and person are held in such low esteem. I would deem that an act of deplorable cruelty.'

'I . . . I shall have to consider matters further.'

'Do so. I would suggest that you make your peace with her, Bishop, for she is a calm, sensible lady. All she requires, I believe, is the money the King promised her for her upkeep while she was here in France looking after her son. *Their* son. And you hold the purse. You can release the money.'

'The King ordered me to hold on to it until she agreed to return to England,' Bishop Walter said wretchedly.

'Then I fear you are gripped on the horns of a dilemma. I do not envy your position.'

'There is no choice. I am a servant of my King,' the Bishop said firmly. 'I will obey my King's commands. I would prefer to make peace with the Queen, but if I may not, I may not.'

'Then go in peace, Bishop. I will pray for you.'

The Bishop nodded, but then his attention was drawn to the goblet. 'What a marvellous piece of workmanship. May I look at it?'

'Yes. It is one of a kind, I think. You like such trinkets?'

'I have seen its like only once before,' the Bishop said absently.

'Where was that?'

'I used to be the chaplain to Pope Clement V. He had a pair like this. I remember them clearly.'

'Made by the same man, I have no doubt,' the Cardinal said shortly. He took his goblet back, weighing it in his hand with pleasure. 'I have had this for these twenty years past. Those which you saw are probably the ones which I myself gave to him. Clement was always a shrewd and kindly man to those who respected him.'

'Yes,' the Bishop said. But he could recall the terror of the destruction of the Templars, wrought largely at the instigation of Clement. That was still a matter of shame, he thought.

The Bishop had a short walk to his chamber, and he marched quickly with a couple of boys holding lanterns. Ever since the murder of Walter de Lechelade in Exeter Cathedral Close some forty-five years before by the Dean's men, the Bishops of Exeter had been made aware of the dangers of walking about at night in the dark without aid.

He paid little attention to the way, for he was still smarting at the Cardinal's attitude. It was remarkable to him that a fellow striver in the service of God should be so unhelpful. If he himself had been asked to assist a man like the Cardinal, he would have done all he could to support him. To be thus ejected, almost as though he was some form of beggar at the door, was humiliating in the extreme. He was a Bishop, in God's name, not some humble penitent who deserved a flea in his ear.

The door to the passage that led to his rooms was just here. He thanked the boys, gave them a few coins for their trouble, and entered.

He felt exhausted. Travelling here to France had unnerved him in the first place, because he knew how unpopular he had become. But to arrive here and have that harridan the Queen rail at him before everyone in the French court, that had brought home to him how fragile his position was. If possible, it had been made even more so by the effect of the French official's death. To have people accuse him, to actually believe that he was capable of such a vile attack – that was repellent! And meanwhile he still had little idea how on earth he could make his way homewards, for he dare not return to the King without Queen Isabella, or at the very least, some kind of promise from her that she would soon follow him.

The passage was lit by occasional candles, set widely apart. He walked along, careful to avoid stepping too close to them. It would not be the first time a man had accidentally brushed against a candle and either scorched a great hole in an expensive robe, or even had a smudge of molten tallow stain his sleeves.

Her behaviour was *intolerable*, he told himself. How the woman could think that she . . .

He was at a narrower part of the corridor when a hand reached about his throat, yanking him off his feet and drawing his body over a large chest. The man had been hiding in the shadows beyond the chest, and by pushing the Bishop over it, Stapledon could not defend himself in any way whatever. His legs were taken away by the chest's lid, and his head fell back to crash against the wall behind, giving him a sickening sensation.

'Bishop Walter, I am so glad to see you,' a voice hissed.

The Bishop looked up, but it might have been a demon who gripped him for all he could see. All he was aware of was a blackness, as of the cowl of a hood with nothing inside. It was a terrifying sight. He grabbed for his crucifix, preparing to jab it upwards, when suddenly he felt a prick at his throat. A knife!

Strangely enough, this made him less fearful. He was petrified at the thought of a devil, or any minion of hell, but a man was a different matter. Now, he could see the glitter of reflected candlelight in his attacker's eyes. They looked familiar – but from where?

'Release me, churl,' Bishop Walter said.

'Silence! Call me churl? You'll be buried here in a pauper's grave if you are not careful, Bishop. The Queen just wants her money, but there are plenty of others here in Paris who would like nothing better than to skin you alive and feed your body to the crows. You have dispossessed so many, robbed so many – you have enemies everywhere.'

'It is a lie!'

The dagger pressed upwards a little. 'You dare to contradict me? Before God, you craven, quaking thing! You will die here unless you unbend. Perhaps it is too late already. You should fly from France. Remain here, and you will soon be dead.'

Bishop Walter felt the hand gripping his throat thrust forward, and it was only by flinging his arms wide and latching his fingers on to the lid of the chest that he stopped himself from falling. Sitting up shakily, he kissed his crucifix as he gazed first one way, then the other. The corridor appeared empty.

It was some moments before he could stand. His legs were

unharmed, but he was uncertain whether they might support his weight or not. When he put his hand on the chest lid, his arms began shaking and he sat there, looking down, nausea washing over him, until a servant hurried past, checking the candles.

'Are you all right, Bishop?' he asked.

'I am perfectly well, I thank you,' Bishop Walter said.

The boy tutted to himself. 'Someone's snuffed all these candles. They will keep doing that. I'll soon have them ready again.'

With a spill, he brought a flame from another set of candles further along the corridor, and relit those in the candelabra nearest the chest. 'Are you sure you are all right, Bishop?'

'Yes. I am fine,' Bishop Walter said, and now his voice was fully under control. 'You came from that direction?' he asked, pointing back towards the Cardinal's rooms.

'Yes, my Lord.'

'Tell me – did you pass a man as you came this way? A tall man, strong, with a hood over his head?'

The boy considered. 'There's no one about at this time of day,' he said after a moment. 'Was there someone you wanted to see?'

'No. That is well, I thank you,' Bishop Walter said. If the man had not gone that way, he must be along this corridor – but if he was, there was only the Bishop's own chamber at the end. The man must have gone the other way, surely.

His voice . . . it had sounded more English than French, he realised suddenly. Conversing had been easy. And the voice had been oddly familiar.

He stood, gripping his crucifix again, and made his way to his rooms.

And then his legs began to shiver and wobble as though they could no longer support him. He had never before felt so fearful. Someone had been here, in this corridor, an Englishman, someone who had cause to detest him, and someone who had been able to fly away like a wisp of smoke, and just as silently. He might have been a ghost, were it not for the sore bruising the Bishop felt at his neck.

Bishop Walter stood at his door, and then shot a glance behind him, almost scared of what be might there. He half-expected to see that looming shape again.

Chapter Twenty-Nine

Louvre

Baldwin was still considering the sad tale of the cook the next morning when the summons came for him to hurry to the Bishop's chamber.

'What ails him now?' he muttered.

'He is prey to fears of a natural kind,' Simon said more graciously.

'Aye, well, if he is that keen to see us, we would be churlish indeed not to go. And then, on the return, the bar may be open,' Sir Richard said hopefully.

They found the Bishop sitting on a large chair facing them as they walked into his room. There was a clerk at his side holding a slate board, while two others sat at a desk behind.

'Sir Baldwin, Sir Richard, Simon, I am very grateful that you could come so swiftly.'

'It was our pleasure, my Lord Bishop. The Duke is being entertained by his tutor for a little, and then will go to his mother. Sir Henry is with him, so we have our morning free,' Baldwin said.

'That is good,' the Bishop said. He then stood and

---

[1] Thursday, 3 October 1325

paced before turning and facing them. 'I am very anxious,' he blurted out. 'I fear an attempt may be made upon my life.'

'My Lord Bishop, I am sure you need have no such alarms. There is no one here who could wish you harm,' Baldwin said, and he felt irritation that the Bishop had called them to him for such a foolish reason.

'Look at this, Sir Baldwin,' the Bishop said, and drew down the collar of his robe.

There, at his thin neck, the flesh somewhat pale, rather like a plucked chicken, there were four large bruises on his right side, one on the left.

'Dear Jesus!' Baldwin hissed. 'Sir Richard?'

The Coroner joined him. 'A goodly-sized fist, that man'll have, if I'm any judge. A good, great paw to mangle you in that manner, me Lord. Who was it?'

'I have no idea,' the Bishop said. 'I was attacked in the dark. And yet there was something familiar about the man's voice. He was English, I think.'

'Has anyone else tried to warn you away from here?' Baldwin asked.

Almost everyone, the Bishop thought to himself sadly. 'No one for certain, no. But I think that all would prefer to see me gone. I am an embarrassment to the Duke, an irritant to the Queen, and a shameful beggar in the eyes of King Charles. No one wishes me here, and yet I may not go home. All I want is to return to Exeter and rest my weary bones, but I must remain here until the Queen concedes that her place is with her husband. What may I do?'

'First, you should be better guarded,' Baldwin said firmly. 'We do not want you harmed, my Lord Bishop. Second, I think that King Charles should be informed that your life has been threatened. The King has accepted you as his guest, and safe-conducts have been issued. If you are harmed here, it will reflect most disastrously upon the French King.'

'That is true,' the Bishop murmured.

'But that fact alone makes me wonder who'd be stupid enough to try to threaten Bishop Walter,' Sir Richard said.

Simon shrugged. 'There are any number of Frenchmen who dislike the Bishop for his diplomatic efforts.'

'Aye, and some English, too,' the knight grunted.

Baldwin smiled. 'We know where the threat may lie, but the important thing just now is to make sure that the Bishop is protected. We will have to mount guard ourselves, and also see whomsoever else we may enlist to help us.'

Paris, near the River Seine

Vital shrugged his cloak around his shoulders. Here in the alleyway, no sun could reach them, and it felt as though they were living in a perpetual chill.

'I hope he's not just testing our cupidity.'

'More likely he is looking to see how to get himself out. I wouldn't be surprised if he'd thought we'd bring him along without chains, and he'd try to run for it,' Pons said.

Vital gave him a sidelong look. His companion was dressed all in shabby brown, like a worker along the shores. It was only the sword which made him stand out, and that was mostly hidden under his cloak.

'Bring him up here!' Pons suddenly barked behind him.

There was a small force of five-and-twenty men, all armed with good polearms and long knives, all picked carefully for the task ahead. In their midst was Le Boeuf, and now he was manhandled up to meet Pons and Vital. 'These chains, can't you—'

'No,' Pons said. 'If this is the genuine place, and your work brings this matter to an end, then I personally will release you.'

If there's nothing there, you will go back to the cell, and I will tell all that you tried to sell me the King, but failed.'

'But they'd flay me, if they thought I'd done that!'

'Then you had best hope that he is in there and that we capture him, eh?'

Le Boeuf stared at him with his one good eye, and then peered over his shoulder. 'It's that one, the third door, the one that looks like it's only got one hinge. That's where he lives.'

'Good,' Pons said, and issued his instructions quickly. The men separated, with one smaller force of eight running off to the rear of the building, at the river's edge. Meanwhile, Pons and Vital waited, watching and muttering, Pons counting to four thousand, which was the amount of time the second force would need to get into position.

'Time's up,' he announced quietly. 'Good luck, boys – good luck, Vital. Mind your nice cloak, eh?'

'You mind your moustaches, old friend,' Vital murmured, and then the two gripped their scabbards in their left fists and ran lightly over the road.

There was no sign of life inside. Pons leaned down to peer in through a gap in the timbers of the door, but could see nothing. No lights, no people, just a mess of broken planks and refuse of all kinds. A rat scurried, suddenly alarmed.

Pons looked over, and Vital shrugged. 'Doesn't look very lived in, eh?' and then he beckoned.

The men rushed over the road and ran at the door. There was a loud crack and splintering as the door gave way, and then they were all inside, pelting up the narrow corridor, up some rickety stairs, men fanning out in all directions, shouting and screaming at the tops of their voices, slamming weapons against closed doors, thundering about up in chambers overhead.

Vital looked down at his feet. 'I think he was wrong about this place, don't you?'

Pons was about to respond, when there came a shout from outside, at the rear of the building.

'There's a body here!'

The King swore and slammed a fist into his cupped hand. 'Who betrayed us? Who dared to tell the officers about us, about our home?'

Amélie was still curled on the bed of furs, and now she stretched, lithe as a cat, curling her fingers over, and staring along the length of her arms and hands with satisfaction. 'Perhaps it was the poor assassin you tried to double-cross? Or one of your men who deserves more money than you paid?'

'Shut up whore! If I need the advice of a bitch like you, I'll ask for it,' the King spat. He returned to the window out over the Seine, watching as the men floundered through the thick river ooze to the figure which still lay out nearer the water.

'It is the dry summer this year. Apart from the rains in the last couple of weeks, it's been dry,' his clerk said nervously.

The King made no comment, but stared silently at the work outside. 'They should have carried him further out,' he hissed. 'The river was dropping already when they put the men out there.'

'We didn't know,' said Peter the peasant. He wasn't going to whine. He'd done all he could, sliding down the rope to kill that man on the flats to stop the officers being called.

'You didn't *know*?'

'It wasn't our fault if the bastard didn't get washed away like all the other refuse from the city. Anyway, a man found out there could have come from anywhere. Didn't have to have been thrown from here.'

'There is much which is interesting about this. First is the stupidity of a man like you leaving a corpse out there for anyone to find. Then there's the way you left it there for three days so the officers could come and find it. But worst of all, there's the incredible dimness of a man like you who can't see that these fellows were told where to go. They walked right in through the house we used to deposit the bodies in, didn't they?'

Peter shrugged. 'It was the nearest house to the body. Where else would they have gone?'

The King nodded and then, in a fluid movement, he turned, drew his knife and slashed it across Peter's face. It left a fine red line that began at Peter's right cheekbone, missed the hollow near his nose, then marked over the nose, to the left cheek, running right across it almost to the man's ear. The line remained until Peter's mouth opened in a shocked bawl, and then a fine spray burst from it.

Peter's hands came up to his face, and his eyes stared down in horror at them as they were bedewed with his blood. He drew a breath to cry out, but by then the King had reversed his blade. His hand snaked out and gripped Peter's neck, suddenly pulling his sergeant towards him. The sobbing man had no time to scream before the knife stabbed upwards three times, two to the lungs, the last to the heart. He was dead even as his body slumped on the blade.

'Take that tub of lard away. I don't want to see his face again,' the King said with cold dispassion. He wiped his knife on his sleeve, unheeding, as two of his men pulled the twitching form out of the room. 'We move from here tonight. We'll go to the rooms near Saint Jacques.'

Amélie pouted. 'But I don't like it there. It stinks of dead animals all the time.'

'You will get used to it or you'll die,' the King said matter-of-factly. He felt his broken teeth with his tongue.

This was the result of being slack. He had been enjoying his life too much. There were times to take leisure, but not when a man dared to defy you. The fool Jacquot had killed his men and brought this on to him, and he wouldn't take it. Whether or not Jacquot had sent the men over there to try to catch the King and his men, he didn't know. Probably not, because Jacquot would have directed them to this, his main residence, not the other house. In the past the King had called that chamber his 'courthouse', because it was where he had his men go when they were accused of some misdemeanour. If they were said to be keeping too much of their whores' money, if they were not declaring the full contents of a purse they'd stolen, if they 'forgot' to mention a gambling game that had paid well, they were taken to the courthouse so that their case could be heard. And then justice was administered according to the King's whim. Sometimes the accused was confirmed as guilty, sometimes the accuser was declared to be at fault, and more often than not, the two were forced to fight to the death to determine the outcome.

The advantage of the courthouse was that it was far enough away from any freeman's habitation. Those who lived down here at the side of the river were the poorest and meanest. They would not go to the Sergent to report a murder or screams. And that meant that his courts could be held in safety, and that the bodies afterwards could be usefully slipped into the Seine, to be taken downriver, far away from the place of their death.

If not Jacquot, someone else must have sent the men to the courthouse. In the last few days all had heard of the arrests and the numbers of men who'd been swept up from the streets. Any of them could have known of the King's courthouse. It was a building of ill-repute because of the stories of screams which emanated from it late into the night.

He clenched his fist and set it on the wall, glowering as the men lifted the body from the mud and began to drag it laboriously towards the shoreline. He might never find out who had tried to inform on him. However, there was one man he could force to pay. He hadn't even begun to think about Jacquot yet. Finding someone to destroy his best killer would be immensely hard. Ideally, it should be a man-at-arms who wore the tabard of the King of France. Someone like that would be able to command respect, and even the true King's men could be attracted to money, the same as any other.

There was one man, of course. Up at the castle . . . Perhaps he could be persuaded, for a good fee.

And then killed, of course.

As an afterthought, he beckoned one of his men. 'Follow them, Mal, and see where they go. I want to know where they came from – and where they take the body. Report to me at Saint Jacques.'

Pons and Vital eyed the mud-sodden body in silence. The wound at his throat proved that he had been killed in a professional manner.

'Executed, certainly,' Pons said.

'Are there any other wounds? Was this the last of many, or the first?' Vital wondered.

'It shows that this building has been used for some killings,' Pons said, looking about him again.

'Likely, yes.'

They had seen that this body had been close to the trap-door which led to the river waters and then they had been called upstairs, where they found a large-sized room. There had been fights in here. Blood lay upon the rough-hewn planks in several places, but it was not fresh. The odour was that dull, dry smell which spoke of old death. A bench with a small trestle sat in one corner of the room, and there was a hook in the middle, while to one side stood a small chest. In that they had found some scraps of cloth, six red, one blue. They were baffled.

'Have him cleaned,' Vital said to the Sergent who stood guard over the dead man. 'At least he has not been here for too long.'

'And not in the water,' Pons observed. 'If he had, his hands would have turned to gloves.'

'Yes. I have seen the bodies too.'

They both had. Murdered men often turned up in the river, where their flesh became so engorged with water that it could slip from the meat beneath. It was one of the more revolting kinds of death.

'Can I go free? You see I wasn't lying. They were here.'

The two turned back to their captive. His milky eye made him look still more beseeching, and he held out his wrists like a supplicant. 'Please?'

Pons considered. 'Very well, you can go free when we get back and can unshackle you. But first, what can you tell us about these cloth strips?'

The man looked wary, but then he nodded. Perhaps the thought of his imminent release gave him courage, Pons thought.

'It is for the voting. When a man is accused of a crime against the King of Thieves, they hold a court here. When the jury votes, one of them is made executioner for the guilty. That is why there is one odd colour. The man who picks that is the one who must kill the guilty party. Not that they use the cloths much. Usually it's a matter of letting the accuser meet the accused man, and they fight it out.'

'You seem to know a lot about them?'

Le Boeuf gave a wry little grin. 'There are few in Paris who don't, other than those who work for the other King.'

'How so?'

'There is little that the King of Thieves doesn't know about. If a man takes your purse, or sells you a woman, or if you buy a loaf of bread that is light, it is certain that the King will make money from you.'

'In that case,' Pons said, 'I'd like you to have a bargain with me. You find out where he is now, and we'll not only release you, we'll pay you too.'

'You can't pay me enough. He would kill me.'

'He is so powerful he can kill you without difficulty?'

'If he heard I had taken you to him, my life would be worth nothing.'

'In that case, you should stay in chains, Le Boeuf. Because it is sure that he will learn you brought us here today, if he is so powerful as you say. You had best ensure that we find him very quickly, before he finds you.'

Louvre

It was late in the afternoon that Hugues heard the knock at his door. 'Yes?'

Amélie wandered in, a faint smile at her mouth. She crossed the floor to his table, and hitched a hip on to it.

'I haven't time, woman. Go and find another suitor,' he muttered dismissively, but his eyes were fixed on her inner thigh. That glorious, soft sweep of perfect white flesh was so close to him, he could lean forward and lick it, bite it . . .

There was a rattle of coins, and he stared at the little leather purse she placed before him.

'I'm here for the King,' she said with amusement as he drew back from her and pulled at the drawstrings.

'What is this for?' Hugues demanded. 'Twenty livres Parisis?'

'There is a man he would like removed, Sieur Hugues,' she replied, and began to explain.

Chapter Thirty

Friday after the Feast of the Archangel Michael[1]

Louvre, Paris

Baldwin knew that the last day had been tiresome for all three of them, but there was no doubt that the Bishop lived in fear of his life.

There was no telling who it was who had given the Bishop such a fright. Baldwin had looked at all of the English knights who were present in the Louvre, but none showed any sign of guilt. That was no surprise, though. The sad truth was, all of them appeared to look with disfavour upon the Bishop now. Even Lord John, who was the commander of the knights and men-at-arms set to protect the Queen, appeared to have taken more to the Queen's side.

It was that which was most alarming to Baldwin. In England all these men had been chosen specifically for their loyalty to the King, and yet now, after only a matter of days for some, they were fallen into the Queen's camp. Could the same thing happen in England itself? If the Queen could so easily sway the men over here in France, could she not take them with her to England and persuade others to her cause? If that were so, and if she could raise a small number of men to go with her, she would be invincible.

---

[1] Friday, 4 October 1325

Naturally there were attractions to such an expedition. Few indeed would complain to hear that Sir Hugh le Despenser had been deposed, and ideally executed for his many crimes, and yet Baldwin was most anxious, for if the Queen were to become so all-powerful, it would mean that the King himself could lose his throne, and Baldwin was not happy at the thought of another civil war. The land had suffered too much from such strife before.

Sir Richard was sitting on a throne-like seat in the Bishop's chamber when Baldwin arrived there that morning. Wolf immediately lumbered across the floor and set a great paw on Sir Richard's lap.

'Geddoffit, ye brute!' he roared, and put a hand on the dog's head to tickle behind Wolf's ears, the action giving the lie to his bellow. Wolf sat and shuffled his arse around until he could sit gazing up soulfully into Sir Richard's face.

'Where is the Bishop?' Baldwin asked.

'Bishop's gone off praying,' the Coroner said, biting into a chicken's leg and waving the bone in the direction of the Bishop's chapel. Wolf eyed the leg with anticipation.

'That is good,' Baldwin said. Not many men would dare to attack a Bishop at prayer.

'Heard something. Could explain some of the mutterin's among the other English here,' Sir Richard said. He sucked the last juices from the chicken bone, then methodically licked each finger before wiping them on his breast. 'Mortimer's said to be in Hainault plannin' an invasion. You heard that? There's talk that the Queen is like to support him. She's hardly enamoured of her old man, is she? Eh?'

He belched and set a booted foot on the table in front of him. 'Makes it difficult for a man to see the best way forward for himself.'

Baldwin nodded. 'A man must think of his own position with care.'

'I mean, what if there was an invasion? The King's ships could destroy any fleet, I'm sure – but there's always the risk that the Queen and her men might land. And that worries me.'

It was a great pity, Baldwin thought, that a man like this, a decent, loyal man, should feel the urge to contemplate forswearing his vows of allegiance. For that was what he was saying: that if the Queen were to invade, that he must turn his coat and become her ally. And up and down the realm, others would think the same.

'I mean,' Sir Richard carried on, 'when the men have been slaughtered, as they will be, I'd hate to see her captured. The Queen herself held in gaol? A terrible thought.'

'You mean . . .' Baldwin gaped, although he quickly recovered. There were times when he felt that his ability to understand his fellow man was sorely damaged. 'You would remain loyal to the King, then?'

Sir Richard's eyes narrowed with humour. 'And what else would you expect a man to say in these times, me old friend?'

Baldwin was about to laugh aloud, when there came a knock at the door. He crossed the floor and opened it to find Simon outside. 'Hello, Simon.'

'I've just been asked by the Cardinal, Thomas of Anjou, to send you to meet him,' Simon said. 'He was most insistent.'

'I'd best go, then,' Baldwin sighed. He eyed his dog and said, 'Look after him, would you?'

'I will,' said Sir Richard.

'I was not talking to you, old friend,' Baldwin chuckled.

Tavern near Grand Châtelet

Pons sat at the tavern's one table on a bench that felt as though it had been carved from stone and peered across the street, waiting. There was a howling gale coming through the unglazed window, or so it felt, and he wàs forced to pull his cotte closer about his breast. The weather certainly had changed in the last days, he thought. There was a fire in the room behind him, but he preferred to remain here where he could see who was walking up and down the street. At last he saw three men marching, his friend Vital in their midst.

'I hope I see you well?' he said when Vital had sat and the tavern-keeper had been sent to fetch a jug of hot wine.

'Yes – not that you'd guess it after the night I've had,' Vital replied, pulling his cloak about him. 'It is damned cold in those gaols, you know.'

'How was it?'

Vital reached for the jug as it arrived. His normally sombre mood had turned positively melancholic in the last few hours.

They had agreed that one of them must go to the gaols where the different men had been installed after their arrests, and try to learn more about this elusive 'King of Thieves'. Both knew that Pons was the more competent at interrogation, but this time they had another duty – to follow after Le Boeuf and ensure that he didn't make a run for it, or go straight to this 'King' and tell him all. It was Pons again who was best at concealing himself and following their man without being observed, so this was what he had done.

'I learned that there is a King of the Seine who lives deep in the water, but he only comes out once in a while. Oh, and there is a man in the Temple who believes that his arm is being slowly eaten by pink lions the size of a man's thumb. He kept pulling them off to show me.'

'That is the sum of your news?'

'Oh, no. There is a great deal more. I haven't begun yet. Did you know that Paris is sinking into the mud? Or that the Royal

Family is dead? The King was apparently murdered some years ago, with his wife, and there is no heir. We are waiting for the happy time when the anti-Christ appears and slays us all in his period of misrule, apparently. And one man told me, in all seriousness, that the stars are all the souls of the dead. I asked him why it was that the number didn't jump and leave us in bright starlight after the Famine when so many died, and he muttered that they were sent far away. Ach! I am exhausted and have nothing to show for it.'

'And I have little better,' Pons said regretfully. 'Our Le Boeuf wandered off to his lodging and remained there. There was no way in or out without him being seen, and we kept a close watch on him. This morning I left André there.'

'So we have learned nothing, then.'

'There is one thing. I am still perplexed as to why this King might have ordered the death of Jean. The Procureur was a most determined man. Surely he was killed because of the way that one of his investigations affected the King – or a man who paid the King.'

'And that helps us?' Vital demanded lugubriously.

'No, perhaps not. But it is a thought to be kept.'

'We did learn that Jean was investigating the deaths of the man at the Louvre and his wife.'

'Quite so. De Nogaret and his wife. Perhaps this King of Thieves was responsible for one or both murders?'

Vital nodded slowly. 'In that case, we need to see what we may learn of them, too. De Poissy's servant should have any relevant information, surely?'

'And meanwhile we have to hope that our man brings us some news, too.'

His hopes were quickly to be dashed.

*

Paris

Jacquot wandered apparently idly as he sought food. The place was full this morning, and he was bumped and shoved as he went, but the blows scarcely registered.

With a thick pottage and hunk of bread inside him, he felt more rational, but his mind was still racing. There were men who would kill him now, for the money which the King had offered. He had the choice of going to the King and attempting to make some peace, but he knew that the door was barred to him before he could even test the way. The King had been humiliated by him. It was, in truth, astonishing that he was not yet dead.

So his earlier resolution, to fight it out, was the only way to get through this.

There were many in the city who lived like rats, scavenging, thieving, killing. Not all were in the pay of the King, and it was one of these whom Jacquot sought now, a churl who knew neither mother nor father, but who scraped a living on the streets. 'Little Hound' he was named, for his skill at sniffing out targets. He would invariably win a purse or trinket from a walker without their realising his knife had liberated them of their wealth. A skilled and practised thief, Little Hound was one of that rare number who preferred a life of obscurity to one in the King's ranks.

'You are alive, then?' Little Hound said.

'Last time I looked,' Jacquot agreed.

'Sounds like your master's in trouble, though.'

'How so?'

'Hadn't you heard? His rooms were stormed yesterday. The law is on to him, it seems.' The man picked his nose, eyed the residue on his finger with disgust, and wiped it on the wall beside him. He was a short, skinny man of perhaps four and twenty years, and dirt was ingrained in each wrinkle of his flesh, making him appear more dark-skinned than he truly was. One eye was whitened, where a man had stabbed him in a bar fight, but the other was bright blue, and very shrewd.

'What else?' Jacquot said.

'A quick man might be able to learn much . . .'

Jacquot disliked the man, but he was undeniably useful at giving out information. Wearily, he tugged a livre Parisis from his purse and held it up.

'Very good. Even a small hound must eat, *hein*?' Little Hound said with a grin of discoloured teeth. 'Well, it seems the officers were seeking the murderer of the city Procureur. Somehow they had gained the impression that it was the King himself who had arranged Jean de Poissy's death, so they went there to arrest him. But he was elsewhere. All they discovered was a dead man in the river.'

'How did they know to go there?'

'How do they learn anything? They found a man and threatened to break all the bones in his body. He soon agreed to help them.'

'What else?'

'What else should there be? Isn't that enough?'

Jacquot said nothing, but stood very still and silent, watching him.

'Oh, very well. From what I've heard, the instruction to attack the King came from within the Louvre.'

'Who?'

'I don't know, but everyone knows that the King's latest whore visits the castle as well.'

'Does she?' Jacquot murmured. That was interesting.

After paying him another livre, Jacquot left him a short while later.

So, someone was selling the King, he mused as he walked. That would make life easier. Now he had an idea that could work to his advantage. His only problem was the next person he must visit.

Amélie was not someone he had ever wanted to see again, but just now she might well be useful. After all, it seemed she had better contacts than he had realised.

Louvre

Baldwin entered the room with an awareness of danger. It was only slightly less pronounced than the time he had walked in on Despenser in his new home, the Temple in London.

In the case of Despenser there was no concealment of his nature and the danger to all who crossed him; in the Cardinal's the threat was much more subtle. Baldwin knew that this room belonged to one of the most powerful men in the French King's realm and that meant, by extension, in the whole of Christendom.

He was not an intimidating man, though. Almost as tall as Baldwin, he was not stooped, and gave the impression of having all his faculties unimpaired, which was itself surprising, in Baldwin's experience. He held out his hand with his ring, and Baldwin obediently bent to kiss it, all the while keeping his eyes fixed on the Cardinal's.

In them he could discern only friendliness, which was itself reassuring.

'Sir Baldwin, I am glad that you could come to see me, especially at such short notice.'

'I am happy to be of service.'

'Good. Because I would like you to listen to a few words. It concerns your King.'

Baldwin felt his breath stop in his throat. 'I think that any matter concerning him could be better put to another.'

'Sir Baldwin, you are an intelligent man. Of this on all sides I am assured.'

The contraction of the sentence was almost enough to make Baldwin smile, but he kept his face straight. 'I would hope not to be considered a complete fool.'

'Your King is a wise and good monarch, you think?'

'He is my King.'

The Cardinal gave a dry smile. It was as brittle as a dried leaf. 'I would expect a knight to say nothing foul about his liege-lord. However, you must be aware that your loyalty is not being rewarded. Excuse me one moment.' He strode quickly over the floor of the chamber and left by a door in the farther wall.

Baldwin felt his hackles rise. He stepped away from the middle of the room, his hand reaching for his sword, his eyes casting about for danger. It was impossible not to feel the malice in this room, he thought. It would be best to walk from the place, go back to his Bishop and continue his vigil there, but if he were to do that, he would not only have snubbed the Cardinal, but also demonstrated that he truly believed the man was capable of attempting to harm him – and that would be a grave insult to the French King.

Backed to the wall, he stood a while, listening. From here the noises of the courtyard were muted. The hammering of the smiths, the cries and shrieks of all the servants, the bellows of the stewards, the agonised squealing of the pigs being slaughtered, all were far off, as though in a different building altogether, and that fact alone made him feel more anxious. What he would have given for his sergeant, Edgar, or Simon to be at his side. For he was sure that he was about to be attacked.

There was a slight waft of air. He felt it on the right-hand side of his beard, and saw the tapestry near his shoulder ripple. There was a secret door behind it.

Moving with elaborate slowness, he began to draw his

sword. It was half out of the scabbard when the tapestries parted and he saw a familiar figure.

'Ah, Sir Baldwin. I know already that you are a loyal servant of my husband. Do you intend to slay me?' the Queen asked.

Chapter Thirty-One

Slums east and north,
Paris

André was no novice to the art of watching a house. Any man who had been in the service of Pons would soon learn that his post was usually to stand in the rain and the chill wind without cover of any sort, and normally in the dead of night.

In his time André had watched suspected thieves, murderers and traitors as well as those who were thought to be at risk, but this was the first time he had been told to watch someone who potentially fulfilled *all* the criteria.

Le Boeuf was not a pleasant character. André had already been asking a few of the people nearby about him, while Pons was originally watching their quarry. Sending André was as clear as pinning a notice to the door announcing that the King's men were investigating little Le Boeuf. Pons wanted him to realise that he was being watched.

The doorway where he was standing was dark enough, he thought. There wasn't much likelihood that he'd be seen. His dark cloak and tan clothing would help, too, as would his swarthy features and beard. He only hoped and prayed that no inquisitive Sergent would come along and ask what he was doing there, loitering with such obvious contempt for the laws of the city.

There was little to watch, in truth. The chamber in which Le Boeuf lived remained dark. It had been so since the early morning when Pons had set him here. There was nothing happening, no one to see. André was here, freezing off both ballocks, and all for no purpose. It already felt as though the whole of his left hand had frozen solid, and he wasn't so sure that his face was safe. If only it was still summer. At least in the summer he didn't freeze.

Nor did he die. He felt the thread around his throat rather than seeing it slip over his head, and felt it tighten about his skin before he even had time to raise a hand to try to stop it. He tried to scrabble with his fingers to reach under it, but it was already beneath his flesh, cutting into it. There was nothing he could do to pull at it; nothing on which to gain purchase. All he could do was scrape at his throat ineffectually, while the hideous cord crushed his windpipe and stopped the breath in his neck. And then there was a sensation of collapse, and the madness rose in his mind as he felt his life draining away, because his mind was working normally, and rationally it knew that he was going to die, and die now – slowly, painfully, his lungs screaming, his mouth gaping.

He fell back, his heels striking frantically at the ground, while his eyes bulged and his tongue thickened in his mouth, blocking what little airway there was. His hands reached behind him at last, trying in desperation to claw at his killer's face, eyes, throat.

And he failed. The man waited a little longer as the heels stilled, the fingers relaxed, the shoulders eased and the breast stopped its mad jerking. He let the cord go, and very gently stroked André's face, his hair, stroking down to his neck, which he took suddenly in both hands, and twisted while pulling, until there was an audible crunching of bone.

Then Hugues the castellan stood again and looked over the road towards the house where Le Boeuf lived.

Le Boeuf would have to die. He was a problem, and problems were there to be resolved.

Louvre

'Sit, Sir Baldwin.'

He rose from his bow, and backed himself to a stool. 'Your Highness, I am terribly sorry. I had no idea . . .'

'. . . that the good Cardinal could have brought you here for some ulterior motive of your Queen? I am not surprised. But there is much which may surprise *you*.'

'I am sure you are right.'

'You know my husband has ordered my return, but you are not surprised that I am still here?'

'No.'

'Why?'

'Because you have enemies in England.'

'Despenser, naturally. And Bishop Walter. He is a particular enemy of mine. He hates me.'

'I would not say . . .' Baldwin was silenced by a look. Shame-facedly, he grinned. 'Well, just now, with you refusing his King's command, perhaps yes, he does dislike you a little.'

'Or a lot. But thank you for not lying to me, Sir Baldwin. Tell me – what would you do in my position?'

'Me? Either return immediately and beg forgiveness, or petition the Pope to annul your marriage and remain here.'

She looked at him quickly. 'Did you know that the Despenser has already attempted that? Ah, but almost everyone knows. Why should I delude myself that I have any secrets any more?'

'Your Royal Highness, you have many friends. Could you not merely go home and discuss this with the King, and petition your friends to help you?'

'Which friends do you think would help me? The King has

disbanded my own household. In England I am as free as a caged lark. I may sing, but only because if I do not, I will starve. And no one dares to speak up for me. Not while the King and Despenser reject me. Do you think I am stupid?'

'No, my Lady. Never. But I do hope that you do not intend to harm so many people in our country. If you wait over here, that is one thing. It will delight the King's enemies, and serve only to weaken him. That may mean that your son's inheritance is endangered.'

'What else might I do?'

'You know that as well as I. There are rumours of Mortimer.'

'There are?'

'Sir Roger Mortimer is already the King's most detested enemy, my Lady. If you go to him, you will cause a great deal of anger and resentment. Again, that must put your son's future at risk.'

'You think that the King would dare to suggest that I was a whore? That he would say our son was a bastard?'

Her voice had risen with her rage, and now she stood, quivering with fury before him.

He bowed his head. 'My Lady, I do not accuse, I merely say what others will. The King will have poison poured into his ears by the Despenser. You know that already. And the realm will be riven with anger, with mistrust and disloyalty. For some will follow you, and others will follow the King. But at the end, when all the men in your host and in the King's are dead, the people will still follow the King. Because they trust in him. He is anointed by God.'

'My son could be, too. If the King were persuaded to leave his throne, if he could be pensioned off, to a monastery, perhaps, then my boy could be crowned in his stead.'

'Lady, do you really believe that the men of England would

suffer a child on the throne? Your son is old enough to be wedded, I know, but he is not old enough yet to be able to defend himself from the barons. What would the Marcher Lords make of him? If you disrupt the kingdom, if you show people that the King is able to be deposed, they will take the message that the throne may be taken by any with authority and power. And your son will not find his way to a monastery, I would wager.'

'So I have no choice? Yours is the counsel of despair, Sir Baldwin.'

'No, it is the counsel of honour, your Royal Highness. You do not wish to throw the kingdom into war and decline. Better to return and accept your place. You will be honoured for it.'

She said nothing for a moment, and then she spoke, musingly eyeing the hallings before her. 'You know, I did all in my power to have him love me, Sir Baldwin. I made no complaint when I arrived in England, all alone, and found that my own jewels had been taken and given to that primping cretin, Piers Gaveston. I did not mind, because I was so young, I only sought to win his approval. At twelve years, all I knew was that my place was at the side of my husband, to comfort him. But he wanted nothing of my company. He did not care for my comforts, only those of his friend Piers.

'And when I grew older, when Gaveston was dead, and I gave Edward a son, at last, I thought, I had the love of my husband. But then, that despicable excrescence Despenser came and inveigled his way into my husband's affections. You know how that snake works. My husband took a little longer to throw me aside, and at least I have had the comfort of a number of children, but then at last Despenser won, and I lost all. Position, trust, wealth, friends, even my children. And if I return to England, what exactly will be returned to me?'

'My Lady—'

'Nothing, Sir Baldwin. *Nothing!* You ask me not to go home to husband and lover, but to gaol. You tell me I have to do this, or that, and yet what you offer to me in return is the bars of a cell. Tell me honestly – why should I go there? If I was your daughter, would you in faith order me to go back to a husband who is despised by all? I am nine-and-twenty years. You are older. You could be my father! What would you have me do?'

'My Queen, you torment me. I am a loyal subject, I cannot in conscience say aught else but that you should go to your husband.'

'Yes. You are loyal. But fools may be loyal. And if I were to be so loyal that I would put my life once more in the Despenser's hands, I would be a fool. A complete fool. I cannot do that, Sir Baldwin. And more, I most certainly cannot allow my son to be taken back. Despenser wants total power. Would you have me, a mother, place my own son's life in danger? I will not. I cannot.'

'Then what, Lady?'

'My course is set, I think. I do not wish it, but I see no choice. That is what the good Bishop said, was it not? That my husband had left me no choice? He meant that I should go back with him, immediately. But when a man tries to force one course, sometimes God will show another.'

'What will it be?'

'For now, I will remain here. Sir Roger Mortimer has been most kind to me, in the absence of my own money or the support of my husband. I shall remain here with him.'

'Your Royal Highness, I am deeply sorry to hear it.'

'Perhaps you are. Can you not understand the appalling hurt I have suffered at my husband's hands?'

'Yes, I can comprehend the hideous injustice you feel. I detest injustice as much as any man.'

'But you do not think that I should protect myself?'

'You are in a most difficult position. As Queen you are the embodiment of all the womanly virtues. How could I advise you to do other than return to your position as Queen?'

'That is most sad, Sir Baldwin. You see, I wish to ask you to remain here with me. To serve and guard me.'

Tavern near Grand Châtelet

Vital had just demanded a fresh jug of wine when the portly Sergent from Le Boeuf's street appeared in the road outside. He was out of breath and wheezing with the unaccustomed exercise, but he did not halt until he was at the table beside Pons, and then he stood, head hanging, as he composed himself.

'Come, man! What is the matter with you?'

'André – he is dead. A man has killed him!'

The two gaped for an instant, but then they were on their feet, bellowing for the tavern-keeper, thrusting the table from their paths as they rushed towards the door.

André lay in a doorway, his neck broken, his eyes staring, his tongue swollen and protruding a little. A gaggle of people had gathered nearby, a woman holding a little boy as though she could protect him from the memory of the sight – although it was more likely that she wanted to be saved from the sight herself. 'It was my little Henri who found him, Master,' she said.

'When?'

The boy had been playing with a top, apparently, and found the dead man only a matter of moments after he had come from the church at the end of the Mass. They had sent for the Sergent immediately, and he had arrived very soon because he too had been at church.

'What of Le Boeuf?' Pons asked the Sergent.

He shrugged. 'I came to fetch you as soon as this body was found.'

Pons had a feeling of dread as he glanced across the road, but would not admit to such feelings before these others. 'Come!' he said, and set off to Le Boeuf's house.

The door was open, and Pons felt his shoulders droop. He made no pretence of caution. There was no point. He knew that the man was dead already. It was a small house, with only one large chamber below, and a ladder to climb to a smaller room up in the eaves. Pons went up, filled with dread at what he would find in the bedchamber, but when he reached it, there was nothing to be seen. Only rumpled clothing which reeked, and a rotten palliasse with straw so ancient, most was turned to dust.

'Well?' Vital called up to him.

'Nothing. He's not here.'

'Shit of a witch!' Vital swore.

Chapter Thirty-Two

Louvre

The Bishop of Exeter returned to his chamber with little sense of his alarm and concern being allayed. All that his prayers appeared to have achieved was a conviction that his position here was intolerable.

It was all the Queen's fault! The woman should have agreed to go back to her husband without argument or delay, but no! She had to remain here and try to seek some additional damned concessions. Well, there would be none. And meanwhile, the Bishop's own life was in danger, as he had predicted before coming here. Dear God, what he would give now for that prediction to be proved false!

'Sir Richard, where is Sir Baldwin?' he asked as he entered his chamber.

'He's been called to speak with the Cardinal, me Lord.'

'Perhaps the Cardinal is to persuade him to go to the Queen's side, then,' Bishop Walter said musingly. 'I should not be surprised. She is tempting all others here in France.'

'I wouldn't worry. With Simon and Baldwin and me, you'll be secure enough,' the imperturbable knight declared, peering with interest at a plate piled high with different dried meats.

'Yes, Simon – where is he?'

'He went out to the privy a little while ago.'

'Oh. I see.' The Bishop nodded, and walked to a chair, in which he sat and brooded a while.

'You look worried still, me Lord Bishop,' Sir Richard said, chewing at a sausage with an expression of distrust on his face. 'Pah! Too little salt in that.'

'I am concerned for the kingdom. The Queen's irrational behaviour could bring untold damage to the King.'

'What harm can she do? She's here, the King's there. Unless she tried to marry their son off to some princess, there's not much she can achieve. She's a woman, when all's said and done.'

'Women can be most capable at deceit and dissembling, don't forget, Sir Richard . . . and this one is French,' the Bishop added.

'And alone.'

The Bishop clenched his fist and held it in the air. 'Alone? She has persuaded many to rally to her. It was bad enough with a few contrary men who could not remain in the King's realm at peace, but now I am convinced that she has succeeded in calling Lord John Cromwell to her side, and I believe de Beaumont will remain here with her. In England she has managed to convince many that she has been wronged – and yet look at her! Does she appear to be a woman who's distressed?'

'I wouldn't know,' Sir Richard said.

'No,' the Bishop agreed quietly. 'Neither do I. Yet I do know that she is a friend of the Cardinal.'

'You speak his title as if it's poison in your mouth, me Lord.'

Walter Stapledon glanced over at the honest-faced knight. 'I do not like that Cardinal. He strikes me as the kind of man who is too keen to provide for himself, and less likely to invest in the general good. Do you know, some years ago I had the duty of attending to the Pope. Clement was not the most rigorous man in his works, and I was occasionally forced to wonder about his motives in constantly acquiring new assets. Such jewels, such quantities of gold and silver . . . and one item I adored: a set of goblets which were quite extraordinary. Lovely workmanship. Pewter, but with delightful gilding.'

'Aye.' Sir Richard nodded politely, trying to concentrate.

'And I saw the mate of those goblets in the Cardinal's room. You see, I think he is as avaricious as any other. It is partly that which makes me fear him, for if the Queen were to offer him money, or Mortimer – God save us! – we would be entirely at the mercy of a man who would not scruple to remove obstacles.'

'Hmm. You think he might attempt to kill you?'

'I greatly fear it, yes. And if it would suit him, he would be happy to remove me by allowing rumours of my guilt in the death of the Procureur to flourish. Ah, me! What can I do?'

'Sit and have some wine, me Lord. It's very good.'

The Bishop smiled wearily. 'I think my need is greater for spiritual support. And right now, I must leave and emulate Simon. Excuse me.'

'D'you wish me to walk with you? After all you've said, surely it's not safe for you to be alone? What if that man from the corridor should meet you again?'

'I should be safe enough in broad daylight,' the Bishop said with a grateful smile. 'Even the Cardinal would not dare to attack me in the King's castle in the sun.'

Outside, a little of his bleak mood left him. In truth, it was hard to be miserable while in a marvellous place like this. The Louvre was one of the most magnificent castles in the whole of Christendom, with the white stone making it shine in the afternoon light. Approaching it in broad sunlight was quite dazzling, because the white stonework mingled with the water of the immense moat to blind a man. Lovely, quite lovely.

After relieving himself, he wandered a little while, his mind running on the work he must yet complete before he could go home. It was the first time in a long time that he had been able to leave matters of state alone. Perhaps, he reflected, it was the result of the discussion with God in the chapel. He had seen fit to calm Bishop Walter's fears and lend him a little ease.

'Bishop? Are you all right?'

He turned to see Simon Puttock hurrying towards him, a look of concern twisting his features. 'You are an extraordinary guard, Master Puttock,' he smiled. 'You leave me in my chapel, and then make the effort to seek me out while I'm enjoying the sun.'

'Yes, that's right. Would you like to come back now?'

'No, it is good to take the air for a little.'

'The air here is not so wholesome as that in your chamber, Bishop,' Simon said firmly.

'You wish me to be inside, where you may protect me more easily, and there is logic in that. But the cool air here seems to make my mind function more effectively.'

'Yes, I have no doubt. However, I would like you to come with me *right now*.'

There was an edge to his voice that made Bishop Walter stop and look at him with a sudden alarm. 'What is it, Simon? Is there another disaster to mar this lovely morning?'

'Only one thing, Bishop. Sir Roger Mortimer is here.'

Upper chamber near St Jacques la Boucherie

He woke with acid in his belly, and Le Boeuf began to puke before he knew where he was, before he remembered anything about the evening.

'Christ's boils!' he muttered, spitting and cursing.

There was a pain that began right behind his eyeballs and spread from there to encompass his entire skull. He must have been beaten up badly for his body and head to feel like this, he told himself. And then there was the soreness about his belly. He must have been drinking too, then.

There was light now, but he daren't open his eyes yet. The pain was going to be too intense, sod it, so he rolled himself over, avoiding the direct sun. But something was very wrong. He wasn't on his palliasse. Maybe he'd fallen from it, and was just on the planks of the bedchamber, then. There was rough timber under his cheek, and he experimented with his good eye, opening it to glance down.

Where was he? This wasn't his floor. It wasn't his home. Where had he got to? In a mild panic, he sat upright, and then he realised his wrists were bound. 'God's ballocks! What the . . .'

'Awake, are you? Good. I like to have someone awake when I consider what to do with him. Although in your case I don't feel the need to worry myself. Can you understand that?'

Le Boeuf closed his eye and shook his head, hoping that this might be a mere bad dream, but the dream didn't go away. He felt an ungentle prod against his back, and then a pain that seemed to slam into his kidney and made his eyes jerk wide. A whimper left his drooling mouth.

'Aha, Le Boeuf, so you do know who I am, eh?'

The King of Thieves crouched down to smile at him. Behind him, Le Boeuf could see a woman, a dark beauty with a look of interest on her face as she watched the King draw a dagger. He allowed it to rest against Le Boeuf's cheek, the point down on his skin. It made his flesh creep. He could feel the sharpness, sense the ease with which it could be thrust down, where it would jar against his teeth, then slip softly into his mouth, through his tongue, through even the other cheek, until it pierced the wooden floor, where it would hold him entirely; he'd be unable to move without slicing through the whole of both cheeks, losing his tongue in the process. This was torture of a sort King Charles's own executioners could not have dreamed of. He had heard of the King of Thieves using it against many of his own men.

'Who did you speak to when you decided to sell me and my men?' the King asked in a mild, soft tone.

'I didn't tell anyone . . .'

The knife was pressed down. There was a spurt in his mouth, and he screamed into his closed lips, eyes wide and panicked. Blood in his mouth. A chip of tooth where the dagger's blade had connected. 'No! No!'

'You'll tell me, of course,' the King said. 'Because it's easy. And if you don't, I'll have your body cut into tiny pieces, one by one, even as you watch. You'll be able to see it all. So you need to answer.'

'The King's Sergent. I had to! I had to tell him. And he brought two officers of the King, a man called Pons and another called Vital. They were going to . . .'

'Yes, they were going to kill you, weren't they? Well, it doesn't really matter now, because you will die for what you have told them. You have put me to a lot of trouble, you see. So I think I shall kill you – but not yet. No, I think you need to consider your crimes first, and so I shall wait until later. But to make sure you don't try to escape, I shall need a hammer, please.'

He wanted to shake his head, to plead, but the King had no compassion. There was nothing in his eyes except the desire to inflict as much pain as possible on the man before him. Le Boeuf saw the heavy leaden hammer being passed, and only just had time to open his jaw before the dagger's hilt was struck. His horrified screams were almost muted by the dull thudding of the hammer against the dagger as it was pounded through Le Boeuf's mouth and into the floor.

'There,' the King said, when he was done. He eyed the

sobbing, bleeding thing on the floor before him, and drew back his boot to slam it with all his malice into Le Boeuf's belly, making the man spew again, the vomit pooling near his mouth, the acid burning at the fresh wounds in his cheeks, the blood mingling with the greenish-yellow swirls. 'Feel free to rise, if you want,' the King said quietly.

He kicked again, and Le Boeuf felt it hammer at his upper belly, his body convulsing to eject all the fluid left in his stomach, desperate not to move his mouth and slash all to pieces.

But it wasn't the King's ferocity towards him that scared him most. It was the look in the woman's eyes as she watched, licking her lips as though contemplating a sexual encounter, rather than the destruction of a poor beggar.

Bruised, his kidney ruined, his face pinned to the wooden plank of the floor, Le Boeuf sobbed for his life and for his approaching death.

Louvre

Baldwin was leaving the Cardinal's chamber, when the Cardinal himself approached him from the corridor. 'Sir Baldwin? Would you object to my walking with you?'

'By all means,' Baldwin said with an entirely false smile.

'The Queen is a most determined lady.'

'Yes. I was growing aware of that,' Baldwin said.

'She would have the King relinquish his unnatural obsession with this man Despenser and return to her marital bed. Is that such a dreadful desire?'

'Of course not. However, it is her methodology which I question. She has been commanded to go to her husband, and that rightful order she is refusing to obey. That itself is *petit* treason. No woman has the right to deny her husband's command. But this is worse – her husband is the King. That makes her refusal an act of genuine treason. It is impossible to condone such behaviour.'

'You would have her go to a home which is repugnant to her? You would have her throw herself at her husband, no matter how undeserving?'

'Yes. She is married to him. It may be painful, but better that than the inevitable shame and humiliation of being *forced* to go back.'

The Cardinal looked at him from under frowning brows. 'You think someone could force her?'

'Your King will have to in the end. The Pope will not wish for any further enmity between your King and ours.'

'The Pope will be keen to see the issue resolved, it is true.'

'You don't think he'll demand that she returns to her husband?'

'The Pope? No. I know his mind, I think, as well as anyone does.'

'Why not?' Baldwin asked, genuinely confused by the man's arrogant conviction.

The Cardinal looked at him. 'Do you understand much about the workings of power?' he asked, pointedly looking at Baldwin's patched and threadbare tunic. 'I used to be a poor man, but I managed to achieve some prominence by application and taking some risks. Some years ago I helped the French King to capture the treacherous Pope Boniface. I was soon afterwards able to advance myself. It is how all do so, Sir Knight. The Pope is another such self-made man who managed to win an election. God did His part – but who is to say that men themselves did not influence His choice? The Pope, when all is said and done, is only a man. He wants his life to be eased, not complicated. Now, from his perspective, how safe will it be for Queen Isabella to return to her husband? It will lead to strife in their relationships. It may even lead to her being chastised.

'And now consider this. If she were to be publicly rebuked, how would the King of France view such treatment of his sister? Would you be happy, were she your sister, and you the King of such a land as this? It may well lead to a war, and one which could only have dire consequences for the rest of the Christian world, and which must also delay the possible expeditionary force to the Holy Land to begin a new Crusade. If you were Pope, would you wish for such an eventuality? Or would you prefer to keep the couple separate, perhaps even until the King himself died and his son could take the throne. Then the mother could return.'

Baldwin stopped now and gaped. 'You do not mean to suggest that the Queen could keep her son here with her, against the express command of her husband?'

'Why not? Good Christ, man!' The Cardinal drew away, but then turned back, hissing, 'Do you think every life is as easy as yours? There are *responsibilities*. You worry about your Queen and the feelings of your King, but we are talking about the lives of *thousands*, the souls of perhaps *millions*. We have more to worry about than merely the strict application of the laws of domestic bliss. If the Queen stays here, she may well persuade her son to remain with her. And then the father becomes really rather irrelevant.'

'Cardinal, it is your duty to uphold God's laws, surely.'

'I have many duties. I have served four Popes now. They each were different men, but the main thing was, they were *practical* men.'

Baldwin nodded, a curious empty feeling in his belly at the thought of the man's words.

'It may be best for you personally if you accepted the realities and remained here with the Queen. That is all I wished to say,' the Cardinal concluded.

'I cannot, in all conscience.'

'That is a great pity. For, remember this: the Queen is the younger. She will live longer than the King. It is her largesse which a man should consider.'

'I seek nothing. Only to serve my liege lord as I should.'

The Cardinal eyed him doubtfully. 'In truth? Then I am surprised. You are that rare thing, a knight who is truly chivalric. I have not known many. You are a dangerous man.'

Baldwin ignored that. 'You have served four Popes, you say?'

'Yes.'

'And you say that Boniface VIII was a practical man?'

The Cardinal smiled thinly. 'He was practical in the things he sought to achieve . . . although he did not quite know how to apply himself.'

'I disagree,' Baldwin said, but without smiling in response. 'He knew how to apply himself perfectly. He sought wealth. That was why he deposed Celestine V, for the pursuit of his own profit. Celestine was entirely devoted to the Kingdom of Heaven, not to this poor, fractured world. And Boniface had him killed as payment. So you were part of the army that had Boniface killed in his turn?'

'You are correct about the piety of Celestine, I suppose, but he had little idea of how to achieve anything. He was no manager. The Church is a large organisation, Sir Baldwin. It requires a firm hand on the reins. His successors have all been more . . . single-minded. Boniface did have the failings you mention, but he was removed when those failings became clear.'

'Of course. And so those whom God has seen elected can be removed, deposed, or merely murdered when expedient? You say the others have been more single-minded. I would prefer to call them more ruthless,' Baldwin said, thinking of Clement V, who had destroyed the Templars. 'Some of them sought their own reward without concern for those upon whom they might trample.'

'You accuse the Pope of corruption?'

'Oh, no!' Baldwin evaded the suggestion. 'I accuse no one. I am only a rural knight, with no ambition to be anything else.'

'Well, Sir Rural Knight, you should understand that the world looks a different place when considered from a position of authority.'

'And you are the adviser to King Charles?'

'I am.'

'And his confessor?'

Cardinal Thomas halted. 'I am confessor to many, Sir Baldwin.'

'And you have interests in the French monarchy. You will excuse me, Cardinal. I have interests only in the affairs of my own King. Not yours.'

'I see. Then I think we know each other's position, Sir Baldwin. I am sad, though. You would have been a most useful addition to the Queen's circle of friends.'

'Does she need another?' Baldwin said lightly.

'No,' the Cardinal said flatly. 'She needs no one more.'

Chapter Thirty-Three

Tavern at eastern wall near the Seine

Jacquot found Amélie in the same small tavern where he had been before.

'He has a man there. Did you hear?' she asked.

'I had heard that he suffered an embarrassment,' Jacquot said. He leaned back on his stool and eyed the room behind her.

'You think I have brought the King's men with me? That I want to see you dead?'

He kept his eyes on the men in the room. 'I have no idea.'

'Jacquot, I want to see you in the King's place. And I can help you take it.'

'Oh, really,' he said.

'I've already begun the process,' she said, and smiled.

Jacquot looked at her, and slowly an answering smile spread over his own features. He understood her now.

And trusted her not at all.

Bishop's chamber, Louvre

Simon pulled the door open and almost pushed the Bishop of Exeter inside.

The Bishop turned to protest. 'Master Puttock, what are you doing?'

Simon ignored him, but spoke directly to Sir Richard, who sat back on a seat, his hands comfortably behind his head, his feet on a stool before him. 'Sir Richard, has anyone tried to come in here?'

'No – why?'

'Never mind that now. Can you please go and see if you can find Baldwin?'

'I am here, Simon,' Baldwin said, closing the door behind him and looking about him wearily. The meeting with the Queen, followed by what had felt like a dreadfully intimidating talk with the Cardinal, had left him exhausted. 'What is the matter?'

'I have learned why there is so much activity from the Queen and her friends, Baldwin. The Mortimer is here.'

Sir Richard's feet left the bench where they had been resting, to clatter to the ground. 'That treacherous dog?'

Baldwin held up his hand. 'You are sure of this, Simon?'

'You think I could forget him?'

It was only earlier that year that Sir Roger Mortimer had had Simon captured in Paris and taken to a house so that Baldwin could be persuaded to go there for a talk with Mortimer, the King's enemy.

'Of course,' Baldwin said. Then a thought struck him. 'My Lord Bishop, do you think that the man who grasped your throat might have been Sir Roger? Do you know Mortimer?'

'Of course I know him,' Bishop Walter said. 'He was the King's most important military leader for years, and until his fall, I must have met him many times.' And suddenly his mind was taken back to the figure in the dark, the hissed words that had seemed so familiar. Sir Roger Mortimer . . . could it have been he who grasped his throat, who threatened his life?

'How did you get along with him?'

'With Sir Roger? I would say generally quite well. We were

never close companions, but we neither of us had a cause to be angry with each other.'

'No? Not even when his assets were taken apart?'

Sir Roger Mortimer had been one of those who had been arrested and imprisoned in the Tower after the Marcher Lords were squashed by the King. His lands and belongings were all forfeit to the Crown.

The Bishop looked at him with a haughtily raised chin. 'I benefited not a whit by his destruction.'

'I see. That's good, then.'

'It is?'

'I was fearful that, if he had a debt to settle with you, your life might have been at risk. But so long as you are sure that is not the case, nothing has changed,' Baldwin breathed.

'Nothing has changed,' the Bishop repeated.

But it had, although he did not realise by how much.

Upper chamber near St Jacques la Boucherie

It was the afternoon. The sun had passed over the rear of the house and now was lighting the window hole on the other side, in front of Le Boeuf.

His entire body was a mass of bruises and lacerations. The thought of food made his belly rebel, but he could have killed for a mouthful of water. Or two mouthfuls, the first just to wash the vomit and blood away, the second to sip and swallow. Cold, clear water.

His mouth was a mass of soreness. The taste of blood and bile was unbearable, and Le Boeuf wept with despair at the agony of the acid eating away at the wounds.

It was growing dark, and his trepidation increased with every moment. There were sounds from below him, of men arriving. He knew how the meeting would be conducted: the men would all gather, and when they were ready, the King

would call them upstairs to take their places. Le Boeuf would
be entitled to defend himself against any accusations, and then
the votes would be cast. And his life would end.

There was no sympathy in a meeting like this. The men
were all perfectly aware of his agonies, and they would enjoy
witnessing his terror. And he *would* be terrified. He wanted to
pray that it was quick, but he didn't want to die. A man with
so much life left in him still, it was cruel, unfair.

His life was not so wretched that he would willingly cast it
aside.

Looking about him again, he saw that there was no one in the
room yet. He could just pull away from the knife, allow it to cut
through his cheeks, tug himself free, and then cut his bonds
with it before fleeing. The alternative was death. But the idea of
pulling his head away, feeling the knife slice, was so hideous
that he couldn't. At one point he had been close. Very close. The
house had been silent for a while, and he had sobbed silently,
closed his eye, and tried. God, how he had tried. All he needed
to do was jerk his head back. There would be a short, sharp
pain, no doubt, but then peace. An escape. He could go to the
white monks, who were happy to cleanse a man's wounds and
help him on his way. And after that, when he was healed again,
he could run. He would never be able to stop running, of course.
There could be no escape for a man like him. If the King ever
heard where he had gone, he would be dead. Death would,
however, come quickly. A knife in the back, or a sudden
clubbing at night. Better that than this long, drawn-out hell.

Yes, so he had opened his mouth, clenched his fists, and
prepared to jerk his head away. Only to find that the flesh
would not yield up the blade. It was left intentionally blunt,
with only the point sharpened, so that a man would only be
able to escape the knife if he was prepared to slowly rip
himself wide open.

He couldn't do it.

He could remember now, hearing of a wolf that had been trapped, caught with one paw in a snare. In terror and despair, it had chewed through its own foreleg and escaped. The paw remained. If only he too had that sort of courage.

But it was too late. He could already hear the men coming. Setting his hands on the hilt of the dagger, he tried for the very last time to withdraw the knife, but the leaden hammer had done its job well. The blade had penetrated the plank by more than an inch. Try as he might, he could not shift it.

The door opened. There was a giggle, high and scary, and then more boots marched in.

'Is your name Le Boeuf?' the giggling voice demanded. It was the King.

'Yes.'

'You have to speak up, fellow. We can't understand you,' the King said. For good measure, he kicked Le Boeuf in the spine again.

'I ang Le Boeuf,' he said as clearly as he could.

'You betrayed my home, didn't you?' the King said. His voice had gone very quiet, suddenly. It was somehow even more alarming than his giggling.

'I didn't mean to, it was—'

'Just "yes" will do.'

'I . . .'

'That's a yes, then,' the King said. 'So you see, my friends – that is the sort of man we have here. A coward, who chose to go and sell us to his friends. I think that is a shame, because he has cost us our home. We've had to move to this dump. And it's not so pleasant, is it?'

He kicked Le Boeuf again, and this time the knife tore at his mouth, a fresh eruption of blood making him gag.

'He *sold* us to his *friends*, my comrades. *Us!*' With each emphasis, he kicked again, and Le Boeuf wept as the dagger ripped at his cheeks. There was nothing he could do to defend himself, nothing he could do to save himself from the pain.

'Look at him. Who can doubt he deserves death? But how: that is the question.'

Le Boeuf stared across the room. All the men were behind him, and he could imagine them drawing their knives, all preparing to stab at the same time, each participating in the killing, a bonding of the gang. And it made him want to close his eyes.

But he kept them open a little longer. Long enough to see the woman. She walked into his field of view with a curious look in her eyes, as though she was intrigued to see his reaction to the pain. Seeing him, she gave a little smile, with half-lidded eyes, like a woman making love, but then she looked away, and left the room.

It made him feel still more lonely.

Pons saw the light as the door opened, the flash of the candle before it was snuffed and clouted his neighbour on the back. *'Now!'*

They ran low along the road, clubs and maces muffled with strips of linen to prevent rattling or clattering against walls and pillars, and then they were at the door. Amélie slipped out, muttered, 'Top floor. Room at the very top,' and they were off, at first trying to be silent as they hurried up, but gradually the need for silence was overruled by the need for speed. They all felt it, the mad, urgent demand of action.

Their boots pounded on up the stairs, Pons in the front, and when he came to the uppermost chamber, he found himself surrounded by a group of nine or ten. Three had lost ears, one had a lip split, and Pons felt a grim delight to know that these were indeed the felons he'd sought. One man was directing the others – he must be the King! He was crouched at the side of a huddle on the floor, screaming at the others, his mouth moving, a foam forming in the corners, but Pons could hear not a word. The blood was rushing in his ears, deafening him.

He launched himself inside, his thighs complaining at the effort, and his sword was in his right hand, a club in his left. He was aware of the others entering behind him, was aware of clubs falling, boots kicking, fists flying, daggers stabbing and the fine mist of blood spraying from a dozen wounds; he was aware of all, but his concentration was fixed on the man before him. The King was too great a prize to risk losing him.

The fellow was scrawny as an old chicken. He was bare-chested, even in this weather, up in this unheated room, and Pons guessed that he was keen to be undressed so that the blood wouldn't show when he left to go into the street again. A man with blood all over his shirt would be a target for the interest of the Sergents and other officers. There was already blood on him, but now he reached down to the huddle and pulled free a dagger that lay stabbed in it.

'Put down the knife,' Pons snarled, and launched himself at him, his sword flicking up to the right and, catching the dagger and cutting through the King's fingers. His forefinger and second finger were swept off, and Pons sensed them both flying up and away, even as his attention remained on the face of the man in front of him. There was an expression of utter shock on it. Never before had he suffered the pain and indignity of punishment. He stood now, frozen in impotent rage as Pons's point rested on his throat.

And then his fury knew no bounds. He slammed the blade away with his ruined hand, the spray flying across Pons's face, and hurtled forward.

Pons stepped back, then to his side, grasped the King's wrist as he moved forward, stamped on his foot, and as he fell to the ground, slammed his pommel into the felon's head, hard.

Bishop's chamber, Louvre

Bishop Walter took a deep breath and walked to his great chair.

'If you are right, then there is need to get news of this to the King,' he said with conviction. 'He will wish to see Mortimer found and destroyed.'

'I expect the King will already know he's here,' Sir Richard said.

'Alas, likely not,' the Bishop disagreed. 'Earlier this year, the French had a success in the diplomatic arena and managed to capture all the King's spies. It was appallingly embarrassing. Just at the time that His Majesty needed all his spies operating at their most effective, so that he might know how to negotiate the truce, they had all been discovered. In truth, the King relies on Prior Eastry at Canterbury for his news these days, for the Prior hears from all travellers as they pass through. Some of that can be useful to the King, and is sent on to him.'

'He relies on a *Prior* to keep him informed?' Baldwin said disbelievingly. 'Then it will be necessary to send to the King to let him know.'

'I will put my mind to it.' The Bishop sat down at his great table with two of his clerks to write the letter and look into his correspondence. There was much for him to study, the more so now that he had a new view of it. Sir Roger's appearance on the scene was enough to throw much of the rest of his information into a different focus.

'Sir Baldwin,' he said heavily, looking up from the documents, 'you know my political career has given me a most exciting life. I do not regret any of it. But there is little doubt that it does force a man to hold a different perspective on matters which associates may often not appreciate. Such as the destruction of the Lords Marcher and the arrest of Sir Roger Mortimer.'

'I am sure that is true, my Lord Bishop.'

'He was a good warrior, it's true. And he did perhaps deserve more from a grateful sovereign. But he would have been a disruptive influence, I fear.'

'I could not say. I didn't know him, really,' Baldwin said. He had met Mortimer after Simon had been captured by him, and in his opinion, the man had not appeared to be a menace to the realm.

'He is another rather similar to Despenser in many ways. Too avaricious – both for money and for power. Such greed is always dangerous. A man who demands too much will inevitably fall.'

Baldwin smiled but forbore to mention the Bishop's own wealth. 'I suppose you mean that there was not enough space for two men of such greed in the King's household at the same time?'

'I do not think so, no,' the Bishop said. He was sitting, peering out of the window with a slight frown on his face.

'My Lord Bishop?'

'I was reflecting on the nature of Mortimer. The King has declared him a traitor and enemy of the realm – I just wonder how dangerous he is. If he is so confident of his welcome here in Paris, has he been plotting something new? If he has, it must surely be to the detriment of the King.'

'What could *he* do, that could harm the King?' Baldwin shrugged. And his judgement was that Mortimer could indeed do little. The man was broken: his lands confiscated, his treasure taken, his men scattered.

'I have no doubt you are right,' the Bishop agreed, but Baldwin could see that a little frown remained on his brow.

Alley near St Jacques la Boucherie

Jacquot tapped Little Hound on the shoulder and took a delight in the sight of the man springing about, startled as a faun when the dogs appear. 'Oh, it's you!'

'I want to know what you have learned,' Jacquot said softly.

The Hound looked up briefly at the darkening sky, then nodded and led the way to a small tavern. It was quiet in there, and the only light came from stinking tallow candles and a few thin rushlights set about the walls.

'She is a hard worker, that Amélie. And she knows a great deal.'

'Such as?'

'She has some pillow-talk from the castellan, you know? And she isn't above boasting about what he lets on. Did you know he made his money by robbing a Pope? Yes, thought that would surprise you. Our Sieur Hugues was one of a small force King Philippe sent to some town near Rome to capture a Pope, but instead he found the Pope's treasure, and stole it away. Enterprising fellow, that. And he has much to lose, if news of that robbery ever comes to the ear of our King, who might think it would be a good idea to take all that money for himself.'

'What of it?'

'Well, Guillaume de Nogaret, the dead man's name, was also the name of the man in charge of the force sent to Rome, or wherever it was. This is going back some twenty odd years, mind. Perhaps this fellow who was killed in the Louvre was his son, come to blackmail Sieur Hugues. The castellan would have good cause to remove and silence him then, wouldn't he?'

Jacquot whistled. Then he reached into his purse and slid a coin over the table. 'Well done.'

The Hound sat back and eyed Jacquot speculatively, as

though assessing what he would think of the next piece of information. 'There is more. This same Amélie had met the young de Nogaret when he first arrived here in the city. I wouldn't mind betting she gave the castellan warning about the man's appearance, and—'

'And gave him time to plan to kill the lad,' Jacquot said. 'Yes, that makes much sense!'

Chapter Thirty-Four

Saturday after the Feast of the Archangel Michael[1]

Tavern near Grand Châtelet

Pons lifted his tankard in a toast, and Vital did the same in return. There was a celebratory air to their meal as they broke their thick loaves and soaked up the juices from the pottage that morning. It was satisfying enough merely to have captured the man who had killed Jean the Procureur, but at the same time they were both content that their efforts had seen to the destruction of a larger force of criminals. The King of Thieves was a man who had controlled much of the crime in Paris, and without him, it was likely that the city would grow more peaceful.

After a leisurely breakfast, they strolled together northwards, until they came to the wall. From here they carried on to the bleak fortress of the Temple, where they entered and made their way to the gaols.

'Fetch them,' Pons ordered.

Two gaolers hurried about their business, bringing one after the other of the men and latching their irons to rings in the walls. The last to be brought was the King.

In this darkened chamber, his ribs stood out more, and the hollows at his cheeks looked deeper, the lines at brow and

---

[1] Saturday, 5 October 1325

mouth more heavily engraved, perhaps, but the night in the cold and damp of the gaol had not served to break his spirit.

'You have never been found guilty of a crime here in the King's demesne,' Pons said, walking about the King. 'You have not been branded, or had your nose, lips or ears clipped. How can that be, I wonder?'

There was no answer. The King spent his time staring into the distance as though listening to another conversation.

'There are many like you,' Pons said contemptuously, 'who prefer to pay someone else to do their dirty work for them. No need for you to risk your own precious skin, is there?'

'He's not listening, Pons,' Vital said, walking over to the King and eyeing him. 'Now, that's not very respectful, is it?' All of a sudden, he slammed his fist into the King's belly. 'André was a friend of mine,' he said through gritted teeth. 'I want to know who killed him, you scum.'

The gaolers heard a knock at the door, and one hurried to open it. Outside were two more men, one wearing a shirt that was filthy with stains, while the other had on a thick, smith's leather apron. They walked in and began to make a fire at the pit. Metal tools were set about this, just as they would be at a smithy, but the tools were lighter. Their purpose was not to bend hot metal but to sear human flesh.

'Do you know these two men?' Pons asked politely. He waved a hand at the newcomers. 'They are the King's executioners. You have your own men, I am sure, Your Highness, but no one who is quite so expert at squeezing responses from the recalcitrant. And that is what they will do with you. You had our friend Jean the Procureur killed. I will know why, and who paid you for that.'

For the first time, the King turned to him. There was a flickering rage in his eyes, and he gave the impression of danger still – no, Pons had to amend that. It wasn't danger, exactly. It was more the aura of power and command. Like some General captured after a battle – bloody and beaten, perhaps, but still a man confident of his own position.

'Someone betrayed me,' he said. 'The fool who gave away my house at the Seine, he was one.'

'And you murdered him. That will cost you your life,' Pons said affably.

'And now there is another. Someone who told you where to find me yesterday. Few knew where I would be.' His voice was cold, but rational as he mused on the problem.

'It was her – the whore, Amélie. *She* led you to me, didn't she?' he said of a sudden. 'No one else would have known where to go – only her. When I see her again, I shall show her her own entrails.'

Pons smiled without humour. 'An interesting suggestion. However, you are here to answer, not gain answers. Who paid you to have Jean le Procureur killed? Who paid you to have Guillaume de Nogaret and his wife killed? Oh, and who was it who slew André? Was it you?'

The King slowly let his gaze fall from Pons's face, to run down his old green tunic, all the way to his boots, and then up again to his face. There was no emotion in his look, only a cold disdain. And then, he turned his attention from Pons to the wall.

'You won't answer? No matter,' Pons said with a shrug. 'Get the fires good and hot, lads. We'll be able to show this so-called "King" what will be waiting for him after the hangman's finished with him at Montfaucon.'

Louvre

The Cardinal crossed the great hall with his clerks, his head bowed as he absorbed the news he had received.

That Sir Roger Mortimer had returned was not so

surprising. It was something, in fact, which he and the Pope had urged upon the King of France. King Charles was less keen to have the man here, but then he was also unhappy about his sister remaining in France. It was one thing to have her irritating the hell out of her husband, a man for whom Charles had little respect and less liking, but quite another to keep her here. The King of England was correct – it was wrong for her to remain away from him. Her place was at his side.

However, the Cardinal thought that the Queen could herself usefully become the focus of all those who had cause to resent the King and his associate – his 'friend', Sir Hugh le Despenser, may God fill his bones with liquid lead! That foul pirate deserved to be deposed, and were the Queen able to build a small force, the Cardinal felt sure that it would be received well in England. There were so many desperate to see an end to the reign of the disreputable Despenser. That was also what the Pope and Cardinal Thomas fervently desired. And whatever the Pope wanted must be good for all Christendom.

The Cardinal prided himself on his worldliness. He was a practical man, when all was said and done. Among those in the Church, there were some few who were able, like him, to take harsh political decisions, but few who also had the clarity of purpose and the determination to do all they might for the good of the Church. The Pope himself appreciated his single-mindedness.

But now he had a strange feeling that there were matters which were advancing without his involvement, which was a little alarming.

In one of the King of France's smaller chambers, there was a gathering already when he arrived.

'Cardinal,' Queen Isabella said, rising from her chair and bowing, as gracious as ever. She was a lovely thing, this

Queen, quite the sort of woman who could tempt a saint, the Cardinal considered. She kissed his ring with every sign of humility, but none of her display convinced the Cardinal. Women were utterly dangerous, and ones like this, with brains and beauty as well as the heady air of command which surrounded her like a canopy, were the most dangerous of all.

The Duke of Aquitaine was next. The young man bowed with as much respect as the Cardinal could hope for. His tutor was behind him, and Lord Cromwell too. But it was the other man who attracted the Cardinal's attention.

'Sir Roger,' he said.

The Queen smiled winningly. 'Cardinal, we hope and pray that you will listen to us for a moment or two.'

'I am happy to listen,' the Cardinal said flatly. He would certainly make no further commitment.

'Sir Roger and I are desolate at the terrible way that the kingdom of England has been laid waste by the avarice of one man,' she said. 'There is every risk that my son's inheritance will be thrown away. If the Despenser saw an opportunity, he would not hesitate to kill my son; if he saw profit, I believe he would even slay my husband. I hope I do not shock you?'

'On the contrary. I am fully convinced of the truth of your words.'

'In order to protect my son, I do not dare send him back to his own land. I think it would be dangerous in the extreme. And I dare not leave him here alone. There are enemies in the pay of the Despenser all over France. I am sure you understand this?'

'So you intend to remain here in Paris? What of your expenses, my Lady?'

'Cardinal, I confess, I rely on the support of my brother in his kindness.'

'And you intend to remain here for how long? Until your

husband is dead? Would you deprive him of your companionship, of the companionship of his son?'

'I can see no other way to protect my son.'

The Cardinal nodded, glancing at the boy. And he *was* only a boy. In God's name, he might be a Duke, but the title had been bestowed on a child. Not yet thirteen, was he?

'You wonder at my commitment, Cardinal?' Duke Edward asked calmly.

'I entertain no such doubts, Duke. No, I was reflecting that yours is a hard choice.'

'You mean, to stay here with my mother, or go home to my father?' the Duke said with a wry grin. 'Is it so hard? I have the choice of a loving, gentle and kindly mother, or a father who is so twisted with his fears and his love of his adviser that he has no time to speak to me. He spends all his waking moments fearing the plots of his enemies within his realm, and cannot see that the one sure means of protecting himself is to remove the man whom all despise. To remain here, or to return home – the choice is easy.'

'And if your father should disinherit you for your betrayal?'

The Queen said sharply, 'If he were to try that, his attempt would . . .'

It was Sir Roger who took a half-pace forward. 'His attempt would fail. I would take the country in the defence of the Duke.' So saying, he bent his knee and bowed his head at the Duke.

'Very impressive. But if you intend to do that, you will need men,' the Cardinal said.

'I will ask my brother,' the Queen said eagerly.

'And he will refuse you.'

'He may not – he may allow me to use some of his men.'

'No, because I will speak with him and advise him not to,' the Cardinal said firmly. He looked at the Duke, then at Sir

Roger. 'You must understand, this is one venture that the King of France cannot assist. For him to intervene in the national affairs of your country would be seen as despicable, for he would be harming his own brother-in-law. It may not be.'

'But I am his sister,' the Queen said with a winning smile.

It did not disarm the Cardinal. He was immune to such wiles. 'You are the responsibility of his brother-in-law. You are King Edward's wife.'

'So the King will not aid us?' Duke Edward asked.

There was a coldness in his manner which the Cardinal did not like to hear. The boy should have been whipped more often if he would show such disrespect to his betters. 'I shall advise him not to,' he repeated.

'What of other Christian Kings?' the Queen asked quietly.

'If you were to seek assistance from others, that would be no business of the King of France,' the Cardinal said. 'I only advise the King.'

'That is good,' the Duke said, with a quick look at his mother. 'Then our future is clear. We must bide our time.'

The Cardinal shook his head. 'Not for long. I declare, I do not trust the Despenser to remain satisfied for long.'

Queen Isabella averted her face slightly. 'My husband was a good father, a good King for a while. But now his friendships are perverted by that evil man. I would that I could command that Despenser had never been born. Without him, my husband might have remained at my side, and not sought the affection of others.'

'I fear that had he not found Despenser, he would have found another.'

'True,' the Queen sighed. She dabbed at her eye. 'So, there! I must remain here in exile, clad as a widow for a while longer. And I require a General who can find me a band of men to

wrest the kingdom from the Despenser, to save the King, and
to save the realm for my son.'

The Cardinal nodded. 'So be it.'

But as he looked at Mortimer, the Queen, and the Duke her
son, he was sure he could see a different tale unfolding. And
he saw that there could be good profit for a man who was
prepared to help.

Chapter Thirty-Five

Second Monday following the Feast of the Archangel Michael[1]

Temple, Paris

It was late in the afternoon when the King finally broke.

Every man had his limit. That was what Pons privately believed. He was experienced in the use of torture as a regrettable, but necessary means of gaining answers in many investigations. This time, however, he was actually enjoying it. Pons was one of many who had been glad to call Jean the Procureur a friend.

They had begun by interrogating the three others who had been taken with the King. Each had endured a while, but it was clear enough that they knew nothing of value. As soon as the brands approached them, they began to gabble all they knew. It was scarcely surprising, Pons reflected, bearing in mind that they had all the marks of the executioner's tools on them from previous offences. They knew how much they could endure.

The King was different. He stared at Pons coldly as he listened to the agonised breath of the others, knowing that it would soon be his turn.

Still, he had some courage. Even when his nerve broke, it was not a complete submission. Each word was forced from

---

[1] Monday, 7 October 1325

him by the application of a little more pain, each partial confession dragged out with chains.

'The . . . man . . . of . . . God. He paid. The priest at the Louvre.'

'What is his name? Which priest?'

'He swore death to Jean.'

Second Tuesday following the Feast of the Archangel Michael[1]

Louvre

Stapledon had no idea of the approaching crisis as he prepared to leave his chamber that morning with Simon, Baldwin and Sir Richard.

'Heard a new joke yesterday,' Sir Richard was saying. 'This old fellow was asked how old his son was, and he said, "Me Lord, he's seven and twenty." "How so? Why is he not twenty and seven?" "Because, me Lord, he was seven afore he was twenty." Ha! A good joke, eh?'

Simon eyed him balefully. 'Yes, most amusing.'

'Your head bad again, Bailiff?'

Simon winced at the loud tone. 'I have a slight liverish complaint, I think.'

'You should be more careful, my friend,' Baldwin said with a smile.

'You try being careful when you're out with him,' Simon said quietly. 'It's impossible. The man soaks up drinks like a towel.'

'I believe even a towel must reach the limit of its absorption,' the Bishop said, making a rare joke.

'I've seen no evidence,' Simon grumbled.

---

[1] Tuesday, 8 October 1325

'Eh?' Sir Richard said. 'I missed something?'

Baldwin was about to answer when there came a loud knocking at the door, and he watched as Simon marched to it and opened it wide.

'I would like to speak with the Bishop, if I may,' Pons said.

The King of France eyed the group before him without comment for a long time. 'This is very serious, you appreciate?' he said finally.

'Of course we appreciate that!' Bishop Walter snapped. 'I am being accused of a major crime, on the flimsiest evidence imaginable . . . If it were not such an insult, it would be laughable.'

'Evidence based upon the statement of a man who was suffering torture,' Pons said meaningfully.

'A man suffering torture may say anything to save himself,' Baldwin replied coolly. In his mind he could imagine the agony of the fellow as the tools were deployed about him. He had heard too much of the tortures which had been inflicted upon the Templars.

'You were not popular when you first arrived here, my Lord Bishop,' the King continued. 'When you were rude to your Queen, you angered many of my people; when you then argued with the Procureur as he was attempting to do his job, you made still more enemies. I do not think your stay in Paris should continue for any longer than is absolutely necessary.'

'I cannot leave without the Queen, and she refuses to return with me.'

'I say nothing of that. It is none of my business. But the peace of my realm is very dear to me. I will not have mayhem and other infractions of my law as a result of an unwelcome guest. You must consider your position, my Lord Bishop, and also consider whether you are aiding or thwarting your King's ambitions.'

They were dismissed. As they left the King's presence, Pons made a mocking bow to the Bishop, but Stapledon was unworried by that. He was more alarmed by the reaction of the people outside as he left the audience chamber.

Not one stirred. No one spoke or moved to disturb the silence. It created a monstrously intimidating atmosphere, and Baldwin felt like a deer forced to walk between two packs of hounds – and all that held the hounds at bay was the will of the berner.

Back in the Bishop's room, Stapledon crossed to his chair and sat shakily, passing his hand over his brow. 'What have I done to deserve all this? I swear to you all, I had nothing to do with that man's death. I couldn't have! I wouldn't know where to find him if I'd wanted to!'

Baldwin shot a look at Simon and Sir Richard. 'I believe you, my Lord Bishop. But the man's death happened a little while after he left the castle here, and that was the very same day that you argued with him. It does make the matter look black against you. Perhaps, though, Simon and I with Sir Richard here could look into it and clear your name? There must be some sort of evidence that would show who was in truth responsible.'

'Please do go and see what you may uncover, then,' the Bishop said. He had taken a jug of wine from one of his clerks, and now he sipped the strong red liquid. 'I would have my innocence proved. I am here among my enemies against my wishes, and I must demonstrate that I am guiltless!'

A while later, Baldwin and Simon stood in the courtyard and watched the people hurrying back and forth.

'What do you make of it, Baldwin?' Simon asked.

'I think that whoever wished to make the Bishop appear guilty did a very good job of work. There can be few in the castle now who haven't heard about Bishop Walter's verbal attack on the Procureur. And yet that day there were only a few men about here. Someone chose to spread the story, and when the next morning there was news of the Procureur's death, people put the two tales together. But that was the result of gossip, perhaps. Not all rumours are started maliciously.'

'How can we begin to learn what truly happened, do you think?'

Baldwin looked up at the sun. 'I think the first thing we should do is speak to this man who has been tortured.'

'We would need permission for that.'

'Yes,' Baldwin said. He strolled over to the main gate. In the doorway was Arnaud with two of his men. 'Master Porter? May I speak with you a moment?'

'If you wish.'

'You know the man Pons who has been investigating the death of the Procureur?'

'Yes, indeed.'

'Has he left the castle yet?'

'No, he is still in the hall, I think.'

'When he comes, would you ask him most politely whether he would accept a pint of wine with me? I shall be in the tavern over there,' Baldwin said, pointing.

The coin passed to Arnaud was enough to guarantee his compliance, and Simon and Baldwin enjoyed a pint of wine between them before Pons appeared in the courtyard, walking swiftly to the gate. There he was approached by Arnaud, and turned to glance in their direction before nodding and striding to join them.

'Well, my friends, it is not every day that I am offered a

good drop of the King's finest wine, so I'd be delighted to drink some with you both.'

'That is good,' Baldwin said. He poured a cup full. 'And then we shall exact payment.'

'Aha! I had thought as much,' Pons said. 'What is it?'

'Only this: we should like to meet your informant to see what else he may tell us about the Bishop and the death of the Procureur.'

'I do not object – but what do you want from him? To ask him to change his tale?'

'No, only to confirm his story. We are convinced that our Bishop is not guilty of killing the Procureur.'

'Perhaps he did not wield the knife, but he paid the man who could.'

'The Bishop is a new man to this city, m'Sieur. He does not know it well. Was this villain so famous that a foreigner could find him this swiftly?'

Pons hesitated. 'Perhaps he has visited the country before?'

'He has, I am sure, but not for many years. He knew that he was not popular, because he is no ally to Queen Isabella. Many friends of your Royal Family despise him.'

'He may, perhaps, have come to know of the killers a while ago, then?'

'He is more likely to be the victim of your city's killers than a sponsor of them,' Baldwin said with certainty.

Pons considered, nodding slowly. 'Perhaps.'

'Is there anyone else who has been involved with this fellow?'

'The "King of Thieves", as he calls himself, has been associated with almost all those who've been involved in any crimes for the last few years.'

'But recently, is there anyone who has knowledge of him?'

Pons shrugged. 'Our helper was a woman. A whore who's

lost interest in him as he grew more violent, I think. She took us to him so that we could catch him.'

'And she came to find you?'

'Through another man here in the Louvre. He told us and set a meeting with her.'

'Another of her clients, then?'

'It is possible.'

'May we speak with this "King"?'

'Very well. Perhaps tomorrow you could join me in a visit to the gaol where he is being held? It is the old Templar preceptory north of the city.'

Baldwin's face froze. 'Yes,' he said at last. 'That would be most kind of you.'

'Are you all right, Baldwin?' Simon asked as they made to leave the tavern.

'Yes. It was merely a shock to hear that they are still using that fortress as a centre for torture,' he said.

'Ho! Thought I'd find ye both here. Fancy a little nibble?' Sir Richard said, somewhat indistinctly as they passed the entrance. The knight was sitting outside on a bench, a roasted capon on a platter before him, which he was gradually dismembering, one leg already in his mouth.

'What are you doing here? I thought you were guarding the Bishop,' Simon said.

'Well, I was, but the Queen's man came and fetched him. Lord Cromwell was there, and if I know Lord John, he'll not see any harm come to the fellow while the Bishop's in his charge.'

'What did the Queen want with him?' Baldwin asked.

'To talk about money and the like, I think. Poor Walter groaned and sighed to himself when he heard the summons, but when all's said and done, she is the Queen, and he is her legal guardian while she's here, so he had little enough choice. Now, how about some capon? The man here cooks damn well – are you a thigh man or a breast man, ha ha, eh?'

Although he had little desire for food, at least Sir Richard's company was a distraction from the concerns which assailed him at present, Baldwin decided. He sat down and stabbed a lump of breast with his small eating knife.

Sir Richard smiled broadly. 'Excellent! I always knew you'd prefer a good sizeable breast! So, Sir Baldwin,' he continued, finishing a leg and throwing the bones towards a cat who sat, purring loudly, on a wall nearby. 'What d'you reckon to this story of the Bishop? As much moonshine as saying the castle's mastiff did for the fellow, I'd guess. Yes?'

'Absolutely,' Baldwin said. 'I can see no justification for suspecting the poor Bishop whatever. He would not know how to find this assassin, he would not have had the time to find the man and give his orders in the time available. He is an important guest here, after all. His time has been bound up in visits to others or to chapel.'

'Quite right. That's what I thought too. So I was musin' as I wandered about the castle, whether there was someone else who could have a reason to kill the Procureur. Did you know he was the city's leading prosecutor of felons? You did? Oh. Well, it just occurred to me that surely the man's worst enemy is goin' to be the one who sought his death – and that must mean that there was an affair the fellow was looking at which could have embarrassed someone enough for that someone to pay someone to have the fellow killed. Eh?'

Baldwin half-closed his eyes as he tried to differentiate between the 'someones' and the 'fellows'. 'Yes,' he said at last.

'Good. Glad you said that. Did you know that in the days before he was murdered, this Jean fellow had a talk with the

King himself, and was told to get his finger out of his arse and find the killer of a man at the Louvre?'

'Yes. Jean's servant told us: it was the man de Nogaret,' Baldwin said flatly.

'Perhaps we should search for him, then?' Simon said. 'The man who had this fellow de Nogaret killed?'

'Yes.'

'Ye'll pardon me, Sir Baldwin,' Sir Richard said rather reproachfully, 'if I observe that you don't seem all that bothered to find the fellow's murderer.'

Baldwin looked at the ground, then back to the building behind him. 'I do not think that it is our place to find the killer of de Nogaret.'

It was Simon who glanced at Wolf, pacing so near. 'Baldwin, if a man were to harm Wolf, you would seek his killer no matter whom it might be. Do you really mean to tell us that you wouldn't try to do the same for a man you have never met?'

For the very first time in their long friendship, Baldwin could not hold Simon's gaze. As Sir Richard protested that, 'Of course if Sir Baldwin had met the fellow, it would make a difference,' Baldwin looked away.

'You may think what you like of the father, Baldwin,' Simon went on steadily, 'and you can allow that to colour your feelings towards the son, if you want. But think on a moment. If a man killed the son to avenge some crime, that was unjust. The boy had nothing to do with his father's offences. And think further – the same fellow, perhaps, killed the son's wife. What did *she* have to do with any of those crimes? She was at two removes from the father's offences. It'd be like Despenser punishing me by killing my daughter and her husband. Is that to be borne?'

'No,' Baldwin muttered. He could not curb his loathing for

the family name of de Nogaret, but Simon was correct. The idea that the son and his wife should be slaughtered for the father's offence was disgusting.

'And there is another aspect to this. If I am correct, the Bishop is standing to suffer punishment because he is suspected of the killing of the Procureur, when the true culprit is the man who killed him to silence him about the de Nogaret murders. By allowing the killer of that couple to escape, you are aiding a man to put all the blame on to our Bishop. Can you stand by and permit that?'

'No. No, you are quite right, Simon,' Baldwin said quietly.

'Ha! Glad to hear it,' said the Coroner, and belched long and loud. 'Don't know what in God's name you two are muttering about, but if you're both content to stop blathering and come and help prove the Bishop's innocence, that makes good hearing to my ears!'

'So, what do we do?' Simon asked.

Baldwin frowned. 'On the day that the Bishop had his argument with the Procureur, it was inside the main gate of the castle, was it not? The Procureur was apparently standing and staring at the gate, which was enough to make Bishop Walter think he was staring at *him*. But what else might he have been gazing at?'

'The gate itself?' Simon hazarded.

'Aye. Or the people at it,' was Sir Richard's contribution.

'One or the other, certainly. I feel we should begin to think about these deaths there,' Baldwin said. He took a bite of the chicken breast, then watched as the pale, anxious-looking cook walked on by.

'What is it, Baldwin?' Simon asked, noting the expression on his face.

'That cook. You remember the dead boy? Yet another murder in this castle. Is no one safe?'

*

They had all three surveyed the main gate to the castle after
finishing their capon, but after the fourth muttering of 'God's
faith!' from Sir Richard, even Simon had to admit that there
was little to see. Only the steady inrush of men and a few
women, while a number left by the same route.

'Baldwin, this is pointless,' he muttered.

'Perhaps. And yet there was something which the Procureur
thought was important enough for him to spend much time
right here, watching,' Baldwin said distractedly. 'What could
it have been?'

'Maybe he was just gazing into the distance? Men do when
they're thinking about tough questions,' Simon hazarded.

'He was not that sort of man, I think,' Baldwin said slowly.
'Surely a man with a brain like his, shrewd and quick, would
not have stood here idly. There would have been a good
reason, I am sure.'

'Well, aye, that's possible, but then again,' Sir Richard said,
his thumbs hooked in his belt and glowering about him like a
bear waiting for the mastiffs, 'he may have been staring into
thin air, like Simon said. Perhaps he'd been invited to a lady's
chamber? Eh? Or challenged to a fight? There's any number
of innocent distractions.'

Baldwin threw him a despairing look. Neither sounded
particularly 'innocent' to him. 'What if we—' He checked
himself and frowned. There, in the gateway, he could see the
furious face of the porter. 'Wait a moment. I shall speak with
the gatekeeper.' And in a moment he was stalking towards
Arnaud.

Chapter Thirty-Six

House near the Seine, east Paris

Jacquot was aware that the King would have placed a price upon his head, but there were other considerations just now. With the King and his main cohorts in gaol, and perhaps some of them already dangling on the King's everlasting tree at Montfaucon, there was work to be done if he was to guarantee his position as the King's successor.

The first essential was to ensure that any rivals to the King were dissuaded from attempting a full takeover of the city. After the years of the King's rule, there were not many who stood in any position of authority, but some could try to ease themselves in on the prostitution, or the thief-taking and fencing businesses. Jacquot was not happy to see the efficiency of the group being degraded.

This chamber was the undercroft and storeroom to a tavern over near the eastern wall. He sat on a barrel as the four men walked inside. All were from high up in the King's organisation. All were well-known to Jacquot.

'You are here with me because the King is dead,' he announced.

'How do you know this?' demanded a heavy-set man with a scowl of suspicion blackening his face. He was known as 'the Gascon' for his birthplace, but Jacquot only thought of him as 'the bastard'. He was unreliable, short-tempered, and full of malice. He would be the first to be removed when Jacquot's position was secured.

'He is in the Temple and has been for over a day. You think he'll be happy and content in there?'

'Then what's going to happen?' This was a taller, languid-looking man with a round face and deceptively smiling eyes. Called the 'Avocat' within the gang, he was the one who kept his eye on the money. He would be a useful ally, Jacquot knew.

'I am taking over. If there's a delay, other gangs will move in and cause trouble. All of you will be thrown out and be found floating in the Seine later. This way, all continues as before. It's better for everyone.'

'For you, perhaps,' the Gascon said, and spat. He moved around to Jacquot's flank. Jacquot ignored him.

'You can wrangle and fight, if you want. But if you do, it will put an end to the whole group, and there will be no gang to rule. You will lose everything. You want to carry on as it is now? Then fall in with me. I'll keep the money coming.'

The Avocat was smiling, looking more like a benign old priest than ever. 'And you can promise this?'

'There are not many who will dare to resist me,' Jacquot said. 'I have a reputation.'

'So did the King,' said the Gascon, and drew his knife.

Jacquot's dagger was already out and resting on the barrel before him. He snatched it up, and the tip rested within the hollow of the Gascon's throat. 'I could kill you now, but I won't. If I do that, it will spark internal fighting, and I need you around to squash all feuding like that. You are in charge of discipline, Gascon. Your money will be increased by a fourth, and I will have you as my own Sergent. But only if you are loyal to me now.'

The Gascon looked down the length of the blade, and then he nodded.

Within an hour, Jacquot had his oaths of loyalty from all four.

Louvre

Arnaud looked at the tatty knight with ill-concealed disdain. 'You want to know about the Procureur? You should ask the Bishop of Exeter. He is the man who had him killed. Even the felon admits that. You know of him? He was arrested, and he—'

'Yes, yes, yes, I know of this man and his testimony,' Baldwin said irritably 'However, it was not only the death of the Procureur that concerned me. I was thinking also of the murder before that. The Procureur stood here and appeared to be much taken with something, and I feel sure that it had something to do with his death or the death of de Nogaret. Did he say anything to you about the threat to him, or the other death?'

'No. Nothing I can think of. Only that he was interested in the way that the man de Nogaret arrived that day. He kept asking who'd taken him up to the chamber where he got himself killed.'

'Could you help him?'

Arnaud shrugged. 'It was a boy – a cook's knave called Jehanin. He was here and took the man from the gate to the room.'

Brothel, west of city wall, Paris

Hélias could not weep any more. She had gone to the funeral as a mark of respect for her old friend, but it had given her no consolation. It only reinforced her urge to seek revenge.

The surprise arrest of the King had made many of her whores gasp with shock. No one had thought that the King could be removed so easily; he had appeared to be untouchable. And today there was a set of rumours flying about: a man from outside town was to take over from the King – a man who was even more ruthless than his predecessor. That idea was enough to send some of the wenches into fits of the vapours.

'Calm yourself,' Hélias said yet again as little Katérine dissolved, petrified that one of her most profitable punters, a 'planter,' who supplied false jewels to the unwary, would never come to see her again. The idea that he might be killed now that there was a new master trying to impose his rule, made the girl realise the transient nature of life's little delights.

'He'll clear off out of Paris, and then I won't get the bolt of wool he promised me!' she wailed, until Hélias caught her a smart cut across the rump with a riding switch she kept handy for that purpose. 'Ow!'

'Shut up! Go and find another fellow and stop that whining, you slut! You want to be thrown from my home? Find yourself another room somewhere else? Just now, when your favourite punters may disappear into the Seine? Eh? Then be still and leave me alone to *think*!'

There were few of the strumpets on whom she could rely, but one was Little Bernadette, the girl from whom she had first received the news about poor Jean.

It was rare for Hélias to be sensitive when it came to men. Jean had initially been just another one of her clients important to her only for as long as he kept paying – but then as she grew to know him, the usual sense of contempt which Hélias felt for her customers began to peel away, and in its place was a feeling of warm companionship. Jean had not been coming to her to slake his natural desires for quite some while, in truth, and yet the times when he did visit were usually more enjoyable for the lack of sex. Instead they would discuss the city, the law, affairs of corruption or moral degeneracy, without rancour or irony. And then they would laugh as they raised their glasses. She would miss him hugely.

And he would be avenged.

'Bernadette? Has your man heard anything about Jean's murder?'

The man, one of the girl's regular clients, was a known thief-taker. He would work to find men guilty of specific crimes for a bounty, handing them over to the city's law officers when the cash was ready for him. Often that was an end to the business, but on some occasions there could be better profits. Sometimes the King would pay handsomely for a man to be brought to him – either because the man was to be released, or because he was guilty of an offence against him, in which case the Seine would claim him. At other times the King would merely point to those who were his enemies. There were many who wanted to set up business in Paris. So much easier for the King and his comrades if such people were removed. All the better if they were removed by King Charles's Sergents.

'Yes, he's been here,' the girl said.

'And?' Helias prompted, reaching into her purse for a coin.

Bernadette shook her head and made Hélias put the money away. 'Not for this. I want Jean's killer as much as you. My man said that the new leader was probably the one responsible. There are rumours about him trailing after Jean for some days, so most think he did it.'

'On his own?'

'There was a contract between an unknown man and the King.'

'Find out who it was. I want to know who put the money on Jean's head. Once he's found, we can arrange for him to be made to regret his decision.'

Louvre

Simon and Sir Richard walked along after Baldwin, crossing

the courtyard and peering inside when they reached the kitchen.

Baldwin had to search for the cook. The kitchen had all the fires roaring, and the heat and noise was appalling. The boys lay on the floor, winding the great handles that kept the spits turning, or stood preparing vegetables and stirring pans full of stews and pottages. The flames were like small demons teasing new souls into hell, and the bellowing of the cooks and thin, reedy responses of the knaves, the clatter of pans and bowls, the roars of anger at failures, the snapping and crackling of twigs blazing in the ovens, all combined to create a cacophony so intense that Baldwin felt his head must burst.

Eventually he saw the cook. He was over at the farther end of the room, clouting a boy about the head for some misdemeanour, and when he noticed Sir Baldwin, he came straight over.

'You again,' he said with resignation.

Baldwin nodded. 'Has anybody learned who could have killed your kitchen boy?'

'No. Who cares about a nonentity like him? Poor little monster.'

'You were fond of him?'

'Of course I was! I thought of him – I think of most of the knaves in there—' he said, jerking a thumb over his shoulder, 'as my family. There's not one of them I wouldn't fight for. Not one.' He fingered his heavy cook's knife as he spoke, a faraway look in his eye that told of his feelings about the boy's killing.

'There was another man who was killed here,' Baldwin said gently.

'Yes. The man found in the Cardinal's room. That was the same day poor Jehanin went missing.'

Baldwin looked at Simon. The Bailiff had not missed the relevant comment.

'So,' Simon said, 'if the lad disappeared that same day, what part of the day was it? Morning? Afternoon?'

'It was the same time as the body was discovered. That man, de Nogaret, was found just as I was bellowing for Jehanin. I was trying to find the scallywag, because he was supposed to be back, not off skiving somewhere.'

'Where had he gone?' Simon pressed him.

'I had a need of some ortolans, and sent him to the poulterer, but the lad never returned.'

'Did he get back to the castle?'

'Well, Arnaud was certain he had at first. Told me he remembered little Jehanin walking in – but, then I wondered if he was right. After all, if Jehanin had returned, why hadn't I seen him?'

Baldwin wore an expression of dawning realisation. He explained: 'Because as soon as he came into the courtyard, he was asked to take a man to a room, intending to deliver him to a meeting, as had been planned, but that meeting was to be a murder . . . and your Jehanin was slain in order to ensure his silence.'

'The man was there, though. Why kill my Jehanin? And why conceal his body while leaving the man's on full display?'

'Good questions, to which I have no answer as yet. But I shall before long,' Baldwin said with certainty. 'And now, we will take our leave of you.'

Sir Richard hastily swallowed the piece of tartlet he had stolen from a tray. 'What was that all about, then?' he asked Sir Baldwin, spraying crumbs as he spoke. 'Why'd the fellow tell us all that about his knave?'

Baldwin stopped and glanced back at the cook, still

standing, shoulders slumped, at the doorway to the kitchen. 'Because he truly cares for his apprentices and knaves. And at last I am beginning to gain an understanding for the story here.'

Chapter Thirty-Seven

Queen's chambers, Louvre

Bishop Walter received the invitation to the Queen's chambers for a meal with distinct reluctance. It was impossible to refuse, naturally, but he would have preferred to have waited for Baldwin and the others, and then rested more quietly, content in the knowledge that all three were outside his door.

But it was not to be, and with any fortune, perhaps the woman had begun to see reason. Yes, that must be it. She was going to agree to return with him. Her resolve had waned after seeing how futile her petty rebellion was, and she had grown to understand that her place was naturally at the side of her husband.

So it was with a degree of confidence that he commanded his clerks to join him, and set off along the corridors to find the Queen's chambers.

'Her Royal Highness is expecting me,' he said pompously to the door-guards, and they stood back to allow him to pass.

'My Lady,' he said as he entered, bowing his head in the briefest display of respect he could manage. 'You commanded me to come?'

'Please, my Lord Bishop, take a seat,' the Queen said graciously, waving a hand at the table ready set for their meal.

The Bishop took his seat at the head, and gazed about him. 'There is another place set here?'

'Yes. And I think the Cardinal is here already. Such a punctual man,' she murmured.

As she greeted her second guest, Bishop Walter looked around him. The table was gleaming with fresh, clean linen. No trenchers and bowls for the Queen and her guests: instead her best silver plates were ready to be filled. Spoons of a delicate pattern were set out beside them – lovely things, the craftsmanship excellent. It was actually hard to see where the tail of the handle was affixed to the spoon's bowl.

About the room were the Queen's guards, most of them originally entirely safe and honourable. All had been picked by the King and Lord Cromwell – but now there were rumours, *strong* rumours, that more than half had been won over by Isabella's charming manner, her largesse and her delicate femininity. True, she was the greatest beauty in all France and England together.

Her ladies were standing at the rear of the room. There was no sign of Lord Cromwell, which was a surprise, but the Bishop assumed that this was to be a farewell meal for the Cardinal, so it made good sense to have as few people present as possible, so that any . . . *delicate* matters could be discussed safe in the knowledge that there were few ears to listen.

The food was as excellent as he had hoped. He remembered that as a fact afterwards: as he took the first mouthfuls, he felt a warm glow fill his soul. The dishes were superb, the wine still better, and yet afterwards he could not recall what he had eaten or drunk.

'An excellent meal,' he said as he fell back from the table, sated.

'I am glad.'

He looked over the tablecloths at the array of gold, silver and heavy pewter lying on it. 'You have a table fit for a King, your Highness.'

'The Cardinal has such expensive tastes, Bishop.'

'Not always, my Lady,' Cardinal Thomas said respectfully. 'And never on this level.'

'You are too modest.'

The Cardinal smiled in reply. 'I was born to humble surroundings, and could never aspire to such magnificence.'

Bishop Walter took a sip of wine. Humility was not a trait he would have associated with the Cardinal.

'So, Bishop. How much longer do you intend to make me wait?' the Queen suddenly asked.

The Bishop glanced up at her. Even in her widow's weeds she was a stunningly beautiful creature. For a woman in such a situation, she was dressed fabulously well. Her clothing might be all in black, but for a woman with her perfect features, pale skin and wonderful, almost luminous eyes, it set off her looks to best effect. 'Well, we can be off as soon as you decide, my Lady. It will take little time to prepare all my books and goods.'

She set her head on one side. 'You mean to tell me you think that I shall join you on your journey?'

'But of course . . . is that not why we are all here?' the Bishop smiled, and then he felt the first stirrings of concern as she exchanged a look with the Cardinal.

'My Lord Bishop,' the Cardinal began, sitting back and steepling his fingers 'I think you have missed the point of the meeting here. The Queen had considered that your position had become clear to you, and a sensible end to this impasse was now at hand.'

Bishop Walter smiled still, but behind his smile was a growing rage. That he should be so brow-beaten was *intolerable*! He was the Bishop of a large diocese. He was the King's trusted emissary, his special adviser on so many matters, especially financial, and now he was here to be persuaded to submit? He would not.

'I have clearly been the unwitting cause of embarrassment,' he said. 'Excuse me, but I must return to my own rooms.'

'No, Bishop. I am a Cardinal, and I *order* you to remain here and listen.' Thomas d'Anjou's voice did not rise, but there was no need for it to. 'You see,' he went on, 'many of us are coming to the conclusion that the Queen's situation here is quite unacceptable. It is you who prevent her from gaining access to the funds which she reasonably demands. It is a gross insult to the people of France, to the realm, and to the Crown itself. It will not continue.'

'What do you propose?' the Bishop asked, his jaw clenched.

'Just this: you came here with authority to release monies to the Queen. I suggest you do so.'

'I may not. I was told only to do so when she agreed to return to England, to her husband, her King, as he has ordered. Will she do so?'

'No!' Queen Isabella stated, and her eyes flashed with anger.

'Then there is nothing more to discuss,' the Bishop said.

'There *is* one thing, Bishop,' Thomas d'Anjou said. 'You insult our Lady at your own peril. We are a proud race, we French. We do not tolerate foreign ambassadors, no matter how senior, arriving here and insulting her.'

'I have letters of safe conduct.'

'So you may do. And yet, I think you would find that they would aid you not one whit!'

It was now that the Cardinal dropped his hands to his lap and stared at Bishop Walter. His face was blank. There was no sympathy written on it, for felons deserve none; there was no understanding of the impossible position in which the Bishop found himself, only a firm resolve.

'You suggest I pass the Queen such funds as I hold under

my hand, and then what? I return to England, a disgraced and dispossessed man ready to be flung into gaol on arrival? Or perhaps you would have me remain here as an exile. To be reviled and despised by all who cross my path, neither French, nor English, merely a soulless, unwanted fool who gave up his life for the promise of extending it. Do you think me a fool?'

'I have always been persuaded that there are compensations for the worst insults,' the Cardinal told him. 'In my time, I have been persuaded to leave the side of one Pope for another, I've been persuaded to join the service of the French Crown, and the Pope, and I've been able to rise. Look at me! I have the best-filled coffers outside the Vatican. And I live well – yet I was born a poor fellow with a father who had barely two sous to rub together. You could do the same.'

'Not with honour,' Bishop Walter said flatly. He turned from the Cardinal and stared directly at the Queen. 'This is your last word on the matter?'

'No, not quite. I say this too,' the Queen said, thoughtfully running a finger about the rim of her goblet. 'If you refuse my reasonable demands, I shall leave you to the wolves, Bishop Walter. The truth is, your life is not your own any more. I can control it. If you do not join me, you may thwart me. I will not have that.'

'Then so be it.'

Bishop Walter stood, bowed curtly to each, and walked from the room. And as soon as he was outside, he felt the sweat break out on his brow.

'Sweet Jesus protect me!' he pleaded, crossing himself.

'So that is that, my Lady,' Cardinal Thomas said. He selected a grape from the pile before him and chewed it carefully, the seeds crunching. 'He will not submit to your eminently fair requests.'

'I knew it! I knew it before he entered. Did I not say to you that he was the most stubborn and foolish of all the priests in the realm? If he thinks it is not to his profit, nor that of his damned college in Oxford, nor to his little schools for children, nor to the good of his cathedral, he will have nought to do with it,' the Queen spat petulantly. 'He is so irrational!'

'He must have a letter about him for the money,' the Cardinal said pensively.

'Yes. But the only way to acquire it would be to capture him, ask where it is hidden and steal it from him.'

'Quite. Exactly as I was thinking,' the Cardinal said very softly.

'You are serious?'

'Never more so.'

The Queen frowned with perplexity, looking away. 'I would prefer not to have a Bishop's death on my conscience.'

'And the alternative? That you salve your conscience at the risk of your son's inheritance? Not the best option, my Lady.'

'How may a lady find a man capable of such . . .'

'Please leave it in my hands, my Lady. I can easily find the man for you.'

She was no fool, and now she looked at him very directly. 'And what will you desire for this aid, Cardinal?'

'My Lady, all I wish for is an opportunity to serve you, of course,' he smiled. 'And, perhaps, when you have the money in your hands, you will seek to reward with your largesse those who have helped you?'

Bishop Walter's chamber, Louvre

Bishop Walter was enormously relieved to find Baldwin and Simon in his chamber waiting for him.

'Lock the door,' he burst out, as he crossed the room to his sideboard. On it was a jug, and a servant hurried to try to pour him a goblet of wine, but the Bishop merely slapped him away and poured for himself. Draining the first goblet, he refreshed it and stood silently a moment, staring at the wall before him, thinking desperately.

'Bishop? My Lord?' Simon said tentatively. 'What is the matter?'

'The bitch! The she-wolf! It's all her,' Bishop Walter said, and drank deeply again. Then, quickly, he made up his mind and turned to face the others. 'He sits there and tells me, that Cardinal, that he was born to humble surroundings! Well, all I can say is, it is a great shame no humility wore off on him as a result!'

'Bishop, we do not understand what you're on about.' Simon tried again. 'What has happened?'

'That Cardinal! The Queen! Very well. So be it! Simon, Baldwin, I have to leave here most urgently. Tonight you will sleep here with me. At first light, as soon as the gates are opened, I shall flee the city. We have need of haste – to warn the King of the treachery that is so alive here in Paris.'

Baldwin shot a look at Simon, then approached the Bishop. 'What has happened? You are distressed, but when you left us earlier, you appeared content and satisfied.'

'She threatened me, Sir Baldwin. The Queen suggested that I would not be permitted to stand in her way. She threatened me – *me*, a Bishop in Holy Orders, in God's name! The whore is no more loyal than a feral cat. While it suits her, she treats others with respect, but the next moment, she forgets all trust and faith and honour—'

'Bishop, please be still,' Baldwin said sharply. 'This is her city, do not forget, and there are many people who would be happy to spy on you and spread malicious stories about your conversations. Please moderate your tone.'

The Bishop was about to snap back, but then he grew

uncomfortably aware of the servants in the chamber. There was the steward at his sideboard, chamber servant over by the door, and a scribe sitting with his head bowed at his desk. Taking a deep breath, he nodded, and ordered the servants to leave them alone.

'My apologies, Sir Baldwin. I am sure that those men are safe – they are all English, but you are right to be cautious.'

'Even an Englishman could be tempted by a bribe,' Baldwin said.

'True. Well, Queen Isabella has made it clear that I am not to try to thwart her any more. She wishes for the money which I can authorise from the banks, and I will *not* comply. For that reason I must leave here. I was threatened with death. And offered a bribe, too! The Cardinal suggested I might enrich myself, as he has. Well, I will not!'

'Very well. We shall prepare ourselves,' Baldwin said.

'No. You will remain here. If we travel as a group, there is little possibility that we shall escape the nets the Queen will throw in our path. I shall wander alone, clad as a pilgrim. That way, perhaps, I can reach the coast safely.'

'You will need some men to go with you,' Baldwin protested.

'I shall have my clerks,' the Bishop said firmly. 'That will be enough to confuse any search. If I were to go with a larger party it would be too easy to find me.'

Simon was frowning with incomprehension. 'But what if they do find you? They would surely not dare to hurt you while you have letters of safe conduct?'

'Simon, my friend, while I am in France, I am in enormous danger,' the Bishop explained. 'There are too many people here who detest me and would be keen to see me dead. The Queen for one, but since these rumours about the Procureur dying because of me, there are many others who would also like to see me die.'

Baldwin nodded. 'There are risks in setting off with only a few clerks in attendance, but you would be safer, perhaps, in the guise of a pilgrim than in travelling with a large retinue. Are you sure you do not wish for a sword at your side?'

'I will have my own sword,' the Bishop said shortly. 'I am a knight's son, and have experience of combat. And two of my clerks have had their training in weapons. We should be safe enough.'

'Then it is decided,' Baldwin said. 'And it is the more crucial since it will give you the opportunity to bring news of Mortimer to the King.'

'Yes,' the Bishop said, pausing suddenly. 'I had forgotten him.'

'What of him?' Simon asked.

'You remember I said that he and I had had no disputes in the past? Well, now I wonder whether he has a hand in all this. How else could the Queen have grown so poisoned against me?'

'It is possible that she and he are allied,' Baldwin agreed, glancing at Simon. During their last visit to Paris they had witnessed Mortimer and the Queen holding a private conference, but then there had not appeared to be any danger in two exiles talking. Now it seemed that there might be more to it. 'But Sir Roger Mortimer was always very devoted to his wife, I am sure.'

'He was – but he hasn't seen her in years,' the Bishop muttered. 'The King has her held tighter than a whore's purse.' He looked up, suddenly ashamed. 'I am sorry, friends. These last days have been tormenting to me.'

'We understand,' Baldwin said. 'Now, if you are to leave at first light, there is much to plan.'

Chapter Thirty-Eight

Outside Paris, north of the Louvre
Hélias heard running feet and looked up in time to see Bernadette pelt in through the door.

'Hélias! Hélias!' she gasped.

'Well? What have you found out?'

'There was a contract between the Cardinal and the King, and the King had his best killer put on the job. A man called Jacquot.'

Louvre
In the castellan's chamber, Hugues was startled by the sudden opening of his door. He rolled over to grab for his sword, and Amélie squeaked as she was thrown from him.

'Get rid of the whore, Hugues – we have business,' the Cardinal said coldly.

Second Tuesday following the Feast of the Archangel Michael[1]

Courtyard of the Louvre
Baldwin and Simon were outside as dawn broke, and they watched as the small party of pilgrims walked across the

---

[1] Tuesday, 8 October 1325

grounds to the gate as it was opened by Arnaud. He paid no attention to them as they set off on their way.

'That is that, then,' Simon said.

'Yes. Godspeed to the Bishop,' Baldwin said with feeling. 'I only pray that he makes it safely to the coast. It would be a dreadful disaster, were he to be found on his way and killed.'

'I would miss him,' Simon said.

'I too,' Baldwin said, but with less sympathy. The truth was that Walter Stapledon had been an ally of the Despenser for too long now, and Baldwin was not certain where the Bishop's loyalties lay. He was worried that Sir Walter's main interests were all too self-centred. Only earlier this year, when Baldwin and Simon had found evidence which showed Sir Hugh le Despenser in a less than attractive light, the Bishop had promised to hold it in safe-keeping, and then had given it to Despenser himself, who had promptly destroyed it.

But no matter what his thoughts of the Bishop's personal actions and his integrity in matters of politics, the man had the gift of inspiring others. All too often in the past he had inspired Baldwin himself. It was only more recently that Baldwin had found his blandishments more easy to ignore – or try to. Somehow the Bishop usually managed to get his own way.

Not here in Paris, though, Baldwin reminded himself.

'Baldwin?' Simon nudged him out of his reverie. 'Yesterday, while we were talking to the cook, you seemed to think you were getting an insight into the killings here. Is that right?'

'Partly, I think, yes. I have some idea about the boy Jehanin's death. He was at the gate when de Nogaret entered the castle, and when de Nogaret asked where to go, the boy was told to show him there. And here we have the mystery: all at the gate must know where the Cardinal's chamber was, so why instruct the lad to take a guest so far away from it – unless the motive was murder.'

'True – which means that de Nogaret must have been known to his killer. Someone inside the castle knew he was coming, and knew the time – thus was able to plan to have the man directed to the chamber.'

'Precisely, Simon. The killer did know de Nogaret was arriving. And he had his victim brought to the room where he would be able to slay him in peace. He couldn't afford to take him there himself, as it would have been witnessed. And that, I think . . .'

'. . . Is why the poor lad was murdered in his turn. Just to keep his mouth shut,' Simon breathed.

'I believe so. This killer is cold-blooded enough to remove any who could prove to be dangerous to him. First de Nogaret, then the kitchen knave, then Madame de Nogaret, and I think probably Jean the Procureur. Perhaps because Jean was getting too close to the truth.'

'Did he not make any notes in the scroll?'

'I have looked at it in detail,' Baldwin said regretfully, 'but I can find nothing important. I think our only hope is that this appalling King of Thieves will finally tell us what he knows.'

'It is possible, I suppose,' Simon said without conviction.

'Yes. Just,' Baldwin sighed. 'Ach, come, Simon. Let us go to the Temple and see what the good Pons may show us. We may even be granted some uplifting news there – one never knows.'

Chamber near St Jacques la Boucherie

Jacquot was moderately happy with the way his takeover had gone. The sudden removal of the King was achieved with a minimum of fuss, the transfer of power to him had been implemented, and most of the men in the gang were happy to see some form of continuity rather than out-and-out gang warfare between rivals. That would be bad for business.

'How did you alert the officers to the King's location?' he asked Amélie.

The chamber was small, low-ceilinged and cold. They had been forced to light a small brazier, and the coals glowed reassuringly in the dull light.

She was standing at the side of it, clad in a soft linen material with a heavier woollen robe of red velvet over the top. Looking at him, she smiled. 'It was easy. I told the officer I knew where the killer of the Procureur was to be found.'

He nodded. It was all a game to her. This was her attempt at subtlety, no doubt, to remind him that she knew what he had done, that he had killed the Procureur. With information like that, she could try to run the whole of the gang, if she wanted. But she couldn't, because by some mysterious quirk of fate, she had been born a woman. Despite having been given the mind of a cruel and unfeeling man, she could never rule the Parisian underworld because none of the men would accept a female ruler. Therefore, she must have a figurehead – a puppet to rule in her stead – and he was the one she had selected.

'You would betray me without blinking, wouldn't you?' he said rhetorically.

She smiled at him, that slow, feral twitch of the lips which he had seen so often before. It was the practised smile of the whore, he thought, that signified the slow awakening of desire. She had beguiled the King with it, just as she had sorely tempted other men in the gang.

He shrugged. 'Don't bother. You know it doesn't work with me.'

'No? Why not? Other men love me – don't you?'

'As much as I'd love a snake. You are as smooth, and as lethal.'

She smiled more broadly now, and began to lift her linen skirts. 'You mean you'd refuse me?' she murmured.

'I would not dare to trust you.'

'You are so hurtful,' she laughed. The skirt was already about her waist, but she held the material in her hands, bunched before her belly, so that the cloth hung down concealing her sex. 'Don't you want this?' she taunted him, gently waving it from side to side.

'When I want a whore, I'll go to old Angeline,' he said without rancour.

She dropped her skirts. 'Why not. The raddled old cow could do with a man again. What do you intend now?'

'Now?' he repeated. 'I have the business to continue, woman. The old King was adept at all forms of work. I needs must emulate him.'

'Well, do not work yourself too hard, will you?' she said. 'I have great plans for us while we rule the gang. I wouldn't want you to be too exhausted.'

As she turned and made her way from the chamber, he was sorely tempted to reach for his knife and put an end to her there and then. There was something about her that grated on him all the time. She was so knowing, so ruthless, so bloodthirsty. There were none of the feminine traits in her; only those of violence and destruction. If she had been born a man, he was confident that she would be the new King – and that he, Jacquot, would already be dead.

At the gate to the Louvre

Sir Richard caught up with them as Baldwin and Simon were leaving the castle, Wolf bounding at his side.

'You trying to avoid me?' Sir Richard demanded, only half-joking.

'Not at all,' Baldwin smiled.

'Has he gone?'

They had spoken to Sir Richard as soon as they had been

able, late the previous night, so he knew that Bishop Walter
was intending to leave that morning.

Baldwin looked over his shoulder at a pair of French guards
who appeared a little too interested in them. 'Let us go and
meet with our friend Pons at the Temple as he suggested. We
can speak on the way.'

It took them only a short while to confirm that the Bishop
had indeed left at first light.

'Hmm. A shame. When Bishop Walter was here, a man
could always lay his fist on a good pint of wine. What will we
do now? Perhaps we'll even have to resort to buying our own
barrel or two.' With that thought, the knight's mood lightened
considerably, and he began to look about him with a great deal
more interest. Not from any desire to see more of the splendid
city in which he found himself, Baldwin was convinced, but
more from a wish to spot the first wine merchant's building
with a view to ordering as much stock as he could.

They were soon outside the city's northern walls, and
before them loomed the great blank-sided towers of the
Temple. There was one towering donjon, with four turrets
about it, so far as Simon could see, and the whole was clad in
a dark grey stone that dominated the sky all about here, while
also intimidating the city itself. It lay in the midst of wild
swamplands, with tussocks of greying grasses and bright
reeds. Occasional tufts of white showed where the reeds had
grown their beards, just like Raybarrow Pool in Simon's
Dartmoor, the landscape where he felt most at home.

This was no soft undulating landscape. Here was the great
Templar castle; further along was the hill of Montfaucon,
where the French King had erected his magnificent gallows, on
which he could hang sixty-four felons simultaneously. It lent a
grim, lowering air to the whole area.

Simon was not surprised to see that his friend Baldwin was

growing more and more tense as they approached. This was the place in which the Templars had been arrested on that fateful Friday, and in which so many had been tortured, some so brutally that they died of their wounds or were forever crippled. It was mere good fortune that he himself was not present in the Preceptory on that day, and thus evaded the arrest and subsequent punishment.

The walls were tall and strong, much like those Baldwin had described in the Holy Land, all built to the glory of God and for the protection of pilgrims, but Simon felt no easing of his spirit as he walked in through the main gate. No, he was aware only of a heaviness of spirit, as though the souls of all those who had died in here were calling out to him.

Pons was sitting on a bench near a stable-block. He sat up at the sight of them, tipping his broad-brimmed hat back over his head, and rose to welcome them. 'You are earlier than I'd expected.'

'We have much to do today,' Simon said.

'Where is the man?' Baldwin demanded more bluntly.

'Follow me,' Pons said. He took them around the main tower and out to a smaller series of chambers at the northern wall. A door opened into a dingy little staircase that wound downwards. 'I would have kept him in the same room as normal, but since the murder of the Stammerer, I've been reluctant to stick to the old rooms.'

Simon was not particularly scared of narrow spaces, but that journey was one which would remain with him a long time. There was a lingering damp chill to the air, and the sound of drips. He had enough experience of lands like this to know that the water was seeping through the walls from the marshlands beyond. Foul eruptions of sodden vegetation stood in every available crack. Puddles pooled on the ground, and where there were lanterns flickering with candlelight, water gleamed from every surface. The cold was deadening to the body, but also to the soul.

It was with great relief that he saw Pons had stopped. The man was opening a door that gave onto a new corridor – and this looked more like the passage between gaol cells. On either side were doors, and Pons strode down until he reached one on the left, roughly halfway along. He took out a key, inserted it, and opened the door. 'Here, masters, is the man you wanted to see: Paris's own "King of Thieves".'

Bare-chested, the prisoner sprawled on the floor, his hands yoked to a beam that lay across his shoulders. A scabbed beard marked his jaws, while his right eye was blackened and swollen, the cheek beneath grotesquely deformed where a blow had broken his cheekbone. Blood marked his thighs and breast from a multitude of wounds where tiny squares of his flesh had been systematically cut away, and now all wept in unison.

'No more! No more! You swore!'

'No,' Pons said calmly. 'You begged. I didn't promise anything, King.'

Baldwin was frozen in horror at the sight. It was as though he was seeing for himself – and for the very first time – the result of the attacks on the Templars themselves. The knights had been held in rooms like this, in all probability, and tortured before each other in the same way, so Baldwin had heard tell, just as the Muslims had tortured, mocked, and executed their predecessors at Safed.

'Release him,' Baldwin said, in a voice like death itself.

Street near St Jacques la Boucherie

Jacquot was aware of them as soon as he left his room. Used to following others without detection, he was perfectly aware when someone else was trailing him.

There were three of them – that he was certain of. Two

behind and one up ahead on the left. This lane was narrow, little more than an alley, really, and he could have sworn at himself for being so careless. He'd thought himself safe enough, but now he realised his error. The bitch Amélie had put them on to him and he had walked merrily into her trap. Not again, though. This was the last time she would seal a man's death warrant.

He would have to escape these three first, and the very first thing to do was bunch them up so he knew where they all were.

There was a short alley back behind him, which led up west to the Grande Rue; he would have to get to it somehow. Turning, he marched swiftly towards the two. One displayed no interest in him, but the other was younger, less experienced. Jacquot was surprised Amélie didn't pay a little more and get a more competent set of men. Be that as it may, he had a good look at both, committed their faces to his memory, and then swiftly turned again and shot up the little alley.

Behind him there was a cry, then a patter of boots on the filth of the alley. He threw a quick look over his shoulder, already feeling the pain in his chest from shortness of breath. He was too old for this sort of activity. *She would pay for this.*

Louvre

Hugues was not up early. The discussion with the Cardinal had taken some while, and by the time the man left him, Amélie had disappeared. Probably returned to her little pit in the city itself. No matter.

Today, though, he had business. He would have to trail after the Bishop and wait for a suitable opportunity to kill him, but that wouldn't be too hard. Even if his assassination was seen, the King himself wanted the troublesome priest out of the way, so it was likely that witnesses would hold their tongues.

The large block allocated to the guests and their servants was to the west of the main castle, inside the enormous curtain walls, and he walked along the building idly, keeping an eye open for the Bishop. Surely this was the time he would be returning from his morning prayers in the chapel? But there was no sign of him as the people poured from the little church. After some while, Hugues went to the door to peer inside, but there was no one there, and when he asked the priest inside, he was told that the Bishop had not appeared.

Cursing to himself, he wandered back to the block and leaned against a wall, prepared to wait, glancing up at the sun every so often.

Temple

The King of Thieves turned out to be quite a young man, perhaps only five-and-twenty years old. He may once have been mannerly, from the way in which he tried to bow when the yoke had been cut away from him, but all he could achieve was a vague flourish of the hand, before his legs buckled beneath him.

Baldwin wordlessly passed him a cup of water from the bucket near the door. The King peered into it with a grimace, but sipped at it, knowing and accepting that there would be nothing better in this life. 'I am most grateful to you, my lords,' he said in a cracked voice. 'I suppose you have come to experience my hospitality here in my chamber? Pray, try the wine. It is exquisite, and the food is beyond compare, if you like weevils in your loaf and enjoy sharing it with the cockroaches each day.'

'I want to know all you can tell me of the murder of the Procureur,' Baldwin said.

'Ah . . . him. And why not the others, Sir Knight? Was this one man so important that his death is worth mine – and the deaths of others? What, do you think, makes this man so important?'

'He was an officer of the law,' Baldwin said. Pons was silent, keeping in the shadows nearby, listening but making no contribution.

'An officer?' the King said with mild pain on his features. 'What of it? Does it make him a better man? I think not!'

'Perhaps not, but surely it made him more valuable?' Baldwin said.

The King stretched back his head until all his tendons and muscles were taut, and suddenly gave a burst of laughter. 'Valuable? Yes. In God's name, *yes*! I was paid a great deal to remove him.'

'You were successful. Did you kill him yourself?'

'I am "King", Sieur Knight. Do I look as though I get my own hands bloody?'

'So you told one of your men to do it for you?'

'I was contracted to kill him, I took the money, and passed some on to the assassin. But he was greedy, and demanded more, so I tried to have him punished for his presumption. He hurt several of my own guards, the son of a hog!'

'There was a body in the Seine . . . ?' Pons murmured.

'It was one of my men, whom the assassin killed.'

'This assassin is no friend of yours,' Baldwin said.

'He is the cause of my suffering today.'

'Will you tell us who he was?'

'No. I want my own justice for him,' the King spat. He stood, not quickly with his wounds, but with determination. 'And it's not him you want, it's the priest who paid for the Procureur to be killed, as well as the girl.'

'What girl?' Baldwin asked.

'The one over at the Grand Châtelet two months ago.'

'She was one of your victims, too?'

'Yes. I was paid for her killing, and I always fulfil my contracts.'

'You did it personally?'

'No. As I said, my way is to always pay another.'

'What,' Baldwin asked tentatively, 'about the man de Nogaret in the Louvre?'

'That was nothing to do with me. I wouldn't kill in the King's own palace,' the other King said. 'What, do you think me a fool? To antagonise King Charles can only lead to destruction. I wouldn't risk that.'

'So who did?'

'If I knew that, I'd trade it for my release,' the King of Thieves spat.

'You see the problem with him?' Pons grumbled when they were back in the open air once more. 'He will wander in his mind, and then dry up and refuse to speak any more, and it takes all the effort of more torture to make him get to the point again.'

'And yet there were some useful pieces of information he gave us. He said that the same priest ordered the death of the girl as well as that of Jean,' Baldwin said. 'And that means it could not be Bishop Walter. He was not in the country when Madame de Nogaret was killed.'

'Perhaps, but the word of a thief and murderer like that is hardly to be taken as entirely valid,' Pons scoffed.

'Not entirely, no. But why would he lie? He knows he's going to die.'

'So he finds he can distract us and make us look fools, too!'

Simon interrupted. 'What of this man he mentioned – this assassin?'

'One of his own men gone bad, I dare say,' Pons said. He considered, and then shrugged. 'If the King in there has decided the man will end his days in the Seine, that's what'll likely happen to him.'

'So he wasn't responsible for the death of de Nogaret himself, but he did kill the wife,' Baldwin noted. 'Which is interesting, eh, Pons?'

'Why?'

'Let us return to the Louvre. There is a man I wish to speak to – the messenger who brought news of the visitor to the Cardinal.'

Chapter Thirty-Nine

Louvre

The Cardinal glared as Hugues slammed the door wide and burst into the room.

'He's gone!'

Cardinal Thomas motioned to the three clerks to close their work and leave him alone with the castellan. When they had gone, he asked curtly, 'What is the meaning of this?'

'You wanted the Bishop dead so he couldn't embarrass you. He's gone. I have checked with his servants. All are agreed that he and his clerks are nowhere to be seen, and the Bishop's two most prized possessions are missing: his spectacles and a book he always carried with him. He's left! Fled the castle and the city.'

'You must be mistaken,' the Cardinal said automatically. Gone? The *crétin* could not have taken flight, surely. He had been alarmed last night after the meal, but that appeared only to make him more determined not to leave without the Queen. To go back alone was tantamount to admitting failure, and there was the matter of the Duke, too, the King's son. King Edward would hardly be glad to see his son's guardian turn up in England without his charge. 'No, you must be mistaken. He wouldn't dare.'

'You ask the servants, then. I hunted about the castle, and no one's seen him.'

'Go and ask Arnaud. If the Bishop has left, Arnaud's men will have seen him.'

'Very well. But if he's escaped, you'd best start making plans for what you should do.'

The Cardinal stretched and smiled lazily. 'Me? No. I will be perfectly safe. There is nothing the Bishop can tell the English about me that matters even remotely. *I* am safe.'

Baldwin and Simon were the first to reach the gatehouse, and Baldwin immediately knocked on Arnaud's door. 'Porter? Ah, good. I hope you can help me. I would like to speak with the messenger Raoulet.'

'I'll have him brought to you.'

When he arrived, Baldwin and Simon studied Raoulet with interest. Pons affected boredom, however, and Sir Richard found it hard to keep his eyes on the lad.

Baldwin nodded towards some benches near the tavern, and Sir Richard's spirits lifted. 'You want a drink?' he asked hopefully.

The others made no response, but the big Coroner had soon acquired a large pot of wine, which he slurped as the others spoke.

Raoulet was not an impressive witness, Baldwin reckoned. He was young, skinny and spotty, had the sort of baleful resentfulness that could so easily flare into rage, as was common with many young men nowadays. He had little to add to what they knew. Still, there was one aspect which intrigued Baldwin.

'So you were at the gatehouse and received warning that a man called de Nogaret had come here to meet the Cardinal?'

'Yes. I was told that by a kitchen knave. He said that he'd installed the man in a small chamber, the one where he was found later.'

'Do you know the kitchen knave's name?'

'Yes. He was young Jehanin. Why?'

'He's dead. You know that?'

'Of course. Lots of us have been talking about it. Sad.' His face tended to disagree with his words.

'I am glad there is nothing else to tell us,' Simon said.

'So am I,' Raoulet said. Then he hesitated, his natural inquisitiveness getting the better of him. 'Why?'

'No reason. Except all those who knew anything about this meeting between the Cardinal and the man de Nogaret appear to have died. If you knew anything too, you might be next to die, mightn't you?'

Then, seeing the young man's expression, he added insincerely, 'There is probably nothing to worry about. After all, you don't know anything about it – so there's no need for you to ask us to protect you, is there?'

Raoulet was looking darkly anxious now. 'No, I don't know anything,' he repeated nervously.

'That's good,' Baldwin said. 'Because if you did, and anyone saw you here with us, they might think you were telling us all sorts of secrets.'

'There was nothing! Honest! All I know, I've told you. The knave came to fetch me, and I went to get the Cardinal. And when we got to the chamber, the man was dead.'

'Was the Cardinal still in his chamber?' Baldwin asked.

'Yes. He was there.'

'Good. Then you have no secret to worry about.' But the lad appeared worried about something still. Something that niggled at him. 'Boy, what is it?' Baldwin sighed.

Raoulet set his head to one side. 'It was just a little thing, but I couldn't help but think about it afterwards. You see, when Jehanin came to get me, he didn't come the normal way, the way I'd have expected. He actually seemed to come from the Cardinal's direction.'

Baldwin shot a look at Pons. The Frenchman was alert, staring fixedly at the messenger. 'You sure of that?' he asked gruffly.

Raoulet looked across at him, disdain returning to his features. 'Look, the Cardinal's chamber is there,' he said, making a scuffmark in the dust of the path. 'The man was found dead *here*, and I was over here. Why did Jehanin come from the Cardinal's rooms, then send me back the same way? At the time I thought he was just being lazy – that he was passing, saw me and thought he might as well get *me* to take the message to the Cardinal instead of him. But now, well, I'm not so sure.'

'All right, you can wait for us outside now, lad,' said Pons. Once Raoulet had gone, Pons turned to the others. 'We should speak with the Cardinal,' he said.

Baldwin was frowning. 'Why would a Cardinal want to seek the death of a young man like de Nogaret? It makes no sense.'

Simon was eyeing him speculatively. 'You told me that the older de Nogaret was involved in the destruction of the Templars and the thefts from the Jews. Perhaps it was something to do with one of them. After all, do you remember Bishop Walter last night saying that the Cardinal had said he was born to humble stock or something? How did he amass his wealth, if that's true?'

Pons sniffed. 'A man may amass a large treasure if he's ruthless enough.'

'The Bishop also said he had a cup, the brother to a set he had seen in the Pope's palace,' Baldwin remembered. 'But that was surely not a Templar artefact. Perhaps it was Jewish, and the Cardinal acquired it from the Jews?'

'The Jews were expelled from France in the year before the Templars were arrested,' Pons agreed. 'It was a wonderful time for the King. He took on all their loans and demanded immediate payment, confiscated their houses and assets, everything. Just like the Templars.'

'Let us go and see him, then,' Baldwin said. He opened the door and motioned to Raoulet. 'You know the way to the Cardinal's chamber. Why not lead us?'

Hugues saw them pass him, but he had more pressing matters to look into than where the English might be going. He continued on his way to Arnaud. 'Hoi, Porter! Have you seen the Bishop – the English ambassador, Stapledon? He looks to have disappeared into thin air.'

'Not here, no.'

'He couldn't have come past you in disguise?'

'No. There's been no one like him. Only the usual tranters and merchants coming in and a few pilgrims and travellers leaving.'

'Travellers? What travellers?'

Cardinal's Chamber

The Cardinal greeted them effusively as they entered, which in itself was enough to make Baldwin eye the man askance. His manner grated on the knight's nerves.

'My Lords, it is most kind of you to come here and visit me. Please, allow me to offer you refreshment.'

'We have not had to travel,' Pons said. 'We are here to ask you a little about the day on which you were called to the chamber where you found the dead man de Nogaret.'

'A terrible day, yes,' the Cardinal said soberly. 'I had known his father, but I never expected to know his son.'

'You had not met before?' Baldwin asked.

'No. Never.'

'Where did you meet his father, then?'

'On diplomatic tasks. Here in court,' the Cardinal said.

'You had a humble upbringing, I understand?' Baldwin continued.

The Cardinal beckoned a servant and soon had his favourite goblet in his hands. 'Yes. I was not born to a family of wealth and privilege.'

'A lovely goblet,' Baldwin said. 'May I see it?' He took the weighty cup and peered at it. 'Wonderful workmanship. And Biblical scenes, too. Is it true that the Pope has some similar to this?'

'Yes. I made him a gift of them when he took the Papal throne. That was this Pope's predecessor, of course.'

'Pope Clement – the Pope who oversaw the destruction of the Templars?'

'Yes.'

'That would mean that you did not acquire this cup and the others from Jews, then. The scenes are entirely Christian, are they not?'

The Cardinal was staring at him with some perplexity. 'What of it?'

'I merely wondered where a man with such a humble background could have found these cups.'

'It was while I was at Anagni.'

'You were there,' Baldwin said, 'when Pope Boniface was captured and his treasure taken? He died within the week, did he not?'

'I believe so, yes. A pity, no doubt, but the man was seriously unbalanced. He tried to set himself up as a competitor to the King of France. Clearly that would never be tolerated, and so he was chastised and removed.'

'I suppose that by "chastised", you mean he was beaten up, tortured, robbed and killed?' Baldwin said tensely.

'I suppose I do,' the Cardinal said easily.

'Did he deserve it?' Pons asked.

'Many thought so,' Cardinal Thomas said. He picked up his goblet and glanced into it, motioning to a servant for more wine.

'He probably did deserve punishment,' Baldwin said with a firm restraint. 'He deserved it as much as any who have stolen or killed, Cardinal. But he *didn't* deserve to be beaten and slaughtered without trial. His death was not a punishment – it was a waylaying just as an outlaw might attempt.'

'It seemed suitable at the time,' the Cardinal said flatly, staring straight at Baldwin.

There was a sudden thunderous pounding on the door, and Hugues and Lord John Cromwell strode inside.

It was Lord John who barked, 'Cardinal, the Bishop has fled the city!'

'When did he go? Where?'

'At first light – as soon as the gates were opened.'

'Sweet Jesus!' Hugues spat. 'We must go and find him! If he gets back to the coast with news of . . .' He suddenly noticed the other men in the room and curled back his lips from his teeth in a snarl. 'At least these will remain here to help "protect" the English whelp, eh?'

Baldwin felt Simon stiffen at his side, but his concern was more for the apparently affable Sir Richard, who was already half out of his seat, his hand moving dangerously close to his sword.

'There is no reason to expect us to leave our charge,' Baldwin said, stepping quickly before the other knight and blocking his path. 'We are men of honour.'

'Oh, yes?' the castellan said sarcastically.

It was enough to make even Lord John, who was no friend to Bishop Walter, scowl. 'They are honourable men who are respected by the Queen, man. You would do well to remember that.'

The Cardinal spoke in a mollifying tone. 'Gentlemen, please. There is no need to argue and bicker, just as there was no need for the good Bishop to fly from the city like a man in fear of his life. What is the reason for this? We must certainly send men to protect him. If he wishes to continue to the coast and leave the Queen and her son here, it is not for us to criticise. It is a matter for him and for the King who sent him. But he will need protection on his way, that is for certain. We must gather men to follow after him.'

There was a suppressed urgency in Hugues as he nodded, turned and hurried off along the corridors. Lord John grunted and made his way after him, and the Cardinal rose graciously, finishing his wine and motioning to the others to follow him.

'You were telling us about Anagni?' Baldwin said.

'Yes. Well, I was there, and it made me my fortune. I was one of those under Guillaume de Nogaret in the French team. We joined up with Giacomo Colonna, the man they called the "Quarreller", or "Sciarra", because he was so bellicose. He was keen to come to blows with the Pope, because Pope Boniface was from the Gaetani family, and the Colonnas hated them with a ferocity that must be seen to be believed.'

They descended a staircase, and then were out in the cool, autumnal sunshine. A number of horses were already gathered about, and men were shouting commands, dogs barking or yelping, while from all parts of the castle other men stood gaping at the excitement.

Baldwin continued, 'So you were there with the French contingent, and you found a pot of money?'

'We found some chests of cash. And that was enough for me to buy my Cardinal's hat. Does that surprise you?'

'There is nothing in the corruption of the Church in Rome which could shock me,' Baldwin said icily.

The Cardinal recalled it so vividly. The chests opening – he and Hugues gaping in shock at the money inside, while Paolo held Toscanello by the throat. For a moment all the sounds outside, all the noise inside, were dimmed. Time itself seemed to stand still, and Thomas reached into the nearest chest and touched a goblet, the one he still had with him here. Later he gave the matching goblets and plates to the Pope for his Cardinal's hat. For that moment, though, there was no thought in his mind of giving up any of this hoard.

'Our leader was a man called Paolo. It was he who caused the treasure to come to me, really,' he said. 'Paolo had another man with him, and he slashed the boy's throat, purely because he didn't want to share the loot. Well, there were two of us there at the time, and we didn't need to talk about it. It was plain as a knife in a hand that Paolo wouldn't share with anyone. So we two attacked him, and soon had him on the ground.'

'And the treasure was split only two ways?'

'That is right.'

'And let me guess,' Simon said. 'You didn't want to share it with another – say, Guillaume de Nogaret?'

'Actually, no. That wasn't such a problem,' the Cardinal said. 'We did share a little with him. But not with the King.'

'So this is the money that de Nogaret's son was talking about,' Simon breathed.

'Yes. I think he may have intended to come here to blackmail us into giving him some more. The fool! Why on earth would he think we'd pay now?'

'Perhaps because he was sure that his word would count with the King,' Baldwin said. 'I think that's what you also feared, so that was why you killed him.'

'Aha! So you accuse me? But the messenger found me in my chamber. You know that.'

'And we also know that the messenger was called to fetch you by a young kitchen knave called Jehanin. I wonder why that could have been? We have heard that Jehanin came to Raoulet from *your* rooms, not from the little chamber where the man was killed. It seems likely to me that you met de Nogaret down here, you led him to a separate chamber, where you killed him, and then you left him there, found Jehanin later, and told him to find a messenger to fetch you. I expect he was surprised by the request. Perhaps he questioned it? Perhaps he sought to ask for money later? Whatever the reason, you killed him too, and hid his body for a while, later throwing it into a box in the kitchen, so it could not be associated with you.'

'A marvellous spinning of half-truths and invention. I congratulate you!'

'Well I accuse *you*, Cardinal – I accuse you of having a hand in the murder of Guillaume de Nogaret, and in the murder of the kitchen knave Jehanin. What do you say?'

Pons had stepped nearer and was listening carefully.

'I deny it, of course. And unless I am mistaken, you have no authority in this city. And you too can keep your hand from your knife, Master Pons. I am a Cardinal, and that means I answer only to ecclesiastical officers, not the lay courts.'

Several men had overheard the conversation, especially the accusation. There was a muttering from some groups, and a young lad was standing in the forefront, scowling furiously at the Cardinal. Baldwin thought he recognised the lad from the kitchen.

'You can at least save any other man from being accused and punished,' he said. 'Do you deny killing the two?'

'How would I have managed it? Come, it is hardly likely, is it?'

'You do not deny it, then?'

'I have had more than enough of this. You wish to contemplate my participation in these deaths, you may feel free. It is nothing to me.'

Pons shook his head now. 'No, because the next question is, who ordered the murder of Jean le Procureur? He was investigating the killing of the two de Nogarets, and someone from here, a religious man, is said to have commanded that Jean must die.'

Baldwin looked about him as a gasp burst from the onlookers. He was relieved to see the kitchen boy was gone. It could not have been pleasant for a young fellow to hear about the murder of his companion. The rest were drawing nearer, though, and there was a tide of anger rising all about him.

'First you say that I am capable of killing two, and then that I must hire an assassin? Be logical.'

'You deny the killing of Jean le Procureur?'

'It is nothing to do with me. As I said before, I answer only to the ecclesiastical court. I may be tried for a crime in Rome, if the Pope sees fit to accuse me, but I do not answer for anything here in Paris. There is no court which can hear evidence against me, none with the power to punish me.'

Baldwin would later regret that he didn't look about him. The mumbling had increased within the group of men, and even Sir Richard had grown aware of it, and was warily watching the crowd. If a mob were to form, there would be nothing they could do. Meanwhile, though, Baldwin spent his time concentrating on the Cardinal, watching his face, assessing his mannerisms, his nervousness, his apparent guilt.

But then the Cardinal's face changed. All anger and confidence left in an instant, to be replaced by a dawning horror. He opened his mouth, staring at a point over Baldwin's shoulder, and a curious little sigh burst from him.

It was a sound Baldwin had heard all too often. No scream, no shriek of terror could bring more anguish than that. It was the last gasp of a man as he died.

Even as Baldwin stepped forward to try to help the tottering figure, he saw the point of the cook's long knife appear to the right of the Cardinal's breast, the sudden flowering of blood as it seeped from the wound, and saw the Cardinal's face whiten as he began to shake all over, falling forward into Baldwin's arms.

Four men had already punched, kicked and hammered the cook to the ground, but he lay with an expression of satisfaction on his face as the Cardinal began to gurgle and thrash about in his death throes.

'He killed my boy,' the cook said, just before Hugues kicked him in the face.

Any possibility of an immediate hunt for the Bishop was gone with the death of the Cardinal. The men who had been mounting their horses so enthusiastically, were now milling about aimlessly. It was as though the removal of the Cardinal had taken away their collective will.

Hugues crouched over the body of the Cardinal and wept, while the cook was dragged away to the castle's cells. There was nothing Baldwin could do to protect him. He had murdered a priest in full view of half the Louvre's staff. There could be no mitigation in a case like that.

'I am sorry,' Baldwin said.

Hugues shook his head. 'He was my only friend.'

'You were at Anagni with him, weren't you?'

'Yes. It's how I came to have this position. I know Thomas did better, but I was happy enough. Food, a roof, women whenever I wanted. There's everything I need.'

'The money from Anagni paid for it?'

'It meant I could become a baron in my own right. Thomas was right to go into the Church, because a man could buy more advancement for less money, but he had the training too. He was bright enough to make his way in the Church. I couldn't have done that. But I was a good fighter. The King had need of a good baron, and with the help of de Nogaret's father, I was knighted and became castellan here.'

'Did you see de Nogaret here before he died?'

'No. I didn't know he was coming – I'd have welcomed him if I had. I didn't realise Thomas would have him killed. I didn't agree with that.'

'You knew he had killed de Nogaret?' Simon interrupted.

'Who else would have done it? There was no need, though. The lad was no real threat. What was he going to do? Ask us about money we took twenty-three years ago? I doubt the King himself cares about it. It was money confiscated from his father's enemy, anyway, so he'd be glad enough.'

'You think so? In my experience,' Baldwin said, 'Kings tend to be quite happy to take money no matter where it comes from. If the Cardinal had thought that de Nogaret was going to report him or blackmail him, it could well have led him to kill the young man, to keep his secret. And the same goes for the kitchen knave.'

'Him? He was just a *boy*,' he said dismissively.

'At least his master, the cook, thought differently,' Baldwin said. 'He thought the boy worth killing for.'

'Perhaps the cook is a catamite? How should I know?' Hugues snarled and returned to cradling Thomas's body. 'There was no need to do this for the brat.'

Any sympathy which Baldwin had been forming for the man's grief dissipated like morning mist.

He turned and saw the horses waiting. 'My Lord Cromwell,

will you order them to stand down? There has been enough killing for one day.'

Lord John nodded and began bellowing at the men to instruct them to return their horses to the stables, and meanwhile Pons stood over Hugues and the body, eyeing them thoughtfully. 'You know, my friend, this still leaves me wondering about the other murders. There was the death of Madame de Nogaret. She surely died at the hands of some other. If the Cardinal killed her husband and the boy, it is less likely that he killed the woman. And Jean le Procureur was despatched by a professional. I suppose that must have been the assassin the King spoke of.'

'The man who will soon also be dead,' Baldwin noted.

'Precisely. And yet, who killed my guard and took Le Boeuf? That was another, certainly, for I doubt me that the Cardinal would have left the castle so early in the morning as to do that.'

'The assassin was in the pay of the robber King,' Simon pointed out. 'No doubt it was him again.'

'And yet the assassin was already bitterly angry with the King, and it was mutual, because the one tried to withhold the money owed to the other. There was a body in the Seine when we got to his house, and the King told us that it was a man killed by the assassin. Would the latter have gone back to do the King's bidding after that?'

The others nodded, and Simon said, 'So we may have another killer? It is an unlikely scenario.'

'But something we shall have to consider. Something to keep in our minds,' Pons said with grave deliberation.

Chapter Forty

Arnaud had seen it all. The Cardinal's proud comments, the way that the group formed around him, the sudden appearance of the cook, the flash of the blade and the violence that followed . . . yes, he had seen it all.

'You take care of this,' he muttered to his men and strode away into the main courtyard after Hugues. He could see the castellan's form up ahead; Hugues had the look of a broken man.

'Sieur Hugues? I am so sorry, so sorry.'

'What? Oh, Arnaud.' Even his irascibility appeared to have been eroded. For Hugues looked like an older man, drawn in upon himself, the lines on his face more prominent, his eyes watery and unseeing. 'You mean Thomas.'

'I had never thought . . . I know he was a friend of yours.'

'For more years than I can remember. My only friend. That cook will roast in hell!'

'But why did he stab the Cardinal?'

'Because Thomas killed the cook's boy,' Hugues snapped. 'Didn't you hear?'

'No,' Arnaud said, and he was frowning. 'But I don't understand . . .'

'What?'

'I told you before – I saw your woman with that lad. You told me not to be stupid at the time, because she wouldn't have killed the man de Nogaret, but she may have killed the lad.'

Hugues opened his mouth, but then closed it again. His eyes

dropped, and he studied the dirt for a moment. Then, 'Tell them,' was all he said.

He turned on his heel and left the courtyard, walking to his chamber.

When Hugues entered his room, he closed the door and stood in front of it, breathing deeply, eyes screwed tight shut, feeling as though his heart was about to burst.

There was a smell in there. A smell he recognised.

'Where are you?' he rasped, opening his eyes again.

'Here, lover.'

Her throaty voice sent a chill along his spine. Pushing himself away from the door, he peered around his table. She was lying, naked, on the palliasse. She was as desirable as she had ever been, all whiteness and pinkness and softness. Everything he had ever wanted was there. He wanted to throw himself on top of her now, and find once again the release she offered. Even as he had the thought, she held up a hand invitingly, and he groaned and fell back on to his table, covering his face with his hands.

'It was you, wasn't it?' he said.

She slowly came to a sitting position, leaning back on both arms. 'Me? What have I done?'

'You murdered the boy from the kitchen.'

'I don't know what you mean, Hugues. Why don't you come down here and tell me?'

'You saw the lad out there, you paid him to get the other one, Raoulet, and had him go to the Cardinal. And then you killed the boy to cover your actions.'

'Why would I have done that?'

'For mischief. I know you.'

'You think me so evil?'

'I know you.'

'But why would I do such a thing? I must have had a reason.'

He looked at her. 'You wanted to run the King of Thieves' men, didn't you? You set us all up. You had Thomas kill de Nogaret, *you* killed the kitchen knave to make it look as though Thomas had killed him too, and then you spoke to the King on Thomas's behalf. The perfect go-between. You told him Thomas wanted a contract on de Nogaret's wife, didn't you? And then you made sure that Thomas was worried to death about the Procureur, and arranged another contract for his death.'

She stretched luxuriously and lay back on the palliasse, smiling.

'What then? Oh, you were involved in seeing to the arrest of the King himself, weren't you? Why? So you could take over?'

'I was always a lot cleverer than him. He is a fool.'

'But you couldn't run a gang like his. That'd be impossible. They'd cut you into minced meat for a pie.'

'I could do it with an assistant.'

'Who?' Hugues sneered, letting his hands fall to his thighs. He eyed her with revulsion.

'The King's best man, of course,' she said. 'Jacquot.'

'You persuaded him to rebel against the King?'

'No. I persuaded the King to betray Jacquot. And that meant Jacquot would find himself in charge, if he was careful. And he was. So now he and I run it.'

'You are evil. Is there no one you wouldn't deceive?'

'I haven't deceived you, Hugues. If you wanted, you could join me,' she said, and her hand wandered over her belly now, cupping a breast, rubbing gently, flicking, stirring herself and Hugues. 'You would make more money than here, and you'd have me. Think of it. You could be in charge, once we get rid of Jacquot.'

Hugues stared at her for a moment, and then said wearily, 'Get out, deceiver. I trust nothing you say. Your very words are poison. *Out!* And never return to me.'

A street near the Louvre

Jacquot was still alive. That was, he felt, surprising.

They had almost caught him three times. Once he fell over a startled cat, the bastard, and only just got to his feet in time to scarper before they caught up with him. There was another near-miss when he went the wrong way down an alley and found himself in a dead end. It had taken all his energy to clamber up a wall and escape. And finally there was that moment of dull shock when a man suddenly appeared in front of him, his head lowered and legs braced, a stick in his fist. He glared at Jacquot, and Jacquot in that moment knew that he was dead. He had no chance of escape with this man blocking his path.

And then – miracle of miracles – the fellow apologised, bent his head politely, and stood aside to let Jacquot slip past.

He had made it to this, the Grande Rue, and now, among the thronging crowds he could at least breathe. All the while, he cast about him for any sign of the men following, but there was nothing. They would spot him soon, no doubt. He must find an escape somehow. Somewhere . . .

No. First he would find that poisonous bitch Amélie and slit her throat. This was a betrayal too far. She may have lived after ensuring the King was caught, but she should have realised Jacquot was different.

There were only a few places she was likely to be at this time of the day. He knew that she would go to the tavern later, when she felt the need of food and drink, but before that she would usually go and whore at the Louvre. There were plenty of men there who would pay for her services, and Jacquot knew that she had made good use of her contacts there, bringing jobs and messages to the King. Truth be told, it was probably she who had taken the instructions from the Cardinal to have the Procureur murdered. And then, there were the other jobs. The woman killed down by the Grand Châtelet . . . she was the wife of the man slain in the Louvre, wasn't she? And what about the man who had been set on Jacquot – the incompetent Stammerer. He would have been ordered to do that by someone. Perhaps she'd organised that, too, seeing the potential destruction of the King if she riled Jacquot enough. There were few lengths to which she would not go. And then she'd called the officers herself to the King's hideaway, and ensured that he was taken.

He had reached the gate of the city now, and moved with the crush, out towards the castle, which gleamed white and pure in the flashes of sunlight.

And as he approached the enormous gatehouse, he saw her. Walking towards him.

Louvre gatehouse

She saw him quite clearly, and her smile was unaffected.

That old goat Hugues was past his best. She wanted a partner of more stamina and power. Hugues was always half in the barrel. Too often, he would fall from her to snore when she was only partly satiated. That was why she came to him more often in the morning. At least then it was more likely that she would receive a decent service.

But Jacquot, for all that he was the same age as Hugues, was more deserving of her attention. He had that cold, rational perspective. With his abilities and her ruthlessness, they would forge a partnership that would rock the whole of Paris.

'Jacquot,' she purred as he came closer.

He smiled. 'You really shouldn't have tried to kill me,' he said.

His hand moved so quickly, she hardly had time to register it. The blade was a long one, and it slid in under her right breast. There was a little snagging sensation, an odd feeling that made her frown a little, and then a smooth gliding that was less pain, more itching. She felt the material at her back draw away as though in disgust, and then his hand was removed, and he was walking away from her. She stopped and glared at him, without registering for the moment what had happened. Jacquot, she saw, had his right hand under his cloaked left side, as though settling something. The knife, of course.

She opened her mouth to shout at him, and then full realisation struck her as she gagged. Falling forwards, she retched and brought up a vast effusion of blood on to the dirt of the road before her. No! No! This wasn't happening to her. It was a dream – a wild, ridiculous nightmare. She must wake in a moment and find herself in the King's bed, or in Jacquot's, or in Hugues's. She couldn't die here, lying in the street and watching her blood seep away from her to run in a thick stream down to the gutter.

Unable to call, to shout, to accuse, she lifted her leaden head to watch as he stopped near the city gates. He gave her an unsmiling look, long and deliberate, before walking away again.

She felt the pain growing, a spreading anguish that began in the wound and moved ever outwards until it encompassed her entire body, and then she began to roll and thrash in the roadway, the blood running freely from breast and back and mouth, until her struggles against death grew more slow and disjointed, while men-at-arms ran and called for aid, and women wailed and shrieked, and children bawled . . . and then she knew peace.

Chapter Forty-One

City gate, Paris

Jacquot was almost at the gate itself when the two men appeared in it. One pointed at him, while the other bellowed for help. Time to run again.

The third, the one who had been in front, seemed to materialise from nowhere over to his right. That was fine. He had not intended to run that way anyway. It only led down to the river. No, he would take the path up past the Louvre and out to the open country north. These bumbling fools wouldn't follow him up there. He could stay out overnight, then make his way back in the morning, perhaps. And he'd have these arses discovered and punished for trying to attack him – the new King.

He walked at a rapid pace, throwing his long legs out in front of him and striding powerfully, for all the feeling of exhaustion creeping into his muscles. There was no getting away from it, he was an old man now. There had been a time when he would have done a march like this without thinking, but many barrels of wine had gone under his belt since then.

Glancing over his shoulder, he saw that they were not apparently gaining on him. That was good. If he could only make it up past the main thoroughfares here, he should be all right.

He was past the northernmost section of the Louvre now, and the streets were smaller and less crowded. His pursuers were catching up now. They were more confident, the further they went from the main roads of the city. Especially now that the way was more potholed and muddy. The people all around were the shifty sort who wouldn't meet a man's eye – as clear a sign of danger as any.

A fine drizzle began to fall, and he hoped that this might be the onset of a heavier downpour. A man could hide in a really heavy storm. He tried to urge his legs on faster, but there was a problem. They seemed unwilling to obey his brain. Already he had hurried halfway across the city; there was a feeling of burning in his lungs, and he felt sure that if he didn't get away soon, they would be on him.

There was a shout from behind him, and when he turned, he saw the men begin to hurry, urged on by the larger man of the three. He was a hulking figure, his cloak blowing behind him. He was pounding along the road now, each step throwing up mud or worse, on his face a grim snarl.

He looked familiar, Jacquot thought. Where the devil had he seen the bastard before?

Jacquot made to flee, but suddenly two men darted into the street ahead of him. One had a club, which he weighed in his hands, while the other, a much older man, nervously handled a long staff.

Jacquot ran at the younger, ignoring the old man; he was no threat. He shoved out with his hands, thrust the cudgel-man from his path without halting, took a deep breath, and would have continued, but something struck his shin, and he was flying. The ground seemed to gradually rise up to meet him, as though in some form of delayed reality, and he could see a stone directly in his path that must surely break his jaw when he struck it. He tried to lift a hand to protect his chin, but it was too late, and as he hit the roadway, the shock of the impact jarred his entire frame.

A hand grabbed his right wrist and yanked it down and round behind his back. About it was wrapped a thong, then his left was pulled back too, and although he wanted to struggle and fight, there was an odd lightheadedness in his bones and his head. He could make no defence.

It was as they hauled him to his feet and he tottered like a new-born foal, that he recognised the man at last.

He had been a thief-taker. One of the old King of Thieves' contacts. This was a man who could be hired by any to seek out and arrest or murder an enemy.

'Oh, shit!' he murmured through slackened lips. 'The bastard got me in the end!'

Louvre

The commotion outside the gate made all the men stop and stare, and then Simon was running with Sir Richard and Baldwin for the entrance.

A group of men had gathered about the dying woman, and the three, with Pons puffing behind them, had to push them away.

'Dear God!' Pons muttered under his breath, and crossed himself.

'Do you know her?' Baldwin demanded.

'She used to be the wench of the King of Thieves,' Pons said.

She was still moving, but it was obvious that there was nothing anyone could do for her now. A priest knelt by her, his features pinched and blanched by the reality of the woman's death, and he was doing the best he could, muttering his prayers, trying to get her to utter the words that would save her soul.

'Did anyone see who did this? Eh? Anyone here see who killed this girl?' Pons roared.

'He went off up there, with three men chasing after him,' a voice said from the crowd.

Pons nodded and set off at a trot. After glancing at each other, Baldwin and the others followed.

Baldwin called, 'You seem very angered by this. Was she known to you?'

'You recall we arrested the King of Thieves? It was her took us to him. Looks like he's had his revenge already.'

'What makes you think *he* has done this?' Baldwin asked, puffing slightly.

'Who else would?'

Baldwin made no answer to that. Already they were past the castle, and now only a few tens of yards away, they could see a huddle of men outside a little house further up the road.

Pons had seen it too. Now he gave a great roar and redoubled his speed. Clattering and splashing, the three Englishmen raced after him as quickly as they could.

'Leave him alone!' Pons bellowed.

Hélias motioned to Bernadette and the young girl went to the thief-taker and took his arm, murmuring in his ear. He nodded, bent and kissed her on the mouth, and then stood back, snapping an order to the two with him.

In the roadway in front of her little tavern, Jacquot lay rolling in the filth, gripping his belly. His face was already swelling from the beating he had taken, and as she looked over, she saw old Michel preparing to whack him again with his long staff. She gave a hissed order, and he looked around with surprise. Seeing Pons, he stepped back, and soon Jacquot was alone.

'What is this, Hélias? You taken to waylaying men as they pass? You need the business that much?' Pons demanded. Jacquot tried to shift himself to a sitting position, and Pons nudged him hard with an ungentle foot, knocking him down again, where he remained, groaning gently.

'I want to help the law, Pons. This one, he should have been arrested an age ago.'

'I will be the judge of that. I do know he's likely to be taken soon anyway. He's just murdered a young woman.'

'Well, you should listen more carefully to people who know your business, like me.'

Pons spat. 'Really? Why?'

'Because this fellow lying at your side is the murderer of Jean le Procureur.'

'How do you know?'

Hélias looked at him. 'We have our own means of finding answers.'

Jacquot held up a hand weakly. 'Can I have a say in this? I'm innocent!'

'No! Shut up!' Pons said. 'Hélias?'

'I had customers ask around. They led me to him.'

Jacquot tried again. 'You want to know who really killed le Procureur? Who killed the de Nogarets? Who also killed the man watching the fellow who was taken and murdered by . . .'

'You mean my watchman, André?' Pons snapped.

'Yes. All were the result of the scheming bitch back there. I killed her, I confess it! I killed her to save people.'

Baldwin was shaking his head. 'What do you know of this, fellow? Who are you?'

'My name is Jacquot, and I have nothing to lose by confessing all. Will you hear me out?'

Pons scowled at the name. 'I have heard of you, Jacquot. You are a killer.'

'Only in my own defence. That woman was called Amélie. She was the lover of the King of Thieves, as well as of the castellan in the Louvre. Some weeks ago she met the man de

Nogaret and his wife, and she heard them say that they were
coming to the Louvre. De Nogaret's father was a man high in
the King's esteem, and he wanted to plead for a little of the
King's largesse. But he made a terrible mistake. He told *her* –
and Amélie was always in search of money. She decided to kill
them both, I think, and take their money when they had some.
But then she learned from them that de Nogaret's father had
mentioned a pair of men who stole a large sum from the Pope
years ago. Two men called Hugues and Thomas d'Anjou.'

'The Cardinal and the castellan,' Baldwin said, looking at
Pons.

'Yes. And it gave her an idea – to take the money
herself. To get the two to pay her to keep her silent about their
past.'

Simon was frowning. 'Why? What would it matter what
they did to the Pope all those years ago?'

'Not much,' Baldwin responded thoughtfully. 'Unless the
King felt that the money rightfully belonged to him. And that
might lead to his taking it for himself.'

'Which is what she reasoned,' Jacquot agreed. He eased
himself up to a sitting position, ruefully eyeing the old man
with the staff. 'That stick has hurt my head, old man.'

'What then? Do you have anything other than speculation
to support this tale?' Pons rasped. 'I tell you now, I believe
little of what you say. You are an assassin, a man who relies on
night for your evil.'

'I don't know who told you all that. I am just a peasant and
beggar in this city,' Jacquot said. 'All I'm doing is trying to
help you!'

'Continue, then,' Baldwin said. 'What happened with this
woman?'

Jacquot hawked and spat. 'The first thing was, she was
bumped by the Cardinal. He told her, if she wanted to spread

tales about him, he would have her arrested by the Church and imprisoned. Then the castellan told her she would do well to leave them both alone. But he liked her. And he bedded her. And to keep bedding her, he would have to do her bidding. He thought she only wanted money. She didn't. She wanted power as well. Power over other people. So she killed the de Nogarets to gain power over the Cardinal.'

'A woman did that?' Pons scoffed. 'This man's a fool. Take him to the Temple . . .'

'Wait a moment,' Baldwin said. 'Continue.'

'She killed the first somehow, and when the Cardinal reached the man, he realised he'd be blamed. Worse, he knew that the money which he had taken would be claimed by the King if it was thought he had killed de Nogaret. So he chose to conceal all. And when the Procureur came close to realising there was a link between the Cardinal and the dead man, the Cardinal sought to silence that enquiry too. He paid the King of Thieves to remove this embarrassment.'

'And the girl?'

Jacquot looked up at Baldwin. 'She wanted power, as I said. So she was sworn to kill me too and remove another possible obstacle to her authority.'

'So, as you say, you killed in self-defence.' Pons's voice was dripping with acid. 'Take him to the Temple. Have him held there until we know what to do with him.'

The thief-taker nodded and took Jacquot's arm. He gave a short nod to Pons, another to Baldwin, and then a brief bow to Hélias. Baldwin was sure that he saw him wink too, which made him frown a moment, but then Pons was chivying them back towards the Louvre. 'Come! There is little more to be discussed here. We must find a jug of good wine to celebrate the discovery of the murderer and her death at last!'

*

Jacquot was a pathetic figure, the thief-taker thought to himself. There was nothing about him to inspire fear or awe. Still, there was the fact that he was worth money. That alone was enough to make him look entirely delightful.

'Slower, friend,' Jacquot said. 'I am tired and failing after the way they beat me.'

'Piss on you! Get a move on!'

'Am I a danger to you? Am I a threat? Do you need to hurry me to my death? Let a man enjoy his last walk.'

'I said, get a . . .'

The blade sank in silently, swiftly, and only when he withdrew it did it make a little sound, like a liquid belch. But there was no possibility that anyone would have heard it. Jacquot helped the body to the ground, rolling it over a few times to shove it nearer a wall, before wiping his blade on the man's back and setting off quickly towards the city's north gate. He still had much to do.

Arnaud was nervous as the men appeared in the gateway. He didn't care about the English, but Pons was a different matter. 'Master, I . . .'

'What is the matter with the fellow?' Sir Richard demanded. Even Wolf appeared surprised. He sat near Arnaud and gazed up, panting with mild reproof, or so Baldwin felt.

'Do you have something to say?' Pons said. 'We are in a hurry.'

'It's the castellan, Sieur. I am not sure, but I think the day that de Nogaret was killed, that woman out there who was slain today – I saw her with the boy, the kitchen knave who died. Little Jehanin.'

'And you said nothing?'

'What could I say?'

'Anything else?' Baldwin snapped angrily. If this man had spoken earlier, much of his work in the last few days could have been reduced.

'I did not think of it at the time, but some days after the murder, I spoke with her. She mentioned that she had met de Nogaret in a tavern or wine shop.'

'Who did you tell?' Pons demanded.

'No one. She was speaking about the Cardinal, saying how the boy had told her he was coming to the castle to get money from the Cardinal and would soon be rich, because the Cardinal had stolen some and—'

'What of the castellan?' Baldwin interrupted sharply. 'What of him?'

'He told me to tell you. He was her lover, and he was very upset to learn that she had been with the lad.'

'Why?' Pons wondered.

'I think we should speak to him,' Baldwin said urgently. 'Come!'

But it was too late. The body of the castellan swung gently from the rope about his neck, the hemp creaking with the regular pendulum swing.

'Cut him down,' Pons said quietly.

'Why did he do that?' Arnaud said. He was standing in the doorway behind them as Simon clambered on to the desk and ran his dagger's edge along the rope while Sir Richard gripped the body in a hug. It was soon lying on the floor, a disjointed huddle of clothing.

'He knew his position here was soon to end,' Baldwin said, and sighed. 'This man and his comrade, the Cardinal, both knew that once their past offences were bruited about, they would be ruined. The King would demand their money, and would almost certainly punish them for stealing treasure that should have come to the King himself.'

'The money from the Pope?' Simon objected. 'That was no more the King's than it was theirs.'

'No more it was. But Kings have a habit of ignoring little details of that nature,' Baldwin said with a dry smile. 'The King would remember that his father sent Guillaume de Nogaret with his little force to capture the Pope, and were any man to make a profit, he would expect it to be himself. I have no doubt that Sieur Hugues would have been punished. The Cardinal, of course, would probably survive owing to his religious position. That would give him immunity.'

'Then why would he bother to kill de Nogaret?' Simon asked.

'How do you think the present Pope would react to learning that one of his Cardinals had a part in the capture, ill-treatment, robbery and subsequent death of his predecessor?' Baldwin asked.

'Oh.'

'And the ironic thing is, he didn't harm de Nogaret.'

Pons frowned. 'What?'

'That is what this man died for, I think,' Baldwin said, eyeing Hugues's body. 'He introduced his whore to his past. He let the girl know how he got his money, I expect. And in return she threatened to blackmail him and his friend the Cardinal. And when they proved less than susceptible, she killed the young de Nogaret herself, and sent a little boy to find a messenger to go to the Cardinal to ask him to visit the room where she had done it. Then she killed the boy, the kitchen knave, so that no one would be able to show that she had any connection with the dead man. She was adept at covering her tracks. I admit that.'

'And the Cardinal paid to have Jean killed because he could see how all pointed to him,' Pons agreed.

'Yes. And this same Amélie, I expect, likely also killed the wife of de Nogaret.'

'How so?'

Baldwin jerked his head towards the other side of the castle. 'You told me that the de Nogaret boy died with a knife in his back, yes? He turned his back on the woman because he knew full well that a woman was less of a threat. Especially a woman he already knew from drinking with her. Just as his wife knew her too, and perhaps made no complaint when Amélie asked her to walk with her. But a woman walking with another is less likely to be entirely trusting. Men are more innocent, I have often observed.'

'So was this Amélie guilty of *all* the murders here?' Pons said.

'I think so. And this man killed himself because the idea of losing all was so hateful to him.'

'His money and position, you mean?' Pons said, looking down at Hugues too.

It was Arnaud who tentatively added what Baldwin was thinking. 'And his woman, mon Sieur. He loved her, in despite of all.'

Epilogue

Queen Isabella's chamber, Louvre

'I hear you wish to leave us,' the Queen said flatly.

Baldwin and Simon stood before her, Sir Richard a pace or two behind. She was sitting in a pleasant little chair with decorative cushions that looked more comfortable than the down pillow on the bed behind her, Baldwin thought. She was a picture of regal authority, sitting there so serious, rather like a judge.

It was Simon who answered. His voice was a little choked. 'My Lady, I came here to protect your son on the orders of the Bishop Walter, and I would not leave your service if I thought that there was aught I could do to keep him safe. But the truth is, there is nothing for me to do here. I would remain at your command if there was anything I felt I could add, but you know full well that you have many men to guard you here.'

'And you, Sir Baldwin?'

'My Lady, I have been away from my wife and little children too long. You can surely understand a parent's need to see them. You have suffered from being removed from your own.'

---

[1] Wednesday, 9 October 1325

'You do not need to remind me,' she hissed, eyes blazing. 'But you would leave me and return like that mediocre cleric Stapledon, wouldn't you? Bishop Walter de Stapledon has fled and left me here in dire need, all because he refused to pass to me the money that my husband had already allocated for my use. It is because of him that I am forced to remain here. I could scarcely leave France while my debts were still outstanding, could I?'

So that, Baldwin considered, was to be her excuse. Now that Bishop Walter had run from the city with the letter from the King providing funds, she was forced to remain. It was the Bishop's fault.

She looked them over. 'You have other matters which concern you?'

'What could there be?'

In answer the Queen stood. She waved her hands and all her servants walked from the chamber, leaving only herself and her son with them. 'You know all the stories. The Despenser's most implacable enemy is here in France.'

'Yes. We had heard that the threats issued against the Bishop were probably made by him,' Simon said bluntly. This was no time for prevarication.

'You believe that? You believe Sir Roger Mortimer is here?'

'We do,' Baldwin said. 'My Lady, this is none of our affair.'

'And yet you refuse to aid me. You will remain a man of the King's?'

'The King's, yes. Not Sir Hugh le Despenser's. And I am not your enemy, Lady, merely a man who seeks not to break his oath of allegiance. Do not think the worse of me for that. Sir Roger Mortimer himself refused to raise his standard against that of the King. If he had, the King would have been defeated by him and his host, I am sure. But Sir Roger chose the path of honour and lowered his standard, surrendering himself.'

It was no more than the truth. Sir Roger had been the King's most successful General. When he rose with the other Lords Marcher from the Welsh borders, they could easily have squashed the force sent against them, and yet Sir Roger Mortimer and the others would not fight the King. They were not traitors or rebels, but honourable men protecting what was theirs against an intolerably avaricious man – Sir Hugh le Despenser. So Sir Roger surrendered to the King's standard and was imprisoned. Escaping when his death warrant was signed, he had no choice but to take the path of flight. And now open rebellion, perhaps.

'You think to suggest you are the same as he?'

'I think to persuade you that I am a mere rural knight who has been caught up in affairs which are nothing to do with me, which are not of my making, which are of no interest to me. I have done my duty to you and to your son this year, and all I seek is an opportunity to return to my home. Simon and I both fear for our estates.'

'So you will return to your homes, not to the King?'

'We shall perhaps report that you are both safe, but no more.'

'You say so, too, Bailiff?'

Simon swallowed. 'Majesty, my wife and my home are threatened by the same man who threatens you. I have a duty to get back home to protect them.'

'Despenser threatens you?'

'He threatens both of us,' Baldwin explained, 'but he has bought Simon's house. Our fear is that he may try to evict Simon's family while he is abroad. His covetousness does not know any limit.'

'That is true enough,' the Queen said. 'Very well. Sir Richard, you have been most unnaturally silent today. What will you do?'

'Me Lady, I'm a simple knight from the King's own manor. I can't think to oppose him. So if the truth be told, I'll ride back, report, and then go home. And damn glad I'll be to see it!'

His bluff manner satisfied her, plainly. She smiled and sat again. 'You are all released from my son's service, if he agrees.'

The Duke of Aquitaine was silent for some while, staring at the men in turn. 'All right. I can accept their departure. But only on one condition. When I call for their help, they will come to my aid. Is that clear? I wish you all to swear it.'

Second Thursday following the Feast of the Archangel Michael[1]

Road to Beauvais

He was utterly exhausted. The last two days had really taken it out of him. Bishop Walter was inured to travel: a man who must regularly ride from one side of his diocese to another, and who was so involved in national politics that he must ride to London often, could hardly be otherwise. But this panicky flight was a different thing.

The road here was a rock-strewn track with grass in the middle and low hedges on either side, not unlike the roads in Wiltshire. There had been some very straight sections, but this part was as curving as a rope thrown upon the floor. It meant that they could not be seen from afar, but it also meant that they were unaware of other travellers until they were almost upon them.

There was a need for haste, that much was certain. They had to march fast, and yet avoid the appearance of urgency. If any

---

[1] Thursday, 10 October 1325

should notice them and their hurry, any pursuit would find it too easy to track them down and capture them – if capture was the worst that could happen. It was more likely that they would be taken and executed on the spot, with outlaws accused of the heinous crime. It is what he himself would have done in the King of France's position.

All the while on the road, while his staff tap-tap-tapped the way, and his clerks and servants followed with quiet anxiety, he was aware of the pressing fear that drove them all. The French could appear at any time, swords waving. There was nothing that he and the others could do about it. And Mortimer and the Queen would be delighted to see him dead.

Not that the Queen had actually threatened him. Not directly, anyway, so far as he could remember. It was merely the hints. And the fact of that man gripping him by the throat. That incident had set the fear of death in his heart. It was not something he had ever been aware of before, this terror of being slain like a dog. He supposed it was how many peasants lived, with the constant awareness that the slightest infraction or error could lead to a dagger in the back or a sudden overwhelming assault from a group of men in armour. For the first time he felt an appreciation for the grinding, numbing terror that was a part of so many lives.

They had stopped for a late breakfast of porridge and some bread a few miles back, and now they had full bellies after chewing on some pease pudding which they had secreted in their purses that morning. But Bishop Walter would not give them much time to rest. They must continue. He only prayed that the rain would hold off for a few more days. He dared not ask for rooms at an inn, in case they were followed and their passage reported, so although they could halt and ask for bread or pudding, he would not allow them to use a bed. Their mattresses were the fields and the hollows under hedges.

'Bishop? My Lord?'

He turned with a scowl as the clerk called out. The road was clear of tranters and carters just now, but he had ordered them all not to shout too loudly in case their voices were recognised as English.

'What?'

'Riders!'

The group huddled closer together as the sound of horses came to them. Bishop Walter was in the middle like a general with his troops about him, and he peered back the way they had come with trepidation. This was not the usual route from Paris, he reckoned, which was partly why they had come this way. Also, it was a popular pilgrim route, so they should have been safe enough. This sounded like two large horses, maybe more. But they were hidden by a bend in the road.

And then he felt a lightening of his spirits as he recognised three riders on great rounseys.

'Sir Baldwin! Sir Richard! And Simon, too! This is good news beyond all hope. You are all most welcome!'

Second Friday following the Feast of the Archangel Michael[1]

Furnshill

Jeanne woke to a grey morning in which the rain splattered against the shutters and the wind howled around the doorframes. Autumn was almost over, and winter was battling to take over. It made her shudder. Raised in the French territories, her blood was too thin for these colder climates, especially during the worst of the wintry weather.

Margaret was not in the bed beside her, which was a

---

[1] Friday, 11 October 1325

surprise, and she quickly climbed out of the bed and walked downstairs.

Meg had set the fire, and sat beside it, huddled with her arms around her legs, chin resting on her knees. She didn't look up as Jeanne entered.

'Margaret? Couldn't you sleep?'

'I don't believe we will ever find peace in our house again, Jeanne. I'll always fear that someone is going to come and take it away.'

'Did you wake early?'

'I don't know that I slept. I just keep thinking of that man Wattere. He makes my skin creep, like looking at a snake. I am so scared that if we go back, he'll come again and kill Simon and Peterkin.' She burst into tears.

Jeanne sat beside her and put her arms around her old friend. 'I know it's terrifying, but you have to believe in the justice of your case, Margaret. It's wrong that he should try to take your house from you. No one can do that. When Simon and Baldwin are back, all will be well again. Trust me.'

But even as she spoke her soothing words, she could feel Margaret shudder with silent sobs.

Paris

Jacquot had worked until late last night, sorting out some details of a deal with a smith for gold stolen from a house near the Seine, and when the goldsmith had tried to take a little more than he deserved, Jacquot had used his menacing stare to make the man back down in a hurry. Yes, life was good, and looking better every day now.

In the morning, he packed a small selection of clothes into a shirt and tied it together into a bundle. At his hip was a leather wallet, and into it he placed a little hard cheese, a thick slab of cured meat, and a loaf of bread. Enough for two days, if treated sparingly. He took up a staff and went down the stairs.

Years ago he had come here to this town, unknown, with no family left, nothing. All he now had, he had taken – much of it from the still-warm bodies of those he had killed. There was a wineskin on the floor near his door, and he slipped the thong over his neck as he passed, allowing the skin to dangle over his breast.

Yes, years ago he had come here, seeking an extension to a life that had grown over-burdensome in his home country. But it had taken a whore and the King of Thieves to show him how empty life could become. And since their deaths, he had grown more and more aware of the void in his own life. In the countryside there was abundance. Wildlife, grains, fruit, vegetables – all provided a man with everything he needed, so long as the man himself would merely put in a little effort to till the soil, spread the seed, and cultivate the plants. Here in the city, the only creatures that survived were the human weeds that fed on the dead bodies of other men, that strangled and slew all in their paths. He could exist here, but without pleasure.

He left the house for the last time and took a deep breath in the lane outside. The air today smelled cleaner, purer. This was the day he would leave Paris and make his way to his old home – the little hamlet in the south. The place where his family had lived with him until they all died. Perhaps there were some neighbours still alive?

If there were, he would find them.

As Jacquot left the door, Michel turned to the others and nodded. Quiet as rats, keeping low, they scurried forward, and when Michel raised his cudgel, they moved in for the kill.

'Hey, King! I've a message from Hélias: *remember Jean le*

Procureur!' Michel hissed, and his cudgel swung. Jacquot felt the club slam into him, but there was no pain. His mind was so fixed on memories of his village that the blow caused only a dull incomprehension. He had no rage to defend himself, because he was not Jacquot the Parisian assassin, he was Jacquot, father of three, husband to his darling Maria. In his mind he saw his lovely Maria, and Louisa, Jacques and little Frou-Frou. All his family, his woman and children, those whom he had loved, those who had been his life. He had left the Parisian killer behind him in the house as he had slammed the door, and he felt only shock as the club thudded heavily into his shoulder, spinning him.

He could probably have saved himself even then, if he had been prepared. But as Michel and the others thrust forward, shoving him against the wall, his mind could not quite respond. The first prick of a blade at his breast almost woke him to his danger, almost stirred him to the anger that had protected him for so long, but it failed. He was too surprised.

The blade pierced his chemise, the point striking a rib, and he felt the wash of fluid all over his belly, knowing that this must be the end. For such an effusion, his death must follow swiftly. But there was no regret. Because to die must mean that he would meet his children again, that he would find Maria once more, that this miserable existence was at last over. At last he could hope for a better life to come, as the priests had always promised. So, Jacquot wore an expression of ineffable relief as he met the gaze of Michel, and behind him, Hélias.

But then he realised that the dampness was not blood, it was wine from his skin. He felt the hot despair return. Would he never *die*? Was he doomed to a long, solitary life? Must he continue to exist without the solace of any woman he could trust? Life without his Maria was nothing.

The red, raw wrathful frenzy took him over at last, and he lifted his fist.

Hélias watched as the man stared at his breast. She thought he looked strangely magnificent. True, he was small and scrawny, like so many who had starved, but he had some dignity. Even her men seemed a little overawed by him as he slowly stared down his body, and then his head snapped up again, suddenly gaving a hoarse bellow of pure ferocity, like a bear baited by the hounds.

Jacquot tried to punch, but he was too late. Michel moved in, his club swinging, and she saw little Petit André lift his hatchet, saw the flashing of blades rising and falling, then the boots swinging as Jacquot collapsed. A few moments later there was nothing except the pattering of boots along the cobbles, as her men fled. That, and the soft, liquid soughing of the last breaths of the man who lay bleeding to death.

She walked to him. Not out of sympathy. She wanted to spit in his face as he expired, to tell him that this was all because he had killed a man she had respected – a man she had loved. But she couldn't.

Because as she looked down at him, all she could see in his eyes was a kind of gratitude as his soul left his body to go and greet his family.

It was a look that made her envious.

The Templar, the Queen and Her Lover

Michael Jecks

1325: An atmosphere of dread and suspicion hangs over England.

The last years have been god-awful. A man was hard pushed just to survive with the realm stretched so taut with treachery and mistrust and the war with France.

When Isabella, Queen of England, is dispatched to Paris to negotiate peace with the French King, Sir Baldwin de Furnshill and his companion Simon Puttock travel with her to ensure her safety. But it seems no one can be trusted, not least those in the Queen's own retinue. Murder, betrayal, adultery and cold, calculating evil are just the beginning of Baldwin's tempestuous journey into the dark heart of the world's most powerful realm. Baldwin and Simon must fight to survive as the Queen struggles to stop a vicious war between her husband and her brother . . .

Acclaim for Michael Jecks' mysteries:

'The most wickedly plotted medieval mystery novels' *The Times*

'Atmospheric and cleverly plotted' *Observer*

978 0 7553 3284 7

headline